PRAISE FOR

Gabriel's Redemption

"The Professor is sexy and sophisticated . . . . I can't get enough of him!"

—*USA Today* bestselling author Kristen Proby

"[In *Gabriel's Inferno* and *Gabriel's Rapture*] I found myself enraptured by Sylvain Reynard's flawless writing. *Gabriel's Inferno* and *Gabriel's Rapture* are books I will always treasure and are among my top ten reads of last year. Although they will be missed, I am anxiously waiting for the conclusion of Gabriel and Julia's story in *Gabriel's Redemption*."

—*The Autumn Review*

"An unforgettable and riveting love story that will sweep readers off their feet."

—*Nina's Literary Escape*

"Emotionally intense and lyrical, Sylvain Reynard's words bleed from the pages straight into the heart of the reader."

—*Totally Booked Blog*

"Sylvain Reynard's writing is captivating and intense . . . . It's hard not to be drawn to the darkly passionate and mysterious Gabriel, a character you'll be drooling and pining for!

—*Waves of Fiction*

Books by Sylvain Reynard

GABRIEL'S INFERNO
GABRIEL'S RAPTURE
GABRIEL'S REDEMPTION

SYLVAIN REYNARD

BERKLEY BOOKS, NEW YORK

THE BERKLEY PUBLISHING GROUP
Published by the Penguin Group
Penguin Group (USA) LLC
375 Hudson Street, New York, New York 10014

USA • Canada • UK • Ireland • Australia • New Zealand • India • South Africa • China

penguin.com

A Penguin Random House Company

This book is an original publication of The Berkley Publishing Group.

Library of Congress Cataloging-in-Publication Data

Reynard, Sylvain.
Gabriel's redemption / Sylvain Reynard.—First edition.
p. cm.—(Gabriel's inferno trilogy)
ISBN 978-0-425-26651-9 (pbk.)
1. College teachers—Fiction. 2. Newlyweds—Fiction. 3. Family secrets—Fiction. I. Title.
PR9199.4.R4667G35 2013
813'.6—dc23
2013030022

FIRST EDITION: December 2013

PRINTED IN THE UNITED STATES OF AMERICA

10 9 8 7 6 5 4 3 2 1

Cover design by Lesley Worrell
Cover art: couple: Claudio Marinesco; man: Pali Rao / Getty Images
Interior text design by Tiffany Estreicher

To my readers,
with gratitude.

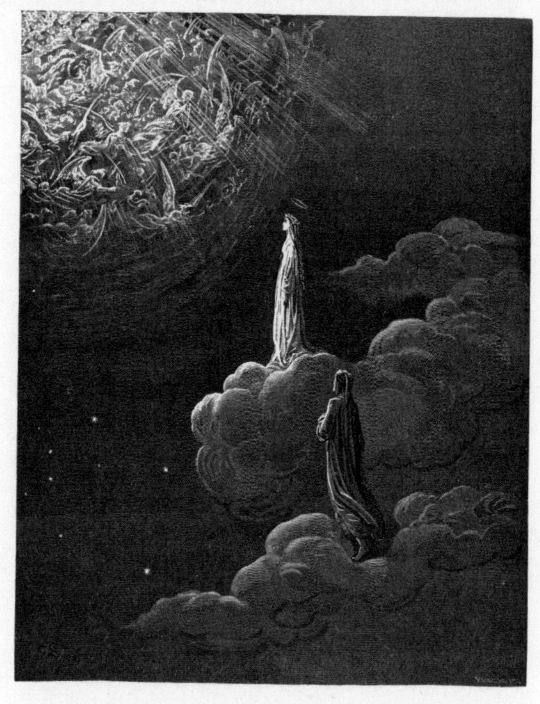

Dante and Beatrice ascend to the sphere of Mars.
Engraving by Gustav Doré, c. 1868

"Hope," said I, "is the certain expectation
Of future glory, which is the effect
Of grace divine and merit precedent."

—DANTE ALIGHIERI, *PARADISO*,
CANTO *XXV.067-069*.

Prologue

1292
Florence, Italy

The poet pushed back from the table and looked out the window at his beloved city. Though her architecture and streets called to him, they did so with hollow voices. It was as if a great light had been extinguished, not just from the city, but from the world.

"Quomodo sedet sola civitas plena populo! Facta est quasi vidua domina gentium . . ."

His eyes scanned the Lamentation he'd quoted only moments previous. The words of the prophet Jeremiah were woefully inadequate.

"Beatrice," he whispered, his heart seizing in his chest. Even now, two years after her death, he had difficulty writing about his loss.

She would remain forever young, forever noble, forever his blessedness, and not all the poetry in the world could express his devotion to her. But for the sake of her memory and their love, he would try.

Chapter One

June 2011
Selinsgrove, Pennsylvania

Professor Gabriel Emerson stood in the doorway of his study, hands in his pockets, gazing on his wife with no little heat. His tall, athletic form was striking, as were his rugged features and sapphire eyes.

He'd met her when she was seventeen (ten years his junior) and fallen in love with her. They'd been separated by time and circumstances, not least of which was his indulgent lifestyle.

Yet Heaven smiled on them. She became his graduate student in Toronto six years later and they'd rekindled their affection, marrying a year and a half after that. Almost six months into their marriage he loved her even more than before. He envied the very air she breathed.

He'd waited long enough for what he was about to do. It was possible she'd need to be seduced, but Gabriel prided himself in his expertise at seduction.

The strains of Bruce Cockburn's song "Mango" floated in the air, casting his memory back to their trip to Belize before they were married. They'd made love outside in a variety of places, including the beach.

Julia sat at a desk, oblivious to the music and his scrutiny. She was typing on her laptop, surrounded by books, file folders, and two boxes of papers Gabriel had dutifully carried from the downstairs of what had been his parents' house.

They'd been resident in Selinsgrove a week—a respite from their busy lives in Cambridge, Massachusetts. Gabriel was a professor at

Boston University while Julia had just finished her first year of a PhD at Harvard, under the supervision of a brilliant scholar, formerly of Oxford. They'd fled Cambridge because their home in Harvard Square was in upheaval, as an addition to the house was under construction.

The Clark house in Selinsgrove had been renovated to accord with Gabriel's exacting standards prior to their arrival. Much of the furniture left behind by Richard, Gabriel's adoptive father, had been placed in storage.

Julia had chosen new furniture and curtains and persuaded Gabriel to help her paint the walls. Whereas his aesthetic ran to dark wood and rich, brown leather, Julia preferred the light colors of a seaside cottage, with whitewashed walls and furniture, accented with various shades of Santorini blue.

In the study, she'd hung reproductions of paintings that were displayed in their house in Harvard Square—Henry Holiday's *Dante Meets Beatrice at Ponte Santa Trinita*, Botticelli's *Primavera*, and *Madonna and Child with Angels* by Fra Filippo Lippi. Gabriel found himself staring at the latter painting intently.

It could be said that the paintings illustrated the stages of their relationship. The first figured their meeting and Gabriel's increasing obsession. The second represented Cupid's arrow, striking Julia when he no longer remembered her, and also their courtship and subsequent marriage. Finally, the painting of the Madonna represented what Gabriel hoped might be.

This was the third evening Julia had spent at her desk, writing her first public lecture, which she would deliver at Oxford next month. Four days ago, they'd made love on the bedroom floor, covered in paint, before the furniture had been delivered.

(Julia had decided that body painting with Gabriel was her new favorite sport.)

With memories of their physical connection in mind, and the music increasing its tempo, Gabriel's patience had come to an end. They were newlyweds. He had no intention of allowing her to ignore him for another evening.

He prowled over to her, his footfalls silent. He moved her shoulder-length hair aside, exposing her neck. The slight stubble of his unshaved face rasped against her skin, intensifying his kisses.

"*Come*," he whispered.

Goose pimples rose on her skin. His long, thin fingers traced the arch of her neck as he waited.

"My lecture isn't finished." She lifted her pretty face to look at him. "I don't want to embarrass Professor Picton, especially when she invited me. I'm the youngest person on the program."

"You won't embarrass her. And you'll have plenty of time to finish the lecture."

"I need to get the house ready for your family. They're arriving in two days."

"They aren't my family." Gabriel gave her a blazing look. "They're *our* family. And I'll hire a maid. Come. Bring the blanket."

Julia turned and saw a familiar-looking plaid blanket resting on the white overstuffed chair that sat under the window. She peered out into the woods that bordered the backyard. "It's dark."

"I'll protect you." He helped her to her feet, clasping his arms momentarily around her waist and bringing their chests together.

She felt his warmth through the thin material of her sundress, the temperature comforting and alluring.

"Why do you want to visit the orchard in the dark?" she teased, pulling his glasses from his face and placing them on the desk.

Gabriel fixed her with a look that would have melted snow. Then he brought his lips to her ear. "I want to see your naked skin glow in the moonlight *while I'm inside you*."

He drew part of her earlobe into his mouth, nibbling it gently. He began to explore her neck, kissing and nipping as her heart rate increased.

"A declaration of desire," he whispered.

Julia gave herself over to the sensations, finally becoming conscious of the music in the air. Gabriel's scent, a mixture of peppermint and Aramis, filled her nostrils.

He released her, watching her the way a cat watches a mouse, as she picked up the blanket.

"I suppose Guido da Montefeltro can wait." She glanced down at her notes.

"He's been dead over seven hundred years. I'd say he's practiced at waiting."

Julia returned his smile, shifting the blanket so that she could take his proffered hand.

As they journeyed downstairs and across the yard, his expression grew playful.

"Have you ever made love in an orchard before?"

Her eyes widened and she shook her head.

"Then I'm glad I'm your first."

She tightened her grip on his hand. "You're my last, Gabriel. My only."

He quickened his pace, switching on the flashlight as they entered the woods behind the house. He led the way, navigating over roots and uneven ground.

It was June in Pennsylvania and very warm. The woods were thick and the canopy of leaves blocked much of the light from the moon and the stars. The air was alive with the evening song of birds and the sound of katydids.

Soon they were entering the clearing. Wildflowers littered the expanse of green. At the far edge of the area stood several aged apple trees. Extending back into the remains of the old orchard, the new trees that Gabriel had planted were spreading their boughs toward the sky.

As they walked to the center of the clearing, his body relaxed. Something about this space, sacred or otherwise, always soothed him.

Julia watched as he spread the blanket carefully over the thick grass, then turned off the flashlight. Darkness wrapped around them like a velvet cloak.

Overhead, the full moon shone, its pale face occasionally muted by wisps of cloud. A clutch of stars twinkled above them.

Gabriel brushed his hands up and down her arms before tracing the modest neckline of her sundress.

"I like this," he murmured.

He took his time admiring his wife's beauty, visible even in the shadows: the arch of her cheekbones, the pout of her mouth, her large, expressive eyes. He lifted her chin and brought their lips together.

It was the kiss of an ardent lover, communicating with his mouth that he desired her. Gabriel pressed his tall body against her petite one, his fingers tangling in her soft brown hair.

"What if someone sees us?" she panted, before slipping her tongue into his mouth.

She explored him earnestly until he retreated.

"These woods are private. And as you mentioned, it's dark." His hands found her waist, spanning her lower back.

He traced the space where her dimples lay, as if they were landmarks that pleased him, before sliding up to her shoulders. Without ceremony, he slowly removed her dress, dropping it to the blanket. Then he unfastened her bra with a mere flick of his fingers.

She giggled at his practiced move, while holding the bra up to cover herself. It was made of black lace and was attractively transparent.

"You're very good at that," she observed.

"At what?" His large hands moved to cup her breasts over her bra.

"At removing bras in the dark."

Gabriel's silence echoed around them. He didn't like being reminded of his past.

She reached up on tiptoes to press a kiss to his angular jaw.

"I'm not complaining. After all, I'm the beneficiary of your skill."

At this, he traced her breasts through the lace.

"While I appreciate your lingerie, Julianne, I prefer you naked."

"I'm not sure about this." She peered over his shoulder, scanning the perimeter of the clearing. "I keep expecting someone to interrupt us."

"Look at me."

Her eyes met his.

"There's no one here but us. And what I see is breathtaking."

With another provocative move, his hands left her breasts to trace the hills and valleys of her spine before covering her hips. His thumbs hovered over her skin. "I'll cover you."

"With what? The blanket?"

"With my body. Even if someone were to stumble upon us, I won't let anyone see you. I promise."

The edges of her lips turned up.

"You think of everything."

"I simply think of you. You are everything."

Gabriel took her offered lips and with great restraint slowly peeled the lace bra away from her body. He kissed her deeply, languidly exploring her mouth, before tugging her panties down.

Now she was naked before him in their orchard.

O gods of all orchard sex, she thought. *Please don't let anyone interrupt us.*

She removed his shirt eagerly, her fingers playing in the few strands of chest hair before sliding over his abdominal muscles to unbuckle his belt.

When they were both naked, he wrapped his arms around her and she breathed out a sigh.

"It's a good thing it's warm tonight," he whispered. "We only brought one blanket."

With a smile she lowered herself to the ground and he covered her with his body. His blue eyes bore into hers as he placed a hand on either side of her face.

"'*To the Nuptial Bowre I led her blushing like the Morn: all Heav'n,*
And happie Constellations on that houre.'"

"*Paradise Lost*," she whispered, stroking the stubble on his chin. "But in this place, I can only think of Paradise found."

"We should have been married here. We should have made love here for the first time."

She ran her fingers through his hair.

"We're here now."

"This is where I discovered true beauty."

He kissed her again, his hands gently exploring. Julia reciprocated, and their passion kindled and burned.

In the months since their marriage, their desire had not abated, nor had the sweetness of their coupling. All speech melted into motion and touch and the bliss of physical love.

Gabriel knew his wife—he knew her arousal and excitement, her impatience and release. They made love in the night air surrounded by darkness and the greenness of life.

At the edge of the clearing, the old apple trees that had observed their chaste love in the past politely averted their gaze.

When at last they'd caught their breaths, Julia lay weightless, admiring the stars.

"I have something for you." He felt around for the flashlight and used it to locate his trousers. When he returned to her side he slipped something cool around her neck.

Julia glanced down to see a necklace made of individual rings. Three charms hung from the necklace—a heart, an apple, and a book.

"It's beautiful." She breathed, fingering the charms one by one.

"It came from London. The rings and charms are silver, except for the apple, which is made of gold. It represents when we met."

"And the book?"

"*Dante* is engraved on the cover."

She looked at him coyly. "Is there a special occasion I've forgotten about?"

"No, I just enjoy giving you things."

Julia kissed him deeply and he moved her to her back, once again putting the flashlight aside.

When they separated, he placed his palm against her flat stomach and brought his lips to the indentation that lay just beyond his thumb.

"I want to plant my child here."

As his words echoed in the clearing, Julia froze.

"What?"

"I'd like to have a child with you."

She caught her breath. "So soon?"

His thumb moved over her skin. "We never know how much time we have."

Julia thought of Grace, his adoptive mother, and of her biological mother, Sharon. Both died at younger ages, but under very different circumstances.

"Dante lost Beatrice when she was twenty-four," he continued. "Losing you would be devastating."

Julia reached up to touch the slight dimple in his chin. "No morbid talk. Not here, after we've celebrated life and love."

Gabriel spread repentant kisses across her abdomen before reclining on his side.

"I've almost outlived Beatrice and I'm healthy." She placed her hand on his chest, over his tattoo, and touched the name on the bleeding heart. "Is your anxiety because of Maia?"

Gabriel's features tightened. "No."

"It's all right if it is."

"I know she's happy."

"I believe that too." Julia hesitated, as if she were going to say something more.

"What?"

"I was thinking about Sharon."

"And?"

"She wasn't a good role model as a mother."

He leaned forward to brush his lips against hers.

"You'd be an excellent mother. You're loving, patient, and kind."

"I wouldn't know what I was doing."

"We'd figure it out together. I'm the one who should be worried. My biological parents were the definition of dysfunctional, and I haven't exactly lived a sterling moral life."

Julia shook her head. "You're very good with Tammy's little boy. Even your brother says so. But it's too soon for a baby, Gabriel. We've only been married six months. And I want to finish my PhD."

"I agreed to that, if you remember." He traced the arch of her ribs with a single finger.

"Married life is wonderful, but it's been an adjustment. For both of us."

He paused his movements. "Agreed. But we need to talk about the future. It would be best if I began having conversations with my doctor sooner rather than later. It's been so long since my vasectomy, a reversal might not be possible."

"There's more than one way to make a family. We can discuss other medical options. We could adopt a child from the Franciscan orphanage in Florence. When the time is right." Her expression grew hopeful.

He smoothed a lock of hair away from her face. "We can do all those things. I intend to take you to Umbria after the conference, before we go to the exhibition in Florence. But when we get back from Europe, I'd like to speak to my doctor."

"Okay."

He pulled her on top of him. A strange charge seemed to jump between their skin as he gripped her hips.

"When you're ready, we'll start trying."

She grinned.

"We should probably practice a lot in preparation."

"Absolutely."

Chapter Two

Julia startled awake early the next morning. Dawn had yet to break and the bedroom was quiet, the silence broken only by the sound of Gabriel's rhythmic breathing and the distant chattering of birds outside.

She clutched the sheet to her naked chest and closed her eyes, forcing her breathing to slow. The act only brought the scenes from her nightmare into stark relief.

She'd been at Harvard, running across campus to find the location of her general exam for her PhD. She stopped person after person, begging for help, but no one seemed to know where the exam was being held.

She heard the sounds of crying and was shocked to find an infant in her arms. She clutched the child to her chest, trying to shush him, but he wouldn't stop crying.

Suddenly, she was standing in front of Professor Matthews, the chair of her department. A large sign at his left indicated that the general exam was taking place in the classroom behind him. He blocked the doorway, telling her that children weren't allowed.

She argued. She promised she'd keep the baby from crying. She begged him to give her a chance. All her hopes and dreams of completing her PhD and becoming a Dante specialist rested on the exam. Without it, she'd be dismissed from the program.

At that moment, the infant in her arms began to wail. Professor Matthews scowled, pointing to the stairwell nearby and ordering her to leave.

An arm reached across her body, hugging her. She looked down to see that Gabriel was still asleep. Something in his unconscious state must have prompted him to comfort her. She watched him with a mixture of love and anxiety, her body still trembling from the nightmare.

She stumbled to the bathroom and switched on the lights and the shower. She hoped the hot water would calm her. Certainly, the brightness of the bathroom helped dispel some the darkness.

As she stood under the tropical rain shower, she tried to forget the nightmare and the other worries that fought to breach the surface of her consciousness—her lecture, their family's impending visit, Gabriel's sudden urge to have a baby . . .

Her fingers went to the silver necklace clasped around her throat. She knew that Gabriel wanted children with her. They'd discussed it prior to their engagement. But they'd agreed to wait until she graduated. Graduation was still a good five or six years away.

Why is he bringing up the subject of children now?

She was anxious enough over her studies. Come September, she'd be taking courses and looking ahead to her general exams, which would have to be completed the following year.

More pressing was her lecture, which was to be delivered at Oxford in a few weeks. Julia had completed a paper on Guido da Montefeltro in Professor Marinelli's graduate seminar that past semester. The professor liked the paper so much, she'd mentioned it to Professor Picton, who encouraged Julia to submit an abstract to the conference.

Julia had been overjoyed when her paper proposal was accepted. But the thought of standing in front of a room of Dante specialists and lecturing them on topics they were far more expert in was daunting.

Now Gabriel was talking about having his vasectomy reversed when they returned from Europe in August.

What if the vasectomy reversal is successful?

Guilt washed over her. Of course she wanted to have his child. And she knew that undoing the vasectomy was more than just a physical procedure. It would be a symbolic gesture—that he'd finally forgiven himself for what happened with Paulina and Maia. That he'd finally begun to believe that he was worthy of fathering and parenting children.

They'd prayed for children. After their wedding, they'd approached the tomb of St. Francis and said spontaneous, private prayers, asking for God's blessing on their marriage and the gift of children.

If God wants to answer our prayers, how can I say, "Wait"?

Julia worried she was being selfish. Maybe she should prioritize having a child over her education and aspirations. Harvard wasn't going anywhere. Lots of people went back to university after starting a family.

What if Gabriel doesn't want to wait?

He was correct to point out that life was short. The loss of Grace was testament to that. Once Gabriel knew he was able to father a child, he'd probably want to do so immediately. How could she say no?

Gabriel was a consuming fire. His passion, his desires, all seemed to overtake the desires of those around him. He'd told her once that she was the only woman who'd ever said no to him. He was probably correct.

Julia worried about her ability to say no to his deepest longing. She'd be overwhelmed with the desire to please him, to make him happy, and in so doing would sacrifice her own happiness.

She hadn't had much growing up. She'd been poor and neglected when she lived with Sharon in St. Louis. But she'd distinguished herself in school. Her intelligence and discipline had served her well through Saint Joseph's University and the University of Toronto.

Her first year at Harvard had been successful. Now was not the time to quit or drop out. Now was not the time to have a child.

Julia covered her face with her hands and prayed for strength.

❧❧

A few hours later, Gabriel walked into the kitchen, carrying his running shoes and socks. He was clad in a Harvard T-shirt and shorts and was about to retrieve a bottle of water from the fridge when he saw Julia sitting at the kitchen island, her head in her hands.

"There you are." He dropped his shoes and socks to the floor and greeted her with an insistent kiss. "I wondered where you'd gone."

He remarked her tired eyes and the purple smudges below them. She looked distressed.

"What's wrong?"

"Nothing. I just finished cleaning the kitchen and the fridge, and now I'm making a list for the grocery store." She pointed to a large piece of paper that was covered in her flowing script. It sat next to a cup of coffee that was stone cold and half empty, along with another equally long list of to-do items.

Gabriel looked around at the kitchen, which was sparkling within an inch of its life. Even the floors were immaculate.

"It's seven o'clock. Isn't it a bit early for housekeeping?"

"I have a lot to do." She didn't sound enthusiastic.

Gabriel took her hand, stroking his thumb across her palm. "You look tired. Didn't you sleep well?"

"I woke up early and couldn't get back to sleep. I need to make up the bedrooms and clean the bathrooms. Then I need to go shopping and plan the meals. And . . ." She heaved a shuddering sigh.

"And?" he prompted, lowering his head so he could meet her eyes, which had moved to the long to-do list.

"I need to keep moving. I'm not even dressed." She tugged the edges of her pale blue silk bathrobe together and moved to stand.

Gabriel stopped her.

"You don't need to do anything. I said I'd find someone to clean the house, and I will." He gestured to the grocery list. "I'll go to the store after my run."

Her shoulders relaxed slightly. "That will help. Thank you."

He cupped her cheek with his hand. "Go back to bed. You look exhausted."

"There's still too much to do," she whispered.

"I'll look after it. You need to work on your lecture." He offered her a half-smile. "But get some sleep first. A tired mind doesn't work very well."

He kissed her once again and led her upstairs. He pulled the covers back on their bed and watched her settle before tucking her in.

"I know this is the first time we've had houseguests. I don't expect you to be the maid. And I certainly don't want our relatives to keep you from meeting your deadline. Work in the study for the rest of the day. Forget about everything else. I'll handle it."

He pressed his lips to her forehead and turned out the light, leaving Julia to her slumber.

Gabriel usually listened to music when he jogged, but on this morning his mind was distracted. Julianne was overwhelmed; it was obvious.

She wasn't an early riser and from the looks of her this morning, she'd been awake for hours.

They probably shouldn't have invited their relatives to visit prior to her conference. But since they were going to Italy for most of the summer, this was the only time everyone could be together.

He'd forgotten how time consuming it was to have company. He'd never entertained more than one or two people at a time, and then only with the support of a housekeeper and a bank account that permitted him to take his guests out for meals.

Poor Julianne. Gabriel recalled his own years at Harvard: how vacations were never true holidays since there was always work to do, languages to learn, and exams to prepare for.

He was relieved to be tenured. He wouldn't trade places with Julia for anything. Especially since he'd coped with the pressures of grad school by drinking, doing cocaine and P—

Gabriel stumbled, pitching forward as the toe of his shoe caught on the sidewalk. He righted himself quickly and regained his stride, forcing himself to concentrate on his steps.

He didn't like to think about his years at Harvard. Since his move back to Cambridge, he'd experienced drug flashbacks so vivid, he would swear he could feel the cocaine entering his nostrils. He'd drive down a street or enter a building on the Harvard campus and feel a craving that was so sharp it was painful.

Thus far, with the grace of God, he'd resisted. Certainly, his weekly Narcotics Anonymous meetings had helped, as had his monthly appointments with his therapist.

And then, of course, there was Julianne.

If Gabriel found his higher power in Assisi last year, Julianne was his guardian angel. She loved him, inspired him, made his house a home. But he could not shake the fear that Heaven had smiled on him only to bide its time before snatching her away.

Gabriel had changed in myriad ways since Julianne was his student. But he had yet to abandon his belief that he was not worthy of sustained happiness. As his therapist had warned, Gabriel had a pattern of self-sabotage.

His adoptive mother, Grace, had died of cancer almost two years previous. Her untimely death symbolized the shortness and uncertainty of life. If he were to lose Julianne . . .

If you had a child with her, you'd never lose her.

A still, small voice spoke in his ear.

Gabriel quickened his pace. The voice was right, but it didn't express his primary motivation for wanting a baby with Julianne. He wanted a family that included children—a life filled with laughter and the knowledge that he could right the wrongs done by his own parents.

He'd kept his internal struggles from his wife. She was burdened with her own concerns and he was loath to add to them. She'd worry about his addictions and his fears, and he'd already given her too much anguish.

While Gabriel jogged the familiar circuit of his old neighborhood, he began to wonder why she'd been so dispirited this morning. They'd spent an incredible night together, celebrating their love in the orchard and later, in bed. He racked his brain, trying to figure out if he'd done something to hurt her. But their lovemaking had been, as usual, both passionate and tender.

There was at least one other possibility, and Gabriel cursed himself for not having thought of it sooner. Julianne always carried with her a degree of anxiety about being back in Selinsgrove. A year and a half ago, her ex-boyfriend, Simon, had broken into her father's home and assaulted her. Subsequently, his current girlfriend, Natalie, had confronted Julia at a local diner, threatening to release lewd pictures of her if she didn't withdraw her assault complaint.

Julianne had convinced Natalie that it was not in her interest to release the pictures, since they'd implicate Simon, as well. His father was a U.S. senator who was running for president, and Natalie was working for his campaign.

At the time, Gabriel kept his doubts about Julia's success to himself. He knew that once a person acquired a taste for blackmail, he or she would keep trying to draw from that well.

Gabriel cursed again, now running at a punishing rate of speed. He'd never told Julia what he'd done. He didn't want to do so now. But if she was worrying about Simon and Natalie, then perhaps it was time to tell her the truth . . .

❧❧

When Gabriel returned from his run, Julia was sleeping. He chuckled, noticing that her bare feet were sticking out from under the covers. Julia didn't like it when her feet grew hot and so she'd bare them to the air while snuggled under several blankets.

Leaning over, he tucked the covers around her feet and walked to the shower. After he dressed he checked on her, but she was still asleep. He hurried down the stairs, grabbing her lists from the kitchen and heading to the Range Rover. With any luck, he'd be able to complete the shopping and secure a maid before she awoke.

❧❧

At eleven o'clock that evening, Julia finally descended the stairs from the second floor. She found Gabriel seated in the living room, reading. He was in a leather club chair, his feet resting on a footstool, his eyes moving behind his glasses.

"Why, hello there." He greeted her with a smile, closing his book.

"What are you reading?"

He showed her the cover. *The Way of a Pilgrim.*

"Is it good?"

"Very. Did you ever read J.D. Salinger's *Franny and Zooey*?"

"A long time ago. Why?"

"Franny reads this book and it troubles her. That's where I first heard about it."

"What's it about?" She picked up the book, glancing at the back cover.

"It's about a Russian Orthodox man who tries to learn what it means to pray without ceasing."

Julia arched an eyebrow. "And?"

"And I'm reading it to discover what he learned."

"Are you praying for something?"

He rubbed at his chin. "I'm praying for a good many things."

"Such as?"

"For me to become a good man, a good husband, and, someday, a good father."

She smiled a little and looked at the book again. "I suppose we're all on our own spiritual journeys."

"Some of us are further along than others."

She put the book down and climbed into his lap. "I don't think of it that way. I think we chase God until He catches us."

Gabriel chuckled. "Like *The Hound of Heaven*?"

"Something like that."

"One of the things I admire most about you is your compassion for human frailty."

"I have my own vices, Gabriel. They're just hidden."

She looked around the room, noting the vacuum marks in the carpet and the freshly dusted furniture. The air smelled of lemon and pine.

"The house looks great. Thank you for finding someone else to clean it. I was able to get a lot of work done today."

"Good." He looked at her over the rims of his glasses. "How are you feeling?"

"Much better. Thanks for making dinner." She rested her head on his shoulder.

"You weren't hungry when I brought it up to you." He ran his fingers through her hair.

"I finished it eventually. I ran into a problem with my paper, so I had trouble stopping long enough to eat."

"Can I help?" He removed his glasses, resting them on top of his book.

"No. I don't want people thinking that you're the brains behind my research."

"That wasn't what I was offering." Gabriel sounded offended.

"I need to do this myself."

He sniffed. "I think you worry a little too much about what other people think."

"I have to," she said sharply. "If I present a paper that sounds like you wrote it, people will notice. Christa Peterson has already been spreading rumors about us. Paul told me."

Gabriel scowled. "Christa is a jealous bitch. She's going backward in her career, not forward. Columbia made her enroll in the M.Phil program in Italian. They wouldn't admit her directly into their PhD. I've already spoken to the head of her department at Columbia. She slanders us at her peril." He shifted in his chair. "And when were you speaking to Paul?"

"He emailed me after the conference he went to at UCLA. That's where he saw Christa and heard the rumors she was spreading."

"You haven't even let me read your paper. Although we've discussed Guido so much I'm sure I know what you'll say."

Julia chewed on the edge of her thumbnail but said nothing.

He hugged her more closely.

"Has my book been helpful?"

"Yes, but I'm taking a different tack," she hedged.

"That can be a double-edged sword, Julianne. Originality is admired, but sometimes established methods are established for a reason."

"I'll let you read it tomorrow, if you have time."

"Of course I'll have time." He began rubbing her back, up and down. "In fact, I'm looking forward to it. My goal is to help you, not hurt you. You know that, right?"

"Of course." She kissed him again before burrowing against his chest. "I just worry about what you'll think."

"I'll be honest, but supportive. I promise."

"That's the best I can hope for." She smiled up at him. "Now I need you to take me to bed and cheer me up."

His eyes narrowed thoughtfully. "What would cheering you up entail?"

"Taking my mind off my troubles by tantalizing me with your naked body."

"What if I'm not ready for bed?"

"Then I guess I'll have to go to bed by myself. And maybe cheer myself up." She stood and stretched, glancing at him out of the corner of her eye.

In a flash he was behind her, scooping her into his arms and racing for the stairs.

Chapter Three

"You can't present this." Gabriel strode into the study the following afternoon, clutching a printout of Julia's lecture.

She looked up from her laptop in horror. "Why not?"

"You're wrong." He set the pages down and pulled off his glasses, tossing them on top of her desk. "St. Francis comes for the soul of Guido da Montefeltro after he dies. We discussed this. You agreed with me."

Julia crossed her arms defensively.

"I changed my mind."

"But it's the only interpretation that makes sense!"

She swallowed hard, shaking her head.

He began to pace in front of her desk.

"We talked about this in Belize. I sent you an illustration of the scene while we were separated, for God's sake! Now you're going to stand in front of a room full of people and say that it never happened?"

"If you'd read my footnotes, you'd—"

He stopped pacing and turned to face her.

"I read the footnotes. None of those sources go as far as you. You're merely speculating."

"Merely?" Julia pushed back from her desk. "I found several reputable sources that agree with most of what I say. Professor Marinelli liked my paper."

"She's too easy on you."

Julia's mouth dropped open. "Too easy? And I suppose you think that Professor Picton invited me to the conference *merely* out of charity?"

Gabriel's expression softened. "Of course not. She thinks well of you. But I don't want you to get up in front of a crowd of senior professors and offer a naïve interpretation. If you'd read my book, you'd—"

"I read your book, *Professor Emerson*. You only mention the text I'm analyzing in passing. And you *naïvely* adopt the standard interpretation, without reflecting on whether you should."

Gabriel's eyes narrowed.

"I accept the interpretation that makes sense." His tone was glacial. "I never naïvely adopt anything."

Julia stood, huffing in frustration.

"Don't you want me to have my own ideas? Or do you think I have to repeat what everyone else has already said just because I'm a lowly grad student?"

Gabriel's face reddened. "I never said that. I was a grad student once, too, if you'll recall. But I'm not anymore. You could benefit from my experience."

"Oh, here we go." Julia threw up her hands in disgust and walked out of the study.

Gabriel followed.

"What do you mean, *here we go*?"

She didn't bother turning around.

"You're just upset that I'm going to disagree with you in public."

"Bullshit."

"Bullshit?" She turned around. "Then why are you telling me to change my paper so I fall in line with your book?"

He placed a hand on her arm. "I'm not trying to get you to fall in line. I'm trying to help so that you won't make a fool—" He stopped abruptly.

"What was that?" She shook off his hand.

"Nothing."

He closed his eyes and inhaled deeply.

When he opened his eyes, he appeared calmer. "If you start now, you should be able to rewrite your paper in time for the conference. I can help."

"I don't want your help. And I can't change my thesis. They've already published the abstract on the conference website."

"I'll call Katherine." He gave her an encouraging smile. "She'll understand."

"No, you won't. I'm not changing it."

Gabriel's lips pressed together into a thin line.

"This is not the time to be stubborn."

"Oh, yes, it is. It's my paper!"

"Julianne, listen—"

"You're worried I'll make a fool of myself. And embarrass you."

"I didn't say that."

She gave him a look that was wounded if not betrayed. "You just did."

She stalked into the bedroom, attempting to close the door behind her. His hand shot out, stopping the door.

"What are you doing?"

"I'm trying to get away from you."

"Julianne, stop." He gazed around helplessly. "We can talk about this."

"No, we can't." She jabbed a finger into his chest. "I'm not your student anymore. I'm allowed to have my own ideas."

"That isn't what I was saying at all."

She ignored him and walked toward the bathroom.

"Julianne, damn it. Stop!" he bellowed from the doorway.

She whirled around.

"Don't yell at me!"

He held his hands up in an expression of surrender and drew a deep breath.

"I'm sorry. Let's sit down and talk."

"I can't talk to you right now without saying something I'll regret. And you obviously need to cool down."

"Where are you going?"

"To the bathroom. I'm locking the door and I'm going to avoid you for the rest of the day. If you don't leave me alone, I'm going to my dad's."

Gabriel winced. She hadn't stayed with her father since before they were married.

"How would you get there?"

She rolled her eyes.

"Don't worry, I won't leave you without a car. I'll call a cab."

"There aren't any cabs in town. You'll have to call one in Sunbury."

Julia glared. "I know that, Gabriel. I used to live here, remember? You must really think I'm an idiot."

She walked into the bathroom, slamming the door behind her.

Gabriel heard the lock click into place.

He paused for a moment before knocking on the door. "Rachel, Aaron, and Richard are arriving soon. What will I tell them?"

"Tell them I'm an idiot. Obviously."

"Julianne, just listen to me. Please."

He heard water running from behind the door.

"Fine!" He shouted. "Avoid me. Our first fight and you lock yourself in the God damned bathroom." He smacked his palm against the door.

Abruptly, the water shut off.

She raised her voice in order to be heard. "My first public lecture and you tell me it's shit. And not because it is, but because I didn't agree with you and your own God damned book!"

❧❧

After a lengthy hot bath, Julia emerged. The bedroom was empty.

She dressed quickly before entering the hall. She padded over to the staircase, listening.

Satisfied that the house was empty, she walked to the study and closed the door. Then she sat behind her desk, turned on some soft jazz as background noise, and returned to her paper.

❧❧

"Where's Julia?" Rachel hugged her brother before rolling her small suitcase and that of her husband, Aaron, into the living room. Her tall and willowy form was clad in a pair of khaki pants and a V-necked white T-shirt. Her long blond hair hung straight and perfect, pushed back from her attractive face by large black sunglasses. She looked like she could have starred in a Gap ad.

Gabriel's expression tightened.

"She's working on her paper."

"Did you tell her we arrived?" Rachel moved to the foot of the stairs. "Jules! Get your ass down here!"

"Rachel, please," her father said reprovingly before greeting Gabriel with a hug.

Richard stood an inch or two shorter than his son and had light hair and gray eyes. He was quiet and serious, and his intelligence and kindness engendered respect in all who knew him.

When there was no movement upstairs, Rachel turned to her brother, gray eyes narrowed.

"Why is she hiding?"

Gabriel shook Aaron's hand in greeting. "She isn't. She probably didn't hear you.

"Your rooms are ready and there are fresh towels in the guest bathroom. Dad, you're welcome to stay in your old room."

"I'll be fine in the guest room." Richard picked up his bag and began climbing the stairs.

"Are you and Julia fighting?" Rachel gave Gabriel a suspicious look.

He pressed his lips together. "You can say hello when you go upstairs. Then we'll meet for drinks on the back porch. I'm barbecuing ribs for dinner."

"Ribs? Fantastic." Aaron clapped an appreciative hand to Gabriel's back. "I was going to stop to pick up some Corona before we arrived, but Rachel wanted to come straight to the house. I'll be back in a few."

He picked up his car keys and was about to head to the door when his wife stopped him. She shook her head.

Gabriel watched the exchange between Rachel and Aaron and decided that was his opportunity to excuse himself.

"See you on the patio in a few minutes." He walked toward the kitchen.

Rachel shook her head at her husband. "They're fighting. I'll go talk to Jules and you talk to Gabriel. Then you can pick up the Corona."

"What could they be fighting about?" Aaron ran a hand through his dark curly hair.

"Who knows? Maybe Julia rearranged his collection of bow ties without asking him."

❧❧

"Hey." Rachel opened the door to her father's former study.

Julia greeted her best friend with a wide smile. "Rach! Hi."

The two women embraced and Rachel settled herself in one of the comfortable chairs by the window.

"How's it going?"

"Fine."

"So what's up with you and Gabriel?"

"Nothing."

"You lie like a carpet."

Julia turned away. "What makes you think something is up?"

"Gabriel is downstairs looking unhappy and you're up here looking unhappy. There's tension in the house. I don't need to be a psychic to pick up on it."

"I don't want to talk about it."

"Men are jerks."

"I can't argue with that." Julia collapsed in the chair opposite her best friend, flinging her legs over the arm.

"I fight with Aaron, sometimes. He'll get mad and take off for a couple of hours, but he always comes back." Rachel looked at her friend carefully. "Do you want me to go and beat Gabriel up?"

"No. But you're right. We're fighting."

"What happened?"

"I made the mistake of letting him read the lecture I'm working on. He told me it's terrible."

"He said that?" Rachel sat up in her chair, her voice raised.

"Not in so many words."

"What's wrong with him? I would have thrown something at his head."

Julia grinned wryly. "I thought about it, but I didn't want to have to clean up the blood."

Rachel laughed.

"Why does he think your paper is terrible?"

"He thinks I'm wrong. He said he was trying to help."

"Sounds like Gabriel is trying to control your paper like he tries to control everything else. I thought he was in therapy for that."

Julia was quiet for a moment.

"I don't want him to lie to me just to spare my feelings. If the paper needs work, I need to know that."

"He should know how to help you without saying your paper is terrible."

Julia exhaled in frustration. "Exactly. He says he wants to start a family with me. Then he turns around and acts like a condescending ass."

Rachel lifted her hand and gestured for her friend to stop. "Wait a minute. He wants to have kids?"

Julia squirmed. "Yes."

"Jules, that's huge! I'm so happy for you. When are you going to start trying?"

"Not for a while. We agreed to wait until I graduate."

"That's a long time." Rachel's voice grew quiet.

"It would be too difficult to work on a PhD and have a baby."

Rachel nodded. She fidgeted with the hem of her T-shirt.

"We'd like to have a baby."

Julia moved so that she could see her friend better. "What, now?"

"Maybe."

"How did you know you were ready?"

Rachel smiled. "I don't, really. I've always wanted kids, and Aaron feels the same way. We've been talking about it since high school. I love Aaron. I would be happy to live with him, just the two of us. But when I envision the future, I see kids. I want us to have someone who will come home for Christmas. If I learned anything from losing my mother, it's that life is uncertain. I don't want to wait to start a family and then lose my chance."

Julia felt tears threatening, but she blinked them back. "You have yearly mammograms, right?"

"Yes, and I've had genetic testing. I don't have the breast cancer gene, but I don't think Mom had it, either. Even if she did, by the time they would have realized it, it was too late."

"I'm so sorry."

Rachel sighed and looked out the window. "I don't like talking about it, but it weighs on me. What happens if we have kids, and I get cancer? It's always in the back of my mind."

She turned to face her friend. "Having kids is one way to rid Gabriel of his condescending attitude."

"Why's that?"

"He won't be condescending when the baby empties a dirty diaper on him. He'll be shouting your name, begging for help."

Julia laughed. But all too soon, she grew sober.

"I just want him to think that my ideas are important. They're just as important as his."

"Of course they are. Tell him that."

"I will. But right now, I'm not speaking to him."

Rachel ran her hand over the armrest, back and forth.

"He's come a long way. To see him married and talking about starting a family—it's remarkable. Mom told me that when they first brought Gabriel home, he used to hide food in his room. No matter what they said or did, he pocketed something at every meal."

"Was he hungry?"

"He was afraid of *being* hungry. He didn't trust that Mom and Dad would feed him. So he was building up a reserve for when they stopped. He didn't unpack his bags, either. Not until after they adopted him. He kept expecting them to send him away."

"I didn't know that." Julia's heart felt heavy.

Rachel offered her a sympathetic look. "He's my brother and I love him. But he speaks without thinking. His issue with your paper is probably that you didn't write it the way he would have."

"I'm not going to write things his way. I have my own ideas."

"My advice is to talk to him. Of course, it wouldn't be a bad idea to let him sweat a little. Make him sleep on the couch."

"Unfortunately, I'll probably be the one on the couch." Julia pointed to the sofa that stood against the opposite wall.

❧❧

To say that dinner was awkward would be an understatement.

Julia and Gabriel sat side by side. They even held hands during grace. But there was only painful, detached politeness—no warm glances, no whispered words of affection, no fleeting touches under the table.

Gabriel's spine was ramrod straight, his demeanor cool. Julia was quiet and remote.

Richard, Aaron, and Rachel kept the conversation fluid while the Emersons barely spoke. After dinner, Julia declined dessert and excused herself to work on her lecture.

Gabriel's eyes followed her as she left the table, a muscle jumping in his jaw. But he didn't stop her. He simply watched her walk away.

When Rachel went to the kitchen to make coffee, Aaron decided that he'd had enough. He leaned across the table.

"Man, suck it up and tell her you're sorry."

Gabriel lifted his eyebrows.

"Why are you assuming that I'm at fault?"

"Because you're the one with a dic—" Aaron caught his father-in-law's eye and began coughing. "Um, statistically speaking, eighty percent of fights are the guy's fault. Just apologize and get it over with. I don't want to have to sit through another meal like that. It's so cold in here, I'm going to have to go outside to warm up."

"I think I have to side with Aaron. Not that you're asking." Richard chuckled to himself.

Gabriel looked between the two men with something akin to disgust.

"I tried talking to her. That's how our argument started. She locked herself in the bathroom and told me to get lost."

Richard and Aaron exchanged a knowing look.

"You're in trouble." Aaron whistled. "You'd better talk to her before bed or you're looking at couch time."

He shook his head before moving to the kitchen to join his wife.

Richard tapped the stem of his wine glass thoughtfully.

"*Et tu, Brute?*" Gabriel scowled.

"I didn't say anything." Richard looked at his son kindly. "I've been trying to stay out of it."

"Thank you."

"But there's a reason why old married couples tell the young ones not to let the sun go down on their anger. Dealing with problems when they're small will make both of your lives easier."

"I can't exactly have a conversation through a locked door."

"Of course you can. You wooed her once; woo her again."

Gabriel wore an incredulous expression. "You're telling me to woo my wife?"

"I'm telling you to let go of your ego, apologize, and then listen to her. I wasn't always the man you see before you. You can learn from my mistakes."

"You and Mom had the perfect marriage."

Richard laughed.

"Our marriage was far from perfect. But we made a pact early on that we would keep the imperfection out of sight and hearing of you children. Children get anxious when their parents argue. In my experience, couples fight over money, sex, and a lack of respect or attention."

Gabriel began to protest, but Richard lifted a hand. "I'm not asking what your disagreement was about. That's between you and your wife. It's obvious that Julia's feelings have been hurt. She was very withdrawn over dinner, the way she used to be before she began seeing you."

"I'm not the one who shut down rational communication." Gabriel sounded imperious.

"Listen to yourself." Richard's tone turned scolding. "Julia isn't irrational. She's hurt. When someone hurts you, it's rational to withdraw. Especially considering her history."

Gabriel grimaced. "I didn't mean to hurt her."

"I'm sure that's true. But I'm also confident that you don't fight fairly. Learning how to argue with a spouse is an art, not a science. It took your mother and me a long time to figure it out. But once we did, we rarely argued. And when we did, it wasn't ugly or hurtful. If you can argue with Julia while still convincing her that you love her and that she's important to you, your conflicts will be easier to manage." Richard finished his wine and placed the glass on the table.

"Take it from someone who was married a while and who brought up a daughter. When a woman withdraws and is cold, it's because she's protecting herself. My advice is to be gentle with your wife and coax her out of that locked room. Or prepare to spend a lot of lonely nights on the couch."

❧❧

It was after midnight by the time Julia closed her laptop. She knew everyone had gone to bed. She'd heard their footsteps in the hall.

She crept to the door of the study and opened it. Light shone from underneath the closed door to the master bedroom. No doubt Gabriel was awake, reading.

She contemplated going to him. But the distance to his bed seemed interminable.

She grabbed the bottle of bubble bath she'd spirited away from their bathroom after dinner. She'd take another hot bath in the guest bathroom and try to forget her troubles.

A half hour later, Julia reentered the study, shutting the door behind her. She felt refreshed but only marginally more relaxed. Since Gabriel seemed determined to keep his distance, she'd sleep on the couch.

As she lay under the old wool blanket they'd first shared so many years ago in the orchard, she thought of their home back in Cambridge. She thought of their first few months of marriage and how happy they'd been.

She wanted to be a Dante specialist. It was a long road that would require sacrifice, hard work, and humility. She didn't want to be the kind of person who thought herself above criticism. She knew that her writing needed improvement.

But when Gabriel said she was going to make a fool out of herself, the pain was excruciating. She needed him to encourage her, to cheer her on. She didn't need him belittling her. Her belief in herself was shaky enough.

Why can't he see that I need his support?

As her sadness swelled, she wondered why he hadn't come to her.

No doubt he'd spent the evening with his family, smoking a cigar on the porch and talking about old times. She wondered what kind of explanation he'd given to Rachel about their conflict. She wondered why she was lying alone in the dark, close to tears, and he seemed perfectly content to leave her to it.

Just then, she heard a door open down the hall. She heard Gabriel's quick, determined steps. They stopped outside her door.

She sat up, holding her breath. A muted light shone from the hallway, entering the study through the crack beneath the door.

O gods of fighting newlyweds, please make him knock on my door.

She heard what sounded like a pained sigh and a thump that could have been a hand resting against the door. Then she saw a shadow pass across the light as the footsteps retreated.

Julia tightened into a ball but did not cry.

Chapter Four

Very early the next morning, Julia's cell phone rang.

She jerked awake, the sound of the Police's "Message in a Bottle" reverberating around the room. She stared as the phone vibrated against the desk. But she didn't answer.

A few minutes later she heard a chime, indicating she'd received a text.

Curiously, she walked over to the desk and picked up her phone. The text was, remarkably, from Dante Alighieri.

I'm sorry.

While she was contemplating what to type in response, another text arrived.

Forgive me.

She began formulating a reply when she heard movement in the hallway. Someone rapped on her door.

Please let me in.

Julia read the newest text before walking to the door. She opened it a little more than a crack.

"Hi." Gabriel greeted her with a hesitant smile.

She gazed at him, noting that his hair was wet from the shower but that he hadn't shaved. An attractive dark stubble covered his face and he was dressed in a white T-shirt and old jeans, his feet bare. He was, perhaps, the most beautiful sight she'd ever seen.

"Is there a reason you're knocking on my door at six o'clock in the morning?" Her tone was colder than she'd intended.

"I'm sorry, Julianne." His expression was suitably contrite.

(It certainly helped that his eyes were bloodshot and his clothes were rumpled, as if he'd simply lifted them out of a bag destined for the Salvation Army and put them on.)

"You hurt me," she whispered.

"I know. I'm sorry." He took a step forward. "I reread your paper."

She put a hand on her hip. "You knocked on my door to tell me that?"

"I called, but you didn't answer." He grinned. "It reminded me of Toronto, when I had to climb through your window."

Julia's cheeks flamed at the memory of Gabriel standing in her backyard in order to bring her dinner, as she greeted him in a towel, fresh from the shower.

"You forgot something. Something important."

In his hand, he held the illustration of *The Contention for Guido de Montefeltro*. "I found it on the floor of the bedroom last night. I'm not sure which one of us was carrying it, but someone dropped it."

Julia ignored the illustration that he'd left in her mailbox back in Toronto and searched his expression, instead. He appeared agitated, a sharp worry visible in his eyes. He ran his fingers through his wet hair.

"I know you needed to get away from me, but I think we've been separated long enough. Can I come in?"

Julia stepped back.

He entered and she closed the door behind him.

She crossed over to the couch and curled up on it, wrapping the old blanket around her shoulders.

He watched her movements, noticing that her body was now curved into a protective ball. He placed the illustration on top of her computer and shoved his hands into his pockets.

"I read your paper again. I also went back to the *Inferno*." His eyes met hers. "I said some things yesterday I shouldn't have."

"Thank you." Her posture relaxed somewhat.

"I have some suggestions to improve your paper." He leaned back against the desk, resting his hips against the edge. "I know it's important that you stand on your own two feet. But I'm happy to help, if you need me."

"I'd welcome your advice, as long as you don't tell me what to think."

"I would never tell you what to think. How could I?" His face grew gentle. "Your ideas are one of the many things I love about you."

His eyes fell to the illustration.

"I overreacted. I apologize. But the subject of your paper is somewhat personal, Julianne. The story of Francis risking Hell to save Guido's soul represents what I was trying to do when I made my confession to the disciplinary committee back in Toronto."

A lump appeared in Julia's throat. She didn't like thinking about what had happened the previous year. The disciplinary committee and their subsequent separation were far too painful to dwell on.

"I'll admit I wasn't merely reacting to your thesis. I was reacting to what I took to be your dismissal of the story. Our story."

"I never meant to dismiss something so important. I know you risked everything to help me. I know you went through Hell." Her features grew determined. "If the situation had been reversed, I would have descended to Hell to rescue you."

A smile pulled at the edges of Gabriel's lips. "Beatrice knew she couldn't accompany Dante through Hell, so she sent Virgil, instead."

"The only Virgil I know is Paul Norris. I doubt you would have welcomed his help."

Gabriel snorted. "Paul is hardly a candidate for Virgil."

"He was for me."

Gabriel scowled, for the thought of Paul comforting Julia in his absence still rankled.

"I was a bastard. Then and now." He pushed off the desk and stood in front of her, taking his hands out of his pockets.

He glanced at the space next to her. "May I?"

She nodded.

He sat beside her and held out his hand. She took it.

"I didn't mean to hurt you."

"I know. I'm sorry, too."

He pulled her onto his lap and buried his nose in her hair.

"I don't want you to have to lock yourself in the bathroom to get away from me."

He cupped her face and pressed their lips together. After an instant, she responded.

Gabriel kissed her with restraint, his lips warm and inviting. Back and forth and back and forth, he teased and nibbled at her mouth. Finally, she wrapped her hand around his neck, urging him closer.

He traced the seam of her mouth with his tongue. When she opened, he gently slipped inside, touching their tongues together. He'd never been able to lie with his kisses. They communicated far too much of his feelings. Julia felt his contrition and his sadness, but she also felt the undiminished flame of his desire.

His palms slid from her face to her hips, lifting her until she was straddling him. Their upper bodies pressed together as they continued to embrace, mouths eager and exploring.

"Come to bed." Gabriel's voice was a husky plea as he cupped her backside, pushing her over the evidence of his arousal.

"Yes."

"Good." He brought his lips to her ear. "We still have time to make up properly before our houseguests expect breakfast."

Julia pulled away. "We can't make up properly with guests in the house."

"Oh, yes we can." His blue eyes glinted dangerously. "I'll show you."

❧❧

"Last night was terrible." Gabriel lay on his back, one of his arms behind his head. He hadn't bothered to cover himself. Their bedroom was warm and his beloved wife was lying next to him on her stomach, equally naked. In moments like this he wished they could spend their days in bed, unclothed.

"It was." Julia lifted herself on her forearms so she could see his eyes. "Why didn't you come and talk to me?"

"I wanted to read your paper again. And I thought you needed space."

"I don't like fighting with you." Julia ducked her head, the strands of her hair skimming the tops of her breasts. "I hate it."

"I don't like it either, which is surprising, really. I used to love to fight." His lips curled into a pout. "You're turning me into a pacifist."

"I'm not sure you'll ever be a pacifist, Gabriel." Julia's voice wobbled. "Being a grad student is hard enough. I need your support."

"You have it," he whispered fiercely.

"I didn't set out to disagree with you in my paper. It just sort of—happened."

"Come here."

Julia stretched out on top of him and he placed his arms around her.

"We need to figure out a way to disagree without having a repeat of yesterday. My heart can't take it."

"Neither can mine," she whispered.

"I promise not to be a selfish bastard, if you promise not to lock yourself in the bathroom." His eyes bore into hers.

"I promise not to lock myself in the bathroom, if you can give me space. I was trying to get away from you while things were escalating. You wouldn't let me go."

"Point taken. We can take a break during an argument, but we have to promise to talk later on. And not the next morning. I'm not letting you, or myself, sleep on the couch again."

"Agreed. The couch is very uncomfortable. And lonely."

"I didn't express myself very well when we talked about your paper. I'm sorry for that. I wasn't worried about you disagreeing with me. In fact, it's probably better if you're on record as disagreeing with me because it will show everyone that you think for yourself."

"I don't disagree with you for the sake of being contrary." A wrinkle appeared between Julia's delicately arched eyebrows.

Gabriel tried to kiss the wrinkle away, but without success. "Of course not. Much as it may surprise you, I can be wrong, on occasion."

"My Professor? Wrong? Inconceivable." She laughed.

"Yes, it really is surprising, isn't it?" He shook his head wryly. "But by the time I finished your paper the second time, you'd convinced me that the standard interpretation was wrong."

"What?" Julia couldn't believe her ears.

"You heard me. Your paper changed my mind. Although I have some suggestions for how you can strengthen the last part. You didn't quite convince me there."

"I could use a few pointers. I'll give you credit in the footnotes."

His hands slid to her backside. "I'd be honored to appear in one of your footnotes."

She hesitated for a moment. "You don't think the paper is terrible? That I'll make a fool of myself?"

"No. Once I got over my knee-jerk reaction and paid closer attention to your argument, I realized that Professor Marinelli is right. Your paper is good."

"Thank you." Julia pressed her cheek against his chest. "It's hard for me to be a student in the same field as you. I always feel as if I'm trying to catch up."

Gabriel's fingers tangled in her hair.

"I can work harder at being more supportive. We aren't in competition. In fact, I'd like to co-author an article with you, someday."

Julia lifted her head. "Really?"

"I think it would be good for us to create something together, out of our shared love of Dante. And I'm proud of you for having the courage of your convictions. When you defend your paper at Oxford, I'll be sitting in the front row thinking, '*That's my girl.*'"

"It's a dream come true, to hear you say that."

"Then I'll keep saying it."

Chapter Five

The Emersons' relatives wisely refrained from commenting on how relaxed and happy they appeared when they finally exited their bedroom, just before lunch.

Gabriel's brother, Scott, arrived that afternoon with his wife, Tammy, and their son, Quinn. Everyone, including Julia's father, Tom, and his girlfriend, Diane, sat down to an early dinner.

Diane Stewart was an attractive African American woman, with flawless skin, large dark eyes, and shoulder-length curls. At forty, she was almost ten years younger than her boyfriend. She'd known him a long time, having lived in Selinsgrove her entire life.

As dessert was supposed to be served, Diane happened upon the Emersons dancing in the kitchen. Gabriel had wired the house with a central sound system, and the strains of soft Latin jazz filled the air.

The newlyweds were wrapped around one another, swaying softly to the music. Gabriel whispered something in Julia's ear. She seemed embarrassed and turned away, but he chuckled and pulled her close, kissing her.

Diane backed away, intending to return to the living room, but the aging hardwood creaked beneath her feet. The Emersons stopped abruptly and turned to face her.

She grinned.

"Somethin's cookin'. And it ain't the apple pie."

Gabriel laughed, a loud and happy sound, while Julia smiled and rested her forehead against him.

Diane nodded approvingly. "You took so long to make coffee, I thought you'd forgotten how."

Gabriel ran his fingers through his hair, which was mussed because of his wife's earlier explorations. "Darling?" He looked down at her.

"The coffee is ready and the pie is cooling. It won't take a minute." Julia reluctantly stepped away from her husband, who surreptitiously patted her backside.

At that moment, Rachel and Tammy joined them. Tammy was the newest member of the family, having married Gabriel's younger brother Scott a month previous. At five feet eleven inches, she was tall and curvaceous, with long strawberry blond hair and pale blue eyes.

"What's the holdup?" Rachel looked suspiciously at her brother, as if he were the sole cause of the delay.

"We were just making coffee." Julia hid her embarrassment by pouring the beverage into a series of mugs.

"I bet you were." Tammy winked slyly.

"I don't think it was coffee they were making. Mm-hmm." Diane wagged a finger in their direction.

"Right. I'll leave you ladies to it." Gabriel kissed Julia chastely before escaping to the living room.

Rachel examined the apple pies on the center island, testing their temperature with her finger. "Grab a knife, Jules. Let's sample these pies."

"Now you're talking." Diane declined Julia's offer of coffee and parked herself on one of the kitchen stools.

"So what was cooking out here? And please tell me you didn't use the counters." Rachel eyed the granite upgrades that Gabriel had insisted on purchasing.

"Too cold."

Julia clapped her hand over her mouth, but it was too late.

The women burst into peals of laughter and began to tease her unmercifully.

"Is it hot in here, or is it just me?" Diane fanned herself with a paper napkin. "I'm going to start calling this *the house of love*."

"My parents were like that." Rachel looked around the room. "Not on the counters that I know of. But they were very affectionate. It must be something about the kitchen."

Julia didn't disagree. There was something warm and comforting about the space and the house itself. She and Gabriel had trouble keeping their hands off each other, except while she was working on her paper.

"So has my big brother made up for yesterday?" Rachel looked at Julia.

She blushed a little. "Yes."

"Good. I need to have a talk with him, though. He's supposed to buy flowers after a fight. Or diamonds."

Julia looked at her engagement ring, which featured a large center stone surrounded by smaller diamonds. "He's given me enough."

"That's a good-looking ring, honey." Diane turned to Tammy, her eyes focusing on her left hand. "And so is yours. How's married life?"

Tammy watched the halogen lights catch the facets of her engagement ring. "I never thought it would happen."

"Why not?" asked Rachel, her mouth half full.

Tammy's eyes darted toward the doorway. "Shouldn't we serve dessert?"

Rachel swallowed. "The men have working legs. If they want pie, they can come and get it."

Tammy chuckled and picked up her coffee, cradling the mug in both hands.

"Before I started dating Scott, I lived with someone. He was my boyfriend in law school. We talked about getting married, buying a house, the whole white-picket-fence thing. Then I got pregnant."

Julia shifted uncomfortably on the bar stool, her eyes on the floor.

Tammy gave her friends a wistful look. "Scott told me that he was a surprise, but his parents were happy about it. I wish I'd had the chance to meet Grace. She sounds like a wonderful woman."

"She was," said Rachel. "Gabriel wasn't planned either. My parents took him in after his mother died and later adopted him. It isn't the planning that matters. It's what happens after."

Tammy nodded. "We'd talked about having kids. We both wanted children. Then, all of a sudden, Eric decided he wasn't ready. He thought I got pregnant to trap him."

"As if you got pregnant all by yourself." Diane waved her fork in the air.

Julia said nothing, ashamed of the fact that she sympathized with Eric's lack of readiness, although she deplored his actions.

"Eric gave me an ultimatum—the baby or him. When I hesitated, he left."

"Asshole," muttered Rachel.

"I was devastated. I knew the pregnancy wasn't my entire responsibility, but I felt like I should have been more careful. I considered an abortion, but Eric was already gone. And deep down, I was happy about being a mom."

Once again, Julia squirmed, struck by the sincerity of Tammy's tone.

"I couldn't afford the rent on my own, so I moved back with my parents. I felt like such a failure—pregnant, single, living at home. I used to cry myself to sleep thinking that no man would ever want me."

"I'm so sorry." Julia's eyes began to water.

Tammy reached over and hugged her.

"Things got better. But I'll never forgive Eric for signing away his parental rights. Now Quinn will never know his father."

"Sperm donors aren't fathers," Rachel interjected. "Richard didn't contribute genetic material to Gabriel, but he's his father."

"I don't know who contributed genetic material to Gabriel, but he must have been good looking because that boy is *fine*." Diane gestured toward the living room. "Not as fine as my man, but then, no one is."

Julia giggled uncomfortably as she contemplated the notion that someone found her dad to be "fine."

Tammy continued. "I was lucky I had a job. I worked at the district attorney's office with Scott. We went out a couple of times while I was pregnant. We were just friends, but he was so sweet to me. I thought that once I had the baby, I wouldn't hear from him again. But he came to see me a few weeks after Quinn was born. He asked me out and I was smitten."

"He was smitten with you too, as I recall." Rachel grinned. "He was in deep smit."

Tammy touched her engagement ring, moving the band back and forth on her finger. "I was breast-feeding the baby, so I had to pump before he picked me up. My parents babysat. But Scott never made me feel awkward or weird. He saw me as a person, a woman, instead of simply a mom. I guess he had a little crush on me when I was with Eric." She looked at her friends and smiled.

"I was so nervous about meeting you all. I was worried about what you'd think. But you were so welcoming." She glanced at Julia. "I didn't meet Gabriel until later, but he was nice, too. Even when Quinn ruined his suit."

"You should have seen him before he met Julia." Rachel made a face. "He would have handed Quinn the dry cleaning bill."

Julia was about to protest on Gabriel's behalf, when Tammy spoke again. "I can't imagine Gabriel doing that. He's wonderful with Quinn. And Scott? Well, fatherhood does something to a man. To a good man," she clarified. "Scott gets down on the floor and wrestles with Quinn. He's playful and gentle. It's a whole different side to him."

Julia pondered Tammy's remarks, wondering what Gabriel would be like as a father.

"I can't wait to have a girl." Tammy smiled to herself. "Scott will treat her like a princess."

"You want more kids?" Rachel asked, her eyebrows lifting in surprise.

"Yes. I think two kids will be enough for us, but if I have another boy, I'd like to try for a girl."

At that moment, Scott entered the kitchen, carrying a sleepy twenty-one-month-old boy. He nodded at the other women before walking over to Tammy. "I think it's bedtime."

Julia smiled at the contrast between Scott, who was six foot three and strongly built, and the small blond angel he cradled protectively.

"I'll help you." Tammy rose to her feet. She kissed her husband and they went upstairs.

Rachel looked at the stack of dessert plates and at the pies. "I guess I'd better take the men their dessert." She cut two slices of pie, plated them, and carried them into the living room.

Diane looked at Julia and fidgeted with her cup.

"Can we talk for a minute, honey?"

"Of course." Julia shifted her weight on the stool and turned to give Diane her full attention.

"I don't know how to say this, so I'm just going to say it. I've been spending a lot of time with your father."

Julia gave Diane an easy smile. "I think that's great."

"He met my mama and the rest of my family. He's even started coming to church with me on Sundays, to hear me sing in the choir."

Julia hid her surprise at the thought of her father in a church.

"When Dad asked if he could bring you to my wedding, I knew things had to be serious."

"I love him."

Julia's eyes widened. "Wow. Does he know that?"

"Of course. He loves me too." Diane smiled tentatively. "We've been talking about the future. Making plans . . ."

"That's great."

"It is?" Diane's dark eyes searched Julia's.

"I'm happy he's with someone who loves him. As much as I don't want to bring Deb up, I'm sure you know they were together for a long time. Nothing seemed to come of it. And I really didn't like them as a couple."

Diane was quiet, as if she were mulling something over.

"Your dad and I are talking about making things permanent. I want you to know that when we do that, I won't try to take the place of your mama."

Julia stiffened. "Sharon was not my mama."

Diane placed a comforting hand on Julia's arm. "I'm sorry."

"I'm not sure what Dad has told you about her, but I'm guessing it isn't much."

"I've let sleeping dogs lie. When a man's ready to talk, he'll talk."

Julia sipped her coffee in silence. She didn't enjoy talking or thinking about her mother, who died during Julia's senior year of high school. Sharon had been alcoholic and indifferent for most of Julia's life. When she wasn't indifferent, she'd been abusive.

"Grace was like a mother to me. I was closer to her than to Sharon."

"Grace was a good woman."

Julia searched Diane's expression and saw hope in her eyes, mixed with a slight anxiety.

"I'm not worried about you becoming my stepmother. And if you and Dad get married, I'll be there."

"You'll do more than be there, honey. You'll be one of my bridesmaids." Diane wrapped her arms around Julia, hugging her tightly. Eventually, she pulled back, dabbing at her eyes with her fingers. "I always wanted a family. I wanted a husband and a home of my own. I'm forty years old and finally all my dreams are coming true. I was worried about how you'd feel. I wanted you to know that I love your dad so you'd know I'm not with him for his money."

Julia gave her a puzzled look before both women began laughing. "Now I know you're kidding. Dad doesn't have any money."

"He's a good man, he's got a job, and he makes me happy. A woman finds a man like that, who's fine to boot, she holds on to him and doesn't worry about the money."

Before Julia could respond, Tom joined them. When he saw Diane's wet eyes, he strode over to her.

"What's all this?" His hand went to her face, swiping the tears away with his fingers.

"Diane was just telling me how much she loves you." Julia offered her father an approving expression.

"Is that so?" His voice sounded gruff.

"Not that you've asked, but you have my blessing."

He looked down, his dark eyes meeting his daughter's.

"Is that so?" he repeated, his tone softening.

Tom wrapped an arm around both women before pressing a kiss to the tops of their heads.

"My girls," he whispered.

❧❧

A short while later, Julia said good-bye to Diane and her father. She'd thought that perhaps they were living together, at least a few nights a week, and was surprised when Diane explained that they weren't, out of respect for her mama, whom she lived with.

Now Julia began to understand why Diane was in such a hurry to get married and have a home of her own.

❧❧

After dessert was served, Richard Clark sat on the back porch, drinking Scotch and smoking a cigar. The air was cool and quiet. If he closed his eyes he could almost imagine his wife, Grace, coming out the back door and settling in the Adirondack chair next to him.

Heaviness overtook his heart. She would never sit next to him again.

"How are you?"

Richard opened his eyes to see his daughter-in-law, Julia, sitting in the nearest chair. She'd tucked her slim legs up under her and was wrapped in one of Gabriel's old cashmere cardigans.

Richard switched his cigar to his left hand and moved the ashtray so it wouldn't bother her.

"I'm well, how are you?"

"I'm okay."

"Dinner was great," he offered. "Really exceptional."

"I tried to replicate some of the dishes we had in Italy. I'm glad you liked it." She leaned her head back against the chair, staring up at the dark sky.

He tasted the Scotch again, sensing that something was troubling her. But not wishing to force a confidence, he was silent.

"Richard?"

He chuckled. "I thought we'd agreed that you'd call me Dad."

"Of course, Dad. Sorry." She ran a fingernail down the arm of the chair, scoring the wood.

"No need to be sorry. We're family, Julia. And if you ever need anything, I'm here."

"Thank you." She traced a finger across the wound she'd given the chair. "Does it bother you that we've changed things? Inside the house?"

Richard hesitated before answering.

"The bathroom needed to be renovated, and it was smart to add another on the main floor and in the master bedroom. Grace would have liked what you did with the kitchen. She begged me for granite countertops for years."

Julia felt her heart clench.

"We kept a lot of things the same."

"Please don't worry. Grace would have helped you redecorate the house gladly, if she were here."

"Are you comfortable in the guest room? I was wondering if you'd changed your mind about staying there."

"It's good of you to ask, but I'm not bothered by any of these things. It troubles me that Grace is gone and she isn't coming back. I'm afraid that feeling will never go away."

Richard focused on his wedding ring, a plain gold band.

"When I'm inside the house, sometimes, I swear I hear her voice or smell her perfume. I don't feel her when I'm in Philadelphia. My condo has no memory of her." He smiled to himself. "Our separation isn't so bad when I'm here."

"Is it painful?"

"Yes."

Julia sat for a moment, as she thought about how she'd feel if she lost Gabriel. She'd be devastated.

The length of a human life was uncertain. One could get cancer, or die in a car accident, and in the blink of an eye a family would be torn apart.

From somewhere, Julia heard a little voice whisper, *If you had a child with Gabriel, you'd always have a part of him.*

The voice, more than the thought behind it, made her shiver.

Noticing her reaction, Richard stood up and wrapped a blanket around her shoulders.

"Thank you," she murmured. "Do you like living in Philadelphia?"

"My research position isn't quite what I expected. I've been thinking about retiring." He flicked the ashes into the ashtray. "I moved to be closer to Rachel and Scott, but I don't see them much. They're busy with their own lives. All my friends, including your father, are here."

"Move back."

"What's that?" He turned in his chair to face her.

"Move back to Selinsgrove. Live here."

"This is your home now, with my son."

"We're only here during vacations. We can switch bedrooms immediately and you can move your things back from Philadelphia."

He raised his cigar to his lips. "It's kind of you to offer, but I made my choice. I sold the house to Gabriel over a year ago."

"He'd be happier knowing you were where you belong."

Richard shook his head. "I'd never go back on my word."

Julia wracked her brain for a persuasive strategy.

"It would be a mitzvah for us. And we need the blessing."

Richard chuckled.

"That's the kind of thing I used to say to Gabriel, on occasion, when he was being stubborn. What kind of blessing do you need?"

Julia's expression shifted.

"I have an unanswered prayer."

When she didn't comment further, he inhaled from his cigar and exhaled the smoke.

"In my opinion, all prayers are answered eventually. Sometimes the answer is no. But I'll certainly pray that you receive an answer. I can't pretend that the thought of moving back doesn't tempt me. But you've put so much time into making the house yours. You've furnished the downstairs, you've painted walls . . ."

"You mortgaged this house to pay Gabriel's drug debts."

Richard looked at her in surprise.

"He told you about that, did he?"

"Yes."

"It was a long time ago. Gabriel paid us back."

"All the more reason for him to open his home to you now."

"A father would do anything for his child." Richard's expression was grave. "I didn't care about the money. I was trying to save his life."

"You did. You and Grace." Julia looked around the yard. "As long as the house is in the family and we can be together for Thanksgiving and Christmas, it doesn't matter who owns it. Or who lives here."

She tightened the blanket around her as a whisper of a breeze blew across the porch, caressing her face. "Gabriel would never part with the orchard, though. He's hired people to revitalize it. They've planted trees."

"The old trees haven't yielded a good crop in years. I'm afraid he's a bit optimistic."

Julia looked toward the woods, in the direction of the orchard. "Optimism is good for him."

She turned to Richard.

"If you lived here, you could supervise the orchard. It would relieve Gabriel to know it's in capable hands. You'd be helping us out."

Richard was quiet for what seemed like an age. When he spoke, his voice was hoarse. "Thank you."

She squeezed his hand before leaving him to his cigar and his thoughts. As he closed his eyes, a feeling of hope washed over him.

After her guests retired for the evening, Julia sat on the edge of her whirlpool tub testing the temperature of the water. She was looking forward to a few moments of relaxation.

She knew she should be working on her lecture, but the tumult of the day had left her weary. She wondered if she should call her therapist back in Boston. Surely Dr. Walters would have suggestions about how to deal with anxiety, marital conflict, and Gabriel's renewed interest in starting a family.

It wasn't a terrible thing to want a baby. Julia contrasted Gabriel's tender enthusiasm with the cold indifference Tammy described in Eric. Of course, Julia knew which she preferred. She just needed to stand her ground and not let Gabriel's passion overwhelm her and her dreams.

If anything, her conflict with Gabriel the day before illustrated how much they had to learn as a couple. They needed to learn those lessons before bringing a child into the world.

As she waited for the water level to rise, she felt the hairs of her neck stand on end. She turned to find Gabriel standing by the vanity. He'd unbuttoned the top three buttons of his dress shirt; a few strands of chest hair were now visible over the band of his white undershirt.

"I'll never tire of looking at you." He pressed a kiss to her neck before removing the plush towel she'd wrapped around herself.

"I should paint you." He stroked her spine with his fingertips, up and down.

"You painted me the other night, Caravaggio. We got paint all over the floor."

"Ah, yes. It pained me to have to clean it up. I was hoping we could add to it."

"That will have to wait for a night when we don't have guests." She gave him a saucy look. "Care to join me?"

"I prefer to watch."

"Then I'll be sure to put on a show." She lifted her hair from her neck with both hands, arching her back into the pose of a pinup girl.

He groaned and took a step forward.

She held out her hand, stopping him.

"I left my bubble bath in the guest bathroom last night. Would you mind getting it for me?"

"Not at all. *Goddess.*" He tasted her lips before walking away.

It took him a few minutes to locate the bubble bath, because someone had knocked it to the floor and it had rolled next to the wastepaper basket. When he stooped to pick it up, he noticed something wedged in between the basket and the wall.

It was a small, rectangular box.

He read the label. *Pregnancy test.*

But the box was empty.

When he'd overcome his surprise, and double-checked that he'd read the label correctly, he placed the box where he'd found it and returned to his room.

Wordlessly, he handed the bubble bath to Julia, who proceeded to lace the water with its sandalwood-and-satsuma-scented essence before climbing into the tub.

She arranged herself in what she thought would be a provocative pose.

Lost in thought, Gabriel stood motionless.

"What's the matter?" She angled herself in the bathtub so she could see him better.

He passed a hand over his mouth and chin.

"Is Rachel pregnant?"

"Not that I know of. She told me they were trying. Why?"

"I found an empty box for a pregnancy test in the guest bathroom. It looked like someone tried to hide it."

"It was probably her."

"I wish it were you." Gabriel gave her a look that was so intense, she felt its heat on her skin.

"Even after what happened yesterday?"

"Of course. Couples argue. Husbands are asses. We have hot, sweaty makeup sex and move on."

She looked down at the water. "I'd rather have the hot, sweaty makeup sex without the fighting."

His voice dropped to a husky whisper. "That would rather defeat the purpose of making up, wouldn't it?"

She inhaled deeply and lifted her dark eyes to meet his. "I'm not ready for a family."

"Our time will come." He took her hand, pressing his lips to her soapy fingers. "And believe me, I don't want to start another argument tonight or add to your stress."

Julia smiled weakly.

"I suppose the test could be Tammy's."

"She already has a child."

"Quinn will be two in September. I know she wants children with Scott."

Gabriel adjusted the lighting, dimming it before disappearing into the bedroom. A moment later, he returned, and Julia heard the voice of Astrud Gilberto floating from the speaker that was mounted in the ceiling.

Julia gave her husband an appreciative look. "Whoever took the test might have discovered she isn't pregnant. But if she is, you'll be an uncle again. *Uncle Gabriel.*"

Without reacting, he unbuttoned his shirt. He pulled it off and removed his T-shirt, exposing his tattoo and the light dusting of dark hair on his muscled chest.

Julia watched as he hung his shirt on a hook before his hands went to his belt. He smirked as he slowed his movements, teasing her.

She rolled her eyes. "The bathwater will be cold by the time you finish."

"I doubt it. I certainly won't be standing out here when I finish."

"Why not?"

"Because I intend to finish inside you."

With a smirk, he hung up his trousers before divesting himself of his boxers.

Julia knew her husband's body well, but even so, his figure always took her breath away. He had wide shoulders that tapered to a narrow waist and hips, which framed muscular thighs. His arms, along with his abdominals, were well defined, as was the V that sloped to his all-too-prominent sex.

"It kills me when you look at me like that." His eyes fixed hers hungrily.

"Why?" She stared at him shamelessly, moving forward in the bathtub to make room for him.

"Because you look as if you want to lick me. All over."

"I do."

In a flash, Gabriel settled behind her, wrapping his long legs around hers. "That scent is familiar."

"I bought the bubble bath because it reminded me of the massage oil you used in Florence. You rubbed my back, remember?"

"As I recall, I rubbed more than that." Gabriel nuzzled her ear with his nose. "You have no idea what that scent does to me."

"Oh yes, I do." Julia rested against his chest, feeling him hard against her lower back.

"Before we move on to—*ah*—other activities, I'd like you to talk to me."

"About what?" Julia tensed.

He placed his hands on either side of her neck and began to massage her.

"*Relax.* I'm not the enemy. I'm simply trying to persuade you to confide in me a little. You tend to take bubble baths when you're stressed. And you've been taking them daily."

"I just have a lot on my mind."

"Tell me."

She used her left hand to skim the surface of the water, pushing the suds back and forth.

"I worry about grad school and flunking out. I worry about my lecture."

He squeezed her shoulders.

"We've spoken about your lecture and I gave you my honest opinion— it's good. You aren't going to flunk out of your program. You just have to take grad school one semester at a time. You don't have to entertain our relatives this week. Tomorrow, we'll announce that you're spending the day working on your paper. They'll entertain themselves during the day, and tomorrow night I'll grill steaks for dinner. I'm sure Rachel and Tammy will pitch in."

Julia's muscles began to soften under his fingers. "That would help. Thank you."

"I'd do anything for you," he whispered, pressing his lips against her neck. "You know that, don't you?"

"I do." She turned and kissed him earnestly.

When they broke apart, she smiled. "You'll have your birthday when we're in Italy. How would you like to celebrate it?"

"With you. In bed. For a couple of days." He spread his arms around her waist, stroking the skin around her navel.

"Would you like to invite people to join us in Umbria? They could come with us to the exhibition in Florence."

"No, I want you all to myself. We can invite them to Cambridge for your birthday."

Julia placed her hand over his, stopping his movements. "I don't like making a big deal about my birthday."

He leaned back. "I thought we were past that."

"We'll be busy in September."

"Twenty-five is a milestone birthday."

"So is thirty-five."

"My milestones are only important because of you. Without you, they'd be empty days."

Julia buried her face in his chest. "Do you have to be so sweet?"

"Since I've eaten sour for most of my life, yes." With his mouth, he explored the curve of her neck and the soap-slicked skin of her shoulders.

"Then I guess we're having a party in September. We should celebrate Labor Day weekend." She kissed his pectorals before facing forward once again. "What did Richard say when you spoke to him tonight?"

"He'd like to move back, but he doesn't want to buy the house. I think he was counting on the money for his retirement."

"He can live here without buying it. You don't care, do you?"

"Not at all. I'd rather he lived here. But he feels badly about taking advantage of the renovations."

"Now he can enjoy them. The only problem is what to do with the furniture. There's no room for it back in Cambridge."

"We could give it to Tom. His furnishings have seen better days." The Professor sounded prim.

"You'd do that?"

"I'm not going to lie, Julianne. Your father is not my favorite person. But since you are . . ." He kissed her.

"Richard has things he bought with Grace that he doesn't want to part with, and there's some of the furniture he left behind that we put into storage. We'll have to move the new furniture out to make room. We could offer it to Rachel, if you'd rather."

"I think it would be nice to offer it to my dad. He and Diane are talking about getting married."

Gabriel tightened his arm around her middle. "How do you feel about that?"

"She's good to my dad and she's good to me. I'd like him to have someone to grow old with."

"I hate to break it to you, darling, but your father is already growing old. We all are."

"You know what I mean."

He moved her so she was facing him, bringing her legs around his waist.

"Lucky for you, I'm not too old to keep you up all night. I believe this is a room we haven't christened—yet."

Chapter Six

Sometime after midnight, Richard felt the mattress dip as someone crawled under the blankets. He rolled over, spooning the body of his wife. Her figure was familiar and soft, and he sighed loudly as he pressed against her.

She sighed equally in contentment, as she always had in such moments, nestling into him.

"I've missed you." He stroked her hair, kissing it. It didn't seem strange to him that her hair was long and straight, the way it had been before chemotherapy.

"I've missed you, too, darling." Grace reached for his hand and wound their fingers together.

Richard felt her wedding and engagement rings tap against his wedding band. He was glad he hadn't removed it.

"I dream about you."

She kissed where their rings touched. "I know."

"You were so young. We had our lives ahead of us, so many things we wanted to do." His voice caught on the last word.

"Yes."

"I miss this," he whispered. "Holding you in the dark. Hearing your voice. I can't believe I lost you."

Grace freed his left hand and pulled it toward her chest.

Richard steeled himself for the feel of the concave impressions where her breasts had been. Although he was sorrowful over her scars, it never bothered him to look at or touch her there. But she wouldn't permit it.

She'd been planning on having reconstructive surgery, but the cancer returned, making surgery impossible. She was always beautiful to him, always enchanting, even at the end.

As she brought his hand up, his palm met round, full flesh. He hesitated, but only for a moment. She placed her hand over his and pressed.

"I've been healed," she whispered. "It was more wonderful than you can imagine. And it didn't hurt."

Richard's eyes pricked. "Healed?"

"No pain. No tears. And it's so, so beautiful."

"I'm sorry I didn't realize you were sick." His voice caught again. "I should have paid attention. I should have noticed."

"It was my time." She reached down and kissed the back of his hand. "There's so much I want to show you. But not yet. Rest, my love."

❧❧

The next morning, Richard awoke to an empty bed and the knowledge that he'd been given a very precious gift. He felt lighter, more at peace than he had been in a long time. He breakfasted with his family and began making arrangements to resign from his research position in Philadelphia.

In the next week, he put his condo up for sale and hired movers to return his things to the house he'd bought with his wife so many years ago. Gabriel insisted that the items they'd placed in storage also be returned to the house.

When the moving trucks arrived, he directed the movers to the master bedroom, asking them to remove its furniture before bringing in Richard's.

"No." Richard placed his hand on his son's shoulder. "The guest room is mine now."

Gabriel indicated to the movers that they should give him a minute. He turned to his father, eyebrows knitted together.

"Why don't you want your old room?"

"The master bedroom is yours now, with Julia. She's painted it and made it her own. I won't undo that."

Gabriel protested, but Richard lifted his hand to stop him.

"Grace will be with me wherever I sleep. She'll find me in the guest room." He clapped his hand on Gabriel's shoulder once again before calling to the movers and directing them upstairs.

Gabriel wasn't about to argue with his father, especially when he seemed content with his decision. And if he found his father's remarks strange, he kept that to himself.

(But in truth, he didn't find the remarks strange.)

That night, when the house was empty and quiet, Richard could almost imagine Grace getting into bed with him. He rolled onto his side and slept peacefully before meeting her in his dreams.

Chapter Seven

July 2011
Oxford, England

Professor Gabriel O. Emerson peered contemptuously around the modest guest room in staircase five of the Cloisters of Magdalen College. His blue eyes alighted on a pair of twin beds that were situated along the wall, and he pointed at them.

"What the hell are those?"

Julia's eyes followed the path of his accusatory finger. "I think those are beds."

"I can see that. We're leaving."

He picked up their bags and approached the door, but she stopped him.

"It's late, Gabriel. I'm tired."

"Exactly. Where the hell are we supposed to sleep?"

"Where do Magdalen students usually sleep? On the floor?"

He gave her a withering look. "I'm not sleeping in a ridiculous abomination of a single bed ever again. We're checking into the Randolph."

She rubbed her eyes with both hands. "Our reservation isn't until two days from now. And besides, you promised."

"Nigel promised me one of the unused don's rooms, a room with a double bed and an en-suite." He looked around. "Where's the double bed? Where's the en-suite? We'll have to share the bathroom with God knows who else!"

"I don't mind sharing a bathroom with the other guest room for two nights. We'll be at the conference most of the time."

Ignoring her husband's irate sputtering, Julia walked to the window, which overlooked the beautiful quadrangle below. She stared longingly at the strange stone figures that were set above the archways to the right.

"You told me that C.S. Lewis was inspired by those statues when he wrote *The Lion, the Witch and the Wardrobe*."

"That's what they say," Gabriel said in a clipped voice.

She rested her forehead against the leaded glass. "Do you think his ghost ever wanders around here?"

"I doubt he'd haunt a room like this." Gabriel sniffed. "He's probably at the pub."

Julia closed her eyes. It had been a long day, traveling from the hotel in London to the railway station, then to Oxford, and now here. She was so very, very tired.

He took in her subdued form from across the room.

"There's no such thing as ghosts, Julianne. You know that." His voice was gentle.

"What about when you saw Grace and Maia?"

"That was different."

She looked at the statues wistfully before joining him at the door, wearing a defeated expression.

"Would it make you unhappy to stay at the hotel?" His eyes searched hers. "We'd have greater privacy."

"We would, yes." She looked away.

He glanced at the twin beds. "Sex is almost impossible in those things. There isn't enough room."

She smirked. "That isn't how I remember it."

A slow, provocative smile spread across his face, and he brought his lips within inches of hers.

"Is that a challenge, Mrs. Emerson?"

Julia regarded him for a moment. Then she seemed to shrug off her fatigue as she wrapped his silk tie around her hand, pulling his mouth to hers.

Gabriel dropped their luggage and kissed her, forgetting his irritation. Then he reached back with his foot and kicked the door shut behind them.

Chapter Eight

Some time later, Gabriel was entwined with his wife in one of the narrow beds. She breathed his name against his chest.

"You haven't lost your skill. I found your most recent innovation extremely—satisfying."

"Thank you." His chest swelled. "It's late now. Time for sleep."

"I can't."

Gabriel coaxed her chin upward. "Are you worried about your paper?"

"I want to make you proud."

"I will always be proud of you. I *am* proud of you." His blue eyes lasered into hers.

"What about Professor Picton?"

"She wouldn't invite you if she thought you weren't ready."

"What if someone asks me a question and I don't know the answer?"

"You answer it as best you can. If they press you, you can always say they've asked a good question and you'll give the matter some thought."

Julia rested against his chest, her fingers scaling his abdominal muscles.

"Do you think if I asked C.S. Lewis to intercede on my behalf, he'd pray for me?"

Gabriel snorted.

"Lewis was a Protestant from Northern Ireland. He didn't believe in petitioning the saints. Even if he heard you, he'd ignore you. On principle.

"Ask Tolkien. He was Catholic."

"I could ask Dante to pray for me."

"Dante is already praying for you." He spoke against her hair.

Julia closed her eyes, listening to the sound of his heartbeat. She always found its rhythm comforting.

"What if people ask why you left Toronto?"

"We'll say what we always say—I wanted to be in Boston because you were going to Harvard and we were getting married."

"Christa Peterson has been telling a different story."

The Professor's eyes narrowed. "Forget about her. We don't need to worry about her at this conference."

"Promise me you won't lose your temper if you hear something—unsavory."

"Give me a little credit." He sounded exasperated. "We've had to deal with gossip at BU and Harvard and I haven't lost my temper."

"Of course." She kissed his chest. "But academics get bored and like to talk. Nothing is more exciting than a sex scandal."

"I beg to differ, Mrs. Emerson." Gabriel's eyes twinkled.

"Oh, really?"

"Sex with you is more exciting than a scandal."

He flipped her to her back and proceeded to kiss her neck.

❧❧

Before the sun peeked over the horizon, Julia crept back into the room. A shaft of light from the window partially illuminated the naked man in her bed. He was lying on his stomach, his dark hair mussed. The sheet was slung dangerously low, exposing his lower back, his dimples, and the top of his backside.

Julia gazed at him appreciatively, her eyes resting a beat longer than necessary on his muscular back and gluteus maximus. He was beautiful, he was sexy, and he was hers.

She removed her yoga pants and T-shirt, placing her clothes and underthings on an obliging chair. Since they'd been married, she almost always slept naked. She preferred it that way—to sleep skin against skin with her beloved.

Gabriel stirred when he felt the mattress move. He accepted her into his arms immediately, but it took a few moments for him to awake.

"Where did you go?" He began to run his fingers up and down her arm.

"I went to see the stone figures in the quadrangle."

Gabriel's eyes opened. "Why?"

"I read the Narnia books. They were special to me."

He cupped her face.

"So you wanted to stay here because of Lewis?"

"And because of you. I know that Paulina lived here when you did, and I . . ." She stopped, regretting the fact that she'd mentioned someone they were both trying to forget.

"That was before we were involved. I spent very little time with her here." He wrapped Julia in his arms. "I wouldn't have tried to take you to the Randolph tonight, if I'd known your reasons. Why didn't you tell me?"

"I thought you'd think my attachment to the Narnia books was juvenile."

"Anything important to you can't be juvenile."

He thought for a moment as he considered what she'd said.

"I read those books, too. There was a closet in my mother's apartment back in New York that I was convinced would open into Narnia if I was a good boy. Clearly, I wasn't."

He expected her to laugh, but she didn't.

"I know what it's like to be willing to do anything to make the stories real," she whispered.

Gabriel's hold on her tightened. "If you want to see where Lewis lived, I'll take you to The Kilns, his house. Then we'll go to The Bird and Baby, where the Inklings met."

"I'd like that."

He brushed a kiss against her hair. "I said once that you were not my equal, but my better. I'm afraid you didn't believe me."

"It's difficult to believe that you think that, sometimes."

He winced.

"I need to do a better job of showing you," he whispered. "But I'm not sure how."

Chapter Nine

After breakfast in Magdalen's dining room, Gabriel insisted that they take a taxi to St. Anne's, the venue for the conference. He was worried that Julia (and her high heels) wouldn't survive the walk, and there was no way in hell he was asking her to change shoes.

"This is a dream come true," Julia murmured, as they drove through Oxford. "I never imagined being able to visit here, let alone being able to present my research. I can't believe it."

"You've worked very hard." He brought her hand to his lips. "This is your reward."

Julia was silent, as she felt the weight of expectations on her shoulders.

When they passed the Ashmolean Museum, Gabriel's eyes suddenly grew alight.

"I wonder what kind of trouble we can get into in there." He pointed to the museum. "As I recall, there are ample locations for a tryst or two."

Julia blushed and he pulled her into his side, chuckling.

He still had the ability to make her blush, a feat in which he took no little pride. And he'd done more than make her blush a few days previous when they'd tangoed against a wall in the British Museum.

(The Elgin Marbles had yet to recover from their shock.)

The Emersons arrived at St. Anne's College just prior to the beginning of the first session. Inside, a group of fifty academics were milling about the refreshment tables, sipping tea and enjoying cookies while chatting about the extraordinary world of Dante studies.

(For indeed, that world was much more interesting than it appeared to outsiders.)

Gabriel poured Julia some tea before helping himself to coffee. He introduced her to two prominent Oxford professors of his acquaintance as they sipped their drinks.

When it was time to enter the lecture theater, Gabriel placed his hand at the small of Julia's back, urging her forward. She took two steps before she stopped.

A familiar and careless laugh filled her ears, the source of the laughter visible a few feet away. In the center of a group of old and young men dressed primarily in tweed was a raven-haired beauty, holding court. She was tall and lithe, her attractive form clad in a fitted black jacket and skirt. Four-inch heels made her long legs even longer.

(For once in his life, the Professor regarded a pair of elegant designer shoes with something other than appreciation.)

The woman's laugh was curtailed when a man with black hair and very tanned skin began whispering something in her ear, his eyes focusing on the Emersons.

"*Fuck*," said Gabriel, under his breath.

He offered Christa Peterson and Professor Giuseppe Pacciani a thunderous look, while Julia catalogued the reactions of the men who stood nearby. As her eyes drifted from one to the next, a terrible and sinking feeling washed over her.

More than one man stared back at her, their eyes resting longer than was appropriate on her breasts and hips. She released Gabriel's hand and buttoned up her suit jacket so that it covered more of her chest.

A look of visible disappointment marked several of the men's appraisals. Clearly Julia didn't live up to their expectations of a young and delectable graduate student, a woman who'd slept with her professor and become enmeshed in a scandal.

"I'm settling this once and for all." Gabriel surged forward, but Julia dug her fingers into his arm, pressing into the wool of his suit as well as his flesh.

"Can I talk to you for a minute?" she whispered.

"After."

"You can't," Julia hissed. "Not here."

"Trouble in Paradise?" Christa's smug voice reverberated in the room. "I guess the honeymoon didn't last very long."

She fixed her eyes, catlike, on Julia, her attractive mouth curling into a sneer. "Not that I'm surprised."

Julia tried to pull Gabriel away, but he stood his ground, his body vibrating with anger.

"I'd like a word, Miss Peterson."

Christa inched closer to Professor Pacciani. She made a show of appearing to be intimidated by Gabriel.

"Not after what happened in Toronto. If you have something to say you'll have to say it in front of witnesses."

From the safety of Pacciani's side, she leaned forward, dropping her voice. "It isn't in your interest to make a scene, Gabriel. I found out a few things after you resigned, such as your involvement in BDSM. I didn't know that Professor Ann Singer was your Domme."

A hush fell over those closest to the antagonists, their eyes shifting from Christa to Gabriel.

Julia took his hand in hers and tugged. "Let's go. *Please.*"

Despite Gabriel's fury he was conscious, all too conscious, of the now rapt attention of his peers. Still, it took every ounce of his self-control not to lunge forward and seize Christa by the throat.

Stifling a curse, he turned abruptly and took a single step away from his former student.

"I'm looking forward to your paper, Julianne." Christa lifted her voice so more people could hear. "It's unusual for a first-year student to be included in such an important conference. However did you manage it?"

Julia paused, looking at Christa over her shoulder.

"Professor Picton invited me."

"Really?" Christa appeared puzzled. "Wouldn't it have been better to invite Gabriel to speak? I mean, you're probably repeating things you learned from him. Or maybe he simply wrote your paper for you."

"I do my own research." Julia's voice was quiet but steely.

"I'm sure you do." Christa made a point of glancing at Gabriel's back. "But your 'research' can't help you write a lecture. Unless you're planning to tell us about all the professors you slept with in order to get into Harvard."

Gabriel swore and released Julia's hand. He turned around, casting furious eyes in Christa's direction.

"That's enough. You don't speak to my wife. Do you understand?"

"Temper, temper, Gabriel." Christa's dark eyes shone with perverse amusement.

"It's *Professor* Emerson," he snapped.

Julia blocked his path with her body.

"Let's go." She placed a light hand on his chest, just under his bow tie.

"Get out of my way." He looked like a dragon preparing to breathe fire.

"*For me*," she begged, her expression pleading.

Before Gabriel could open his mouth, an authoritative voice sounded at his elbow.

"What is the meaning of this?"

Katherine Picton stood to his right, her white hair short and impeccably styled, her gray-blue eyes flashing behind her glasses. She eyed Professor Pacciani with distaste before turning her attention to Christa.

"Who are you?"

Christa's posture shifted from defensive to ingratiating. She extended her hand.

"I'm Christa Peterson, from Columbia. We met at the University of Toronto."

Katherine ignored the proffered hand. "I'm familiar with the faculty at Columbia. You aren't one of them."

Christa reddened, withdrawing her hand. "I'm a graduate student."

"Then don't present yourself as anything else," Katherine snapped. "You aren't *from* Columbia. You *attend* Columbia. I repeat, why are you here?"

When Christa didn't respond, Professor Picton stepped closer, raising her voice.

"Are you hard of hearing? I asked you a question. What are you doing at my conference, insulting my guests?"

Christa almost faltered, feeling the energy in the room shift under Professor Picton's antipathy. Even Professor Pacciani took a step back.

"I'm here to attend your lecture, like everyone else."

Katherine straightened to her full five feet and looked up at the much taller and half-century younger graduate student.

"Your name isn't on the guest list. I certainly didn't invite you."

"Professor Picton, excuse me. The young lady is a friend." Professor Pacciani smoothly interceded. He bowed and moved to kiss Professor Picton's hand, but she waved at him dismissively.

"As a companion of yours, Giuseppe, her attendance might be excusable. But barely." She glared at him. "You need to teach her some manners."

Katherine turned to address Christa directly.

"I know the havoc you wreaked in Toronto. Your lies almost destroyed my department. You'll follow the rules of decorum here, or I'll have you removed. Do you understand?"

Without waiting for a response, Katherine began scolding Pacciani in fluid Italian, pointing out in no uncertain terms that if his friend made her guests' visit unpleasant in any way, she would hold him personally responsible.

She added that she had a perfect and unforgiving memory.

(It should be mentioned that she was correct.)

"*Capisce?*" She glared at him through her glasses.

"*Certo*, Professor." He bowed, his face drawn and angry.

"I'm the injured party," Christa protested. "When I was in Toronto, Gabriel—"

"Codswallop," Katherine spat. "I'm old, not senile. I recognize a woman scorned when I see one. And so should everyone else." At this, Katherine directed her scathing expression to the men who had surrounded Christa, eager to give ear to her gossip.

"What's more, inviting yourself to an invitation-only event is unprofessional in the extreme. This isn't a fraternity party."

Professor Picton looked around the room once more, pausing as if to challenge anyone to contradict her. Under her withering stare, the prurient onlookers began shuffling their feet and backing away.

Seemingly satisfied, she turned her attention back to Miss Peterson and lifted her chin. "I believe I'm quite finished."

With that, she favored Christa with her back. The other occupants of the room stood by, somewhat shell-shocked by just having witnessed the academic equivalent of a mud-wrestling match, handily won by a small (but feisty) septuagenarian.

"My dear friends, it's good to see you. How was your flight?" Katherine placed her arm around Julia's stiff shoulders, giving her a fraternal squeeze, before shaking Gabriel's hand.

"The flight was fine. We spent a few days in London before arriving by train." Gabriel kissed Professor Picton's cheek. He tried to force a smile but failed.

"I'm not impressed with the fact that they've admitted riffraff." Katherine sniffed. "I must speak to the conference organizers. It's bad enough that you young people should be subjected to such a person, but to have to endure her in public. What a ridiculous girl."

Professor Picton's aged eyes quickly took in Julia's expression of distress, and her demeanor softened.

"I'll buy you a drink this evening, Julianne. I think it's time for us to have a little chat."

The professor's words jarred Julia out of her quietude. A thinly veiled expression of terror flashed across her features.

Gabriel grasped her around the waist. "That's very generous, Katherine, but why don't you join us for dinner, instead?"

"Thank you, I'd enjoy that. But I'll speak to Julianne first." She turned to her former student, her expression kind. "Come and find me after the last lecture and we'll walk to The Bird and Baby."

Professor Picton took her leave and was immediately surrounded by several academic admirers.

It took a moment for Julia to regain her composure, but when she did, she leaned against Gabriel.

"I'm so embarrassed."

"I'm sorry Katherine interrupted when she did. I would have liked to say a few words."

Julia began wringing her hands. "I never should have answered Christa. We should have walked away."

Gabriel's expression tightened. He looked around, then brought his mouth close to her ear. "You stood up for yourself, which was the right thing to do. And I'm not going to stand there and let her call you a whore."

"If we'd walked away, she wouldn't have gotten that far."

"Bullshit. She's already slandering us. You said so yourself."

Julia's face was marked by disappointment. "I asked you to stop."

"And I explained that I wasn't about to let her speak to you that way." He clenched his jaw and released it. "Let's not fight because of that bitch. That's precisely what she wants."

"She was spoiling for a fight. And you gave it to her." Julia glanced around the rapidly emptying room. "Tomorrow I have to stand up in front of everyone, knowing that they witnessed that embarrassing scene."

"If I'd said nothing, if I'd done nothing, then it would look like I agreed with her." Gabriel's voice rumbled, low in his throat.

"I asked you to stop, and you brushed me off." She gave him a wounded look. "I'm your wife. Not a speed bump."

She clutched her old Fendi messenger bag and followed the crowd into the lecture theater.

Chapter Ten

Professor Emerson seethed with anger as he watched his wife walk away. He wanted to drag Christa Peterson outside by her hair and teach her a lesson. Unfortunately, based on her seductive behavior when she was his student, she'd probably enjoy it.

(And take photographs for her scrapbook.)

It was not like him to want to strike a woman.

Or perhaps it was. Perhaps it was precisely like him to want to strike a woman. Anger and violence were written in the bone, the product of DNA. Perhaps Gabriel was just like his father.

He closed his eyes. As quickly as the thought emerged, he tamped it down. Now was not the time to think of what he did and did not know about his biological parents.

Gabriel knew he had a temper. He tried to control it but frequently failed. On one such occasion, to his shame, he'd struck a woman.

He was teaching in Toronto. The women were beautiful and sexy; the city was ripe with diversions of music and art. Yet he'd been depressed. Paulina had been to see him and they'd resumed their sexual relationship—again. After every encounter, he'd swear it would be the last time. But every time she put her hands on him, he gave in.

He knew it was wrong. His continued involvement with her was damaging to both of them. But his spirit, although willing, was tied to flesh that was very, very weak.

After she went back to Boston, he began drinking heavily. He became a VIP at Lobby and fucked a different woman every night. Sometimes fucking more than one in a single Scotch-soaked evening. Sometimes fucking more than one at the same time.

Nothing helped. Haunted by his past, made all the more recent by his few days with Paulina, he felt as if he were one careless moment away from resuming his cocaine habit.

Then he met Ann. They shared an enthusiasm for fencing and fenced a few times at their club, only to retire to a darkened room on the last occasion for a brief but explosive sexual encounter.

Ann Singer promised new, tantalizing diversions. She whispered words of raw, intense pleasure the likes of which he'd never experienced.

He was intrigued. She had the power to drag his mind into his body and keep it there, unable to think or worry. And that was how he found himself in the basement of her town house in Toronto, naked, restrained, and on his knees.

She confused his senses by both pleasing and punishing him. With every strike, all his emotional pain seemed to bleed away. His single errant thought was why had he waited so long to use physical pain to alleviate his mental suffering. But even that thought was soon forgotten.

Then came the humiliation. Ann's dominance was over the mind, as well as the body. As she bruised his flesh, she sought to break his will.

Gabriel realized what she was doing, and his psyche bristled. He desired physical pain and accepted it, but not psychological manipulation. His mind was fucked up enough thanks to his past.

He began to resist.

She accused him of attempting to top from the bottom and redoubled her efforts. She retold his life story, spinning a speculative myth based solely on her own armchair analysis. Some of it came perilously close to the truth. And the rest of it . . .

Without warning, something inside him snapped.

Standing in St. Anne's College, Gabriel couldn't recall exactly what Professor Singer said that set him off. He couldn't remember how long the encounter lasted. He only remembered white-hot, blinding fury.

In one swift motion, he broke the restraint on his right wrist (a considerable feat) and backhanded her across the face. Her diminutive form crumpled to the tiled floor.

He stumbled to his feet and stood over her, breathing heavily. She didn't move.

A door flew open and Gabriel found himself boxing one-handed with her bodyguard, who'd rushed to her defense. Bruised and bloodied, Gabriel was flung outside into the snow, his clothes scattered behind him.

That was his last sexual encounter with Ann and his final experience with BDSM. He was revolted by the fact that he'd lost control and hit her, and he was determined never to strike a woman again. Even now, the shame washed over him.

Gabriel closed his eyes and tried to compose himself. He'd never explained the entirety of what happened with Professor Singer to Julianne. He wasn't about to do so now. Some things were better left unsaid.

He mentally catalogued the eminent Dante specialists who'd overheard Christa's remarks about his past. It was embarrassing, to be sure. But he was tenured and full professor. They could go to hell.

(And study Dante's *Inferno* in person.)

But he needed to neutralize Christa before she damaged Julianne's reputation any further. She'd all but called Julia a whore, suggesting her academic success was won on her knees.

With that thought twisting in his mind, he straightened his bow tie, smoothed his suit jacket, and entered the lecture theater.

Julia watched as her husband approached, his eyes averted, his visage grim.

He glowered at Christa, who sat with Professor Pacciani, before taking the seat between Julia and Professor Picton. Gabriel didn't speak as he pulled his Meisterstück 149 fountain pen and a notepad out of his leather briefcase. His body language was decidedly cross.

Julia tried to concentrate on the lecture, which was on the use of the number three in Dante's *Divine Comedy*. The subject matter and delivery of the presentation could only be described as contravening the Geneva Conventions on cruel and unusual punishment. Worse still was being next to Gabriel and feeling his anger radiating through his handsome three-piece suit.

Out of the corner of her eye, she saw that he was taking copious notes, his elegant script uncharacteristically forceful and angular. There was tension around his mouth and a familiar crease between his dark brows, behind his glasses.

Julia was disappointed in him, but she wasn't angry. She knew it was consonant with his character to be the avenging angel. There had been times when she welcomed that aspect of his personality, such as when he'd beaten Simon senseless after he'd attacked her.

But she didn't like fighting with him, especially in public. She certainly didn't enjoy the sight of him losing his temper and causing a scene in front of so many important people, even if Katherine defended him.

She sighed quietly. His love for her and his desire that she succeed likely fueled his anger.

You're his first serious and committed relationship. You should cut the guy some slack.

She wanted to touch him but was wary of how she might be received. Certainly, she didn't wish to interrupt him. She imagined him peering at her over the rims of his glasses, his expression censorious. Such a reaction would cut her deeply.

It had been a long time since she'd seen him truly angry. Julia thought back to their explosive interactions in his Dante seminar, when she'd challenged him about Paulina. He'd been furious until his anger shifted to passion.

She uncrossed and crossed her legs. Now was not the time to think about passion. She'd wait until they were back in their room at Magdalen before she reached out to him. Otherwise, he might decide to make up with her and drag her into a corner for *conference sex*.

(Conference sex was a peculiar compunction of certain academics. It should be avoided at all costs.)

The next lecture was as torturous as the first. Julia feigned interest while her thoughts fixated on one point. If Gabriel had listened to her, Christa would have been forced to spin her web of slander without a large, focused audience. Now Julia would have to mingle with the other attendees knowing they'd witnessed the embarrassing display. She was shy to begin with. Christa had magnified her unease a hundredfold.

Despite their falling out, Julia would have preferred to spend the day at his side, especially during lunch and the frequent tea and coffee breaks. But they'd agreed the night before to circulate among the conferencegoers, giving Julia the opportunity to network.

She forced herself to make small talk, allowing Professors Marinelli and Picton to introduce her to their old friends, while Gabriel mingled on the other side of the room. He was obviously on a charm offensive—trying to speak to as many conferencegoers as possible. From the glances Julia received, it was clear he was speaking about her.

Women flocked to him. No matter where he was, there were always one or two women standing near him. To his credit, he suffered their attentions patiently without encouraging them.

Julia focused on her own interactions, but she couldn't help but keep apprised of where he was situated and with whom. She also marked Christa's position, but she was never far from Professor Pacciani.

Julia found the fact curious.

Pacciani's eyes seemed to follow her and on one occasion, she was certain he winked. But he made no attempt to approach or speak with her. He seemed content to remain at Christa's side, despite her occasionally flirtatious behavior with other men.

Julia sipped her tea as she listened to professor after professor regale her with tales of their latest research projects, longing for the end of the day.

During the final lecture, Gabriel noticed Julia squirming in her seat. She'd been doing so for an hour, as if she were in desperate need of the ladies' room.

Gabriel had been nursing his irritation with Christa for hours, fanning the embers with myriad justifications for his words and actions. He was in the middle of composing a self-righteous speech that he intended to deliver to Julia when they were back at Magdalen, when she stunned him by passing a note.

I don't want to fight.
I'm sorry.
Thank you for defending me.
I'm sorry she mentioned Professor Pain.

Gabriel reread the note twice.

The sight of Julia's contrition in black and white made his heart constrict. She'd said that she was sorry, even though she'd done almost nothing.

He would have appreciated more support from her. He coveted her compassion—compassion for a plight brought about because of his strong desire to protect her. But he hadn't expected an apology.

Their eyes met and she gave him a tentative smile. The smile, perhaps even more than the note, undid him.

His irritation cooled, under the frigid waters of remorse.

Without delay, he turned her note over and wrote,

Emerson was an ass.
But he hopes you'll forgive him.

It took an instant for her to read it. And when she did, she restrained a laugh, resulting in a strangled snort.

The sound echoed around the room and the lecturer looked up from his notes, wondering how a wild pig had managed to wander into St. Anne's College in order to attend his paper.

Blushing furiously, Julia feigned a coughing fit, while Gabriel patted her back. When the lecture eventually continued, he added to his missive,

I'm sorry I embarrassed you.
I promise I'll do better.
You are not a speed bump.
You're my Beatrice.

Julia's delicate features lightened, and he watched as her shoulders relaxed.

Hesitantly, she reached out her baby finger and linked it with his own. This was her way of holding his hand without others seeing.

He curved his pinky around hers, looking at her from out of the corner of his eye.

Yes, Professor Emerson could be an ass, on occasion. But at least he was sorry.

After the conference ended for the day, Katherine spirited Julia away to The Eagle and Child pub for a drink. The pub was referred to locally as "The Bird and Baby," or "The Fowl and Foetus." It was, perhaps, the most famous pub in Oxford. Julia was eager to see it because it had been one of the meeting places of the Inklings, the literary group that included C.S. Lewis, J.R.R. Tolkien, and Charles Williams.

Inside, Katherine purchased two pints of Caledonian ale and piloted her former student to a back corner. Once they were comfortable, she clinked their glasses together and took a long pull from her pint.

"It's good to see you, Julianne. You're looking well." Katherine took in her former student's appearance with a single glance. "Your wedding was a triumph. I haven't had that much fun in years."

"I'm so glad you could join us." Julia gripped her glass a little too tightly, the whiteness of her knuckles telegraphing her nervousness.

"Are you anxious about your lecture?"

"Somewhat." Julia sipped her ale, wondering why Katherine had insisted on speaking to her alone.

"It's understandable to be apprehensive, but you'll do fine. No doubt you're still a bit shaken after encountering that dreadful woman."

Julia's stomach flipped, and she nodded.

Katherine noted that the other patrons were engaged in their own conversations before continuing.

"Did Gabriel ever explain how I came to be in his debt?"

"He mentioned something about doing you a favor, but he wasn't specific."

Katherine tapped her pint thoughtfully with a single unpainted fingernail.

"I would have thought he'd have told you. But it's like him to keep another person's confidence."

She removed her glasses, placing them on the table.

"Six years ago, I was in phased retirement in Toronto. Jeremy Martin hired Gabriel to replace me, but I was still supervising graduate students and teaching a seminar.

"At the beginning of the fall semester, I received an email from an old friend here in Oxford. He told me that our former professor, John Hutton, was in hospice dying of cancer."

"I know Professor Hutton's work. He was one of the sources for my paper."

"Old Hut probably forgot more information about Dante than I ever knew." Katherine's expression grew almost wistful. "When I received news that he was dying, I'd already begun teaching my seminar. And I'd agreed to deliver a series of lectures on Dante and the seven deadly sins for the CBC. I approached Jeremy and asked if it would be possible to take a week off so I could come here."

Katherine's sharp gaze missed very little, and she certainly didn't miss seeing Julia start at the mention of Professor Martin's name.

"Jeremy was an ally to both of you last year. He tried very hard to help Gabriel, but in the end, there was only so much he could do."

Julia shifted in her seat. "I always wondered why he helped Christa transfer to his alma mater. There were rumors they were involved."

"Rumors hurt people. Sometimes, they hurt innocent people. I expect better from you, Mrs. Emerson, than to be listening to gossip about Professor Martin."

Julia grew flustered.

"I'm sorry. You're right, of course."

"I've known Jeremy and his wife for years. Believe me, Christa Peterson couldn't catch his eye if she were naked, holding the original manuscript of *The Decameron* and a case of beer."

Julia stifled a laugh at Professor Picton's imaginative description, such as it was.

"Two days after I explained my situation, Jeremy approached Gabriel. In short order, he volunteered to take over my seminar and any other responsibilities while I was away."

"I didn't know that."

Katherine tipped her head to one side. "But it shouldn't surprise you. Gabriel likes to do his good deeds in secret, I think, but that he does them is unremarkable. When he volunteered to help he was a first-year assistant professor, just out of graduate school. It was an extraordinary kindness on his part for someone he knew only in passing. As it happened, I was away until after Christmas, burdening him with everything for four long months. And then afterward, when I came home, he was a very good friend to me. So as you can appreciate, I owe him a debt."

"I'm sure he was happy to help, Professor. After everything you've done for us, the debt is more than forgotten."

Katherine paused, peering at their surroundings thoughtfully. "Gabriel tells me you're an admirer of the Inklings."

"I am. Did you know them?"

"I met Tolkien once, when I was a little girl. My father was a Beowulf specialist at Leeds and he and Tolkien used to correspond with one another. I came down on the train with my father to visit him."

"What was he like?"

Katherine sat back in her chair and regarded the ceiling.

"I liked him. At the time, I simply thought of him as old, like my father. But I can recall that he coaxed me into telling him a story I'd made up about a family of badgers that lived behind our house. He seemed quite taken by it." She gestured to the corner in which they sat. "This was the exact spot where the Inklings used to meet."

Julia slowly examined the space. As a child, hiding in her room with a stack of Narnia books, she would never have imagined that one day she would be sitting where Lewis sat. It was nothing short of a miracle.

"Thank you for bringing me here." Her voice almost caught in her throat.

"My pleasure."

Katherine's expression shifted.

"It took me almost an entire semester to see Old Hut. When I arrived in Oxford, his wife banned me from the hospice. I showed up every day for weeks, hoping to change her mind, hoping that he wouldn't pass away before I could see him."

"Who would be so cruel?"

"You ask this question after the *Shoah*? After countless instances of genocide? Human beings can be incredibly cruel.

"In the case of Old Hut, I was the cruel one and I paid for it. But that semester, it was Mrs. Hutton's opportunity to exact her revenge, *with interest*."

"I'm so sorry."

Professor Picton waved her hand. "Gabriel gave me the chance to make my peace. I will always be in his debt, which means I feel a special responsibility for you."

"Were you able to see your friend?"

"Mrs. Hutton's aunt fell ill. While she was visiting her, I managed to see the professor. By then, he was near death, but we were able to talk.

"I came back to Toronto and worked through my depression. But I never told Gabriel the entire story, or why it was so important for me to see John before he died." Katherine pursed her lips, looking as if she were divided about something. Then she shrugged.

"All the important players are dead, with the exception of me. There's no point in keeping it a secret." She looked at Julia over her glass. "I don't expect you to keep things from your husband, but I ask that you be discreet."

"Of course, Professor."

Katherine wrapped her aged fingers around her pint.

"Old Hut and I were involved while I was his student, and afterward, when I taught at Cambridge. He was married. Lucky for me, no one found out about us while I was living here in Oxford. But eventually, there were rumors, and the rumors followed me for ten years."

Julia's mouth dropped open.

Katherine glanced at her, her blue eyes sparkling in what could have been amusement.

"I see you're surprised. But I wasn't always this old. In my day, I was considered attractive. And is it really so surprising? People work closely together on something they're passionate about, and that passion has to go somewhere. Dante speaks of it when he describes Paolo and Francesca."

Katherine replaced her glasses on her face.

"When I was trying to get an academic position, the gossip became particularly vicious. There were those among my student colleagues who were jealous of Old Hut's attentions and the fact that he clearly preferred me. Even without evidence of our amour, they began circulating stories that he authored my research. In fact, someone wrote to the University of Cambridge after I'd applied for a job there, claiming that Old Hut wrote a letter of recommendation for me simply because I was sleeping with him."

Julia laughed.

Then she clapped a hand to her mouth.

"I'm so sorry. That isn't funny."

Katherine's eyes twinkled.

"Of course it's funny. You should have seen his recommendation letter. He wrote, *Miss Picton is competent in the study of Dante.* I was his lover, for God's sake. Don't you think he could have troubled himself to write more than one sentence?"

While Julia stared in horror, Professor Picton chuckled.

"I can make light of it now, but I was unhappy for many years. I fell in love with a married man and I mourned not having him all to myself. No marriage, no children. Once I began presenting my research, the rumors died. People heard my lectures, some of which disagreed with Old Hut's positions, and they realized I knew what I was talking about. I worked very hard to make a name for myself and to come out from under his shadow. That's why when he was dying, the only other person who knew what had transpired between me and Old Hut was his wife."

Katherine stared at Julia intently.

"I tried my best to discredit Miss Peterson this morning and I will continue to do so. But even if I fail, eventually everyone will move on to the latest scandal. By the time you have your own faculty position, the rumors will be forgotten."

"That's six years away, Professor."

Professor Picton smiled. "Given what I've shared with you this evening, I think you should call me Katherine."

"Thank you, Katherine." Julia returned her smile shyly.

"You can help people forget the gossip by being excellent. If you prove yourself, all the gossip in the world can't diminish it. It's possible you'll have to work harder than others, but I don't think you're bothered by hard work. Are you?"

"No, I'm not."

"Good." Katherine sat back in her chair. "My next piece of advice will be a little bit more difficult to hear."

Julia braced herself for the words to come.

"You need to be more assertive, academically. I understand that it's your nature to be shy and that you'd prefer to avoid confrontation. But in the academic arena, you cannot do that. When you deliver a paper and someone challenges you, you have to challenge him right back. You can't sustain misguided or malicious criticisms, especially in public. Do you understand?"

"I don't seem to have trouble speaking up in my seminars. Professor Marinelli has been pleased."

"Good. My advice is to be yourself tomorrow. Be bright. Be excellent. And don't let yourself be ravaged by wolves like some diseased moose."

Julia's eyes widened at the strange reference, but she said nothing.

"You mustn't let your husband defend you, either. That will make you look weak. You need to defend yourself and your ideas if you're going to be successful. Gabriel isn't going to like that. But you must make him see that when he comes to your aid, he makes you look helpless, and that does more harm than good. Chivalry in academia is dead."

Julia nodded a bit uncertainly.

Katherine finished her pint.

"Now, let's see if Gabriel has managed to charm the old bastards of the Oxford Dante Society into forgetting what they might have heard this morning." She winked. "For some of them, what they heard would only make him more appealing. I'm afraid your husband is far more interesting than any of them could have imagined."

Gabriel spent his time apart from Julianne wisely. He visited with old friends and new acquaintances at the King's Arms pub, putting his silver tongue to good use. By the end of the hour, he'd succeeded in giving a half a dozen Dante specialists reason to think that Christa Peterson was a jealous ex-student and that he and Julia were the victims of slander.

So it was with a markedly improved mood that he joined Professor Picton and Julia for dinner. Katherine spoke fluidly as the wine flowed, while Gabriel kept up his end of the conversation.

Julia was quiet, even more so than usual, her large eyes tired. She merely picked at her dinner and couldn't even be tempted by dessert. It was clear that the events of the day had caught up with her.

When she excused herself to go to the ladies' room, Katherine gave Gabriel a concerned look.

"She needs rest. The poor girl is worn out."

"Yes." Gabriel's expression was thoughtful, but he didn't comment further.

Katherine nodded at his empty wine glass. "You've stopped drinking."

"I have." He offered her a patient smile.

"Not a bad idea. I go through periods of teetotaling myself." She wiped her lips with her napkin. "Will you accept some maternal advice, from someone who is not your mother?"

Gabriel turned to her abruptly. "About what?"

"I worry sometimes about your ability to handle your detractors. Especially now that you're married."

He started to disagree but she interrupted.

"I'm old, I can behave how I wish. But you cannot be Julianne's champion at academic conferences. If you rise to her defense, you'll make her look weak."

Gabriel folded his napkin and placed it on the table. "The incident this morning with Christa Peterson was anomalous. She tried to destroy our careers."

"Just so. But even in that case, I'm afraid you did more harm than good."

Gabriel frowned, and Katherine decided to change tactics.

"We've been good friends, you and I. I'd like to think that if I'd had a son, he would be your equal in intelligence and talent."

His expression softened. "Thank you, Katherine. Your friendship is important to me."

"I've given Julianne some advice. No doubt she'll tell you all about our conversation. But before she returns, I'd ask that you consider what I've just said. She's a nice young woman and very bright. Let her brightness shine."

"That's all I want." He looked down at his hands. His eyes were drawn to the way the light caught on his wedding band, and he found himself staring at it.

"Good." Katherine tapped her finger on the table, as if to signal that the matter had been decided. "Now, I hope I'll be invited to dinner at your house when I give my lecture series at Harvard in January. Greg Matthews always takes me to these appalling molecular gastronomy restaurants that serve you deconstructed entrées cooked in liquid nitrogen. I can never decide whether I'm having dinner or sitting for an exam in organic chemistry."

After dinner, Gabriel insisted that they escort Katherine to her residence at All Souls, where they bade one another good night and agreed to meet for breakfast the following morning.

"Eight thirty, sharp." Katherine tapped her wristwatch. "Don't be late."

"We wouldn't dream of it." Gabriel bowed.

"See that you don't." With a wave, she disappeared behind the great wooden door of the college, which closed behind her.

Left standing together, Gabriel took Julia's hand, noticing that her fingers had grown cold. He tried to warm them, touching her wedding band and engagement ring.

"I know that you're tired," he said. "But I want to show you something. It will just take a minute."

He led her around the corner to Radcliffe Camera, a great, circular building that had become an icon of the university. The sky was dark, moonless, but a few lights illuminated the impressive structure.

He squeezed her hand as they approached. "I used to spend a lot of time walking around this building. I've always admired it."

"It's fantastic."

Julia eagerly perused the architecture and its interplay of stone and dome and pillar. The sky was the color of ink, and the dome almost seemed to glow against its backdrop.

Gabriel brought his hands to cup her cheeks. "I want to speak to you about what happened this morning."

He felt her tense beneath his touch. His eyes sought hers and he moved his thumbs gently across her cheekbones. "I'm sorry for embarrassing you."

"I know it was difficult for you to walk away from her at first. But you did. And I'm grateful for that." Her dark eyes glinted. "You still like to fight."

Gabriel took her hands in his and pulled them into his chest.

"I like to fight with people other than you. Christa is a bully. The only way to deal with bullies is to confront them."

Julia lifted her chin. "Sometimes, you should let the nastiness speak for itself. Or at least, let her target decide for herself what's to be done."

"I can do that. At least, I can try."

"That's all I ask." Julia brushed her lips against his. "I'm sorry she brought up Professor Pain. I had no idea they knew each other."

Gabriel closed his eyes. When he opened them, they were pained.

"I confessed my past. I left it behind. Must I be reminded of it forever?"

"I'm sorry." She wrapped her arms around his back, bringing their chests together.

They were quiet for a moment and Gabriel pushed his face into her neck, clutching her tightly.

"Caravaggio," she said.

"What's that?"

"I remember what you said about his painting of St. Thomas and Jesus—how our scars might heal but they never disappear. You can't eliminate your past but you don't have to be controlled by it."

"I know that. But I doubt anyone would want their sexual encounters broadcasted to their work colleagues."

"Anyone who would judge you based on old gossip isn't a friend of yours, anyway." She pulled back so she could look into his eyes. "Those of us who know you will ignore the gossip."

"Thank you." He pressed his lips to her forehead before meeting her gaze. "People and circumstances will conspire to alienate us from one another, Julianne. We can't let them do that."

"We won't."

"I didn't mean to ignore you. You mean more to me than anything," he whispered.

"It's the same for me."

She breached the distance between their mouths in order to kiss him, her lips soft and ever moving.

❧❧

Some distance away, Professor Giuseppe Pacciani groaned his release and collapsed on top of his lover's body. Sex with her was always magnificent, and this coupling was no exception.

He mumbled a few phrases in Italian, as was his custom. But instead of welcoming his words, she pushed him aside and rolled away. Sadly, this was not unusual.

"Cara?"

Christa Peterson pulled the sheet over her naked body. "I need the room tomorrow night. You'll have to stay somewhere else."

With a curse, Giuseppe eased his bare feet to the floor. He walked to the bathroom to dispose of the condom. "This is my room."

"No," she called to him. "It's my room. You always pay for my accommodations. And I'll be entertaining tomorrow night."

He returned to the bed and soon she was under him again, his forearms on either side of her shoulders.

"You'd take someone to your bed so soon? The sheets will still be warm."

Her dark eyes flashed.

"Don't judge me. You're married. Who I fuck is none of your business."

He bent down and kissed her, his lips insistent until she opened her mouth.

"Such a dirty mouth, Cristina."

"You love it when I'm dirty."

He sighed, and his expression morphed into a wry smile.

"Sì."

He moved to his back, taking her with him.

"I want to get up." She pulled against his arms.

"No."

She struggled but he would not let her go. Finally, she relented, resting her head against him.

He toyed with her hair. This was part of their arrangement. Afterward, she had to let him hold her.

Perhaps he did so simply to satisfy himself that there was something affectionate about their fucking. Perhaps he did so because he was not an entirely ruthless adulterer. But whatever the reason, she always resisted for a moment or two, even though she secretly liked being held.

"I was surprised to hear from you, Cristina. We were supposed to meet a year ago. You never answered."

"I was busy."

He lifted the ends of her raven hair to his nose, inhaling its fragrance.

"I wondered why you insisted I bring you. You're here for revenge."

"We're both getting what we wanted."

His fingers stilled.

"Be careful, Cristina. You don't want Professor Picton as an enemy."

"I don't care."

Pacciani cursed.

"Don't you understand the patronage system? Departments around the world are filled with her admirers. Your chair at Columbia was her student."

"I didn't know that." Christa shrugged. "It's too late. I've already pissed her off."

Pacciani grabbed Christa's chin roughly, forcing her to look at him.

"I'm responsible for you now. So you will stop. I'm trying to get a position in America and I don't need Professor Picton making trouble."

Christa was quiet for a moment as she examined his menacing expression.

"Fine," she pouted. "But I need the room tomorrow night."

"*Va bene.*"

He released her chin and resumed stroking her long, dark hair. "What was his name?"

"Who?"

"The man who made you like this."

Her muscles tensed under his fingers. "I don't know what you mean."

"You know, *tesoro*. Was it your papa? Did he—"

"No." She trained her eyes on his furiously. "He's a good man."

"*Certo, cara. Certo.*

"All the time I've known you, you've had lovers but no suitors. You should be married. You should be having babies. Instead, you fuck old men for expensive gifts."

"I don't fuck you for your gifts. I fuck you because I like to fuck."

He laughed.

"*Grazie.* But still, there must always be gifts." He brought his lips to her forehead. "Why?"

"I like nice things. That isn't a crime. And I'm worth it."

"You know what I think, *tesoro*?"

"Stop calling me that." She pulled away.

His hand wrapped around the back of her neck, holding her in place.

"You don't think you're worth it, which is why you demand gifts. Sad, no?"

"I don't want your pity."

"You have it, all the same."

"Then you're a fool."

His grip on her tightened. "You fuck priests and old, married men because you're afraid. You're afraid of what might happen if you were to sleep with someone who was unattached."

She struggled in his arms.

"Since when did you become a psychiatrist? Don't project your bullshit on me. At least I'm not fucking around on my wife."

"*Attenzione*, Cristina." His tone was a warning. "So who is the man you fuck tomorrow night? A priest? A professor?"

She regarded him for a moment, then traced her finger across his lower lip. "Who said it was a man?"

Giuseppe gave her a ravenous look.

"Then I expect you to share."

Chapter Eleven

"Wake up, darling." Gabriel ran his thumb over Julia's eyebrows. "You need to get ready."

She buried her face in the pillow and mumbled something unintelligible.

He chuckled, thinking about how adorable she looked.

"Come on, you need to grab the shower before one of our neighbors occupies it."

"You go first."

"I'm already showered, shaved, and dressed, darling." He ran the back of his hand down her naked spine, taking pleasure in the tremor that resulted.

"You kept me up too late," she groaned.

"If you don't get moving, Katherine will be cross with us."

"I'm not taking a shower. I can sleep longer."

Gabriel rolled her over and ran his nose along her collarbone, inhaling her scent.

"You smell like sex," he whispered, flicking out his tongue to taste her skin. "And me."

"That's why I'm not taking a shower. We had incredible makeup sex, which I'd like to remember."

It was all he could do not to pull the sheets off her and engage in wild, passionate (and scent-transferring) sex. But he quickly restrained his impulses.

"You can't deliver a lecture at Oxford smelling of sex."

"Watch me."

Gabriel looked at his wristwatch. Then he looked at his wife.

Then he took off all his clothes and commenced in wild, passionate, scent-transferring (albeit quick) preconference sex.

❧❧

The Emersons were late departing for All Souls College. On the hurried walk over, Julia told Gabriel the story of Katherine and Old Hut.

He was surprised. He knew Professor Hutton by reputation but had never met him. Apparently, he was a bit of a bastard.

(One might wonder how much of a bastard Hutton had been, given the former nature of the professor making the judgment.)

Gabriel was grateful for Professor Picton's support and told her so over breakfast inside All Souls, expressing his hope that Christa would forgo the opportunity to make trouble for Julia at her lecture.

"Applesauce," said Katherine. "Julianne has the situation in hand and we'd all do well to let her see to it."

Julia smiled bravely, fidgeting with the silver necklace Gabriel had given her back in Selinsgrove.

As they entered St. Anne's after breakfast, Gabriel wrapped an arm around Julia's waist, hugging her.

"You look lovely. And you're going to be fine."

She glanced down at her navy suit and plain navy pumps. Gabriel had wanted her to wear Prada or Chanel, but she was wary of flaunting their money. She'd rather people focused on her research than her clothes. So she'd purchased a simple jacket and skirt from Ann Taylor, with modestly high-heeled shoes from Nine West. Even so, given the way some of the other conferencegoers dressed (with the exception of Christa Peterson), she felt a bit overdone.

Underneath her clothes, she knew she wore Gabriel's scent along with the corset he'd bought for her, which bolstered her confidence considerably.

"I'm going to get a coffee. What would you like?" He smiled and released her.

"A bottle of water, please. I'd like to sit down, if you don't mind."

"Not at all. See you in there."

Julia returned his smile and entered the lecture theater alone.

Gabriel exchanged a few pleasantries with some colleagues before he approached the refreshment table. By the time he'd poured his drink and taken a bottle of water, everyone had exited.

Or so he thought.

"Hello, Professor."

A sultry voice behind him arrested his attention. Gabriel turned to find Christa hovering nearby like a malevolent ghost.

"What do you want?" His expression grew murderous.

"You wanted to talk yesterday. So—talk."

Gabriel glanced around the empty room, wondering if their voices would carry into the lecture theater.

Christa stepped closer to him than was appropriate and closed her eyes, inhaling deeply. When she opened them, her eyes were hungry.

"You smell like sex."

"Don't play games with me. I want the slander to stop."

"That isn't going to happen."

"I'll sue you."

Something flitted across her face, but she quickly pulled her features into a relaxed smile.

"For what? Telling the truth?"

"There's no truth to your character assassinations. You weren't harassed back in Toronto. And Julia does her own research, as is obvious to anyone with half a brain."

The sound of laughter echoed from the lecture theater. Gabriel turned in its direction.

Christa lifted her voice to regain his attention.

"You're forgetting the part where you fucked one of your students and were placed on administrative leave. That's a story worth telling. Not to mention the fact that Professor Singer had quite a bit to say about you. It's a pity she didn't take photographs. I would have liked one."

She reached up to brush imaginary lint off the lapels of his navy blue suit.

He caught her hand at the wrist and squeezed. Hard.

"You're playing with fire."

She leaned even closer, bringing her mouth within inches of his. "Oh, I hope so, Professor."

With disgust he released her, stepping back and wiping his hands as if they'd been contaminated. With another glance toward the theater, he decided to end their confrontation.

"You keep your mouth shut. Or I'll make your life a living hell."

"There's no reason to be unfriendly. The power to end this is in your hands." She gestured to his crotch, her lips turning up into an appreciative smile. "Actually, it's a bit lower."

He muttered an expletive and began to walk away, but she followed him.

"Come to my hotel and tomorrow, you won't have to worry about my talented mouth anymore." She placed her hand on his arm, dropping her voice to a seductive whisper. "*I know you.* I know what you like and I know what you want. We'll fuck all night then go our separate ways."

He pushed her hand away roughly.

"No."

"Then what happens next is on your conscience."

Gabriel took a step in her direction. "You stay away from my wife, do you hear me?"

"I'm at the Malmaison. It used to be a prison, which should appeal to you." She reached up to bring her lips to his ear. "I brought handcuffs."

Gabriel was too busy pushing her away to realize that she'd dropped something into his suit pocket.

With a smirk, she waved.

"Tonight is your only chance. Come before midnight."

She turned on her very high heels, swaying seductively as she walked. Then, almost as an afterthought, she paused and looked at him over her shoulder.

"Give my best to your *wife*."

Chapter Twelve

A few minutes later, Gabriel scanned the crowd of the lecture theater, looking for Julia. His eyes widened as he took in the scene at the front of the room. Julia was being hugged. By someone large. By someone male.

By someone—handsome.

Gabriel took the stairs two at a time in order to reach the front of the hall. He watched as Julia pulled back from the man, her face happy, her kissable lips curved up into a smile.

The man reluctantly withdrew his arms from her waist before saying something that caused her to laugh.

Gabriel was ready to strangle the man, and then he was going to challenge him to a duel.

As he approached, Julia's eyes found his. The man turned in the direction of her gaze.

Gabriel stopped short.

"Angelfucker."

"Pardon?"

Paul Norris squinted at his former dissertation supervisor, not quite sure he'd heard what he thought he'd heard. Certainly, he had his own favored descriptors for the Professor, few of which were complimentary.

Studentfucker, Paul thought.

"This conference keeps getting better and better," Gabriel muttered, straightening himself to his full height of six feet two inches.

"Professor Emerson." Paul subconsciously flexed his biceps and broadened his chest.

"Paul." Gabriel moved to Julia's side possessively, handing her the bottle of water.

"Shake hands, gentlemen." She frowned, looking between her friend and her husband.

The men followed her suggestion less than enthusiastically.

"I didn't know you were coming." Gabriel looked pointedly at Paul.

"I wasn't. One of the presenters backed out, so Professor Picton invited me. I'm giving the paper just before Julia's."

Julia smiled. "That's great. Congratulations."

Paul beamed in return.

"Can I take you to lunch?" He focused solely on Julia.

"I'm afraid she already has plans."

Julia gave her husband what could only be referred to as *the look* before nodding at Paul.

"I'd love to go to lunch with you. Thank you."

Gabriel clutched Julia's elbow.

"I don't think that's appropriate," he whispered.

"*Darling*," she whispered back a warning.

"Hello, Mr. Norris," Katherine interrupted. She shook Paul's hand firmly before turning to Gabriel. "Mr. Norris and I are having dinner this evening. I'd like you and Julianne to join us."

"We'd be delighted." Gabriel's voice was strained. "Since we'll be dining with you this evening, Mr. Norris, I'll claim my wife for lunch." He smiled, showing all his gleaming white teeth.

"Darling, can I have a word?" Julia asked. She turned to Katherine and Paul. "We'll be right back."

Julia took Gabriel's hand and led him to a quiet corner of the room.

"I want to have lunch with him."

"Over my dead body." Gabriel crossed his arms over his chest.

"He's an old friend."

"An old friend who kissed you."

"That was after you left me. As you may recall, I turned him down." She crossed her arms, mirroring his posture.

Gabriel scowled. "He wants you."

"Paul is not someone who would make a pass at a married woman. It's just lunch. So I'm asking you, please, don't make a big deal out of this."

"It *is* a big deal."

"I haven't seen him in a year. I'd like to talk to him and see how he's doing. Maybe he's back together with Allison."

"He's still in love with you."

"No, he isn't."

Gabriel crowded her, dropping his voice.

"You forget that women who are beautiful, intelligent, and kind are in short supply. A man would do anything to have a woman like you. Including stealing you from your husband."

Julia squared her shoulders.

"You forget that when a woman finds a good man, a man who loves her and makes her happy, she doesn't fuck around."

Gabriel flinched.

He couldn't help it—his eyes found Christa's and he watched as she taunted him, looking between himself and Julia smugly.

Gabriel turned back to his wife and uncrossed his arms.

"I'm not happy about this."

Julia reached up to kiss his cheek. "I can live with that. Thank you."

Within minutes, Gabriel found himself in the unhappy position of having to watch his wife sit next to the Angelfucker, while he sat on her other side. She and her friend exchanged a few playful words before the session began, and Gabriel resented each and every one of them.

This conference is like a tour through the various levels of Hell, he thought. *The only things missing are a respectable Virgil and hordes of people screaming.*

It was one thing to suffer the slings and arrows of Miss Peterson. It was quite another to find his wife in the arms of another man. And in the arms of the Angelfucker, of all people.

Gabriel started reciting the prayer of St. Francis in Italian in an effort to calm down.

He knew that he should tell Julia about his confrontation with Christa. But he also knew that it would upset her, potentially ruining her opportunity to appear poised and self-confident in front of the conference attendees. So he kept the distasteful details to himself.

Besides, he had Mr. Norris to worry about.

Paul had been a good and loyal friend to Julia, especially when she'd needed him. But he'd made a play for her, something Gabriel understood but would never forgive.

He wanted to keep Julia as far away from him as possible. But the look on her face when she saw him killed that possibility. She'd had precious little to smile about the day before. Gabriel was not about to kill that look.

He tapped his foot quietly as the first conference speaker began her presentation. He was absolutely oblivious to the distracting noise his handmade Italian shoes were making against the floor until Julia laid a gentle hand on top of his knee.

He took out his Meisterstück 149 and toyed with it, trying in vain to flip it over his fingers in a single motion.

In an effort to distract himself from a paper he swore he'd heard before, he thought back to his very public fight with Julia, when she'd been a student in his seminar. She'd provoked him in front of Paul, Christa, and the rest of the class. He'd been horribly embarrassed and furious. In his rage, he'd even destroyed what had been a very serviceable Ikea chair.

He'd learned a great deal from Julia in the interim, not least of which was the importance of forgiving others and one's self. But Julia's pacifist tendencies were too extreme. Without him, or someone like him, she'd been broken and abused.

Gabriel watched her thoughtfully. Perhaps she'd become a pacifist *because* she'd been abused. Perhaps the bearer of scars was all too aware of the damage that could be done by vicious words and deeds. He pondered that insight for some time, staring at her, until she squirmed.

Julianne was beautiful, with clear skin and large eyes, but she didn't know it. She didn't see what others saw, and although she'd made much progress since they'd been together, Gabriel knew that her self-image would always be less than it should be. He knew this and because of it, he was careful to protect her, even from himself.

He certainly wouldn't let the Angelfucker capitalize on her weaknesses.

Chapter Thirteen

January 2011
Near Essex Junction, Vermont

Paul Norris stepped into a very large pile of cow shit.

"Fuck," he exclaimed, lifting his boot.

Bessie, one of his father's prized Holsteins, cast him a baleful look.

"Sorry, Bessie. I meant *fudge*." He patted the cow on her neck and began to clean off his boot.

As he shoveled manure in his father's barn in the early morning, he contemplated the inner workings of the universe, karma, and what his life had become. Then he thought about *her*.

Julia was going to marry the bastard. By this time tomorrow, the wedding would be over.

He couldn't believe it.

After everything Emerson had put her through . . . after all of his paternalistic, asinine, controlling bullshit. She took him back. Worse—she didn't just take him back; she was marrying him.

Emerson the ass.

Why?

Why do good guys always finish last?

Why do the Emersons of the world always get the girl?

There is no justice in the universe. He gets the girl and I'm shoveling shit.

Julia said that he'd changed, but really, how much could one man change in the space of six months?

He was glad he hadn't accepted the invitation to the wedding. To have to stand there and watch them look into one another's eyes and say their vows, knowing all the while that Emerson was going to take her to a hotel somewhere and . . .

Paul groaned the groan of a man in love who'd lost his beloved.

(At least he had a lot of shit with which to occupy his time.)

He was working on his parents' farm in Vermont because his father was recovering from a heart attack. Despite his recovery, the doctors instructed him to refrain from performing manual labor.

Walking back to the house from the barn at eight o'clock, Paul was ready for breakfast. It was cold and the wind whistled through the trees that a Norris ancestor had planted as a windbreak around the large farmhouse. Even Max, the family's border collie, was cold. He ran in circles, barking at the falling snow and begging to be let inside.

A car traveled up the long drive from the main road, stopping inches from Paul's feet. He recognized the car immediately—a lime green Volkswagen beetle. And he recognized the driver as she opened her door and placed one Ugg-clad foot after the other onto the freshly plowed driveway.

Allison had dark curly hair, freckles, and snapping blue eyes. She was funny, she was smart, and she was a kindergarten teacher in nearby Burlington. She was also Paul's ex-girlfriend.

"Hi." She waved. "I brought coffee from Dunkie's."

Paul saw that she was carrying a tray that had four large coffees from Dunkin' Donuts and a bag that contained mysterious treats. Treats that he hoped included fried dough covered in sugar.

"Go inside. It's freezing out here." Paul waved his gloved hand at the house and followed Allison and Max through the snow.

Paul pulled off his boots and outdoor clothes in the mudroom, placing his gloves on a rack to dry. Then he began washing his hands, scrubbing vigorously under the warm water.

He could hear his mother, Louise, speaking to Allison in low tones in the kitchen. She didn't sound surprised at Ali's sudden appearance. Paul began to wonder if her appearance wasn't all that sudden.

When he entered the kitchen, his mother disappeared with two of the coffees.

"How's your dad?" Allison handed him his cup.

He sipped it quickly, wanting to put off his answer. The coffee was perfect—black with two sugars. Ali knew how he liked his coffee.

"He's better." Paul's voice was stiff as he sat across from her at the kitchen table. "He keeps trying to work, and Mom keeps telling him not to. At least he didn't make it out of the house this morning. She caught him in time."

"We sent flowers to the hospital."

"I saw them. Thanks."

They sat quietly, awkwardly, until Allison reached her hand across the table to take Paul's large paw in hers.

"I heard about the wedding."

He looked at her in surprise.

"Your mom told my mom. They ran into each other at Hannaford's." She rolled her eyes.

He shook his head but said nothing.

"For what it's worth, I'm sorry. She's clearly a fool."

"She isn't, but thanks." He squeezed her hand. He was going to withdraw, but it felt nice to hold her hand. It felt familiar and comfortable and God knew that he needed comfort, so he kept it there.

She smiled and sipped her coffee. "I know this is a bad time. I just wanted to let you know that I'm here."

He shifted his weight, focusing on his coffee cup.

"Do you want to go to a movie?" she blurted. "I mean, sometime. Not right now. It's too early to go to a movie now." Her cheeks pinked up as she searched Paul's expression.

"I don't know." He released her hand and sat back in his chair.

"I don't want things to be weird between us. We've been friends forever and we promised each other we'd always be friends." She began to score the sides of her coffee cup with her fingernail.

"Things are just—difficult right now."

Allison scratched at the surface of the cup.

"I'm not trying to rope you into something. I really want to be friends. I know you're busy and—stuff." She began ripping off small pieces of her coffee cup and placing them neatly on the kitchen table.

"Hey." Paul's hand shot out across the table to catch hers mid-rip. "Relax."

She looked into his eyes and saw acceptance and kindness. She exhaled in relief.

Paul withdrew his hand again, wrapping it around his cup.

"We have a history and it's a good one. But I don't want to jump back into something with you. It would be too easy to do that."

"I've never been easy, Paul." She sounded offended.

He cleared his throat and looked her straight in the eye. "I never said you were. What I mean is it would be tempting to go back to what we had because it was comfortable. You deserve to be with someone who's serious and not half in it."

Paul lost himself in the momentary silence that followed before realizing that Allison was waiting for something.

He blinked at her. "What?"

"Nothing. So are we on for a movie sometime or what? I might even take you to dinner at Leunig's, now that I'm pulling in the big bucks as a teacher."

Paul found himself smiling, and his smile was genuine.

"Only if you let me take you to breakfast at Mirabelle's."

"Great. When?"

"Get your coat."

He followed her to the back door and helped her with her coat. When she nearly toppled over trying to put her Uggs back on, he knelt on the sandy, salt-licked floor and slid them on her feet.

"Half of you is better than the whole of anyone," she whispered, if only to herself.

Chapter Fourteen

July 2011
Oxford, England

At the beginning of the conference's lunch break, Julia excused herself to go to the ladies' room, asking Paul to wait for her return. She was ascending the staircase on her way back to the lecture theater when a pair of Christian Louboutins came into view.

Julia's gaze traveled up a pair of legs clad in silk stockings to a black pencil skirt, to a fitted jacket, and thence to the face of Christa Peterson.

Her expression was hostile but noticeably tense as she clutched the railing with whitened knuckles. She shifted her weight between her feet as if she were uncertain whether to proceed or to retreat.

"I can't wait to hear your paper. I'm sure I'll have a few questions."

Julia ignored her and tried to move forward, but Christa blocked her.

Julia huffed impatiently. "What do you want?"

"You think you're so smart."

"We have nothing to talk about."

"Oh yes, we do."

Julia screwed her eyes shut before opening them incredulously. "Seriously? You want to have this argument here, at a conference? Don't you see how your actions are hurting your career? Gabriel says that Columbia made you enroll in the M.Phil rather than the PhD. You burned bridges in Toronto, and you're burning them here. Don't you think it's time to let things go?"

"I don't give up that easily."

"Your vendetta is ridiculous. I never did anything to you."

Christa laughed darkly.

"It isn't about you. You aren't worth troubling about."

"Then why?"

Christa tossed her hair. "You have something I want. I always get what I want. Always."

"Let me go." Julia lifted her chin defiantly.

Christa's almond-shaped eyes passed over Julia from head to foot.

"I don't understand what he sees in you. You aren't that pretty." She waved a contemptuous hand at Julia's unassuming suit and less-than-designer shoes.

"Gabriel is beautiful. He's a legend. All the women at Lobby knew him and all of them wanted to fuck him." She looked at Julia scornfully. "Yet, somehow out of everyone, he ends up with you. But you won't be able to keep him. He needs to be with a woman whose appetite is as voracious as his."

"He is."

Christa laughed, the sound tinny and brittle. "Hardly. I'm sure he enjoyed the conquest, at the beginning. But now he's had you, his eye will wander and you'll lose him." Her eyes flashed with a knowing light. "He's probably cheated on you already. Or he's planning to."

"If you don't let me go, I'm calling for help. Do you really want to be embarrassed in front of everyone? Again?"

Christa hesitated, and Julia took the opportunity to brush past her. She was two steps from the top of the staircase before she stopped. She turned around.

"Love," she said quietly.

"What?"

"You're wondering what Gabriel sees in me. The answer is love. I know about the other women. He hasn't kept secrets from me. But they aren't a threat."

Christa put her hands on her hips. "You're delusional. So you love him. So what? *Look at yourself.* Why would he want such a vanilla little mouse when he could have a tiger in his bed?"

"Better a loving mouse than an indifferent tiger." Julia straightened her shoulders. "Those women didn't see who he truly is. They didn't care that he was miserable. They would have used him until there was nothing left and then thrown him away. I've loved him since I was seventeen. I love all of him—the light and the dark, the good and the bad. That's why he's with me. He left the others behind and he will never go back. So do your worst, Christa. But if you're planning to seduce my husband, *you—will—fail*."

Julia turned to walk away but stopped again, facing Christa one last time.

"You're right about one thing, though."

"And what's that?" Christa sounded contemptuous.

Julia smiled knowingly. "My husband is an exceptional lover. He's attentive, creative, and absolutely mind-blowing. And tonight and every night, the woman enjoying his adventurous nature will be me."

She gave Christa a long look.

"Not bad for a mouse."

"I'm sorry you had another run-in with Christa." Paul's tone was sympathetic as he escorted Julia from St. Anne's to a small Lebanese restaurant that was within walking distance. "I guess she's only here to harass you."

Julia fidgeted with her wedding ring, moving it back and forth with her thumb.

"She told me she was going to ask questions after my paper. She's going to try to make me look stupid."

Paul wrapped his arm around her shoulders.

"She can't make you look stupid because you aren't stupid. You stand your ground. You'll be fine."

He squeezed her before removing his arm.

"You look good. Much better than the last time I saw you."

She shuddered, recalling when she'd said good-bye to Paul outside her apartment in Cambridge the summer before. She'd been thinner and sadder, but cautiously optimistic that life at Harvard would suit her.

"Married life agrees with me."

Paul grimaced. He didn't want to think about what Julia's married life included, because he couldn't stand the thought of her sleeping with Professor Emerson. He hoped to God Emerson had given up his penchant for BDSM and treated Julia with gentleness.

An image of Emerson tying Julia up flashed through his mind. His stomach rolled.

"Are you all right?" Julia peered up at him. "You look a little green."

"I'm fine." He forced a smile. "I've just noticed that the Rabbit is gone."

"It was about time, don't you think?"

"I'll miss her."

Julia focused her attention on the sidewalk in front of them.

"She returns at tense moments. My legs are wobbly just thinking about standing in front of all those people."

"You can do it. Just pretend you're presenting your paper to me. Ignore everyone else."

Instinctively, Paul reached out to take her hand but stopped himself.

He gestured to her awkwardly, trying to disguise his movement.

"Uh, you cut your hair."

She tugged one of the dark locks that fell short of her shoulders. "I thought it would look more professional. Gabriel doesn't like it."

"I'll bet he doesn't."

(Paul neglected to mention the fact that he agreed with the Professor.)

He gestured to her left hand. "That's quite a rock you have."

"Thank you. Gabriel picked it."

Of course he'd buy her a big-ass ring, Paul thought. *I'm surprised he didn't have his name tattooed on her forehead.*

"I would have married him with a ring from a box of Cracker Jack." Julia looked at her hand wistfully. "I would have married him with a tie from a garbage bag. I don't care about this kind of stuff."

Exactly. I could have never given her a ring like that. But Julia is the kind of girl who would be happy with next to nothing, provided she loved the guy enough.

"He paid off my student loans," she offered quietly.

"What, all of them?"

She nodded. "I was going to consolidate them and start making payments, but he insisted on paying them."

Paul whistled. "That must have cost him."

"It did. It's taken some getting used to—the fact that we share everything including a bank account. I had a very small checking account when we got married. He had . . . more."

"How do you like living in Cambridge?" Paul changed the subject, far from eager to learn how much *more* the Professor had.

"I love it. We live close enough to Harvard so I can walk. Which is good, because I don't drive." Julia sounded sheepish.

"You don't? Why not?"

"I kept getting lost and ending up in sketchy neighborhoods. I called Gabriel from Dorchester one night and he had a fit. And that was after I'd used the GPS."

"How did you end up in Dorchester?"

"The GPS screwed up. It didn't recognize one-way streets. It even told me to do an illegal U-turn while I was driving through one of the underpasses. So I ended up farther and farther away from my house. After that, I quit."

"You don't drive at all?"

"Not in the greater Boston area. Gabriel's Range Rover is difficult to park and I was always worried I was going to hit someone. Boston drivers are crazy. And don't get me started on the pedestrians."

Paul resisted the urge to itemize Gabriel's myriad failings, and settled on one.

"Why doesn't he get you a new car? Obviously, he can afford it."

"I want something small, like a Smart car or one of those new Fiats. Gabriel says they're like driving a can of tuna." She sighed. "He wants me in something bigger, like a Hummer."

He bumped her shoulder playfully. "Planning on invading Baghdad? Or just Charlestown?"

"Very funny. If I can't parallel park the Range Rover, how the hell am I going to park a Hummer?"

Paul laughed, opening the door to the restaurant.

Before he could ask the host for a table for two, a commotion emerged from a nearby table. A little girl, who was probably three or four years old, was hitting a button on her book repeatedly, generating a few bars of a song over and over again.

As the girl continued this behavior, Paul and Julia looked around the restaurant. The other patrons were less than impressed.

A woman who was modestly dressed and wearing a hijab tried to persuade the girl to exchange her musical book for another, nonmusical one. But the girl shrieked in protest.

It was at that moment that an older man who had been sitting near them noisily demanded that the waiter silence the girl. He further complained that she was ruining his lunch and that children *who cannot behave themselves* should not be allowed in restaurants.

The woman flushed a deep red and tried once again to persuade her daughter to switch books. But once again, the girl refused, kicking loudly against the table leg.

At that moment, the host approached them.

"A table for two," said Paul cheerfully.

"By the window?" The host gestured to a table in the far corner, next to the window.

"Yes." Paul moved to follow the host as he retrieved two menus.

As they were walking across the dining room, Julia noticed that the older man was still grumbling about the little girl and that she was still playing her music loudly and erratically. Julia wondered briefly if the little girl was autistic. Regardless, she was appalled at the older man's behavior.

She addressed the host. "Maybe we could trade tables with the girl and her mother? If they don't want to move, that's fine. But the girl might like to look out the window and she'd be able to play with her book in peace."

The host glanced in the direction of Julia's hand, noting the increasing discomfort of the other diners.

"Excuse me," he said, before approaching mother and child.

The mother and the host had a quick exchange in Arabic, and then the mother addressed her daughter in English.

"Maia, we can sit by the window. Isn't that nice? We can look out at the cars."

The little girl followed her mother's gesture to the table in the corner. She blinked a little behind her thick glasses and nodded.

"Maia, can you say thank you?"

The girl's name seemed to carry across the restaurant. At the sound of it, Julia startled. She found herself staring at the child, her body frozen.

Maia looked up at the host and mumbled, while the mother smiled at Julia and Paul.

A few minutes later, mother and child were happily situated in the corner. The little girl pressed her face against the window, looking outside at the cars and pedestrians, her musical book forgotten.

Julia and Paul were seated at the other table, next to the now triumphant older man. They ordered a few plates to share and quietly sipped their drinks.

"You didn't ask me first." Paul's voice broke into Julia's thoughts.

"I knew you wouldn't mind sitting here."

"You're right. In fact, it's better that you dealt with the situation because I was about to walk over to that guy and talk to him. What a jerk."

Julia looked at the man who'd been so censorious and shook her head.

"I don't know why I continue to be surprised by people's insensitivity. But I am."

"I'm glad you are. I know too many cynical people."

"So do I."

Paul's eyes flickered to the mother and child. "Are you planning to have a Maia of your own anytime soon?"

Julia winced, the child's name continuing to jar her.

"No. Um, not yet, I mean."

Paul gazed at her for a moment, his large, dark eyes radiating concern.

"You look panicked. Are you worried about having kids?"

She lowered her eyes.

"No, I want kids. But later on." She sipped her water. "How's your father?"

Paul considered exploring her anxiety but thought better of it.

"He's okay. I'm still at the farm helping out, so I had to let my apartment in Toronto go."

"How's your dissertation coming?"

He snickered. "Terrible. I don't have a lot of time to write, and now Professor Picton is pissed with me. I was supposed to give her one of my chapters two weeks ago and it isn't finished."

"Is there anything I can do?"

"Not unless you want to write the damn thing for me. I'd like to go on the job market this fall, but Picton won't let me unless I'm further along." He sighed loudly. "I'm probably going to be on the farm for at least another year. The longer I'm there, the harder it is to write."

"I'm sorry to hear that."

Julia put her glass down and began rubbing her eyes.

"Are you tired?" Paul sounded concerned.

"A little. My eyes bother me sometimes. It's probably stress." She put her hands in her lap. "Sorry. I don't want this conversation to be all about me. I'd rather hear how you're doing."

"We'll come to that. When did your eyes start bothering you?"

"When I moved to Boston."

"Lots of grad students end up with eyestrain. You should get your eyes checked."

"I hadn't thought of that. Do you wear glasses?"

"No, I drank a lot of milk growing up. It helped my vision."

She appeared puzzled. "I thought carrots did that."

"Milk helps everything."

She laughed.

Paul couldn't help but appreciate Julia's beauty, made even more lovely when she laughed.

He was about to say something but was interrupted by the waiter, who served their lunch. When he withdrew, Julia spoke.

"Are you seeing anyone?"

Paul fought a frown.

"Ali and I go out occasionally. But it's casual."

"She's a nice person. She cares about you."

"I know that." His expression darkened.

"I want you to be happy . . ."

He changed the subject. "How are things in your program?"

Julia toyed with her silverware before answering. "The professors are tough and I'm working all the time, but I love it."

"And the other students?"

Julia made a face.

"They're very competitive. I consider a couple of them friends, but I don't necessarily trust them. I went to the library once and found that someone had hidden a bunch of the Boccaccio resources so the rest of us couldn't use them for our seminar."

"So I guess you aren't spending late nights in the library sharing a carrel?"

"Definitely not." She nibbled on her food.

"Do you go out at all?"

"Rarely. It's awkward because the other students bring their partners and Gabriel won't join me."

"Why not?"

"He doesn't think it's a good idea to socialize with grad students."

Paul bit his tongue. Hard.

"He wants to have a baby," Julia blurted.

She cringed, immediately regretting her lack of discretion.

"It might be a bit difficult, given his biology," Paul teased. When he saw the look on her face, he grew serious. "And you don't?"

"Not right away." She twisted her linen napkin in her lap. "I want to finish my program. I'm worried if we have a baby, I'll never graduate."

She ducked her head, berating herself internally for mentioning so personal a struggle to Paul. Gabriel would be livid if he knew she was sharing these kinds of confidences. But she needed to talk to someone. And Rachel, although sympathetic, did not understand the academic world.

"I'm sorry, Julia. Have you told him?"

"Yes. He said he understood. But it's out there, you know? Once you express that kind of desire, it can't be taken back."

Paul tapped his foot under the table. Their conversation had taken a surprising turn, and truthfully, he didn't know what to say. He quickly thought of something.

"There were some mothers in our program back in Toronto, but only a few."

"Did they finish?"

"Truthfully? Most of them didn't. A lot of the guys had kids. But most of them had wives who either stayed at home or worked part time. . . . Hey." He waited until she lifted her face. "That's a small sample. I wasn't paying a lot of attention to who was getting pregnant and who wasn't. There's probably a group at Harvard that can give you advice about balancing a family and grad school."

"I didn't want to have those conversations now."

"I can understand that."

Paul shook his head.

"Jules, it's none of my business, but don't get pressured into living someone else's life. If you aren't ready for a family, say so. And stick to your decision, otherwise you'll end up miserable."

"I don't think having a baby with my husband would make me miserable." She sounded defensive.

"Dropping out of Harvard would. I know you, Julia. And I know what's important to you. You've been working so hard for this. Don't throw it away."

"I don't want to, but I feel guilty."

Paul cursed obliquely.

"I thought you said he was supportive of you."

"He is."

"Then why would you feel guilty?"

"Because I'm putting myself first. I'm putting my education first, over his happiness."

Paul gave her a hard look. "If he loves you, then he won't be happy at the cost of your happiness."

Julia adjusted the silverware in front of her, lining up the ends so they were perfectly symmetrical.

"Much as I hate to say this, I think you should talk to him again. Tell him what you want and ask him to wait." Paul grinned. "And if he won't, then kick him to the curb."

She looked over at him in surprise.

"Paul, I don't think that—"

He interrupted her. "Seriously, Julia. If your husband loves you, then he needs to wake the fuck up and cut out the barefoot-and-pregnant bullshit."

Her brow furrowed. "He doesn't want that."

"Then you have no reason to feel guilty. You're young. You have your whole life ahead of you. You don't have to choose between grad school and a family. You can have both."

"I'm not the only person whose dreams count."

"Perhaps not." Paul lowered his voice, his eyes fixed on hers. "I'm not exactly objective when it comes to you."

"I know," said Julia, softly. "You've been a good friend. Thank you."

"No thanks needed." His voice grew gruff.

"Friends are in short supply. Yesterday, Christa told almost everyone about what happened in Toronto. I was humiliated."

"I wish someone would shut her up. Permanently."

"Gabriel tried. They made a scene. Then Professor Picton arrived and threatened to throw Christa out."

Paul whistled. "I'm sorry I missed that. Picton and Christa in a steel-cage death match? We could have sold popcorn."

He caught sight of Julia's face, which was lined with distress.

"I don't mean to be a jerk."

"You aren't a jerk."

He continued tapping his foot under the table, an expression of discomfort.

"I said some stupid stuff in the email I sent before you got married. I refused to come to the wedding. That's the behavior of a jerk."

Julia's eyes widened. "You told me you couldn't come because your dad was sick."

The tempo of his foot increased.

"That's true—my dad was sick. But that wasn't the reason I didn't come to your wedding." His eyes met hers. "I couldn't watch you marry him."

Paul took in her troubled expression and pulled his chair closer to the table.

"I know you're married and I would never do anything to mess with that. But God help me, I couldn't watch you marry him. I'm sorry."

"Paul, I—"

He lifted a hand to silence her.

"I'm not waiting in the wings. But it's hard for me to see you with him. And to hear that the rumors are still swirling around you—rumors that are his fault, not yours—and that he's pressuring you to have a baby when you just started your program . . . *Fuck.*" He shook his head. "When is he going to wake up and realize that he married an incredible woman and that he needs to care for her?"

"He *does* care for me. He isn't who you think he is."

Paul leveled his dark eyes at hers.

"For your sake, I hope not."

"He volunteers at the Italian Home for Children. He's done humanitarian work with the poor. He's changed."

"He isn't much of a humanitarian if he can't see that his wife needs time before she becomes a mother."

"He sees it. I'm the one who's struggling. It's hard to withhold something from someone you love, knowing that it would make him happy. And I'm happy, too," she whispered. "You recognized it yourself. I know he has his faults, but so do I. He'd give me the world if he could fit it in his pocket, and he never, ever, lets me fall."

Paul looked away, his knee bouncing under the table.

Chapter Fifteen

Paul's paper was well received, if not a little short in Gabriel's estimation. He noted with grim satisfaction that both Paul and Julia appeared uneasy after their lunch, as if things hadn't gone quite as they'd expected.

If Gabriel wanted to quiz Julia for details, he hid it well. He greeted her warmly when she returned, and they sat together during Paul's presentation.

Soon, it was Julia's turn. Professor Patel, one of the conference organizers, introduced her, dubbing her a rising star at Harvard. Gabriel's grin widened as he saw Christa seethe.

The audience included fifty academics, in various stages of their careers. Professor Picton and Professor Marinelli sat in the front row near Gabriel. All three smiled at Julia encouragingly.

With uncertain fingers, she placed the pages of her paper on top of the lectern. In contrast with it, her petite form seemed even smaller. Professor Patel adjusted the microphone downward so that it would catch her voice.

She looked young and pale and nervous. Gabriel caught her chewing at the inside of her mouth and he silently willed her not to do so. He was grateful when she stopped.

With her eyes fixed on his, she took a deep breath and began.

"The title of my presentation is 'The Silence of St. Francis: A Witness to Fraud.'"

"In *canto* twenty-seven of Dante's *Inferno*, Guido da Montefeltro tells the story of what happened after he died,

'Francis came afterward, when I was dead,
For me; but one of the black Cherubim

Said to him: "Take him not; do me no wrong;
He must come down among my servitors,
Because he gave the fraudulent advice
From which time forth I have been at his hair;
For who repents not cannot be absolved,
Nor can one both repent and will at once,
Because of the contradiction which consents not."
O miserable me ! how I did shudder
When he seized on me, saying: "Peradventure
Thou didst not think that I was a logician!"'

"Guido lived in Italy from about 1220 to 1298. He was a prominent Ghibelline and military strategist before retiring in order to become a Franciscan, around 1296. Afterward, Pope Boniface VIII persuaded him to give fraudulent counsel to the Colonna family, with whom he'd been having trouble.

"Boniface wanted Guido to promise the family amnesty if they would leave the security of their fortress. Guido did so, but only after he secured absolution. As a result of his counsel, the Colonna family left the fortress only to be punished by Boniface. Later, Guido died in the Franciscan monastery in Assisi.

"Guido's account of what happened after his death is dramatic. We can envision St. Francis courageously confronting a demon in order to rescue the soul of his fellow Franciscan."

Her eyes flickered to Gabriel's, which were a lively, expressive blue. A look passed between the two, and for an instant she knew they were both thinking of the ways they had rescued each other.

"But as is usual with Dante's writings, appearances can be deceiving. In life, Guido had a persuasive but deceptive tongue. In death, he inhabits the circle of the fraudulent. So his words should be treated with skepticism. Certainly, skepticism is warranted about Guido's claim that Francis came for his soul. If that was Francis's purpose, he failed.

"Nowhere else in *The Divine Comedy* do we witness evil overcoming goodness. The *Comedy* is so called because the narrative moves from disorder in Hell to order in Paradise. If one soul were to be punished unjustly, it would undermine the entire narrative. So a lot is at stake in this passage. Our interpretation of it has significance for the entire *Comedy*."

Julia paused and took a sip of water, her hand shaking slightly.

"According to Dante, justice motivated God to create Hell. Virgil alludes to this when he explains that justice motivates the souls of the departed to pass over the river Acheron into Hell. Dante seems to take the view that those who inhabit Hell do so justly, because they merit their final destination. Souls aren't in Hell by accident or because of divine caprice. If that's the case, how do we interpret Guido's statements?"

Katherine nodded, her eyes sparkling with pride. The movement caught Julia's attention, and a short look passed between the two women.

"With the understanding that Dante believes the souls that inhabit Hell do so justly, let's reconsider Guido's story. The demon sees Francis and shouts at him, saying that Guido's soul belongs in Hell and that it would be robbery for Francis to take it. If that's true, why would Francis appear?"

Julia paused, hoping that the audience would join her in considering the question.

"A survey of the literature in Dante studies for the past fifty years reveals at least two interpretations of this passage. First, that Guido is truthful and Francis appeared for his soul. Second, that Guido is lying and Francis didn't appear at all.

"I believe that both possibilities are too extreme. For the first interpretation to be the correct, we'd have to attribute either ignorance or injustice to Francis, neither of which is reasonable.

"The second interpretation asserts that Francis didn't appear, but then the demon's speech doesn't make sense, since Guido cannot steal his own soul. So we're left with a puzzling report of Francis's appearance, accompanied by an explanation that strains credulity. The explanation is given by Guido and a demon, neither of whom is trustworthy.

"I believe we can solve the puzzle of Francis's appearance by rejecting Guido's explanation, and substituting one that would be consistent with Francis's life and character. According to my interpretation, Francis appeared and was seen by the demon. But the demon misunderstood why Francis was there."

Julia began to grip the lectern more tightly, as the members of the audience began to murmur. Her mouth felt dry as the desert, but she continued, her eyes locked on Gabriel's.

"Much as it might be . . . comforting to think of Francis coming down from Heaven like an archangel to fight for Guido's soul, that can't be what happened." A look passed between the Emersons before Julia continued.

"Guido capitalizes on Francis's well-known commitment to his brothers, no doubt thinking that reasonable people will believe that he appeared at the death of a fellow Franciscan. Further, Guido wants Dante to spread this tale, so others will think that he was important enough to merit the saint's attention, or that his condemnation to Hell was a mistake.

"The demon, thinking to persuade Francis not to rob him, explains why Guido deserves to be in Hell. Guido sought absolution for the sin of fraudulent counsel *before* he committed the sin. He believed absolution would free him from the consequences of his sin, and so he willingly and unrepentantly committed fraud against the Colonna family.

"The demon points out that absolution only works if the human being repents. You can't sin intentionally and be repentant of your sin at the same time." Julia gave the audience a tentative smile. "Absolution isn't like fire insurance."

(At this, a few members of the audience, including Paul, laughed.)

"Guido cloaks himself in Franciscan robes and preemptive absolution, but he's a fraud. Francis would have known this. If anything, Guido shamed the Franciscans by behaving the way he did.

"Although Francis could have condemned Guido's sin, he remains silent. He can't save Guido. He has to watch as the demon takes Guido by the hair and drags him down.

"The ugliness of the demon's shouting and Guido's false Franciscanism appear even worse when contrasted with Francis's quiet, pious presence. His silence and lack of action give the lie to the demon's explanation that Francis is there to steal. And his silence forces us to reexamine Guido's tale.

"Would Francis have been so passive in trying to rescue a soul that was condemned unjustly? Of course not. But since Guido hasn't repented of his sin, all Francis can offer him is his silent compassion and, possibly, his prayers."

Julia paused and intentionally looked in Christa's direction.

"Francis could have argued with the demon. He could have called him a liar for presenting a false account of his appearance. He could have protested that the demon is simply gossiping about him. But instead of fighting to preserve his good name, Francis is quiet so that the evil can be heard for exactly what it is."

Julia shifted her gaze to the other conferencegoers, noting numerous nods of agreement and Paul's wide, expressive grin.

"Guido would have us believe that St. Francis was either gullible enough to believe that Guido belonged in Heaven or arrogant enough to believe that he could second-guess God. Guido would have us believe that Francis confronted a demon but lost, because he wasn't smart enough to best the demon in a match of logic.

"Francis's life and his actions give the lie to those possibilities. In my view, he comes to the grave of Guido da Montefeltro to mourn him and his life of fraud, not to rescue him. In so doing, Francis manifests compassion and mercy, although it is a severe mercy." At this, Julia's eyes met her husband's.

"Francis was not a thief. He was not deceptive or fraudulent, and he made no attempt to use vain words to further his cause. If anything, Guido captured the essence of Francis's nature by describing him as being present but silent.

"It's surprising, perhaps, that someone so skilled in fraud would be so adept at painting a picture of virtue. But when we reflect on the stories Francis's followers told about his life and works, we see that that's exactly what Guido does, even though he attempts to overshadow the picture with his skillful use of rhetoric.

"In conclusion, I think that the two historical interpretations of this passage are mistaken. Francis appeared at the death of Guido, but not to steal his soul.

"Francis's appearance contrasts true Franciscanism with the false Franciscanism of Guido da Montefeltro. If anything, Dante uses Guido as a foil to praise the piety of St. Francis by providing a stark contrast between the two men. Thank you."

Julia nodded at the audience as they offered her a respectable level of applause. She noticed several of the academics whispering to one another before her eyes found the faces of Professors Picton, Marinelli, and Emerson.

Gabriel winked, and her face broke into a relieved smile.

"Are there any questions?" Julia asked, turning to the audience.

There was a moment that in Julia's mind seemed to last forever, in which no one spoke. She found Christa's face and watched her conflicted expression, and believed that she had escaped unscathed.

Then, as if in slow motion, Christa's expression changed and hardened. She scrambled to her feet.

Out of the corner of her eye, Julia saw Professor Pacciani take hold of Christa's elbow somewhat roughly, trying to pull her back into her seat. But Christa wrenched her arm free.

"I have a question."

Julia bit her lip unconsciously, her heart leaping into her throat.

As if it had been choreographed, every member of the audience turned to look at Christa. Several conferencegoers whispered to their neighbors, their eyes alive with anticipation. Christa's conflict with the Emersons was well known now by almost every attendee. Indeed, the room began to buzz with a kind of nervous energy as everyone wondered what she was going to say.

"There are so many holes in your paper, I don't know where to begin. But let's start with your *research*, such as it is." Christa's tone was contemptuous. "The majority of papers on this passage accept the fact that Francis came for Guido. A few recent papers deny that Francis appeared. But no one"—she paused for emphasis—"*no one* thinks that Francis appeared but not for Guido's soul. Either Guido is lying or he isn't. It can't be half and half, like cream."

She smirked as a few members of the audience laughed.

Julia swallowed hard, her eyes darting around the room, reading everyone's reaction before returning to Christa's.

"Furthermore, you don't even mention the beginning of *canto* twenty-seven, when Guido explains to Dante that he's telling the truth because he thinks that Dante will spend the rest of eternity in Hell and therefore won't be able to tell anyone what really happened. That passage demonstrates that Guido is telling the truth about Francis's appearance.

"Finally, if you'd bothered to read Professor Hutton's seminal work on the organization of the *Inferno*, you'd know that he thought the demon's speech was reliable because his words were historically accurate. So Hutton thought that Francis appeared for Guido's soul, too."

With a proud smile, Christa sat down, waiting for Julia's response.

She was so proud of herself, so self-satisfied, she missed the look that Professor Picton gave to Professor Pacciani. The look indicated very clearly that Katherine was holding Pacciani responsible for the flamboyant behavior of his guest, and that she was not pleased with that behavior. In response, Professor Pacciani whispered in Christa's ear, gesticulating wildly.

Julia simply stood there, blinking rapidly, while every single person in the room waited for her answer.

Gabriel moved forward in his chair, as if he were going to stand. He thought better of it, however, when Professor Picton narrowed her eyes at him. The expression on his face was thunderous as he glared in Christa's direction.

Paul muttered an expletive and folded his arms across his chest.

Professor Picton simply nodded at Julia, her face a picture of confidence.

Julia raised a shaky hand to push her hair behind her ear, the diamonds in her engagement ring catching the light.

"Um, let's begin with your point that some interpreters believe that Francis came for Guido's soul and that this can be shown by his opening lines to Dante."

Julia read the lines in Italian, her pronunciation sure and musical,

"*'S'i' credesse che mia risposta fosse*
a persona che mai tornasse al mondo,
questa fiamma staria stanza più scosse;
ma però che già mai di questo fondo
non torno vivo alcun, s'i' odo il vero,
sanza tema d'infamia ti rispondo.' "

Julia began to stand a little taller.

"In this passage, Guido *says* he's willing to tell the truth since he believes that Dante is one of the damned and thus wouldn't be able to repeat the story. But Guido's tale is self-serving. He blames everyone—the pope, the demon, and by implication, St. Francis—for his fate. There's nothing in his account that he should be embarrassed about. If anything, the story he tells is one he would *want* to have repeated. He simply doesn't want to tip his hand by saying so, which is why he gives the speech I just quoted.

"You're also forgetting this line:

"'*Ora chi se', ti priego che ne conte;*
non esser duro più ch'altri sia stato,
se 'l nome tuo nel mondo tegna fronte.'"

Growing in confidence, Julia resisted the urge to smile, choosing rather to meet Christa's gaze gravely.

"Dante tells Guido that he intends to repeat his tale in the world. It's only after Dante says this that Guido recounts his life story. Also, we know that Dante doesn't resemble the other shades physically. So it's likely that Guido recognized that Dante wasn't dead."

Christa began speaking, but Julia lifted a patient hand, indicating that she wasn't finished.

"There's textual evidence for my interpretation. There's a parallel passage in the fifth *canto* of *Purgatorio*, in which Guido's son talks about how an angel came for his soul at his death. Perhaps it's the responsibility of angels and not saints to ferry souls to Paradise. Thus, Francis appears at Guido's death for quite a different purpose.

"As for your last point, about Professor Hutton's work. If you're referring to *Fire and Ice: Desire and Sin in Dante's* Inferno, then your characterization of his position is incorrect. Although I don't have a copy of the book with me, there's a footnote in chapter ten in which he states that he believed that Francis appeared, because he thinks the words of the demon were directed at someone other than Guido, himself. But Professor Hutton says he has doubts as to whether Francis appeared for Guido's soul or for some other reason. That's all he says on the matter."

Christa stood up as if to argue, but before a word could exit her mouth, an aged professor dressed entirely in tweed turned around to face her. He looked at her contemptuously through his tortoiseshell glasses.

"Can we move on? You've asked your question and the speaker answered it. Adequately, I might add."

Christa was taken aback, but she quickly regrouped, protesting that she should have an opportunity to ask a supplementary question.

Once again, the audience reacted with whispered words, but Julia noticed that the expressions on their faces had changed. Now they were looking at Julia with a kind of muted appreciation.

"Can we move on? I'd like the opportunity to ask a question." The aged professor turned away from Christa and directed his gaze to the moderator, who stepped forward, clearing his throat.

"Ah, if there's time we'll come back to you, miss. But I believe Professor Wodehouse has the floor."

The aged man in tweed muttered a thank-you and stood up. He removed his glasses and waved them in Julia's direction.

"Donald Wodehouse of Magdalen." He introduced himself.

Julia's face paled, for Professor Wodehouse was a Dante specialist whose standing rivaled that of Katherine Picton's.

"I'm familiar with the footnote you're referring to in Old Hut's book. You've summarized it correctly. A different view is taken by Emerson in his volume." At this, Wodehouse gestured in Gabriel's direction. "But I see you haven't been swayed by him, despite the fact that you two share a last name."

Laughter erupted from the crowd, and Gabriel winked at Julia proudly.

"As you point out, it's perplexing to see why Francis would appear at the death of a false Franciscan, but we need to posit Francis's appearance in order to make sense of the demon's speech. So we're left with half-and-half as the woman behind me mentioned. I don't find that problematic. Half-truth, half-falsity seems to pervade all of Guido's words. The ambiguity and rhetorical sophistry is what one would expect in a person guilty of fraudulent counsel. So I tend to agree with much of what you've said, and although I can't speak for him, I surmise that Old Hut would too, if he were here."

Julia exhaled slowly in relief, her fingers loosening their iron grip on the lectern. Her mind was bracing for his next words, but she felt vindicated by the professor's remarks.

Professor Wodehouse glanced at his handwritten notes before continuing.

"You've provided an interpretation that's certainly as good a theory as any, and better than those accounts that would attribute ignorance or injustice to Francis. But let's be clear. It's speculation."

"Yes, it is." Julia's voice was low but determined. "I'd welcome suggestions of alternative interpretations."

Professor Wodehouse shrugged. "Who knows why Francis did anything? Perhaps he was supposed to meet another soul in Assisi and was merely waylaid by an opportunistic fraud."

At this, the audience laughed.

"I do, however, have a question." He replaced his glasses on his face and looked down at his notes. "I'd like you to say more about the agreement that existed between Boniface and Guido. You rather glossed over that part in your paper, and I think the matter merits more attention."

And with that, he sat down.

Julia nodded, frantically trying to gather her thoughts.

"My thesis was on the interpretation of Francis's appearance, not Guido's sin. Nevertheless, I'm happy to expand on that part of the paper."

Julia began a short but fluid summary of Guido's encounter with Pope Boniface VIII and its aftermath, which seemed to satisfy the professor. However, she mentally made note of the fact that he'd thought her paper lacking in that respect. She'd attend to his worry in her revision of the paper for potential publication.

A few more questions were asked and answered, and then the moderator thanked Julia. A round of applause that bordered on the enthusiastic filled the room, and Julia noticed several older professors nodding at her.

When the moderator invited everyone to pause for tea and coffee, Julia watched in surprise as Professor Pacciani took Christa by the hand and led her away.

Julia walked over to Gabriel, eagerly searching his face.

He smiled and linked their pinky fingers surreptitiously.

"That's my smart girl," he whispered.

Chapter Sixteen

Julia made the rounds during the coffee break, speaking to Professor Wodehouse and others about her paper. It was almost universally acknowledged that her research was very good and that she'd handled the questions admirably. In fact, more than one conferencegoer remarked that they were surprised she was only a graduate student and not a junior professor.

While his wife enjoyed her academic triumph, Gabriel strolled outside, sipping his coffee in the Oxford sunshine.

He was grateful for the fine weather and lack of rain. He was also grateful that Julia's presentation had gone so well. Yes, she'd appeared nervous, and as always, there was room for improvement. But given her status as a doctoral freshman, many of the attendees had been duly impressed. He silently offered a prayer of thanks.

Midprayer, Paul Norris approached him, his hands jammed into his pockets.

They made patient, polite small talk at first. Then Gabriel noticed that Paul was regarding him with something akin to agitation.

"Is there a problem?" Gabriel's voice was deceptively soft. Soft like Scotch.

"No." Paul removed his hands from his pockets. He was about to reenter the college when he stopped.

"Fuck it," he muttered.

He squared his shoulders, facing his former dissertation director.

"Professor Picton would like you to be an external reader on my dissertation."

Gabriel regarded Paul coolly. "Yes, she mentioned that."

Paul waited for the Professor to continue, but he didn't.

"Uh, is that something you'd consider?"

Gabriel rocked back on his heels. "I'll consider it. Your dissertation topic is good and I was satisfied with the work that you did for me. I passed you to Katherine for personal reasons, otherwise, I'd still be directing your dissertation."

Paul looked away uncomfortably.

"Julia did well." He changed the subject.

"Yes, she did."

"She even handled Christa."

Gabriel's face wore a look of pride. "Julianne is a remarkable woman. She's much stronger than she looks."

"I know." Paul's eyes hardened into what could have been a glare.

"You seemed to have a lot to say to and about my wife." Gabriel's tone grew progressively cooler.

"What are you doing to put a stop to the rumors? I was out at UCLA in March and people were talking about how Julia boinked you in order to graduate and get into Harvard."

A muscle jumped in Gabriel's jaw.

"Those rumors are the fruits of Miss Peterson's poisonous tree. She will be dealt with, I assure you."

"Well, you need to step it up."

Gabriel's eyes narrowed. "What was that?"

Paul shifted his weight, but he would not be deterred.

"When I arrived yesterday, I overheard a couple of the old folks talking about Julia. They assumed she was a bimbo and that's why she was on the program."

"I think it's safe to say she proved them wrong. Julianne's paper was well presented and well received. There's also the little matter that rather than simply *boinking* her"—at this, Gabriel waved his hand distastefully—"I married her."

"She may be your wife, but you don't deserve her."

Gabriel took a menacing step closer.

"*What did you say?*"

Paul drew himself to his full height, which was an inch taller than his former professor.

"I said you don't deserve her."

"You think I don't know that?"

Gabriel threw his china coffee cup in frustration. It smashed on the pavement.

"Every night when I fall asleep with her in my arms, I thank God she's mine. Every morning when I wake up, my first thought is that I'm grateful she married me. I will never be worthy of her. But I spend every day trying my damnedest. You were her friend when she needed one. But listen to me when I tell you, Paul, you do not want to push me."

A long silence passed between them. Gabriel held on to his temper as the result of a Herculean effort.

Paul was the first to look away.

"When I first met her, she was so jumpy. I felt like I had to whisper just so I wouldn't scare her. She isn't like that anymore."

"No, she isn't."

Paul hunched his shoulders. "She was telling me about her program at Harvard over lunch. She loves it."

"I know that." Gabriel's expression grew even darker. "And I know you want her. I'm telling you, you can't have her."

Paul met his gaze. "You're wrong."

"Wrong?" The Professor challenged him, taking a step forward. They were now mere inches apart, the Professor's posture angry and threatening.

"I don't just want her. I love her. She's the one."

Gabriel stared at him incredulously. "She can't be the one. She's my wife!"

"I know."

Paul looked over the Professor's shoulder at Woodstock Road, shaking his head.

"I met a pretty, sweet, Catholic girl. The kind of woman I could introduce to my parents. The kind of woman I've been looking for my whole life. I treated her right, we became friends, and when an asshole came along and broke her heart, I was there. She cried on my fucking shoulder. She fell asleep on my fucking couch."

Gabriel snapped his jaw shut furiously.

"The semester ended and she followed her dream to Harvard. I helped her move. I found her a part-time job and an apartment. But when I finally told her how I felt, when I finally asked her to choose me, she couldn't. Not because she didn't care about me, or didn't feel anything. But because she was in love with the asshole who broke her heart."

Paul laughed without amusement.

"And this guy, he's bad news. He fucks around. He treats her like dirt. He drinks too much. For all I know, he seduced her for kicks. He was involved with a professor who hits on her students and is into BDSM. So who knows what he does to my girl behind closed doors? When he leaves her, I'm ecstatic, thinking now she has a chance to be with someone who'll be good to her. Someone who'll be gentle with her and never, ever make her cry. Then, to my fucking astonishment, the asshole comes back. He fucking returns. And what does he do? He asks her to marry him. And she accepts!"

He kicked at the pavement in frustration.

"That's my life, in a fucking nutshell. Find the perfect girl, lose the perfect girl to an asshole who broke her heart and will probably break it again and again. And then get a fucking invitation to their big-ass wedding in Italy."

Gabriel ground his teeth together. "In the first place, she is not your girl and she never was. I don't have to justify myself to you or to anyone else. But out of respect for my wife, who seems to care about you, I'll admit I was an asshole. I'm not that man anymore. I never fucked around on her, not even once, and I'm sure as hell not going to break her heart again."

"Good." Paul shuffled his feet. "Then let her finish her program."

"Let her?" Gabriel's voice dropped to a near-whisper. *"Let her?"*

"She might decide to give up or take time off or something. Encourage her to continue."

Gabriel's eyes flashed. "If you have information you want to share, Mr. Norris, I suggest you spit it out."

"Julia feels guilty about making her grad program such a high priority."

Gabriel scowled as the import of Paul's words became clear.

"She told you this?"

"She also said that she doesn't have any friends."

"How convenient for you. Are you interested in continuing to be her friend?"

Paul grimaced. "This isn't fucking convenient. Don't you get it? I love her and because I love her, I have to listen to her worry about making you happy. You, the asshole who left her."

"I'm not exactly happy she chose to confide in you."

"If she had friends in Cambridge, she wouldn't need to. And anyway, my friendship with her has to end."

Gabriel rocked on his heels, momentarily taken aback.

"Did you come to this decision yourself?"

"Yes."

"Have you told her?"

"I wouldn't do that to her before her lecture. That would be cruel."

"When are you planning to tell her?"

Paul sighed deeply. "That's the problem. I can't say it to her face. When I get back to Vermont I'll write to her." He gave Gabriel a resentful look. "I'm sure that will make you happy."

"I don't take pleasure in her suffering, despite what you think." Gabriel looked down at the platinum band on his left hand. "I love her."

Paul's dark eyes shifted to the wedding ring.

The Professor continued, "Your friendship is important to her. She'll be hurt."

"It's time to move on."

"Will you tell her that?"

"I'm not going to lie. It's going to kill me to tell her the truth, but I will."

"That's very noble." An admiring tone crept into Gabriel's voice. "Perhaps I should persuade you to change your mind."

"You can't."

A long look passed between Paul and his former professor.

"I've misjudged you, Paul. And for that I'm sorry."

"I'm not doing this for you. I'm sure as hell not doing this so you'll read my dissertation and write me a recommendation letter. I'll tell Katherine that I spoke to you and you declined."

Paul nodded at Gabriel and began to walk toward the college.

"Mr. Norris," Gabriel called.

He stopped and slowly moved to face the Professor.

"I always intended to be an external reader, whether you continued your friendship with Julianne or not. Your research stands on its own merits." He extended his hand.

Paul considered this for a moment, then strode toward him. They shook hands.

"Thank you."

"You're welcome."

A look passed between the two men that was reminiscent of the look that warriors gave after a battle in which both sides took heavy losses.

Paul was the first to speak.

"I'm not going to interfere in your marriage. But if I learn that you've broken her heart again, we're going to have a problem."

"If I break Julianne's heart, I'll deserve it."

"Good." Paul grinned. "Can we stop touching each other now?"

Gabriel dropped his hand as if it were on fire. "Absolutely."

Chapter Seventeen

Later that afternoon, Julia and Gabriel checked into the Randolph Hotel. They were supposed to meet Katherine and Paul for dinner. But Paul said that he needed to speak to Professor Picton alone and, apologizing, asked the Emersons if they'd mind canceling their dinner plans. So the Emersons were left to dine alone.

After a quiet meal in the Randolph's elegant dining room, they went upstairs to their suite.

"Are you glad the conference is over?" Gabriel held the door open for his wife.

"Very glad." Immediately, Julia took off her suit jacket, draping it over a chair. She sat on the edge of the bed and kicked off her high heels.

She retrieved a square of chocolate from atop one of the pillows and unwrapped it, popping the sweet into her mouth. "They didn't give us chocolates at Magdalen College."

She gazed fondly in the direction of the en-suite. "'I'm kind of in love with the heated towel rack in the bathroom. We need one of those in Cambridge."

Gabriel laughed. "I'll see what I can do."

"But I wouldn't trade our nights at Magdalen for anything. If we come back to Oxford, I hope we can stay there again."

"Of course." He kissed the top of her head. "Magdalen is a special place, but the accommodations are a bit Spartan for my tastes. I think if we split our time between here and there, we'd be doing well."

"I had hoped I'd see a Narnian ghost during our visit."

"You won't find one outside Magdalen. Although I'm told that the actor who played Inspector Morse haunts the bar downstairs. We could go and take a look."

"I think I've had enough of people for one day. I need a hot bath, a hot towel, and an early night."

"Do you feel differently now?" He extended his hand to cup her cheek.

"About?"

"About grad school." He shrugged. "About anything."

"I worked hard on the paper, but I was also lucky. The audience didn't bring their pitchforks."

"They weren't pushovers. I know that crowd. They don't suffer fools."

"I noticed that based on the way they turned on Christa during the question period. I've never seen that happen before." Julia shuddered.

"I've seen it. And worse."

"I wonder where she went."

Gabriel snorted. "Apparently, Pacciani escorted her from the building. I suppose Katherine really did put the fear of God in him. He was furious."

Julia looked up at her husband curiously. "Don't you think it's strange that Paul didn't want to have dinner with us? He seemed to be looking forward to it earlier."

Gabriel traced a light finger down her nose. "Maybe Katherine isn't happy with his dissertation and he wanted to smooth things over without an audience."

"Maybe."

"You still haven't answered my question. Do you feel differently about grad school now? Or are you still enthusiastic about your program?"

She put her hand over his, pressing his palm against her cheek. "It was an intimidating experience. But I'm glad I did it. I'd like to do it again."

"Good, because I think you're gifted, Julianne, and I want to do everything in my power to help you succeed."

She closed her eyes tightly. "Thank you, Gabriel. That means a lot."

"You can always talk to me. If something is troubling you, I'll listen. I promise." He slid his hand to the back of her neck.

"I just want us to be happy."

"I want that too. So if you're ever unhappy, tell me."

She pressed her lips to his wrist.

"I wonder what Beatrice's husband thought of Dante's attentions. You have to admit, that part of the story is sad. Beatrice is married, but she has this poet following her around and writing sonnets about her."

Gabriel's grip on her tightened. "I married *you*. I love *you*. We have what Dante and Beatrice never had." He kissed her again. "I need to go out. But I'll be back."

"Will you be gone long?"

"I don't know. But in the meantime, I have a gift." He pulled a box out of his pocket and placed it in her hand.

Julia read the label. *Cartier.*

She looked up at him wide-eyed.

He opened the box and she saw a beautiful white gold watch shining against folds of creamy silk.

"This is in recognition of a job well done. You're going to have lots of opportunities to present your research, and you need a reliable watch."

He removed it from the box and turned it over, showing her the inscription on the back.

To My Beloved,
With admiration and pride
Gabriel

"A Timex is a reliable watch. This is something else entirely." Julia almost laughed.

"Something entirely deserved, I assure you."

She touched the engraving in awe.

"How did you know?"

"How did I know what?" He clasped the watch around her wrist. It fit perfectly.

"How did you know I'd do a good job?"

"Because I have faith in you." He kissed her slowly. Then, with a determined look, he exited their suite.

❧❧

Christa Peterson sat on the large bed in her hotel room, waiting. She'd managed to find a sexy black basque that laced up the back, and she wore it with gartered stockings and very high heels.

Champagne cooled in a silver container in the corner, provocative music floated through the air, and a series of sensual accessories (including handcuffs) lay on the table next to the bed.

She checked the very expensive watch she'd worn since she'd lost her virginity, resisting the urge to think back to the words Giuseppe had said to her the night before. His ascription had been too close to the mark.

Instead, she focused on what was about to happen. She was finally going to have her heart's desire—Professor Gabriel O. Emerson in her arms, her bed, her body.

At last.

Men never said no to her. And despite Gabriel's attachment to his plain and mousy little wife, he was a man. They'd fuck a few times and go their separate ways. She'd have the satisfaction of knowing her success rate at seduction was one hundred percent.

A knock echoed through the room.

Trying to hide her enthusiasm, Christa straightened the seams of her stockings and walked toward the door.

Chapter Eighteen

"You were wonderful," Gabriel whispered, lazily running the backs of his fingers up and down her spine.

She hugged the pillow, hiding her face. She was lying on her stomach, her back gloriously exposed.

He eyed her bashfulness with concern before leaning over to kiss the slope of her shoulder.

"Darling?"

"Thank you." Julia shifted a little, her eyes meeting his.

"How did you feel about that position?" Gabriel pressed his palm flat just above her backside, resting over two dimples.

"I enjoyed it."

"But?"

"No qualifications."

"Then why are you shy?"

She shrugged.

Gabriel rolled her to her side. "You're safe. I promise, you're safe in my arms and in my bed. Always."

He placed a finger to her chin, lifting it.

"Talk to me."

She avoided his eyes. "I don't want to bring old issues up, but sometimes I worry."

"About what?"

"I worry I'm not adventurous enough for you."

Gabriel would have laughed had she not looked so serious. He forced himself to look grave.

"That's a remarkable worry after the past few hours." His palm rested on the curve of her backside, but he resisted the urge to squeeze.

She blew a lock of hair away from her mouth. "I didn't get a chance to tell you this, but Christa cornered me just before lunch."

Gabriel's eyes flashed. "I don't want to hear that name while we're in bed."

Julia nuzzled against the fine hair of his chest. "I'm sorry."

"What did she say?"

"She said you deserved someone adventurous."

"Don't listen to her poisonous bullshit."

"I told her you deserved love and that's what I gave you."

"That's certainly true." His hand slid up her spine to her neck, where he began massaging her gently. "So why are you worrying?"

"Because I want to keep you."

Gabriel chuckled in spite of himself. "I'm afraid we're in a competition, then, darling, because I want to do my damnedest to keep you."

"Good." She snuggled closer in his arms.

"There are some adventures I experienced before you that I don't wish to repeat."

Julia thought of Professor Pain and winced.

Gabriel's index finger traced the curve of her neck, up and down and up and down, whisper soft. "Other adventures I'd be willing to explore, if you felt the same way. Our bed is for pleasure. My utmost concern is to please you and to find my pleasure with you, not at your expense. You don't need to worry that I'll abandon you if you say no to me. You can always say no. Understand?"

"Yes." She breathed deeply.

"So if I were to suggest something . . . new, and you were to decide you didn't want to try it, that's fine."

"Really?" Her large eyes searched his.

The edges of his lips turned up. "I might attempt to seduce you and change your mind. But I can think of few things more unpleasant than bedding an unwilling woman."

He stroked his thumb across the curve of her cheek.

"And in your case, I can think of nothing more painful than looking into your eyes and seeing discomfort or regret."

He brought their mouths together and they were both momentarily lost in the sweetness of their embrace.

"Do you still feel shy?" He pulled back so he could see her expression.

"No." She pressed her legs together. "But I'm wondering what kind of sexual adventures you have in mind."

"Trust me, Julianne, and I'll show you." He rolled her to her back before pinning her arms above her head and whispering his lips against her throat.

❧

The next morning, the Emersons slept late despite their intention to awake early and visit the Ashmolean Museum. Gabriel left the bed first, kissing Julia before walking to the en-suite.

After he'd showered and shaved, he entered the bedroom, clad only in his glasses and a towel. Julia was still asleep.

He gazed on her with no little satisfaction. She'd been absolutely shattered the night before, the result of an exceptional series of orgasms. His chest swelled with pride.

For Gabriel, it had been a night spent initiating her into activities she'd never done before. He couldn't help the primal possessiveness he felt at being the one to teach her—at being the one to share her pleasure. But his possessiveness was tempered with tenderness, as he recognized how much Julia had come to trust him.

Their couplings were always passionate, always loving. Gabriel watched her relentlessly when they were together, so that any sign of hesitation was immediately addressed. And knowing that she was safe in his bed, she gave herself freely.

Sex could be all-consuming. He knew this and had once been consumed, caught like an animal in a trap. He knew that even with his wife, there were times when he felt the temptation to push everything aside so he could find himself inside her.

Julia could be voracious and passionate. Her confidence in her safety made her brave, and her passion for him made her an enthusiastic lover. Her experience was limited to what he'd taught her, a fact in which he took no little pride. It seemed as if every sexual act between them was fraught with newness.

He didn't know how to communicate his feelings on these matters to her, without bringing up the specter of his past. But he felt the differences among his wife and his lovers in his very flesh and tried to reassure her of how much she pleased him in word as well as deed.

Within the bedroom as without, they followed the wisdom of St. Augustine: *Love and do what you will.*

(They'd loved and willed several times the night before.)

He eyed the remnants of his surprise—strawberries and truffles for both of them, champagne for Julia and sparkling water for him. The concierge had been very obliging when he'd appeared at his desk on impulse the night before.

Gabriel began picking up the clothes they'd discarded. He hung up her things first, smiling at the corset and minuscule panties she'd worn underneath her conservative suit. She knew just how to tantalize him, without losing any of her innate modesty.

He hung up his own suit, emptying his pockets as he did so. Something white fluttered to the ground.

He bent over to retrieve it. It was a business card with printed lettering.

Christa Peterson, M.A.
Graduate Student
Department of Italian
Columbia University
Email: cp24@columbia.edu
Tel. (212) 458-2124

Gabriel stared in disgust at the item, turning it over. On the back of the card he found writing, in a sloping woman's hand,

Malmaison Hotel, Room 209.
Tonight.

With a curse, Gabriel crumpled the card and threw it into the wastepaper basket.

Christa must have slipped it in his pocket the day before. No doubt she'd written on the card before she saw him, having planned her seduction in advance. Perhaps she'd even traveled to Oxford solely for that purpose.

Given that explanation, much of her behavior made sense. Gabriel was the mark, not Julia. Christa's outrageous actions were carefully calculated to entrap him, capitalizing on his desire to protect his wife. Of course, that didn't stop Christa from taunting Julia and suggesting she wouldn't be able to hold on to her husband, as if Christa knew her seduction would be successful.

His stomach lurched.

Gabriel walked to the bed, looking at Julia's face in profile as she slept. They'd enjoyed an evening of tremendous pleasure, and Christa wished to take that away from them. Her lust had turned into envy and treachery as she conspired to become an adulterer and steal him from his wife.

It's a good thing Julia didn't find that card.

Hopefully, she would have confronted him about it and not gone and bared her soul to Paul.

A tremor traveled up and down Gabriel's spine. Julianne's budding career was precious. His marriage was precious. And he wasn't about to let anyone or anything threaten either.

Picking up his cell phone, he strode back to the bathroom, dialing the number for John Green, his lawyer.

❧❧

In the Malmaison Hotel in Oxford Castle, Christa stood in front of the bathroom mirror. She raised a shaking hand to her lip, ghosting over where the skin was split. She winced, slowly inspecting the bruise that was blossoming in her cheek and the marks where his fingers had dug into her flesh.

She looked terrible.

She'd opened the door to her room the night before, expecting to see Professor Emerson. Instead, Giuseppe was standing there, drunk and furious.

He'd pushed past her and locked the door, ranting about how she was going to cost him an academic position in America. His rants were slurred and in Italian.

When she questioned him, he grew even more belligerent, demanding to know whom she was attempting to seduce in the hotel room he'd paid for.

As soon as she said Gabriel's name, he'd backhanded her.

She'd never been struck before. There were a lot of things she'd never experienced before last night and this morning. She looked down between her legs where the flesh was tender and raw. She hadn't consented. She hadn't consented to any of it.

Giuseppe's previous tenderness had disappeared entirely. He'd been in a rage, ripping the fabric from her body and forcing her to the bed. He'd called her names, cursing her and Gabriel, and when she struggled, he'd struck her again.

She stumbled to the toilet as she recalled the assault, emptying the contents of her stomach. When she was finished, she leaned against the counter and drank a glass of water.

She thought she was in control. She decided whom to fuck and what they must give her in return. She was the one who spurned lovers. But last night the control had been taken away from her.

He'd taken more than that. She fought angry, frustrated tears at the memory.

She crept back to the bedroom to make sure that he was still sleeping. When she heard the low sound of his snores, she knew it was time.

Hastily, she pulled on some clothes, not caring if the colors or styles matched. She tossed her belongings in her suitcase, leaving the torn remnants of last night's lingerie on the floor.

She heard a loud intake of breath coming from the bed and spun around, terrified.

Giuseppe muttered something and his snoring recommenced.

Christa located her purse and her passport and grabbed them, along with her coat. She was almost to the door when she realized that her Baume & Mercier watch was sitting on the nightstand. It was mere inches from his head.

She wanted to retrieve it. The watch was very valuable, for sentimental reasons.

As she approached the bed, Pacciani's breathing grew more uneven. A groan escaped his mouth and he rolled toward her.

Without looking back, she fled to the door, opening and closing it quietly.

She left the watch behind.

As she entered the taxi that would whisk her to the railway station, she began plotting her revenge. All thoughts of Professor Gabriel O. Emerson and his young wife, Julianne, fled from her mind.

Chapter Nineteen

"I'm sorry I didn't attend your graduation in Toronto." Gabriel held Julia's hand as they explored the Ashmolean Museum, which was across the street from the Randolph Hotel.

"I searched for you. I was so sure you'd be there."

"I couldn't be in the same room as you and not go to you. To do that in front of Jeremy and Dean Aras . . ." Gabriel shook his head. "I'll go to your next graduation."

"Promise?"

"Absolutely."

She reached up to press their lips together. "Thank you."

They continued walking through the museum, stopping to admire some of the items on display. When they stopped in front of a panel that displayed a medieval painting of St. Lucy, Julia was reminded of Rachel.

"Your sister sent me an email. She asked how my paper went."

"Is she pregnant?"

"She didn't say. If she isn't, it's not for lack of trying."

Gabriel wrinkled his nose. "I don't need that kind of image."

"I'm sure Rachel doesn't need that kind of image of you, either. But she was almost as happy as me when we consummated our relationship."

"I find that hard to believe," he whispered, pulling her into his arms in a dark corner.

"She said she's looking forward to visiting us in Cambridge Labor Day weekend."

"Quiet, now. I'm trying to kiss you."

Julia laughed. "Just a minute. I'm not done."

"Hurry up," he pouted, bringing his lips to within an inch of hers.

"This is important." She gave him a scolding look. "Rachel and

Aaron would like us to light a candle for them in Assisi. They want us to pray that they'll have a baby."

"I think Richard's prayers would be more efficacious than mine. Although I'm still praying for one more thing."

Gabriel couldn't hide the brightness of hope that shone in his eyes, as if his unanswered prayer were a treasure that he desperately desired.

Julia noted the change but said nothing. She'd just celebrated her triumphal coming out into academic society the day before. Now Gabriel was hinting at having a child. Somehow the hope in his eyes made her discomfort all the more painful.

The light in his eyes dimmed.

"Why are you looking at me like that?" He released her from his arms.

"Like what?"

"Like you're repulsed by me."

"I'm not repulsed." She forced a smile.

"Is the thought of having a child with me so repulsive?" Gabriel's features hardened.

"Of course not." She wound their fingers together. "It's difficult for me to think about children when I'd rather focus on conference presentations and grad school."

"It isn't an either-or proposition, Julianne. I'd never make you sacrifice your dreams. I think I've demonstrated that ably enough." His voice was glacial.

"As you may recall, your sacrifice caused us both a great deal of pain."

"Point taken." He released her hand and gestured to the hallway. "Shall we?"

"Gabriel." She placed a light hand on his arm. "I told you before we were married that the thought of having little blue-eyed boys with you made me happy. It still does."

"Then why can't we talk about it? God, Julianne. If we were going to go to Africa, we'd talk about it. If we were going to build a house, we'd talk about it. Why can't we talk about having a child?"

"Because I can't say no to you, not when you look so happy and hopeful." Her eyes filled with tears. "I can't bear to be the one standing between you and your dreams, like a coldhearted wench."

"Darling," he murmured, sweeping her into a tight embrace. "Nothing could be further from my mind."

His hand found the skin of her neck, underneath her hair, and he stroked it tenderly.

"This isn't the best place to have this conversation, but I promise I don't think of you that way. I told you I'd wait. I understand you want to finish your program. Watching you yesterday, I don't know when I've been more proud of you. You were fantastic." He pressed his lips to just below her ear. "When I bring up the subject of a family, I swear I'm not trying to pressure you. I'm simply bringing up a topic that makes me happy, hoping that it will make you happy too. We can talk about the future and make plans without changing our time line. Starting a family is a momentous decision, especially given our backgrounds. I know that you've given the matter some thought. I'm simply asking that we talk about it. But we certainly don't need to talk about it now. I'm sorry for bringing it up on the heels of your lecture. Just promise me we'll talk about it someday, even if it's in the most general of terms."

"Of course, Gabriel. It's just that the topic makes me anxious."

"Then I need to do a better job of bringing up the subject and not springing it on you. But I don't want to hear you refer to yourself as either coldhearted or a wench ever again." He pulled back to make eye contact with her. "Neither of those ascriptions applies to you, and I certainly won't have anyone speak about my wife that way."

She nodded.

"Good." He took her hand and began walking. "Now, as I recall, you were telling me about Rachel's email."

"Her exact words were, 'I'm calling in all my chips. I've got Christians, Muslims, Jews, and even a Zoroastrian praying.'"

Gabriel looked puzzled. "Rachel knows a Zoroastrian? How is that possible? There are less than two hundred thousand Zoroastrians worldwide."

"She works with a woman who's Zoroastrian. How do you know how many Zoroastrians there are?"

"I Wikied it."

Gabriel gazed at her solemnly before giving her a sly wink.

"Don't believe anything you read on Wikipedia, Professor."

"I couldn't have said it better myself, Mrs. Emerson. Someone wrote an entry about me on that damned site, and the content was shocking. *Wikifuckers.*"

He kissed her gently but firmly before they heard someone nearby clearing his throat.

A security guard stood two feet away.

"Move along." He glared at them.

"Sorry." Gabriel sounded far from apologetic as he wound his arm around Julia's waist and ducked into an adjacent room.

"We need to be more discreet." She felt flushed as they continued their tour.

"We need to find a darker corner." Gabriel gazed at her provocatively, and she felt her flush deepen.

"I've asked John Green to send Christa a cease-and-desist letter." Gabriel led her into the hallway.

"Do you think that's a good idea?"

"John did. It's a shot across the bow. We're simply reminding her that we won't tolerate slander. The woman is a menace."

Julia took a deep breath and held it before exhaling slowly. "The conference went better than expected."

He brought her hand to his lips. "You were exceptional."

"So maybe the slander isn't as worrisome as we thought."

"Slander is always worrisome. Don't you know that line from *Othello*:

> "'*Who steals my purse steals trash. . . .*
> *But he that filches from me my good name*
> *Robs me of that which not enriches him*
> *And makes me poor indeed.*'"

"I seem to recall hearing you quote that before. But can you really stop Christa from gossiping about us?"

Gabriel looked at her in resignation. "I don't know. But given her behavior at the conference, I had to try."

Chapter Twenty

July 2011
Minneapolis, Minnesota

Paulina Gruscheva's handwriting was bold and sophisticated, like the woman herself. She wrote with a Montblanc fountain pen, the black ink flowing in curved flourishes over the expensive cream-colored envelope.

She'd had to look up his address. Miraculously, he was in the Cambridge telephone book.

As she peered down at the letters and numbers she'd written, a smile of satisfaction spread across her beautiful features. Then she sealed the envelope and readied herself to take it to the post office.

He was going to be surprised.

Chapter Twenty-one

July 2011
Italy

Julia and Gabriel said good-bye to Katherine, Paul, and Oxford a few days after the conference. The last words exchanged with Paul were especially awkward. Julia knew her friend and consequently knew that something was wrong. But when she asked him about it, he merely referenced his anxiety over his dissertation.

When he hugged her good-bye, he held her tightly and a little too long. Julia said they'd stay in touch, and he nodded but didn't agree. She excused his behavior by telling herself that he was simply being nostalgic about their friendship.

Gabriel distracted Katherine from noticing Paul's exchange with Julia, trying to give them some privacy. He took no pleasure in seeing Paul's discomfort, or the way he tried to appear happy and at ease for Julia's sake.

The Emersons traveled to Rome, celebrating Gabriel's birthday on the seventeenth of July with a special tour of the Vatican Museum. There was, however, a shocking lack of museum sex.

(Not even Gabriel was tempted to indulge himself with Julia inside the Vatican.)

They visited Assisi for a few days, where they prayed and lit candles at the crypt of St. Francis. Although Gabriel and Julia didn't confess the content of their prayers, it was understood that they prayed for each other, for their marriage, and for the eventual gift of a child.

To these prayers, Julia added her own requests for wisdom and strength, while Gabriel asked for goodness and courage. Both of them prayed for Rachel and Aaron, asking that God would bless their attempts to have a baby.

So it was that they arrived at their house near Todi, an Umbrian village, at the end of July. The house was located near a mixed fruit tree orchard and boasted an enclosed pool that was bordered on one edge by lavender. The fragrant flowers perfumed the air, and Julia placed a few sprigs between the sheets of their bed.

When she awoke the next day, Gabriel was gone. With the sun high in the sky and shining in through the balcony windows she was not surprised by his absence, or by the coolness of the sheets on his side. Clutching his pillow, which still retained the scent of Aramis mingled with lavender, she found a handwritten note.

> Good Morning, Darling.
> You were sleeping too peacefully to awaken.
> I've gone into Todi to pick up a few things from the market.
> Call my cell phone if you need anything.
> Love,
> G.
> PS. You're breathtaking.

Julia smiled. It was a simple note, not unlike countless others he'd written for her. But in the bottom corner, almost as an afterthought, he'd sketched her. It was her profile while she slept, transposed into a small pencil drawing. Underneath it he'd written *My Beatrice*.

She hadn't known that he had skill with a pencil, although his dexterity in other respects suggested a multiplicity of manual talents. The sketch was quite good. She wanted to frame it.

Still smiling, she swung her naked feet to the floor and walked gingerly to the closet. She didn't feel like wearing clothes. So she took one of Gabriel's dress shirts and put it on, buttoning only a few of the buttons before searching one of the dresser drawers for some socks.

From downstairs, she heard Gabriel's voice calling. Enthusiastically, she sped down the stairs and toward the kitchen.

"Hello." He kissed her forehead as he set the groceries on the counter. "You look pretty."

Hands free, he pecked first one cheek then the other before trapping her in his arms.

"Did you sleep well?" His lips moved against her hair.

"Very well. Between our stay in Assisi and last night, I think I've slept more than in months." She pressed her mouth to his Adam's apple, and he recoiled slightly as if she'd tickled him. "Thank you for the drawing."

"You're welcome."

"I didn't know you could draw."

"Darling, I'd paint you if I could. *With my fingers.*"

"Stop teasing me, Professor. Every time I think of paint, I think of what we did on the floor back in Selinsgrove. And it gets me hot and bothered." She pouted in jest.

"I'll see to that later, I promise." He released her from his arms, smiling slyly. "I like your socks."

She looked down at her feet and flexed them.

"Argyle is sexy."

"Indeed. A friend once told me that argyle is the fabric of seduction."

"You have strange friends." She shook her head, plucking a grape from the fruit bowl and eating it.

He began unpacking the groceries, watching her from the corner of his eye. "You seem happy."

She hoisted herself up onto the counter and began to swing her legs back and forth.

"I am. The conference is over; we had a great time in Rome and Assisi. I'm in love with my husband and I get to share this fantastic house with him. I'm the luckiest woman in the universe."

Gabriel's eyebrows shot up. "In the universe? Hmmm. I'm sure the inhabitants of the galaxy next door will be sorry to hear that."

She playfully poked him with her argyle-covered foot. "You're a nerd."

He turned on her and grabbed her foot, pulling it upward until her leg was extended to the height of his shoulder. She reclined on her elbows to maintain her balance.

"*What did you just call me?*" He feigned anger, but his sapphire eyes twinkled.

"Um, I called you a nerd."

He raised a single eyebrow.

"Oh, really? Would a nerd do *this*?" Expertly, Gabriel used his fingers to stroke the contours of Julia's instep.

When she sighed at the pleasant sensation, he peeled off her socks before tossing them over his shoulder.

"Let's see if we can get you all hot and bothered, shall we?" His voice was low, and it made Julia quiver.

He slid his hand over her leg, toying with the back of her knee until she groaned.

"Julianne," he growled, his eyes dancing.

"Y-yes?"

"You aren't wearing panties."

With a single finger, he traveled the length of her inner thigh and back again, stroking up and down in a patient rhythm.

She began to breathe rather rapidly as his fingers approached where she was exposed.

"Nerds are not known for their skills in lovemaking." Gabriel withdrew his hand and placed his index finger against her mouth.

She parted her lips and he pressed his finger inside. She closed around him, sucking his finger slightly before releasing it.

He winked at her before using his now-moistened finger to stroke the inside of her upper thigh.

"Would a nerd know to do this?" He leaned over and began to blow across the trail of wetness he'd left with his finger.

When Julia shivered, he smiled wickedly and nuzzled the same trail with his nose.

Standing up again, he kissed her hungrily and then abruptly retreated. Before she had the time to protest, he dropped to his knees in front of her.

"Hmmmm," he said, moving her legs so that they rested on his shoulders again. "This counter seems to be the perfect height. I guess you really are the luckiest woman in the universe."

Chapter Twenty-two

The following evening, Julia awoke in the middle of the night and visited the en-suite. On her return, she heard Gabriel shifting in bed, a few muffled words escaping his lips.

This was not surprising. Gabriel was usually a deep sleeper, but there were nights when he'd toss and turn and even talk in his sleep. Usually, Julia wasn't bothered by it. But on this evening, he started thrashing in bed and cursing.

She was at his side instantly. "Gabriel?"

He continued his erratic movements, punctuated as they were by moments of torpor.

She switched on the lamp. "Gabriel?"

He mumbled. Then, all of a sudden, he tore at the bedclothes, wrestling and flailing until he was free.

His eyes shot open and he sat up, gasping for breath.

"Are you all right?" Julia elected to keep her distance, speaking in a low voice.

He looked at her, disoriented, and clutched his chest.

"Is it your heart? Can you breathe?"

"Nightmare." His voice cracked.

"I'll get you a drink." Julia returned to the en-suite and retrieved a glass, filling it with water from the tap. He accepted it wordlessly.

She sat on the edge of the bed and waited, watching him closely.

"What was your nightmare about?"

He finished his drink, placing the glass on the nightstand.

"Give me a minute."

Julia wanted to brush his dark hair back from his forehead, but she didn't think he would welcome the gesture.

His blue eyes blinked before fixing on the wall behind her.

"My biological parents."

"Oh, sweetie." Julia reached out to hug him, but he stiffened. She paused for a moment, then walked over to her side of the bed.

Gabriel didn't move. He didn't even bother to turn out the light but continued to sit with his back against the headboard.

She slid over to him, underneath the sheets. She wanted to comfort him. But the air around him was charged with a strange kind of energy. Gabriel didn't want to be touched.

She closed her eyes and had almost drifted into sleep, when his voice came out of the darkness.

"I was with my mother in our old apartment in Brooklyn. I could hear her and my father arguing."

Julia's eyes snapped open.

"I heard a crash. I heard my mother crying. I ran into the kitchen."

"Was she okay?"

"She was kneeling on the floor. He was standing over her, shouting. I hit him with my fists. I shouted back. He shoved me and went to the front door. My mother crawled after him, begging him not to leave."

Gabriel's eyes glinted coldly, anger distorting his handsome features.

"Fucking bastard," he spat.

"Sweetheart," Julia murmured. She slid her hand across the sheet, making contact with his hip.

"I hate him. He's been dead for years and still, if I knew where his grave was, I'd piss on it."

Julia pressed her palm into his hip.

"I'm sorry."

When he didn't respond, she stroked his skin softly, an act that was meant to be soothing.

"He hit her. It was bad enough that he seduced her and abandoned us. But the asshole hit her."

"Gabriel," she whispered. "It was only a dream."

He shook his head, still staring off into space.

"I don't think so."

Julia stilled. "You think it was real?"

Gabriel covered his eyes, pressing his fingers into the sockets. "I don't think that was the first time they fought. Or the first time I intervened."

"How old were you?"

"Young. Five or six. I don't know."

"You were a brave boy, defending your mother."

Gabriel dropped his hands into his lap.

"It didn't do any good. He broke her. Can you imagine crawling after a man who hit you? In front of your son?"

"She must have loved him."

"Don't make excuses," he snapped.

"Gabriel, look at me." Her tone was gentle.

He turned in her direction, his eyes blazing fire.

"I stayed with Simon," she remarked quietly.

Gabriel blinked, and slowly the fire in his eyes began to diminish.

"I didn't know your mother. But I know how messed up my head was when I was with Simon."

"That was different. You were young."

"I can't imagine your mother was very old when she had you. How old was she?"

"I don't know," he ground out.

"She thought she loved him. She had a child with him."

"He was married."

Julia fidgeted with the sheet that covered her. "We can't change our pasts. All we can change is the future."

"I'm sorry I woke you." Gabriel pressed a kiss against her hair.

"You didn't."

He pulled back so he could see her face. "Oh, really?"

"I had a female problem to attend to."

After a moment, realization passed over his features. "Oh. Are you feeling all right?"

"I'm not feeling my best but it will pass."

"I thought you seemed a little sensitive earlier." He ghosted a hand over her breasts.

She grabbed his hand, stilling it.

"I'm sorry about your nightmare."

He moved away, turning the light off. Then he slipped under the sheet next to her.

She could hear him bring his teeth together, clenching his jaw.

"Do you really think it's a memory and not just a nightmare?"

"Sometimes I can't tell," he admitted.

"Has it happened before?"

"On occasion. It's been a while."

"You never said anything."

"It isn't something I like to discuss, Julianne. My memories of my childhood are vague at best. And what I remember, I try to forget."

"Have you told Dr. Townsend about them?"

"Briefly, yes." He touched Julia absently, floating his fingertips over her back. "I know very little about my parents."

"I can understand your anger at your parents. But it isn't a healthy thing to hold on to."

"I know that." He stopped touching her and rolled to his side, facing her. "There might be terrible skeletons in my family's closet. Could you love me in spite of them?"

"I'd never love you in spite of anything, Gabriel. I just love you."

He captured her mouth, but only for an instant. They relaxed into the bed, spooning under the covers.

Just as she was about to drift into sleep, Gabriel's voice sounded in her ear.

"Thank you."

❧❧

The next morning, Julia was sunning herself by the pool before it grew too warm. She wore a large sun hat and a very small blue bikini. Gabriel had persuaded her to purchase the bikini during their trip to Belize before they were married. She had had few occasions to wear it.

She thought back to the previous evening and Gabriel's nightmare. It had disturbed them both. She couldn't help but envision what he'd described—his mother on the floor, crawling after the man who fathered her child and abandoned her. Perhaps that image, fictional or otherwise, was part of what generated Gabriel's intense antipathy to the sight of Julia on her knees. Even now, several months into their marriage, that was one position he couldn't countenance.

Perhaps it's because of Paulina.

Julia winced. She didn't like thinking of Gabriel's former lover and the mother of the child they'd lost. But unless Gabriel was hiding something, he hadn't heard from her in over a year.

Julia was inclined to let sleeping dogs lie.

A shadow fell over her legs and she looked through her sunglasses to see him standing over her. He was clad only in black swimming trunks and was carrying a towel.

His muscled chest and arms rippled as he moved, kissing her before placing the towel on a chair and diving into the pool. The water was warm and a welcome respite from the bright Umbrian sun.

Gabriel swam laps, losing himself in the almost-silence of the water. Back and forth and back and forth. During physical exercise, as during sex, he could relieve his mind of all worry and stress, focusing only on his movements.

He actively suppressed all thought or reflection on his nightmare. An intuition had taken hold that told him that the dream was a memory. No amount of reasoning had been able to persuade him otherwise. So he simply turned his attention to something else—the feel of the sun and the water against his flesh, the sound of splashing in his ears, the taste of chlorine, the glorious burn in his muscles as he pushed himself to swim faster.

He was counting laps, flip turn upon flip turn, when the peacefulness of his morning swim was broken by a sudden cry.

He surfaced immediately, his eyes searching for Julia. She was still in her chair, but she'd swung her legs over the side of the lounge and was holding her iPhone to her ear.

"She's *what*?" Julia's voice was unusually shrill.

Gabriel wiped his eyes so he could see her better.

"You're kidding." She paused, mouth gaping. "When is she due?"

Gabriel swam to the ladder and climbed out of the pool. He picked up his towel and began to dry off, his eyes fixed on her.

"No, I'm happy. I'm happy for you both. I just can't believe it." Her tone was sincere, if not surprised, but her body language was notably tense.

Gabriel waved a hand in front of her face. "Who is it?" He pointed at the phone.

My dad, she mouthed.

Now it was Gabriel's turn to gape. If her words meant what he thought they meant, then . . .

"So when is the wedding?" Julia peered up at Gabriel, lifting her eyebrows.

"I don't know. I'll check with him and get back to you. Wow, Dad. This is really sudden."

She laughed. "Yes, for you too. Obviously."

Gabriel reached over and placed a hand on her shoulder. She covered his hand with her own.

"Yes, of course. Put her on." Julia paused. "Hi, Diane. Congratulations."

Gabriel wiped his face with the towel a second time and moved to sit on the lounge next to Julia.

"Of course we'll be there. We just need to sort out the date.

"That's right.

"Of course. Congratulations again. Bye.

"Hi, Dad. I'm happy for you both.

"Yes, of course. Bye."

Julia disconnected the phone and slumped in her seat. "Holy shit."

"What is it?"

"My dad is getting married."

Gabriel's lips twitched. "I gathered that. They spoke to you about it in Selinsgrove."

"Yes, but they want to get married immediately because Diane is pregnant."

Gabriel stifled a grin.

"Hmmm." He stroked the stubble on his chin, pretending to be deep in thought. "A shotgun wedding for Tom, who is probably the only person I know who actually owns a shotgun. I'd label the situation as *ironic*, except I know better." He winked.

Julia adjusted her sunglasses. "Yes, literature professors have an annoying habit of actually using words correctly. It takes all the fun out of a good neologism."

Gabriel laughed.

"And that remark there"—he paused to kiss her mouth—"is precisely why I love you, Mrs. Emerson."

"I thought you loved me for my breasts."

"I am equally partial to all of your assets." He slid his hand down to the edge of her bikini bottom, giving it a playful tug.

"You are entirely too charming for your own good, Professor."

"So I'm told. When's the baby due?"

"End of December."

"Are you upset?" He removed her hat and her sunglasses, so he could see her eyes.

"No, I'm in shock. My dad is having a baby. We didn't light a candle for him in Assisi."

"That's probably a good thing, or God would have sent him twins."

"God help us."

"I'm sure it was a shock for your father. How's he taking it?"

"He sounded excited. I get the impression they were surprised, but I didn't want to ask too many questions."

"That's probably wise. At least I know what to buy him for Christmas."

"What?"

Gabriel's mouth widened into a slow, satisfied smile.

"Condoms."

Julia rolled her eyes.

"So when are they getting married?"

Julia gestured between them. "That depends on us. They want us to be there, so as soon as we can get back."

Gabriel frowned. "I'm not cutting short our vacation for their wedding."

"Easy, tiger. They're asking us to fly to Selinsgrove for a weekend when we get back. They want us to give them some dates and then they'll talk to Diane's family."

"You're going to be a big sister."

A startled look passed over her features.

"I'm going to have a sibling," she breathed. "I always wanted a brother or sister."

"Big sister Julia," said Gabriel. "With all the rights, privileges, and responsibilities. I always hated being an only child. I was glad when

Scott and Rachel became my siblings. Even though Scott was a pest for most of his life."

"I don't know how this happened."

Once again, Gabriel suppressed a grin. "I'm disappointed to hear you say that, Mrs. Emerson. Obviously, our nocturnal activities haven't been—ah—*memorable* enough."

Julia frowned. "You know what I meant. My dad is old."

"He isn't that old. Diane is even younger."

"She's forty. She told me."

"A spring chicken."

Julia looked at him out of the corner of her eye. "Did you just say *spring chicken*?"

"I did. Your dad found himself an attractive young fiancée and now he's about to be a father. Again."

"My dad is going to be a father," Julia repeated, a faraway expression in her eyes.

"I think you're in shock." Gabriel stood up. "Maybe I should get you a drink."

"Rachel wants to have a baby, Dad is having a baby, and we . . ." She didn't finish the sentence.

Gabriel leaned over her. "Look at it this way. There will be lots of older kids for our children to play with during Christmas and summer vacations. Eventually."

"Christmas and summer vacations. All those kids. Holy shit."

"Exactly." Gabriel smiled. "Holy shit."

Chapter Twenty-three

That same day, Christa Peterson strode into the Department of Italian at Columbia University a few minutes early for her appointment with Professor Lucia Barini, the chair. Christa had successfully escaped Professor Pacciani and returned to New York, nursing her wounds (both internal and external) and vowing her revenge.

When she thought about what had happened to her at the Malmaison Hotel in Oxford, she did not use the word *rape*. But she had, in fact, been raped. He'd forced her to have sex and used violence to subdue and overpower her. For various reasons, Christa chose to think of what happened to her as a loss of control. He took power away from her and used it against her. She was going to do the same to him. Only she was going to make sure he suffered more.

He'd sent an email offering a halfhearted apology. She'd ignored it.

In fact, she'd decided to dedicate her considerable energy to ruining him. She wrote a long letter to his wife (in Italian), detailing their affair from the early days when she was Pacciani's student in Florence. She enclosed photographic evidence (some of which was pornographic), along with copies of salacious emails. If that wasn't enough to make his life difficult, she intended to bide her time until she could do something really damaging.

Which was why when she heard a rumor that Professor Pacciani intended to apply for a job in her very department, Christa made an appointment to speak with Professor Barini.

Because she was so intent on revenge, she hadn't had much time or energy to devote to Professor Emerson and Julianne. In fact, she'd almost forgotten about them.

Since she was early for her appointment, Christa decided to check her departmental pigeonhole. From it, she retrieved a business-sized envelope, emblazoned with the name and address of a prominent New York law firm. She hastily ripped open the letter and read the contents.

"Damn it," she muttered.

The Professor hadn't been kidding when he said that he was going to shut her up. She held in her hand a cease-and-desist letter that accused her of several incidents of public defamation of character. Each incident was described in painstaking detail, along with the legal implications of her statements. The letter threatened further action if she persisted in making slanderous remarks about Gabriel or his wife, reserving the right to take action on those incidents that had already occurred.

Fuck, she thought.

Part of her wanted to pen a saucy reply to the law firm. Part of her wanted to continue her crusade to ruin the Emersons simply out of spite.

But as she looked at the other pigeonholes, she realized that such an act would be foolish. If she ever wanted to be admitted to the PhD program and actually graduate, she couldn't do anything that would embarrass her department.

(And besides, she had a much larger fish to fry.)

As she crammed the letter into her purse, she resolved to forget about the Emersons and focus her attention on ending the career of one Professor Pacciani. To do this, she was going to expose her affair with him.

And, playing the part of the insecure and easily controlled graduate student in Professor Barini's office, that was precisely what Christa did.

Chapter Twenty-four

Across the ocean, Gabriel switched the light off before pulling Julia into his arms. He began to kiss her neck ardently.

She tensed.

He paused. "What's the matter?"

"I can't, remember? I'll probably be finished the day after tomorrow."

"I'm not kissing you because I expect sex."

She arched an eyebrow in the darkness.

"I have a fairly good memory. I remembered that you were on your cycle." He pulled away, sounding chippy.

She tugged at his arm. "Sorry. I didn't want you to get your hopes up."

He lowered his voice to a husky whisper. "Hope *springs* eternal."

"So I've heard."

"Tomorrow, I'll show you. Eternally."

She laughed and curved herself into him.

"So much witty repartée, Professor. I can almost imagine I'm in a Cary Grant movie."

"You flatter me." He kissed her eyelids. "Are you excited about being a big sister?"

"Yes. I want the baby to know me. I want to spend time with him or her. I've waited my whole life for a sibling."

"We were planning to spend part of our vacations in Selinsgrove, anyway. As Rachel's and Scott's families expand, we'll want to spend time with them too. Selinsgrove is the best place to do that."

"That's another reason to be glad that Richard decided to move back into the house. We'll all be together."

Gabriel pulled a lock of her hair thoughtfully. "I've come to like your shorter hair. It suits you."

"Thanks."

"Although I like your hair long, too."

"It will grow back, I promise."

Gabriel stopped his movements.

"I have half siblings."

"Oh?" Julia forced herself to sound casual.

"When my mother was upset, she used to say that my father left us because he loved his real family more."

"What a terrible thing to say to a child." Julia's tone was severe.

"Yes. She was troubled, but beautiful. Dark hair and dark eyes."

Julia gave him a questioning look.

"I have my father's eyes, apparently. I remember my mother being tall, but I can't imagine she was more than a few inches taller than you."

"What was her first name?"

"Suzanne. Suzanne Emerson."

"Do you have any photographs of her?"

"A few. There are baby pictures of me, as well."

"You've been holding out on me. Why have I never seen them?"

"They aren't hidden. They're in a drawer back in Cambridge. I even have her diary."

Julia's mouth dropped open. "You have your mother's diary?"

"And her father's pocket watch. I use it, on occasion."

"Did you ever read the diary?"

"No."

"If Sharon had left me a diary, I would have read it."

Gabriel gazed at her quizzically. "I thought you didn't have anything of your mother's."

"They sent my father a box of her stuff when she died."

"And?"

"And I have no idea what's in it. Dad used to keep it in his closet. I'm assuming he still has it. Now that you've reminded me, I should probably ask him to let me see it."

"I'll go with you."

"Thank you. How much do you know about your father?"

"Not much. I seem to remember meeting him once or twice, not counting the content of last night's dream. When he died, I had a few conversations with his lawyer. I know my father lived in New York and had a wife and children. Initially, I declined the inheritance, but when I changed my mind they tried to break the will."

"Did he disinherit them?"

"Far from it. A year before he died, he added me as an equal beneficiary to his other children. His wife also received a substantial inheritance."

"So you never met them?"

Gabriel laughed without amusement. "Do you think they were in a hurry to meet the bastard who was stealing their birthright?"

"I'm sorry," she whispered.

"I don't care. They aren't my family."

"What was your father's name?"

"Owen Davies." Gabriel lifted her chin with his finger. "I've told you these things and I'll share what photos I have when we get home. But I want you to promise you won't look into my family."

His expression was intense, if not severe. But there was something else in his eyes that she couldn't quite decipher.

"I promise."

He brought her head back to rest on his shoulder.

Chapter Twenty-five

August 2011
Near Essex Junction, Vermont

The following evening, Paul sat at the kitchen table in his parents' farmhouse, staring at his laptop. It was almost seven o'clock.

He'd been home from England for two weeks. Every day he sat down to type an email to Julia, and every day he found he couldn't.

Her emails were always cheerful, and the most recent one was no exception. She'd written him from Italy, urging him to visit the Vatican museum the next time he was in Rome. As if he needed urging. As if he needed the reminder that she was married and jet-setting around Europe with her dashing and older husband, who was probably thinking of ways to persuade her to have his baby.

Bastard.

Paul was a rugby player. He was tough. But somehow, this slip of a woman from Selinsgrove, Pennsylvania, had turned his life upside down. Now he was afraid of doing what he'd already determined to do.

"This is ridiculous," he muttered. He started to type, the words just beginning to flow, when he heard a knock at the back door.

Curious, he answered it.

"Hi." Allison greeted him, standing outside and holding two large coffees from Dunkin' Donuts. "I thought you could use one of these."

When he didn't respond, she gave him an uneasy smile. "Are you working on your dissertation? I don't mean to interrupt."

She handed him a coffee. "I'll just go."

"Wait. Come in." He held the screen door open.

She thanked him and walked into the kitchen, pulling out a chair across from where his computer was situated.

"I haven't heard from you since you got back from England."

"I've been busy." His voice had a slight edge to it. "My dissertation director is kicking my ass and I have a lot of ground to cover before September."

"How was your trip?"

Paul sipped his coffee and made an appreciative noise. "It was good. My paper went well and I was able to talk to my director."

Allison nodded, clutching her cup a little too tightly. "Was she there?"

"Her name is Julia." Paul's tone was sharp.

"I know that," she said gently. "I met her in this kitchen, remember?"

"Yes, she was there." He tasted his drink again.

"How is she?"

"She's good. Her husband was there, too."

Allison searched Paul's unusually morose expression.

"You don't sound happy."

He didn't respond.

"I'm sorry."

He gave her a half-smile. "Why are you sorry?"

"Because I don't like to see you pining."

He shrugged but didn't deny it.

"I was trying to compose an email to her when you knocked on the door."

Allison gripped her cup in two hands. "I don't know her. But I think it's weird that she's keeping in touch with you, given your history. It's like she's leading you on."

"You're right, you don't know her." Paul glared.

"I doubt her husband is happy about her emailing you."

Paul muttered something unflattering about the Professor.

Allison sat still for a moment, as if she were waiting for something. Then she stood.

"I'll see myself out."

Her former boyfriend followed her to the back door. "Thanks for the coffee."

"You're welcome." She stepped outside.

"For what it's worth, I'm sorry."

Allison didn't turn around but stood facing the driveway.

"Me, too."

Chapter Twenty-six

August 2011
Umbria, Italy

Every time Julia sat down at her computer, she was tempted to Google Gabriel's parents. But he'd exacted a promise from her and she wouldn't betray him, no matter how difficult it was to keep that promise.

On one such morning, Julia was checking her email when she found something from Paul. She opened it.

After she read the message, she sat back in her chair, stunned.

"Do you want eggs for breakfast? Or fruit and cheese?" Gabriel called from the kitchen, which was next to the living room.

When she didn't respond, he walked over to her.

"Should I make eggs for breakfast, or just fruit and cheese? There's also pastries from the bakery."

She looked up at him in evident distress.

"What's wrong?"

"I just got an email from Paul."

Gabriel resisted the urge to comment on the Angelfucker and his behavior. "What did he say?"

Wordlessly, she pointed at the computer screen.

Gabriel fished around in his pocket for his glasses and put them on.

> Dear Julia,
>
> Thanks for your email. You did a great job with your paper and I thought you handled the questions well, especially Christa's. I was impressed.

Professor Picton was very complimentary. She doesn't praise people often, so you should be proud of yourself.

Please pass along my congratulations to your father and his girlfriend. He's a good guy and I'm happy for them.

I'm back in Vermont. My dad's health continues to improve. Thanks for asking. I'll tell him and Mom that you said hello.

I'm determined to meet Professor Picton's deadlines, so my parents have hired more help at the farm. I hope to go on the job market this fall and pick up some interviews at the Modern Language Association meeting. If I don't get a job, I'm back on the farm for another year.

I'm glad we had a chance to go to lunch. It was good to see you.

There were some things I should have said, but didn't. I guess I should say them now.

I think we need to go our separate ways. You're married and I need to move on.

Maybe it will be easier for me in the future. But in the meantime, we should stop emailing.

I don't mean to hurt you, so please don't take it that way. I care about you, but I've been thinking about this for a while and believe it's for the best.

Be happy, Rabbit.

Paul

Gabriel's eyes focused on hers. She looked stricken.

"I sent him a couple of emails. It took him days to reply. And look at what he said."

Gabriel crouched down, placing his hand on Julia's knee. "He's in love with you. You know that."

"I know he loved me once."

Gabriel looked at her gravely. "Did you stop loving me when I left Toronto?"

She nibbled on the edge of one of her fingernails. "Of course not."

"If he truly loves you, he'll love you for a long time. Maybe forever."

"Then why wouldn't he want to be friends?" She turned troubled eyes in his direction.

"Because it's too painful." Gabriel cupped her cheek. "If I'd lost you to him, I couldn't be friends with you. I'd simply have to love you from a distance."

"I never meant to hurt him," she whispered.

"I'm sure he realizes that."

"Why didn't he try to talk to me about it when we were in Oxford?"

"He didn't want to upset you before your lecture."

Julia turned suspicious eyes in her husband's direction. "Did you know about this?"

Gabriel hesitated, ever so slightly.

"Yes."

"Why didn't you tell me?"

"For the same reason he didn't bring it up. We wanted you to be in the best frame of mind at the conference."

She pushed her chair back from the table. "So you and Paul discussed this? You discussed me?"

"Briefly, yes."

"You should have told me!"

"I'm telling you now. Truthfully, Julianne, I thought he'd change his mind. But once again, Paul has surprised me."

"You dole out information like vitamins."

Gabriel lifted his head, a smile playing about his lips. "Vitamins?"

"You know what I'm saying. You and your secrets." She rose to her feet, but he caught her wrist.

"I don't have secrets from you. We agreed not to disclose everything from our pasts for the sake of moving forward. But if you want full disclosure, I'll give it to you." He lifted his chin in challenge. "And then I'll ask you for full disclosure. For example, did you happen to have a conversation with Paul about dropping out of Harvard?"

"What?"

"He tore a strip off me, telling me I had to make sure you didn't abandon your dreams."

Julia's eyes widened.

"When did he say this?"

"In Oxford, right after your lunch. So don't lecture me on keeping secrets, Julianne. I'm not having lunch with old flames and telling them about our marital conflicts."

"I wasn't doing that."

"Well, what do you call it, then?"

She lifted her hands and then let them drop to her sides. "It just—came out. I was worried and needed someone to talk to."

"Did it ever occur to you that you already have someone to talk to?" Gabriel glanced between them significantly. "Someone infinitely closer?"

"I needed time to think."

"I can understand that. I can even support it. But time to think and going to someone else to talk about our problems are two different things. That was not the right thing to do, Julianne, and you know it." His tone was reproving.

Julia stared, expecting him to explode into temper. Surprisingly, he didn't.

(Which demonstrated, clearly, that the Apocalypse was nigh.)

Gabriel continued. "I don't share our problems with anyone. And yes, sometimes I dole out information, as you so charmingly put it, in order to protect you. But it is always, *always*, done with love."

His fingers slid from her wrist to her hand. "I tried to persuade Paul not to cut off contact with you. Not because that was what I wanted, but because I didn't want to see you hurt."

Julia blinked back tears that had suddenly appeared. "What hurts is the fact that you don't trust me."

"I trust you."

"But not with your family history."

He clenched his teeth. "You know what I know—that my mother's family disowned her and left me to foster care after her death. My father abandoned us. Do you want me to investigate such people? Just so I can discover more unsavory details?"

"They made you, Gabriel. There has to be something in your family history that's worth knowing. And of course I don't want you to be upset. But your family is part of you. If we have children, eventually they'll ask about their grandparents."

Gabriel dropped her hand, his face a mask of stone.

"If I could expunge them from my memory, I would. I won't have our children so polluted."

She lifted her chin. "A man as good and as brilliant as you came from that pollution. And so will our children."

His expression softened. He raised her hand to his lips and kissed the back of it. "Thank you," he whispered.

"You're right, I shouldn't have gone to Paul with my worries. But he was my friend." Julia continued to fight back the tears.

He pressed her face into his chest.

Chapter Twenty-seven

At bedtime, Gabriel strode into the master suite. He was barefoot, clad only in a white shirt and jeans. When he caught sight of Julianne, he began rolling up his sleeves.

"Are you still on your cycle?"

Julia was standing by the washroom, having just finished brushing her teeth and washing her face.

"I finished yesterday."

"Good. Take off your clothes and lie on the bed."

She stared at him.

"Now."

His eyes seemed to burn through her. Without argument, she undressed quickly, dropping her clothes to the floor before climbing onto the bed.

"On your stomach. Eyes closed."

She couldn't help trembling at the tone of his voice, but she did what he said. With eyes closed, her other senses were heightened. She felt the breath of air from the open window. She could hear Gabriel's sure footsteps against the tiled floor.

Soon he chose music to fill the air, "The Look of Love" performed by Diana Krall. Julia opened her eyes and saw that he'd turned the lights out and lit candles next to the bed. A luminescent cloud filled her gaze.

"*Eyes closed*," he commanded.

She did as she was bidden and felt the mattress move. His hands found her waist, lifting her in order to slide a pillow beneath her hips. Seemingly satisfied with her position, his lips blazed a trail from dimple to dimple before coming to rest at the base of her spine.

A single finger traced up to the nape of her neck, gliding across her shoulders. Another pillow was placed under her naked breasts before he stretched her arms above her head.

"A work of art." He breathed in her ear before kissing just behind it, drawing the skin into his mouth. His palm traveled the length of her back twice before exploring her bottom and legs.

The bed shifted and the music changed to Sting's "I Burn for You." Julia felt more than a fluttering of desire.

She could feel his presence next to the bed, but she heard nothing until he set a couple of objects on the table. She turned her head in the direction of the sound, but Gabriel placed a hand over her eyes, blocking her sight.

"Do you trust me?"

"Yes."

"Good." He passed his hand over the back of her head, pulling her hair to one side. "I've missed you these past few days. I've been looking forward to getting reacquainted."

Julia heard him straighten, and after a few moments she heard the rustling of clothing and the sound of his belt hitting the floor. Then she heard the subtle sound of his underwear sliding over his skin.

She opened her left eye, drinking in the sight of her naked husband, watching as he turned his back in order to arrange things on the table. She sighed in appreciation of his form and closed her eyes once again.

She heard something liquid and the sound of his hands rubbing together before the bed moved once again. Then he was massaging her shoulders.

She groaned.

"You like that, do you?"

She hummed. The scent of satsuma and sandalwood filled her nose: the scent of their first time together.

"Thank you."

"I've only just begun."

He took his time, worshipping her body with his hands. On occasion, his nakedness would rub up against her. She would move to deepen the contact, but he would only chuckle and retreat.

After what seemed like hours she drifted into an almost unconscious state, totally and completely relaxed. All thoughts of anything other than Gabriel flew out of her head.

He brought his mouth to her neck, drawing the flesh against his lips and gently sucking. His large hands slid the length of her arms until they took hold of her wrists, stretching them out to her sides like a cross.

Then his naked body was over hers, pressing his front to her back.

She murmured at the contact.

"If it's too much, tell me."

It was an intense feeling. She preferred frontal contact, but there was something about Gabriel spread over her like a second skin that was especially intimate and erotic.

When he heard her breathing grow shallow, he took his weight with his knees, separating her legs. She inhaled and he placed a hand under her to cup her right breast.

Julia moaned her approval.

He moved his left hand beneath her to the junction of her thighs, his fingers sliding against her skin.

He petted her, his hands working in concert, drawing pleasure from both parts of her body. Then, ever so slowly, he pushed inside.

He stilled. The feeling of being inside her in this position was almost overwhelming. They always fit together well, but on this occasion, the sensation of their joining assailed his control.

Julia pushed back against him. "Please."

"Don't move," he rasped.

She froze and he felt her inhale shakily, her back moving against his front.

"You're a goddess. But—don't—move."

Julia smiled against the sheets, and then ever so slowly, she lifted her hips and pressed back against him.

With a groan and a curse, he moved inside her, quickly and forcefully. Within minutes they were joining at a frantic pace, the air alive with the sounds of pleasure.

Julia lifted her hips one last time, and he felt her shudder around him.

He could contain himself no longer and rapidly followed.

When he'd caught his breath, he stretched over her like a banner, his lips smiling against her shoulder.

"This is transcendence," he whispered. "I've never had better."

Julia's heart skipped a beat. "Never?"

"Never."

His palm rested on her backside and he felt her body sink into the bed as a wide, joyous smile spread across her face.

Chapter Twenty-eight

The next morning Julia awoke to the sound of Gabriel snoring. He rarely snored, but when he did, it was a force of nature.

(Even Dante specialists snore, on occasion.)

She'd slept soundly all night. He'd given her a gift—the knowledge that she was the sexual pinnacle for him as he most gloriously was for her. A delicious feeling of anticipation and uncertainty filled her at the prospect of repeating the previous evening's activities.

Gabriel loved her. That fact gave her confidence when it came to ceding control to him. But as C.S. Lewis had once written about Aslan, Gabriel was not tame. There was always a hint of danger and unpredictability surrounding him.

With caution in mind, she elected not to wake him and inform him that he was snoring. Instead, she decided to brave convention and skinny-dip in the hot tub.

The hot tub sat on the balcony just outside their bedroom. Since their closest neighbor was several miles away, Julia didn't worry about dropping her bathrobe. She merely climbed into the tub and allowed the sun and gentle wind to caress her face, while the water soothed her tender spaces and sore muscles.

She'd almost fallen asleep when she heard the sound of Gabriel's voice. She opened her eyes to find him clad only in his boxer shorts, talking on his iPhone.

She took a moment to admire the rugged beauty that was her untamed professor.

With her eyes, she traced the curves of his muscles, the lines and tendons that etched his arms. She watched the strands of hair that decorated his chest, and their cousins that led from his navel to the band of his underwear.

Julia glanced at their surroundings—at the hills and valleys surrounding their villa. No one could see them.

Without warning, Gabriel ended his conversation and put his phone on a table nearby.

"Can I join you? Or are you simply interested in a show?" He flexed his biceps theatrically.

Julia swallowed noisily. "Um, what's included in the price of admission?"

He smiled slowly.

"Whatever you desire. I'm here to please, Mrs. Emerson." He dropped his voice. "So name your pleasure."

Julia indicated that he should approach, and he quickly divested himself of his shorts and joined her in the hot water. She straddled his lap, wrapping her arms around him. "All I want is the pleasure of your company."

Gabriel hugged her and she rested her chin on his shoulder.

"Thank you for last night."

"It is I who should be thanking you, Mrs. Emerson."

"I'm a little dense sometimes. It only just occurred to me that you went to so much trouble last night because you were trying to cheer me up." She toyed with his chest hair.

"That isn't exactly true. We hadn't made love for a few days, since you were on your cycle. That gave me time to think about how I wanted to go about reconnecting with you." He lifted her hair off the back of her neck, and slid his fingers through it.

"I wanted you to know that I appreciate it. I appreciate the care you take in planning our times together and also that you knew I was feeling bad yesterday." She placed her palm over his tattoo, near his heart. "And that you told me you've never had better."

"It's true. Sex is different with you. We have attraction, of course, and chemistry. But we also have affection and love. When all of those things are combined . . ." He trailed off.

"Thank you." She brushed her lips against his. "Who were you talking to on the phone?"

"Scott."

"Oh, really? What did he want?"

"He and Tammy would like to bring Quinn to Boston for a weekend in the fall. They'd like to stay with us."

"That sounds fun."

"I said I'd have to check with you, but we'd be glad to have them."

"I'm happy you and your brother have patched things up." She kissed his neck. "Sometimes I wish we were the same age. We could have gone to the prom together."

Gabriel nuzzled her.

"It would have been an honor to take you to prom, but it's a good thing I didn't know you when I was a teenager."

"Why not?"

"Because I wouldn't have treated you the way you deserve."

She moved so that she could see his eyes. "I don't believe that. You treated me well the first night we met, back in the orchard. You would have behaved the same way when you were younger."

"Perhaps. There's something about you . . ." He smiled. "We can arrange to have a prom here, just the two of us."

Julia laughed. "I'll have to buy a dress that's too short and that will give my father a heart attack."

"I don't recall inviting him," Gabriel growled, kissing her. "How short is too short?"

"For me, just a bit above the knee. I'm shy."

He nipped at her lower lip. "You weren't shy last night."

She stroked the stubble on his jaw. "Your love makes me brave."

"That's good, because I'll keep loving you. Forever." Gabriel slid his hands to her waist and pulled her against his chest. "I'm sorry about what happened with Paul."

"Me too." Her expression turned wistful. "From now on, if we're having problems I'll keep them between us."

"I promise to do the same." He cleared his throat. "I'm afraid that when couples marry, their friendships change."

She shrugged. "I guess so."

"I've neglected our social life. I'll do better, I promise. We can invite people over for dinner and I'll accompany you to the pub nights at Grendel's Den with the other grad students."

Julia's eyes widened. "I thought you didn't like socializing with grad students. You'd never join me before."

Gabriel brushed his thumb across her jaw.

"I'd do almost anything to make you happy. I don't want you to regret a single moment we're together."

His eyes grew dangerous. "So come here."

❧❧

A few hours later, Gabriel heard the house telephone ring. He ignored it.

Curiosity eventually got the best of him and he stuck his head through the study doorway and into the hall. From a distance, he could hear Julia speaking Italian. Wondering who she was speaking with, he left his study to descend to the kitchen.

"No, Fra Silvestro. *Non è necessario.*"

Julia caught Gabriel's eye and lifted a finger, indicating that he should wait.

"Allora dovremmo organizzare una festa per i bambini. Non per me."

Gabriel's eyebrows lifted and he crossed over to her, leaning against the counter.

"Sì, per i bambini. Possiamo festeggiare i loro compleanni." She paused, and Gabriel could hear the Franciscan brother chattering away on the other end of the line.

"Ci dovranno essere regali, palloncini e una torta. E del gelato." Julia laughed. *"Certo. E' proprio quello che vorrei. . . . Ci vediamo, allora. Arrivederci."*

Julia hung up the telephone. "Good grief."

"What was that all about?"

"That was Brother Silvestro from the orphanage in Florence."

"Why is he calling you?"

"He wanted to speak to you but seemed delighted that you were indisposed."

The edges of Gabriel's lips turned up. "Sounds like he wanted to sweet-talk us and thought you'd make a better target."

"Perhaps. He wanted to host a party for us when we visit the orphanage next week."

Gabriel appeared surprised. "And you said no?"

"I asked him to throw a party for the children, instead. We don't need a party."

Julia turned her attention to what she'd been doing before she received the telephone call, which was preparing a light lunch.

Gabriel wrapped his arms around her from behind.

"You're very assertive."

"It's for the children."

"This is something about you that's always puzzled me, Julianne. You give up what you want rather easily. But you're adamant about not giving in when it comes to someone else."

"I don't think I give up what I want so easily. I didn't give up on you, did I? And you were pretty awful in the beginning." Julia peered up at him out of the corner of her eye.

He shifted his feet.

"I had in mind how much you wanted to stay at Magdalen College and how you were willing to leave when I insisted."

She turned back to what she was doing.

"Sometimes I don't have the energy to fight with you. You were upset about the room. I don't like seeing you upset."

Gabriel pressed his lips to her neck.

"I think you need a party."

"I do." She reached up and tangled her fingers in his hair. "I need a private party that involves me peeling my handsome husband out of his favorite pair of jeans."

She moved her mouth to his ear. "But your glasses stay on."

He chuckled and pulled their lower bodies flush. "I didn't know you had a thing for men in glasses."

"Oh, I do. The way you feel about my high heels? That's how I feel about you in glasses. But first I have to call Fra Silvestro's assistant to see if she can rent a pony."

Gabriel straightened.

"A pony?"

"Is that a bad idea?"

"Can you rent ponies? In Florence?"

"I don't know. I'm sure none of the children have ever seen a pony, let alone had the chance to ride one. I thought it would be fun."

Gabriel observed his wife's excitement with no little amount of joy.

"If you look after the gifts for the children, I'll find a pony."

"Thank you." She gave him a saucy wink. "Oh, and while you're at it, see if you can rent a petting zoo."

Chapter Twenty-nine

Julia didn't respond to Paul's email. He'd asked her not to contact him, and she decided to honor his request. She knew that eventually their paths would cross at a conference or a colloquium. She thought that once he became used to the idea that she'd married Gabriel, he'd be able to be friends with her again.

Or so she hoped.

But his request and the way he'd done it—via email—had hurt. So she avoided her email for a couple of days. When she finally checked her account, she found a message from her father.

> Jules,
>
> Call me on my cell phone as soon as you get this message,
>
> Dad.

Tom's emails and telephone messages were usually terse. He was not a man of many words. But the tone of this particular email was so ominous, Julia didn't bother to alert Gabriel as to what was happening. She simply picked up the telephone in the kitchen and dialed her father's cell phone.

He picked it up on the first ring. "Jules."

"Hi, Dad. What's going on?"

Her father paused as if he were struggling to find the words. "We're at the hospital."

"The hospital? Why? What's wrong?"

At that moment, Gabriel walked into the kitchen. Julia pointed to the telephone and mouthed the words *My dad.*

"Yesterday we went to have an ultrasound. We were supposed to find out the sex of the baby. But something was wrong."

"What?"

"His heart."

"His?"

"My son." Tom's voice broke on the last word.

"Dad." Julia sniffled and her eyes filled with tears.

Gabriel stood very close to his wife, so that he could hear both sides of the conversation.

"Where are you now?" she asked.

"At the Children's Hospital in Philadelphia. They agreed to see us right away."

Julia heard a muffled noise in the background, then heard her father whisper, "It's going to be all right, honey. It's going to be all right. Don't cry."

"Is that Diane?"

"Yes." Tom sounded strained.

"I'm so sorry, Dad. What did the doctor say?"

"We just met with the cardiologist. He says that the baby has hypoplastic left heart syndrome."

"I've never heard of that before. What is it?"

"It means he only has half a heart." He inhaled slowly. "It's fatal, Jules."

"Oh my God." A tear spilled onto her cheek.

"He won't survive without surgery. So they'll have to operate after he's born. That is, if Diane can carry him to term. Sometimes . . ." Tom's voice trailed off.

"Can they fix it?"

"The surgery can make his heart do what it needs to do, but it can't give him a normal heart. They say it will take three different surgeries and a lifetime of medication. No one knows how well he'll do or if he'll—" Tom began to cough.

"What can I do?"

"There's nothing anyone can do. Except pray."

Julia began to cry, and Gabriel gently removed the telephone from her hand.

"Tom? It's Gabriel. I'm sorry about the baby. Let me book you a hotel near the hospital."

"We don't need—" Tom stopped abruptly, and Gabriel could hear Diane speaking in the background.

Tom sighed. "Okay. That would be good."

"I'll make the arrangements and email you the information. Do you want to go to New York for a second opinion? I can make airline reservations for both of you. We can get you a referral to another hospital."

"The doctors here seem to know what they're doing. We have a meeting with the pediatric cardiac team tomorrow."

Gabriel's eyes fixed earnestly on his wife's.

"Do you need Julianne?"

"There isn't much she can do right now."

"Be that as it may, she's your daughter and the baby is her brother. You say the word, she'll be there."

"Thanks." Tom sounded gruff. "Things are up in the air right now."

Julia wiped at her tears and gestured to the telephone.

"She wants to speak with you. Take care, Tom."

Gabriel handed her the phone.

"Dad. Please keep in touch and let me know what's going on."

"Will do."

"I hate to bring this up, but what about the wedding?"

"We don't know, Jules."

"We'll plan on spending Labor Day in Selinsgrove. I can be there before that, if you and Diane need me."

"Good."

"Do you want me to tell Richard?"

Tom hesitated.

"Might as well. The fewer people I have to have this conversation with the better. Diane was on the phone with her mother earlier and her sister, Melissa."

A tear slid down Julia's nose.

"I love you, Dad. Give my love to Diane."

"Will do. Bye, Jules."

Julia quietly put down the phone. Then she was in Gabriel's arms.

"They were so happy about the baby."

He squeezed her tightly as she clutched at his shirt.

"They're at a good hospital."

"They're devastated. It sounds like even if the heart problem can be corrected, the baby still will have health problems."

"Doctors make predictions, but they're guided by probabilities. Every patient is different."

He straightened suddenly, as if something had just occurred to him. "Does Tom have any health problems?"

"Not that I know of. Both of his parents had heart disease."

She looked up at him. "You don't think this is genetic, do you?"

"I don't know." He held her more closely. "There are few days when being an MD is infinitely better than being a PhD. This would be one of them."

More tears streaked down Julianne's cheeks. It had never occurred to her that something could be wrong with the baby. She'd been so happy to be having a sibling that any of the risks were unthinkable.

As she cried in the arms of her husband, she realized that whatever grief she was feeling, Tom and Diane must be feeling tenfold.

"How could they have prepared themselves for this?" she croaked. "They're devastated."

Julianne leaned against Gabriel, not noticing the expression on his face or the sudden flash of horror in his eyes.

Chapter Thirty

August 2003
Cambridge, Massachusetts

"Gabriel? Baby, it's time to get up."

A soft, feminine hand stroked the stubble on his face and for a moment, he relaxed. He wasn't sure where he was or who was lying naked beside him, but she had a sexy voice and a light touch. Cautiously, he opened his eyes.

"Hi, baby." Her large blue eyes stared down at him in devotion.

"Paulina," he groaned, closing his eyes. He had a pounding headache and all he wanted to do was sleep. But Professor Pearson didn't accept excuses from his teaching assistants, which meant he needed to drag himself to campus.

(It was possible the professor would have accepted death as an excuse as to why his teaching assistant missed class. Although it was doubtful.)

"It's eight o'clock. You have time for a shower and breakfast. And maybe a little . . ." Her hand slid down his chest to his abdomen. Then she wrapped her fingers around him and . . .

And his morning erection withered in her hand like a dead flower.

He pushed her away. "Not now."

"You always say that. Is it because I'm getting fat?" She sat next to him, her stomach slightly rounded, her generous breasts full.

He didn't answer, which in itself was a kind of response.

"I can make it good for you. You know I can." She hugged him around the shoulders, kissing his neck. "I love you."

"I said *not now*. Fuck. Can't you hear?" He disentangled himself from her arms before sliding his legs over the side of the bed. The hardwood floor was cool beneath his feet but he barely felt it.

All his attention was focused on one thing—the ghost of white powder left on his nightstand. Now he was awake, arranging the mirror and the razor blade and the rolled-up five-dollar bill.

The world around him melted away and he felt his mind and body spring to life, his movements sure and quick.

In the blink of an eye it was up his nose and everything was clear again. He was hyperalert. He could think. He could function.

He lit a cigarette, forgetting that his . . . whatever-she-was-now was in his bed, watching him. She wrapped herself in a robe and fled to the kitchen, not wanting to expose their unborn child to smoke.

He finished his cigarette and showered, pausing to drink the cup of coffee she'd placed next to the sink. He brushed his teeth and shaved, his mind enumerating all the work he had to do on his dissertation, along with the interminable to-do list foisted on him by Professor Pearson.

Gabriel didn't have time to examine his life or his actions. If he did, he would have realized that he was a slave, in chains, to cocaine, nicotine, caffeine, and alcohol.

He was a slave to his passions, also, when his dick was working. Even though he was living with Paulina and she was pregnant, he was still sexually involved with other women. He never bothered to ask himself whether he should stop. In fact, he didn't think about it at all. He simply did it.

"You're handsome." Paulina watched him from the doorway, her hand cradling her protruding abdomen over her black silk robe.

Gabriel ignored her, as he was wont to do. He also ignored the dark circles on his face, his bloodshot eyes, and the fact that he was a good ten to fifteen pounds lighter than his normal, healthy weight.

"I made you breakfast. Scrambled eggs and toast." She sounded hopeful.

"I'm not hungry."

"You have a long day ahead of you and Pearson is going to work you hard."

"Get off my ass," he snapped. "I said I wasn't hungry."

"I'm sorry." She looked down at her stomach contritely. "It's sitting on the table with fruit and a fresh coffee. All you have to do is eat."

His sapphire eyes fixed on hers, watching her through the mirror.

"Fine," he clipped.

She smiled to herself and disappeared into the tiny kitchen.

Soon he was dressed in the respectable uniform of a Harvard graduate student, complete with corduroy jacket and Levi's, and seated at the table, forcing down breakfast. He finished his third cup of coffee and was about to light another cigarette when he noticed that Paulina was staring at him. Hungrily.

"What?"

She moved to sit in his lap, wrapping her arms around his neck.

He made an involuntary groan at her weight, not seeing her wince as he did so.

She brought her mouth to his ear. "I know you're in a hurry. Just kiss me before you leave."

"Paulina, I—"

She cut him off with her lips, her tongue eager and searching as it snaked into his mouth.

His hands came to her waist as he kissed her back, feeling his body beginning to respond.

"Come on, baby." She reached for the button of his jeans. "We'll be quick."

"I don't have time." He placed her on her feet, groaning a little at the exertion. "Maybe tonight."

Her face crumpled. "But you write at night."

"I can make time."

"But you don't." She reached for his hand. "Gabriel, I love you. It's been a while. Please."

Her big blue eyes filled with tears and her lower lip trembled.

He rolled his eyes to the ceiling.

"Fine. But it needs to be fast."

He pushed his chair back from the table and gestured to his crotch. "Get started."

With an eager look on her face, she knelt between his legs and pulled down his zipper.

Chapter Thirty-one

August 2011
Umbria, Italy

Gabriel couldn't sleep, plagued as he was by hazy memories of the past. His mind twisted in several different directions, tugging him to and fro. Finally, he tired of tossing and turning and went downstairs to pour himself a drink.

As he stood in the kitchen he cursed. He'd removed all the alcohol, with the exception of a couple of bottles of white wine reserved for Julianne. But wine would not satisfy his craving. Not tonight.

No, tonight he desired Scotch. The smoothness on his tongue, the quick burn in his mouth and throat, the latent warmth that would spread to his insides.

Just one. I just need one.

But it was no use. The Scotch was gone.

Gabriel thought of Julianne, upstairs in his bed. She was sleeping peacefully, unaware of the demons that plagued him. His very hands shook with desire.

He quickly ran through the twelve steps of Narcotics Anonymous before focusing on step two.

A power greater than myself can restore me.

Help me, God.

Please.

Gabriel closed his eyes and made the sign of the cross, his soul desperate and conflicted.

He knew that the keys to the Mercedes were steps away. He knew that he could drive to a local tavern and drink. Julia was sleeping soundly. He could return to their bed afterward and she would never know.

His eyes opened.

He reached for the keys.

Chapter Thirty-two

"Gabriel?" Julia's voice floated out to where he was seated on the balcony.

He was in a dark corner, brooding. He could hear her feet padding across the tiled floor and through the open doors as she approached him.

"What are you doing?" She eyed the cigarette he held in one of his hands and the drink in the other.

"Nothing." He placed the cigarette to his lips and inhaled slowly before turning his face to the sky and blowing the smoke heavenward.

"You don't smoke."

"Of course I do. Usually, I choose cigars."

She looked from his glass to his face, her eyes troubled.

He lifted his glass in mock salute.

"Don't worry, it's Coke." He grimaced. "I'd prefer Laphroaig."

"There isn't any."

"I know that," he growled. "The house is bereft of alcohol except for wine."

"Only white. You prefer red." Her eyebrows knitted together. "Did you go looking?"

"What if I did?" he snapped.

Julia began chewing at her bottom lip.

Gabriel put his cigarette in the ashtray and reached up, pressing his thumb against her mouth.

"Don't." He freed her lip, then picked up his cigarette, turning away from her.

Silence stretched between them, an immeasurable distance, until finally, she spoke.

"Good night, Gabriel."

"Wait." He placed a hand to her hip, pressing into the gauzy whiteness of her nightgown. "I need to ask you something.

"How healthy are you?"

"It's after midnight and you're asking about my health?"

"Just answer the question." He sounded grim. "Please."

She pushed her hair back from her face. "I'm healthy. I have low blood pressure and I tend to have low iron levels, so I take a supplement."

"I didn't know that."

"My low blood pressure is probably genetic. My mother had it."

"Genetic," he muttered, drawing on his cigarette again. The smoke billowed from his nostrils as if he were a dragon.

"It's a bit odd to ask me about my health while you're out here smoking, don't you think?"

"It's better than cocaine, Julianne." His voice was cold. "How did your mother die?"

"Why are you asking me this?" She pulled away from him.

"You told me your mother died while you were living with your father. I didn't know if she had health problems or if it was an accident." Gabriel's expression was searching, but his eyes were guarded.

"She was drunk and fell down the stairs at her apartment building. Broke her neck." Julia gave him a venomous look. "Happy now?"

She turned to go back into the bedroom, but he caught her arm. *"Julianne."*

"Don't touch me!" She wrenched her arm free and turned on him. "I love you, but you can be a cold son of a bitch."

He was on his feet in an instant, his drink and cigarette discarded on the table. "I don't deny it."

"Something is troubling you, but instead of discussing it with your *wife*, you'd rather discuss it with your drink and your cigarette and the Umbrian landscape. Fine. Sit out here all night by yourself. But don't try to mindfuck me."

She moved toward the doors that led to their bedroom.

"I'm not trying to mindfuck you."

"Then warn me before you start spelunking through my unhappy memories."

Gabriel tried to restrain a chuckle but failed.

She turned and glared. "It isn't funny!"

"Spelunking, Julianne? Really?" His face relaxed into a playful grin, at which she merely frowned.

He closed the space between them. "Don't blame me for laughing. You have an enviable vocabulary."

She struggled against his arms and then his lips were on hers. The dusky taste of smoke and tobacco invaded her mouth. His kiss was gentle but insistent.

In time, her posture softened.

"I'm sorry," he whispered. "I'm in a foul mood. I shouldn't take it out on you."

"That's right, you shouldn't.

"When I'm upset, I talk to you. *Talk to me.*"

He pulled away, running both hands through his hair, making its dark strands even more unruly.

She tugged at his elbow.

"Everyone gets into a foul mood sometime. But you can't bring up certain topics so indelicately."

"Forgive me."

"You're forgiven." She shivered. "But you're scaring me. You're looking for Scotch and talking about cocaine. You're asking me how my mother died. What's going on?"

"Not tonight, Julianne." He scrubbed at his face with his hands. "Haven't we had enough distress for one day? Go to bed. I'm not fit for company."

He returned to his seat, his shoulders slumped.

Julia hesitated, her eyes darting between the doors to the bedroom and his face. Part of her wanted to leave him to brood alone. Part of her believed that he was in distress and that if she didn't attempt to intervene, he would spiral into a depression.

Or worse.

She went to him, holding out a tentative baby finger, linking it with his.

"You're upset."

"Yes." His voice sounded flat.

"Before we were together, when you'd get into a foul mood, what would you do?"

"I'd drink and do coke. And . . ." He began tapping his bare foot against the floor of the balcony.

"And?"

His blue eyes moved to hers. "I'd fuck."

"Did it work?"

He snorted. "Temporarily. My troubles always came back the next morning."

She looked inside the bedroom, toward the large canopied bed.

She lifted her chin. "Let's go."

"Go where?"

"To bed." She tugged at his pinky finger. "To work out our foul moods."

Gabriel's eyes seared into hers. Then he seemed to pull himself back. "That is not a good idea. I told you, I'm not myself."

"Do you love me?"

He frowned. "Of course."

"Would you hurt me?"

"Absolutely not. Who do you think I am?"

"I think you're my husband and I think you need to fuck your bad mood away. So let's go."

His mouth dropped open.

When he'd collected himself, his expression grew harsh. "I don't fuck you, Julianne."

"No, you'd rather I were someone else so you could."

His eyes flashed. "That is not true. You don't know what you're talking about."

"Oh, yes, I do. You didn't touch me when we went to bed. I needed you but you said no." She stretched her arms wide. "Don't you understand? What you crave, I need. Help me forget I'm about to lose the only sibling I've ever had. Please."

He was torn. It was telegraphed in the way his eyes bore into hers and the eagerness that radiated from his skin.

On impulse, Julia wrapped an arm around his back and placed her other in his hair. She tugged his mouth toward hers and kissed him deeply.

He responded quickly, wrapping her legs around his hips. Soon he was controlling their kiss; his tongue in her mouth, insistent and urgent.

"Take me to bed," she begged, when he finally drew breath.

"We aren't going to use the bed."

With a dangerous look, he carried her into the bedroom.

Gabriel didn't bother with lamps or music before he pressed her against the nearest wall. A distant light from the open door to the bathroom lightened the dark bedroom to gray.

Her legs tightened around his hips as he pulled off her robe. The silk sank to the floor.

He placed two fingers in his mouth, wetting them, before reaching down to pet between her legs. She moaned and pressed against his hand. His touching grew more desperate.

"Are you afraid?" He brought his lips to her ear.

"No." She wound her fingers in his hair, pulling his mouth to hers.

He explored her with his tongue, licking at her lips and thrusting inside. His hand slid around to cup her backside, pulling her against him.

"Watch," he rasped, fluttering his mouth along her neck.

"Watch what?"

"Us. In the mirror."

Julia opened her eyes and saw the mirror mounted on the wall on the other side of the room. Somehow, it was perfectly positioned to reflect her husband's magnificent and naked back and the dark-haired woman who was hidden by his body.

"I want you to see what I see when you come."

Gabriel trailed kisses up and down her neck before rubbing his stubble against her chest. He cupped her breast in his hand, worshipping each one with his mouth. Licking and nipping and sucking.

He dropped a hand between her legs again and, using deliberate strokes, petted her as his mouth closed over a rosy peak.

Julia tried very hard to keep her eyes open, but it was difficult. His tongue teased her flesh, his lips tugging and pulling.

She'd never seen what they looked like together. His body long and lean, hers smaller and softer. Their skin had different tones—he was darker while she was fair.

Gabriel lavished her with single-minded attention. As if he were a dying man and this was his last assignation. Her very flesh nearly melted from the heat of his touch.

His focus caused the world to fall away, as it always did in those moments, his probing fingers and impatient erection brushing between her legs.

"I need you," she murmured, pulling back so she could see him. She was clutching his shoulders, almost climbing him.

"I need you to come first. Eyes on the mirror."

He continued to pet her, resisting the urge to speed despite her desperate movements.

Without warning, her rosy lips parted and she gasped, her gaze fixed on their reflection.

Then with a single, deep thrust he was inside her.

She saw her eyes widen, her fingers tighten their grip on his shoulders. She saw his strong hips and lean, beautiful backside moving apace, pushing into her again and again.

She groaned, eyes closing.

"I told you to watch," he growled, nipping her ear.

Her eyes opened and she saw him glaring at her.

She turned to look at the mirror. He kept up his rhythm, moving and thrusting.

Sighs and moans escaped her lips as his pace increased. And still, she did not look away.

"This isn't fucking," he whispered. "Look at me."

Her eyes fled the mirror and met his. The sapphire blue of his irises was barely visible against the wide, black pupils.

"This isn't fucking. It's a hell of a lot more."

His breathing stuttered as he thrust, his pace suddenly uneven.

"Always." She began panting, her exhalations matching his rhythm.

He opened his mouth to say something, but at that moment, she orgasmed. His words were drowned in a sea of sensation. Her eyes closed as the satisfaction flowed through her.

Gabriel thrust deep once more and released, his teeth nipping at her collarbone.

Julia struggled to catch her breath, resting her cheek against his neck.

"Incredible," he rumbled, after he'd caught his breath.

He lifted his head. "Are you all right?"

She closed her eyes, resting her head against the wall. "Yes, but I'm probably bowlegged. Give me a minute before you put me down."

"What makes you think I'm finished with you?"

He pushed her hair behind her shoulder, his mouth finding her ear.

"*One*," he whispered.

⁂

Julia awoke the next morning to an empty bed. Of itself, this was not surprising. But when she discovered that the bathroom and balcony were also empty, she pulled on her robe and went in search of her husband.

He was nowhere to be found.

The keys to the Mercedes were on the kitchen counter, where he'd left them the night before, next to an empty bottle of Coca-Cola. He hadn't left a note.

A wave of hurt washed over her. The night before had been passionate, perhaps more so than any other night previous. They'd made love against the wall, on the bathroom counter, on the floor, and finally on the bed. The sun was almost peeking over the horizon when he'd finally relented and let them sleep.

Julia had wanted to wake up with him and perhaps, to take her time exploring his body before languorously making love. But such was not her good fortune. Gabriel's absence and the absence of a note made her feel twinges of anxiety. He hadn't even left a glass of water or juice at her bedside, as was his custom.

I wonder if this is how his other women felt after spending the night with him. If he even let them spend the night . . .

Her anxiety morphed into unhappiness as she reluctantly climbed the stairs and returned to her room. She changed into her bikini, grabbing her sunglasses and hat before walking to the pool. A swim would keep her occupied.

She swam laps until she'd almost forgotten her conversation with her father the day before, and Gabriel's evident distress the previous evening. Then she set her feet down in the shallow end, her eyes straying to a pair of running shoes that were situated at the edge of the pool.

"I thought I told you I didn't want you swimming alone."

Gabriel stood, holding out a towel. He was dressed in his jogging clothes and he was sweaty, his T-shirt soaked.

"Good morning to you, too." She swam to the edge and plucked the towel from his grasp.

"Good morning."

"I wouldn't have to swim alone if you didn't leave me," she muttered, climbing out of the pool.

"You know I like to run in the mornings."

"It's almost noon." She wrapped herself in the towel and faced him, hands on her hips.

He seemed agitated. He glanced at her but wouldn't make eye contact, and his posture was decidedly uncomfortable.

Julia wondered how a night of fantastic sex could leave her relaxed and weightless and leave him strung as tightly as a bow.

"You could have left a note."

"I could have," he said slowly. "I didn't think of it."

"If you want to run, that's fine. Just let me know when you'll be back."

Gabriel opened his mouth to protest but suddenly decided against it.

"I'm going to have a shower. I made the hotel reservation for your father yesterday and arranged to have the concierge deliver a fruit basket. I'll be in my study for most of the day, working. But I'll take you to dinner in Todi tonight."

"No."

He blinked at her. "No?"

"No, Gabriel. You can't run off to your study after treating me so coldly. No."

His expression shifted.

"I don't mean to be cold, Julianne." His voice was low.

She stared at him.

He scrubbed at the stubble on his chin. "I have a lot on my mind."

"That's what you said last night. I hoped our activities would have helped."

A shadow passed over his features.

He stood in front of her, reaching out to grasp the necklace she was wearing. He ran his thumb over the suspended heart.

"You are always lovely. I could hold you in my arms and make love to you all day, but that wouldn't solve my problems."

Julia placed her hand over his. "Then tell me you love me."

His eyes met hers. "I love you."

She breathed out a heavy sigh. "Go find your solution. But don't forget that you aren't the only person in the house. I don't want to live with a ghost."

Gabriel's eyes grew pained. He kissed her chastely, then exited the enclosed pool area.

❧❧

True to his word, Gabriel spent the afternoon in his study, behind a closed door.

Julia had no idea what he was doing, although she hoped he was solving whatever problem it was that troubled him so deeply.

Several different scenarios flew through her head. Perhaps Paulina had contacted him, hurling him into a tailspin. Perhaps the revelation of her brother's illness had caused him to rethink his own desire for a child. Perhaps he was realizing that married life was not what he'd hoped it would be—that the thought of being tied to one woman, to her, was stifling.

Julia's anxiety increased. She could handle anything, she thought, but Gabriel's coldness. She'd seen contempt in his eyes before. She'd been dismissed from his presence. She'd survived it once, but the mere thought of him leaving her again was crippling.

In an effort to turn her attention elsewhere, she sat at her computer, investigating the Children's Hospital of Philadelphia and hypoplastic left heart syndrome.

The hospital's website gave her some hope. It described several patients who'd received the surgery her little brother would have to have. But each patient testimonial included the caveat that no one, not even the specialists at the hospital, could predict how healthy the patients would be when they became children, teenagers, or adults.

She said a silent prayer for her father and Diane, and, lastly, for her brother. She asked God to help him and to give him health.

Then her thoughts turned to her husband.

She prayed for him. She prayed for their marriage. She'd thought their sexual activities the night before had brought them closer together and that they would free him to communicate with her.

Now she worried they'd had the opposite effect. If Gabriel could communicate to her with his body, perhaps he failed to see the need to communicate with words.

With such thoughts in mind, she returned to her pediatric cardiology research, reading article after article, until the words blurred before her eyes and her head sank down against the chair's armrest.

❧❧

Julia awoke to the sensation that someone was watching her.

She was lying in bed. Seated next to her, his arms around his bent legs, was Gabriel. He regarded her from behind his glasses.

"It's late," he whispered. "Go back to sleep."

She squinted at the clock that sat on the bedside table. It was past midnight.

"I missed dinner."

"You were exhausted. I kept you up too late last night."

She yawned. "Come here."

He avoided her outstretched hand.

"Hey," she whispered. "Don't I get a kiss?"

He brushed his lips against hers in a manner that could only be described as perfunctory.

"That's not a very good kiss," she pouted. "You're perched on the edge of the bed like a gargoyle, glowering at me. What's the matter?"

"I am not glowering."

She sat up and placed her arms around his shoulders.

"Then kiss me like you mean it, non-glowering-gargoyle-like husband of mine."

His dark brows knitted together. "A gargoyle? You're hell on a man's ego, Mrs. Emerson."

"You're far more beautiful than me, Professor. But I'm fine with that."

"Don't blaspheme." His expression darkened.

She sank back against the mattress, groaning in frustration.

"I love you, Gabriel. That means I'll put up with a hell of a lot from you. But I won't let you shut me out. Either talk to me or I'm going home."

She felt his eyes before she met them—two glowing and angry sapphires in the nether darkness.

"What?" he growled.

"If I go and stay with my dad, he'll talk to me. I can take care of him and Diane when they get home from the hospital. You're acting as if you can't stand the sight of me." She rolled to her back, staring up at the canopy.

"Beatrice." His voice was pained. "If you need to see your dad, we'll go together. But I would never let you make that trip alone. I'll be damned if you go home without me."

She hazarded a small smile.

"Now there's the Gabriel I married. I thought I'd lost you." She removed his glasses, placing them on the side table. Then she pulled him under the covers with her.

He rolled onto his side, facing her. Then, ever so lightly, he found her lips in the darkness.

"Finally." She rested her head against his chest. "Tell me why you're so grim."

"I don't think you want to hear this right now."

"Yes, I do."

"Fine. You said you thought I wished you were someone else so I could fuck you." His tone grew sharp. "Never say something like that to me again."

"I'm sorry," she whispered.

"It isn't true. I swear to God, it isn't true. I left that life behind and God help me, I do not want to go back there."

"I wasn't asking you to go back there. I was hoping you'd work out your bad mood with me, instead of sitting outside brooding."

"I wasn't fantasizing about fucking other women, I assure you." He sounded angry. "And what we have is too important to cheapen."

She sat up swiftly.

"There was nothing cheap in what we did last night. We love each other. We'd both received upsetting news. We needed comfort."

"I was selfish."

"It was mutual. Remember? I wanted you. I needed you. If you were selfish, then so was I. But I don't see it that way. Yes, it was more aggressive and vigorous than we usually are. But you promised me I was safe with you. And I felt safe. You promised me we could be adventurous. Last night was one of our adventures. And in giving, we both received."

She tried to keep a straight face. But couldn't.

She smiled widely, trying to restrain a snicker.

In a flash, she was on her back and he was over her, their noses inches apart.

"I don't think St. Francis would approve of you taking part of his prayer and applying it to our sexual activities," he growled.

"Francis believed in love and in marriage. He'd understand. At the very least, if he disapproved, he'd be silent about it."

Gabriel closed his eyes and shook his head. But a smile played across his mouth.

When he opened his eyes, they were tender.

"I could live with you forever and still you would surprise me."

"I'm glad to hear that, Gabriel, because you're stuck with me. Even when you're in a foul mood. I'm not ashamed of what we do with our bodies, because it also involves our souls. I don't want you to be ashamed either."

He nodded and kissed her reverently.

She kissed him back.

"You tell me that I'm safe in your bed. But I want you to know that you're free in mine. All the baggage, all the things from our past, they don't matter here."

He stroked her jaw with his thumb. "Okay."

"Now will you tell me why you were so upset last night?"

"Not yet." A shadow fell across his face. "I just need a little time." He toyed with the diamonds in her ears. "You have my heart. Never doubt that."

Julia rested in his arms, but it was a long while before sleep claimed her.

Chapter Thirty-three

Julia was not a psychologist. She'd spent time in therapy and was familiar with twelve-step programs and recovery. But she tried very hard not to diagnose others. In the case of her husband, she couldn't help herself. Something was troubling him. Something disturbing enough to cause him to return to his old coping mechanisms.

She suspected that whatever was upsetting him was related to the news they'd received from Tom and Diane, but she wasn't certain. Correlation is not causality, and so it was possible that the two events were merely coincidental.

Without knowing what was wrong, she didn't know how to help him. Or how to comfort him. She felt as if a dark cloud hung over them, despite Gabriel's concerted attempts to behave as if nothing were wrong.

She knew better. And his unwillingness to share his burden wounded her.

As their time in Umbria drew to a close and they prepared to travel to Florence, she resolved to do her best to be supportive and loving. But she was determined that if he hadn't confided in her by the time they returned to Cambridge, she would take matters into her own hands.

During the previous summer, Gabriel had volunteered at the Franciscan orphanage in Florence during his separation from Julia. But as the staff quickly discerned, he was not the ideal volunteer. He didn't take direction, he gave it. He didn't hesitate to make changes to the workings of the orphanage, or to make demands about the facilities and food.

And when the staff protested that they didn't have the money to implement his changes, he simply paid for them himself.

In sum, the director of the orphanage, Fra Silvestro, welcomed his donations but was relieved when the Franciscans over at Santa Croce persuaded Gabriel that his skills would be better utilized in leading tours and giving lectures on the life of Dante.

So it was with delight that Fra Silvestro welcomed Julia to the orphanage in August, hoping that she would moderate her husband's more aggressive charity.

When the Emersons arrived, they were met by the director; his assistant, Elena; and an assembly of children. The children, who ranged in age from four to eight, addressed Julia as *Zia Julia* and presented her with a bouquet and a series of drawings they'd made. The illustrations were done in bright colors and featured smiling children and a woman with long, dark hair standing in the center.

For a moment, Gabriel was overwhelmed. In the eyes of the children, especially the older ones, he saw a glimpse of himself as a child. He remembered standing in the waiting room of the hospital in Sunbury after his mother died, trying to get something to eat from the vending machine. He didn't have any money and so he crawled on the ground to check under the machine for lost coins.

Gabriel tamped down the memory. If Grace hadn't come upon him that day, his life would have turned out very, very differently.

Julia greeted all the children, crouching down to their level. She seemed perfectly at ease, chattering and laughing with them in Italian.

After the introductions were made, the Emersons were led to a side yard where the rest of the orphanage's children, ages one to twelve, had gathered. The staff brought out the infants, so that they too could join the party.

Gabriel had been unable to rent a petting zoo but had secured the services of four ponies and their handlers. The ponies were tethered at the far end of the yard, surrounded by a crowd of excited children.

There were balloons and games, and a large, inflated bouncing castle. There were tables of food and desserts, and a large pyramid of wrapped gifts.

"How will they know which gift is for which child?" Gabriel pondered aloud.

Julia glanced at the pyramid. "I'm sure each gift is labeled."

"What if they don't like the present they receive?"

"Elena asked the children what they wanted and wc bought it." Julia squeezed his hand. "Stop fussing. The children will see you frowning and you'll scare them."

Gabriel sniffed at being so maligned but cautiously adjusted his expression.

He watched as she played games with the children, blowing bubbles and batting around balloons. A dark-haired, dark-eyed toddler took a shine to her, and soon Julia was carrying the boy on her hip and wresting her hair from his chubby fists, while avoiding a slight trickle of drool.

Gabriel was seized with a realization so strong it hurt.

Julianne was born to be a mother. She's loving and giving and patient. She has what my biological mother lacked, and what Grace had in abundance.

Maybe she even has enough to compensate for my own shortcomings.

To keep his melancholy at bay, Gabriel helped with the ponies, lifting children on and off their saddles. Julia had been correct. The ponies were the highlight of the event. Children lined up to pet and feed them in between rides.

When it was time to hand out presents, Gabriel stood behind the gift table with Julia.

Brother Silvestro made an announcement to the children, thanking Zio and Zia Emerson for their generosity. Gabriel and Julia nodded to polite applause. Then Julia began handing out the presents, still holding on to the toddler.

Gabriel would have joined her, but a little boy pulled at his trousers in an effort to secure his attention.

"Hello," said Gabriel, in Italian. "How are you?"

"Are you him?" the boy asked.

"Am I whom?"

"Superman."

Gabriel gave the child a puzzled smile. "Why do you think I'm Superman?'

"You look like him. Can I see under your shirt?" The boy pointed to Gabriel's white oxford button-down.

He smiled wryly. "I don't have my suit on today."

"You're wearing Clark Kent's glasses."

Gabriel removed his glasses and frowned at them. He thought his Prada frames were a good deal smarter than the horrific pair that Clark Kent wore.

(Perhaps he'd been mistaken.)

Gabriel didn't have time to be offended, however, because as soon as he took off the glasses, the boy gasped. A small crowd of other children soon gathered around.

"It's Superman," the first boy whispered, triumphantly.

Gabriel replaced his glasses, then reached out to ruffle the boy's hair.

"I'm afraid I'm not Superman. I'm Zio Gabriel from America. Zia Julia is my wife."

The children looked over at Julia, who was continuing to call out names and dispense brightly colored presents. She caught their eyes and smiled prettily.

"That's Lois Lane." A little voice piped up.

"Yes," said the first boy. "We recognize her. That's Lois Lane."

Gabriel examined Julia with new eyes.

"I thought Lois was taller," he mused, half to himself.

"I have a picture. See?" A boy held up a comic book and pointed to the drawing of Lois Lane on the cover. "It's her."

"She cut her hair," said another boy, eyeing Julia with disappointment. "I liked it longer."

"Tell me about it," Gabriel muttered.

"Can you do any tricks?" a girl interjected.

"What kind of tricks?" The Professor fought to hide his amusement.

"Lift something heavy, see through walls, fly."

"Oh, yes, fly!" The children began to jump up and down.

The Professor looked at the ever-increasing crowd of youngsters moving around him and sighed. He held his hands out to quiet them.

Then he leaned forward, dropping his voice.

"No one knows Clark Kent is Superman."

"I know," said one of the boys, lifting his hand high in the air.

Gabriel grinned. "Yes, you know. But none of the adults know. Lois and I are here for the party. So I need you all to help us keep this a secret. Understand?"

Some of the children gazed at him skeptically, but many of them nodded.

"Now Lois has a present for all of you. Why don't you go over and say hello and pick up your gift?"

With a somewhat mixed reaction, the children began to disperse, soon distracted by other pursuits.

Julia, who had been half-listening to the exchange nearby, caught his eye and winked.

Superman? she mouthed.

He shook his head. He'd been called a lot of things in his thirty-five years, but no one had ever accused him of being Superman. Although he had to admit, Julia would make a damn fine Lois Lane.

He wondered if there was a costume shop in Florence that he could visit.

He was contemplating that (and other naughty things) when he felt someone's eyes on him. He looked down and saw a small blond girl. She had her fingers in her mouth and was staring up at him.

He smiled. *"Ciao, tesoro."*

She took her fingers out of her mouth and extended her arms.

At first, he didn't understand what she wanted. She lifted her arms higher and waved them slightly.

"She's asking you to pick her up, Man of Steel." Julia was suddenly beside him.

Gabriel lifted the girl into his arms and she smiled briefly before placing her fingers back in her mouth.

It was at this moment that Julia's eyes met his and a long look passed between them. She greeted the child and patted her on the back. Then she returned to the gift table.

"Maria doesn't speak."

Gabriel turned to face Elena, Brother Silvestro's most capable assistant.

Elena reached out to tuck a blond curl behind the child's ear. "I'm surprised she went to you. She usually avoids strangers."

"How old is she?" Gabriel asked.

"Three." Elena switched to English. "But she hasn't spoken since she arrived almost a year ago."

"Why not?"

"Too much trauma."

Gabriel looked at the cherubic face of the child and suppressed a series of curses.

"Will she ever speak?"

"We hope so. She needs a family, certainly."

Unconsciously, Gabriel held the child more closely.

"Is it difficult to find families?"

"Sometimes." Elena smiled at Maria and spoke Italian, asking if she was enjoying the party.

Maria nodded and pointed in the direction of the ponies.

"Ah. I think you would like a pony ride. Shall I?" Elena gestured as if to take the girl, but Gabriel shook his head.

"I'll take her."

He walked over to the ponies and asked her in Italian which one was her favorite. She pointed to the smallest one, a black pony with white patches on his coat. He had a braided tail with a red ribbon tied to the end of it. He was called *Cioccolato*.

Carefully, Gabriel placed Maria on the saddle and rested his hand on her back while the pony's owner began to lead them in a circle.

Maria smiled and clutched the pony's mane between her tiny fingers.

As Gabriel walked the circuit with the child and the pony, he mused on the fact that his life could have turned out very differently. He was not an orphan, but a man with a family. And he had a family because Grace and Richard had opened their home and their hearts to him.

Although the darkness that was currently eating away at him had not abated, he found himself grateful for the hope that had shone in his life. And he vowed to share that hope with others. Somehow.

❧❧

Julia watched her husband with the crowd of children and later, with the little girl, and found herself transfixed. Something about the sight of a tall, handsome man explaining why he wasn't Superman warmed her.

She hadn't had many opportunities to watch Gabriel interact with children. She never accompanied him on his volunteer work at the Italian Home for Children. She'd seen him interact with Quinn, of course, but only on a few occasions.

Seeing how Gabriel was protective and sweet with Maria tugged at her heart.

The Professor was intimidating. He had his moments when he could be cold and prim. Certainly, there were times such as when she'd found him smoking on the balcony in Umbria when she worried about him. But the surprising gentleness with which he treated children made her wonder what he would be like with their child. He'd ruffle their son's hair and talk about Superman. He'd carry their daughter in his arms and treat her like a princess.

As she saw Gabriel smiling and chattering to the silent child, Julia realized that what Tammy had told her was true—children bring out a special side of a good man.

And Julia desperately wanted to give Gabriel that opportunity.

Someday.

❧❧

At the end of what had been a fulfilling but long day, Julia sat with Gabriel on the terrace of their favorite room at the Gallery Hotel Art. The terrace and the room itself held so many memories for them. It was the place Julia had given him her virginity, and the place he returned to when he felt himself in danger of succumbing to his addictions after their separation.

He was lying on the banquette, hands behind his head, looking up at the star-studded sky. She was next to him, sipping a glass of San Pellegrino.

"You could have wine," he said, pointing to her glass.

"I'm fine with water, Superman."

His mouth twitched. "That was an interesting conversation. I've been called a lot of things in my life. But no one has ever called me Superman."

She ran her fingers up and down his arm.

"Only because they haven't got the nerve. I rather like the idea of you being the handsome but slightly nerdy professor by day, and the sexy Man of Steel by night."

"What did I say about calling me a nerd?" Gabriel caught her wrist, pulling her so she was lying half on him.

The water sloshed in her glass, so he took it from her, setting it aside.

He brought their noses together.

"I can show you some steel tonight."

"I'm counting on it," she whispered.

"I never thought of you as Lois Lane before. But there's a remarkable likeness."

Julia rolled her eyes heavenward. "All this time, I thought you were in love with Beatrice, when really, it was Lois Lane. I need to switch literary genres."

"Hardly. But a little role-playing might be interesting, Miss Lane."

"We'll have to have a Halloween party so we can dress up."

Gabriel traced the line of her jaw with his finger.

"We don't have to wait until Halloween."

A thrill coursed up her spine at his tone.

"I look forward to that. Did you have a good time at the party?"

"Of course." He released her, his gaze returning to the stars.

She sighed, picking up her glass again. She sipped the water as she contemplated how to broach the subject.

"Something happened today, didn't it?"

"Yes."

She waited for him to comment further, but he didn't.

She put her drink on the table and went to him, placing her arm atop his abdomen.

"Do you want to talk about it?"

He shook his head.

Her heart sank. "The list of things you won't share with me is becoming longer."

"My silence isn't meant to hurt you."

"It does." She huffed in frustration. "How can I be your partner when you won't talk to me?"

"Julianne, I'm going to talk to you. I promise I won't do anything without discussing it with you. I just need to—figure out a few things first."

"Can't you figure them out with me? I'm a good listener. I can help."

"You are a good listener. The best. But sometimes a man needs to do things alone."

"Is that man-speak for 'Don't worry your pretty little head, darlin'?"

"*Man-speak?*" He chuckled, pressing his lips to her palm. "You're adorable."

She pulled away, crossing her arms in front of her chest. "Now is not a good time to be patronizing, Gabriel."

He rolled to his side and kissed the wrinkle between her eyebrows. "I'm not patronizing you. You *are* adorable." He paused, his eyes focused and intense. "You need to be a mother. Seeing you with the children—how loving and at ease you are. You're a natural."

"Today was a special day. Your ponies were a hit."

"You were right, as usual."

"Then why are you so sad?"

"I can't stand to leave them there." Gabriel's eyes and tone evidenced his distress.

Julia observed him, realizing that whatever distress he felt at the orphanage had been very well hidden.

"The children are treated nicely. The staff love them. They're safe."

"It's still an orphanage."

"Yes." Julia pushed a curl back from his forehead. She ran her fingers through his hair in an attempt to soothe him.

"I know what it's like," he said quietly. "When my mother died, there were several months when I didn't know where I'd end up. It could have been an orphanage or foster care. I could have been shipped back to New York to live with my mother's family. I was in limbo, never knowing if someone was going to show up to take me away or if Grace and Richard were going to tire of me and pack my bags."

"They would never have done that."

"I didn't know. They were strangers to me. I wasn't especially adoptable. My father disowned me, and my mother's family didn't want me. They would have left me to an orphanage—my own flesh and blood. Now do you understand why I don't want anything to do with them?"

Julia placed her hand against his face. "Yes. But you were very adoptable. Grace and Richard were attached to you from the beginning."

"If they hadn't taken me, what would have happened?"

“There’s no point in going down that road. You have a family that loves you and you have me.”

“You’re everything, Julianne.”

The beauty of his words pierced her heart. She leaned forward to kiss him, trying to show how much his words meant to her.

When she pulled away, he grasped her hand at the wrist. “We could adopt.”

“I thought you wanted to try to have a child first.”

He looked away.

“Has something changed?” she pressed, noting his body language.

“Children like Maria deserve a home. She doesn’t even speak!” Gabriel became visibly agitated.

“Maybe we should try to help Elena find a family for her. You know lots of people.”

“What about us?”

“Us?”

“Why don’t we take her?”

Julia searched his eyes, surprised to discover that he was serious.

“Sweetheart, we aren’t in the best position to take home a toddler.”

“We love each other and we’d love her. We have a house and a yard. We speak Italian.”

“Maria is a toddler with special needs and we’re first-time parents. I’m already worried about making mistakes.”

Gabriel sat up. “How could you make a mistake? You are everything that is good and gentle. Children are drawn to you.”

“I’m not ready.”

“What if you had help? I’m owed a sabbatical. That was part of my agreement with BU when I left Toronto.”

Julia gave him an incredulous look. “You’d use your sabbatical to stay home with me and a baby?”

“Why not? Children aren’t awake all the time. We could take turns. You have to admit that having an extra pair of hands would make things easier.”

“Neither one of us knows very much about caring for a toddler.”

“We have Rebecca.”

Julia laughed. “Rebecca is wonderful, but she’s our housekeeper, not a nanny. Her kids are grown up. I don't think she'd want to help us with a child."

"I think you'd be surprised if you asked her. She's already volunteered to help more when we have a baby."

Julia pulled away from him. "You've spoken to her about this?"

He held his hands up. "No. But before we were married, she mentioned that she hoped she'd be with us for a long time, long enough to see us start a family."

He frowned. "I'm not the enemy, Julianne. I'm not constantly looking for ways to sabotage your education. Or your life."

She ducked her head. "I'm sorry. I feel as if the slightest disturbance will cause me to lose my focus and I'll flunk."

"I think that's the most honest thing you've said about your program."

She lifted her face, eyes narrowing. "What's that supposed to mean?"

"It means, darling, that you're worried about failing. Even though so many people are eager to support and help you. Including me and Rebecca."

She started to protest, but he interrupted.

"Anxiety over starting a family is legitimate. But I think you'd be anxious about your program anyway. That has more to do with how you see yourself than how you see the program."

Julia's eyes widened.

"I—that's not true."

"It is. I know, I felt the same way when I was at Harvard. I think anyone who has an accurate sense of self has the same concern." He moved his hand to the back of her neck, urging her forward. "You can do it, Julianne. I believe in you."

Tears pricked at the back of her eyes and she found herself in his arms, clutching him tightly.

He moved his mouth to her ear.

"I'd like to take Maria home with us. I'd like to take all the kids home with us. But this thing with Harvard is something you need to deal with on your own."

"Is that why you won't tell me what's troubling you?"

Gabriel exhaled loudly.

"No. I'm still working things out in my mind."

"Without me."

"I'll share it with you eventually. As I said in Umbria, I won't do anything without discussing it with you first. I just need some time."

She shook her head but elected not to argue with him.

"Will you continue your work with the Italian Home for Children?"

"Yes. They need me, of course, and I've promised the students that if they graduate high school with an excellent grade point average that I'll send them to Italy."

"You're already changing the lives of children. You should be proud of yourself."

He gave her a half-smile. "Are you sure you aren't ready for adoption? We'd love her."

His eyes were dark with emotion.

Julia thought back to what she'd seen that day—the way Gabriel was with Maria and the other children. At that moment, Julia truly wanted to give him what he was asking for. But she knew it was wrong.

"We would. But if we love her, we need to do what's best for her. And that's probably finding a local family. Not two American newlyweds who don't know what they're doing. You'd have to give up smoking."

"That isn't a problem." He looked at her carefully. "You're worried about the drugs, aren't you?"

She squirmed and he frowned at her.

"You don't seem to have a lot of confidence in me."

"I have every confidence in you. But you have to remember that I watched my mother relapse more than once."

He disentangled himself from her arms. "Well, I'm not going to relapse."

"Good."

"Maybe we should talk about your own relapses. Just last month you were struggling with something and you turned to Paul."

Julia's brown eyes flashed. "You don't get to throw that back in my face. I apologized, remember?"

"You're right. I'm sorry," he said stiffly.

"Are we having an honest and open conversation? Or are you trying to manipulate me?"

Gabriel glared. "We're having an honest and open conversation. I apologize for bringing up Paul."

She sighed.

"I understand that it's difficult to work with the children at the orphanage and to leave them there. I feel it too. But it isn't in Maria's best interest for us to take her now."

"The orphanage is good, but it isn't the same thing as having a family."

"Which is exactly why we shouldn't take her."

Gabriel moved to his feet. "That is not the Julianne I know speaking."

"Oh, yes it is." She stood in front of him.

"The Julianne I know would give the clothes off her back to a homeless person."

She took a step closer, her face flushed with anger.

"I would give the clothes off my back for Maria. But I want her to be with a family who are stable and experienced when it comes to children. She's been traumatized. Taking her to a place where she doesn't know the language, away from her city and her friends, would only upset her. We'd be hurting, not helping. And I won't let you do that. And I don't care if you think that I'm being a coldhearted bitch or whatever the hell you have running through your mind."

She gave him a reproachful look before retreating to the bedroom.

"Fuck!" he shouted, picking up her glass of water and throwing it.

The glass shattered against the floor of the terrace.

From a distance, Gabriel heard the door to the bathroom slam shut.

He placed his hands on the balcony, leaning against the edge, and hung his head.

Chapter Thirty-four

August 2011
Washington, D.C.

Senator Talbot's son Simon stood to his feet and quickly pulled on his jeans.

"Where's my shirt?" He looked in vain for the light blue polo that perfectly matched the color of his eyes.

"It's on the chair." His girlfriend, Natalie, sat up, not bothering to clutch the sheet to her chest.

As usual, his eyes dropped to her breasts, which had been surgically enhanced the year previous. He placed a knee on the bed.

"God, I'm glad I bought these." He dropped his head and drew one of her nipples into his mouth, sucking it strongly before biting with his teeth.

"Come on." She reached out to palm him through his jeans, but he pulled back.

"I have to go. I'll call you." He located his shirt and pulled it over his head before hastily retrieving his shoes and socks.

"When will I see you?" She knelt behind him and pressed her lips to his neck. With a single finger, she traced his jaw, gliding over the scars that were the result of his one and only violent encounter with Gabriel Emerson.

He shook her off. "Stop that."

"I'm sorry." She sat back on her heels repentantly. "No one notices them. I think they make you look rugged."

He turned, his eyes glacial pools.

She tilted her head to one side. "When will I see you?"

"Not for a while."

"Why not?"

"We need to cool off."

"But things have been going well. I work for your father now, for God's sake."

"And I told him we were casual. That was his condition for hiring you. I can't be seen going in and out of your apartment anymore. People are watching."

"Then we can meet at a hotel." She reached for him but caught only air.

Simon walked toward the bedroom door. "He wants me to take Senator Hudson's daughter to dinner."

"What?" She leapt from the bed. She stood in front of him, naked, her green eyes sparking with anger and her long, red hair a riotous mess.

Simon placed one of his hands on the back of her neck.

"Don't get hysterical."

She shivered at the coldness of his voice. "I won't. I'm sorry."

He stroked his thumb along the curve of her neck.

"Good. Because I don't like it when you get hysterical."

He dropped his hand to her ass.

"It's just dinner. She finished her junior year at Duke and she's here for the summer. I'm going to take her out and, hopefully, persuade her to put a good word in for my dad with her father. We could use his endorsement."

"Are you going to fuck her?"

Simon snorted. "Are you kidding? She's a virgin. I had enough of that shit dealing with Julia."

Natalie wrinkled her nose at the mention of her former roommate.

"What makes you think the Hudson girl is a virgin?"

"Her family is religious. They're from the South. It's a guess."

"Religion didn't keep Jules from going down on you." Natalie crossed her arms in front of her.

"Keep your mouth shut about Julia. I don't need her asshole boyfriend fucking things up for me."

"He's her asshole husband now."

"I don't care what he is. You know the score." Simon pulled her closer. "Don't bring them up again."

"How do you think I feel? My boyfriend is being set up with another goody two-shoes because his father thinks I'm a whore."

Simon gripped her ass with both hands.

"We're finally getting what we want. We just need to wait until after the election."

"Oh, I can be patient." She dropped to her knees in front of him, quickly freeing him from the confines of his jeans. "But I think you need a reminder of who you're walking out on."

Chapter Thirty-five

Florence, Italy

Gabriel smoked a lonely cigarette out on the terrace, staring at the shards of a broken water glass. He'd upset Julianne.

She'd seen him throw things before. He'd murdered her old cell phone when that motherfucker Simon called her.

Gabriel inhaled, drawing the air deep into his lungs before exhaling through his nostrils.

He did not think of their relationship as tempestuous. Although they'd had more conflict recently. They'd fought back in Selinsgrove over her paper. They'd fought in Umbria when he'd asked about her mother and she'd told him he was mindfucking her.

Tonight they'd descended to a new low when she accused him of thinking she was a bitch. Nothing was further from the truth. He couldn't even place the word and her name in the same sentence.

But he'd lost his temper before he had the chance to say that.

His secrets were hurting her. He knew that. But he couldn't unburden himself until he'd found a solution. He didn't want to appear weak and undecided, or worse, to watch her compassion change into pity. He'd rather alienate her temporarily than lose her respect.

And he hadn't found a way forward. Not yet. He was caught between two extremes, both of which were unacceptable. At the moment he lacked the courage or the wisdom to find a middle path.

He finished his cigarette and lit another one. Perhaps he lacked both courage and wisdom.

Julianne was correct. If they adopted a child, he'd have to quit. He'd quit cigarettes before, after his stint in rehab. He could quit again.

He thought about Tom and Diane. They'd gone from the elation of discovering they were expecting to the devastation of learning that their child had a life-threatening birth defect. He couldn't imagine how powerless they felt. He'd had a glimpse of such impotence when Paulina—

Gabriel forced himself to focus on the cigarette he held between his fingers. He couldn't allow his mind to wander down that road. Not tonight.

He gazed at the skyline of Florence, at the tower of the Palazzo Vecchio, waiting until he was sure Julia was asleep.

He visited the bathroom, brushing his teeth and dropping his clothes to the floor. He showered quickly, knowing that she'd smell the smoke on his skin.

Naked and with damp hair, he slid between the sheets. He didn't touch her. A quick glimpse of the bed in the lamplight revealed that she was wearing a nightgown and curled on her side, facing away from him.

Message received, sweetheart.

As he settled into bed he thought, perhaps, that he heard a murmur of distress emanating from her direction.

"I'm sorry," he whispered.

When she didn't respond, he switched off the light and turned his back to her.

It only took a moment for Julia to shift so she was spooning him from behind.

"I'm sorry, too."

"We promised we wouldn't go to bed angry anymore."

"I'm not angry, Gabriel, I'm hurt."

He reached back to grasp her wrist and pulled her arm so that it draped over his waist. "You're right about Maria. I just wanted to do something.

"I don't think you're a bitch. I'd never think of you that way. You're my beloved."

"Then I need you to be kind to me. I have to tell you, Gabriel, this past little while has been really difficult. I don't want our marriage to be like this."

His body tightened.

"I'll find a way to make it up to you. I promise."

"I don't want you to make it up to me. Just tell me what's wrong."

"I will. I promise."

"Tell me now." Her tone was harsh.

"Please, Julianne," he whispered. "I'm asking you, please, to give me a little more time."

"So you can come to some momentous decision without me?"

"I wouldn't do anything without talking to you first. But haven't you ever been worried about something and tried to figure out how to deal with it? You can't exactly make those decisions for me." He shook his head. "I'm asking you, Julianne, to have a little compassion."

She searched his eyes and found nothing insincere in them.

"I can give you a little more time. But I want you to call Dr. Townsend."

Gabriel opened his mouth to protest but was interrupted.

"I won't accept your refusal. Either tell me what's troubling you, or tell him. But for both our sakes, Gabriel, tell someone."

With a deep exhalation, he nodded.

Gabriel was awake before sunrise and quit the suite before Julianne awoke. Though it pained him to leave the warmth of her embrace, he was on a mission. The sooner he gathered the information he needed, the closer he would be to a solution.

(Or so he hoped.)

That afternoon, he had an important meeting scheduled with his old friend, *Dottore* Vitali, the director of the Uffizi Gallery. Now Gabriel was more determined than ever to show his wife how much he loved her. And to do so publicly.

As he exited the hotel, he reflected on the fact that he preferred Florence in the morning—the quiet of the streets before the city shook off its slumber.

He stopped at the café at the Gucci Museum in Piazza della Signoria and bought an espresso and a sweet roll. He enjoyed his breakfast outside, along with his newspaper, *La Nazione*, biding his time until he could call for Elena at the orphanage.

At ten o'clock, he rang the doorbell. Elena was surprised to see him and even more surprised when he revealed the reason for his visit.

She thanked him for his concern for Maria and suggested that if he wanted to help, he could assist in covering the costs for the therapist she was seeing in an effort to help her recover her speech.

When Gabriel raised the subject of adoption, Elena quickly explained that adopting a child in Italy could be difficult. Only married couples were permitted to adopt, and they must have been married for at least three years. Even if he and Julianne had decided to adopt Maria, the Italian government wouldn't let them.

Gabriel left the orphanage duly chastened, but not without making a substantial donation to cover Maria's expenses. He made it clear that Elena was to contact him if any needs arose.

Lost in thought, he wandered to a café at Santa Croce. Instead of watching the beautiful women walk by, he made a few phone calls, prevailing upon Florence's finer families to consider supporting the orphanage through foster care or adoption.

Reactions were mixed. Everyone was willing to part with their money for charity, but not a single couple would agree to become foster parents. Adoption was absolutely out of the question.

Once again, Gabriel was confronted with the lavishness of grace as he contemplated all the reasons why Richard and Grace could have said no to adopting him, but didn't.

❦❦

Julianne awoke to an empty bed and a quiet hotel room. But Gabriel had left a glass of water on the nightstand, along with a note,

> *Darling,*
> *I've gone to run errands.*
> *I'll be back in time to get ready for the exhibition opening tonight.*
> *I love you,*
> *And I like my body when it is with your body,*
> *G.*

On the back of the note, Gabriel had transcribed a poem by e. e. cummings: "i like my body when it is with your."

Julia read and reread the poem, wondering what Gabriel's errands were.

In truth, she felt guilty. Gabriel was correct—Maria needed a family to love and care for her. Julia could see why Gabriel was drawn to her.

As all the anxiety about graduate school and her career washed over her, she couldn't shake the suspicion that she was being selfish by valuing her education over the welfare of a child.

Still, it didn't seem right to take Maria from the only country she'd ever known and place her in a house with strangers. Especially since Julia didn't know what Gabriel was troubled about.

Maybe he wants children right away and he's gearing himself up to tell me so.

Julia entertained the thought but put it aside. Gabriel recognized her anxiety about grad school. He wasn't going to add to it.

She'd worked so hard to get herself to this point. His remarks the evening before about "the Julianne he knew" had cut her deeply. She'd tried to be compassionate her whole life. Surely being a good person didn't entail the abandonment of one's dreams.

Much as she wanted to help Maria, she simply couldn't agree to adopt her. Not now. Perhaps in two years when they were better acquainted with her, and Julia was in her fourth year of graduate school. The fourth year was devoted to preparing her dissertation prospectus and then writing her dissertation. Julia could simply work on her research and be a mother, at the same time.

(Or so she thought.)

Still, she worried about her husband—about what secret demons tormented him and why he was so determined to be secretive.

She lifted her iPhone from the nightstand and quickly sent him a text.

G,

I missed waking up with you this morning.

Thank you for your note and the poem.

Looking forward to the opening tonight.

I love you too,

J.

xo

Then, in an effort to exercise her compassion, she dressed and spent the day on her own quest—trying to find the homeless man she'd given money to during her first visit to Florence with Gabriel.

She searched the city center, but no one seemed to know the man she was referring to, and certainly none of the people she asked had seen a man answering his description.

While Julianne was burying her sorrows in a lemon gelato at Bar Perseo, Gabriel was finishing his meeting with *Dottore* Massimo Vitali at the Uffizi. He returned to the hotel to find an empty suite, but the scent of orange blossoms filled the air, remnants of her perfume.

He had happy memories of their first visit to Florence. There was a wall in the suite that he would have liked to enshrine. He thought back to the early days of their relationship and how he'd worked so hard to earn Julianne's trust. He was seized of a sudden by a glimpse of what his life would be like without her—empty, naked, cold.

He had to deal with his problems head on, or the gap between them would grow ever wider until eventually, he lost her.

He picked up his phone and dialed the number for his therapist's office. Then he left a long message.

After he'd hung up the phone, he opened his laptop and pulled up the Google search engine. He typed the following search phrase: "Owen Davies."

A few hours later, Julia was standing in the bathroom, applying makeup, while Gabriel stood at the sink next to her, shaving. As her fingers stroked over part of her throat, she found herself wincing. She could no longer see where Simon had bitten her. But every time she touched the spot, she felt his teeth.

A gentle hand caressed the back of her neck. "He won't hurt you again."

She met Gabriel's eyes in the mirror. "I wish I could believe that. Somehow I suspect he and Natalie aren't finished with me."

"They wouldn't dare." He kissed her forehead.

"How can you be so sure?"

Something flickered across his features, but it was eclipsed by his smile.

"Trust me."

"I heard from my dad today." She traced the marble topped vanity with her finger.

"What did he say?"

"They want to get married Labor Day weekend. It will be a small wedding. Dad feels more comfortable with Diane at his place and Diane doesn't want to move in with him without being married."

"And the baby?"

"Nothing has changed. Diane seems to be doing well, and the baby is about as good as could be expected. They're keeping an eye on both of them." She shook her head. "Dad feels pretty helpless."

"Of course he does. He wants to protect them and there's nothing he can do."

She nodded, looking down at the marble with a fascination unwarranted by its appearance. "I'm sorry about Maria."

"So am I." He leaned against the vanity, contemplating his bare feet. "But at least I tried to help her."

"Maybe one of the families you contacted will change their mind. If they could just meet her, I'm sure they'd fall in love with her."

He nodded, wriggling his toes.

"I won't say that I understand, Gabriel, because I don't. I wasn't adopted and so I don't share that special affinity you have with the children at the orphanage. But if you could just give me until my fourth year, I—"

"We'll have plenty of time to talk about that. There's no rush." He smiled at her gently.

A feeling of relief mixed with dread washed over her.

Gabriel returned to his shaving, while she watched with rapt fascination.

"This reminds me of our first trip to Florence. We were getting ready together before going to the Uffizi." She seemed wistful. "I was just your girlfriend, then."

Gabriel stopped.

"You were never just my girlfriend, Julianne. You were my lover. And we're still lovers."

"How could I forget?" She gestured in the direction of the bedroom, pausing for a moment to remember their first time together. "I was so happy here.

"But tonight I'm going to accompany you to the Uffizi as your wife. We get to open the exhibition of your illustrations together."

"They're *our* illustrations. And I love you even more now than I did before. I didn't think it was possible."

"I love you more, too." She peered down at her toes, admiring the way the red nail polish shimmered in the light. "I think your love has healed me, in many ways."

Gabriel placed his razor on the counter.

"I don't know why you persist in being sweet when I'm shaving." He tried not to get shaving cream on her silk robe, but failed. "We're going to have to have sex now."

She laughed. "We can't. We're due at the Uffizi at seven. The guests of honor can't be late."

"It wouldn't do for one of the guests of honor to be cross all evening because he's hard and wanting. We had a fight. We made up. You owe me makeup sex."

Julia reached out a hand to test his arousal.

"I wouldn't want you to be uncomfortable, Professor. But I really need to get ready. Look at my hair."

He pulled back to see the dark strands, which were now streaked with shaving cream on one side.

"Fine," he huffed. "But don't be surprised if I spirit you off to a corridor and have my way with you."

"I'm counting on it, Superman." She nipped his ear with her teeth before escaping his arms. "And just for the record, I like my body when it's with yours, as well."

❧❧

A short while later, Julia exited the washroom, walking over to where Gabriel was seated in the living area of their suite.

"What do you think?"

He stood up and removed his glasses, tossing aside the book he'd been reading.

He took her hand, spinning her in a circle. Her Valentino dress was very feminine, with a boat neckline, cap sleeves, a slim bodice, and a full skirt. The fabric was a rich red taffeta.

She pulled at the hemline, which sat above her knees. "I think I should have bought something black, instead."

"No." His eyes traveled from her exposed collarbones, across her breasts and down to her long and shapely legs. "Red is perfect."

He peered down at her black Prada peep-toe stilettos.

"You've been holding out on me, Mrs. Emerson. I don't recall seeing those before."

She arched an eyebrow at him.

"You aren't the only one with secrets, Professor."

Gabriel's smile slid off his face.

She looked down at her shoes.

"But I can arrange a private viewing."

"In a dark corner at the Uffizi?"

Their eyes met and she nodded.

He kissed her cheek. "You look lovely. The guests won't be looking at Botticelli. They'll be looking at you."

"Oh, don't say that, Gabriel. I'm nervous enough." She brushed imaginary lint from his shoulders and then straightened his black bow tie. "You're handsome. I don't have the pleasure of seeing you in a tuxedo very often."

"I can arrange a private viewing." He pressed his lips to the inside of her wrist, closing his eyes and inhaling her scent.

"Roses." He opened his eyes. "You've changed your perfume."

"The Noble Rose of Afghanistan. It's beautiful, isn't it? It's fair trade and it encourages development in that country."

"Only you would choose your perfume because of the company's commitment to fair trade. What did I do to deserve you?" Gabriel whispered, his eyes dark and searching.

"You deserve happiness. Why can't you let yourself believe that?"

He gave her a long look, then took her hand in his and led her to the door.

All the while, Julia's heart nearly cracked under the weight of her realization that her love had not healed him.

❧❧

"*Professore. Signora.*" Lorenzo, *Dottore* Vitali's assistant, greeted them at the entrance to the Uffizi.

"We shall gather with the media. You will be invited to open the exhibition. Then we will view the collection, enjoy a reception and later, dinner."

Gabriel acquiesced in Italian, squeezing Julia's hand.

Lorenzo led them to a hallway where a crowd of about a hundred people were gathered. Julia recognized many familiar faces from Gabriel's lecture a year and a half ago. All the men were in tuxedos, save the members of the press; all the women were wearing gowns, many of which swept the floor.

Julia looked down at her bare legs self-consciously.

Soon they were surrounded. Gabriel shook hands and exchanged pleasantries, introducing Julia as his beautiful wife. She watched as he greeted guests in Italian, French, and German, working the room fluidly and comfortably. But he never let her leave his side; his arm remained wrapped around her waist.

They were just about to follow *Dottore* Vitali to the doorway to the exhibition when Julia stopped short. Staring at her, not fifty feet away, was Professor Pacciani, with a tall, dark-haired woman on his arm.

Julia's eyes widened.

For a moment, she thought the woman was Christa Peterson. But on sustained inspection, she realized that although there was a resemblance, Pacciani's companion was older than Christa by about ten years.

Gabriel felt Julia stop, but he'd been speaking with Vitali, getting last-minute instructions on what was to take place. His eyes followed hers and something akin to a growl escaped his chest.

"Ah, you know Professor Pacciani, I assume." Vitali spoke in Gabriel's ear. "We invited the professors from the universities, on your instructions."

"Right," said Gabriel. He rued the fact that he hadn't been more explicit about who should not receive an invitation.

"Shall we?" *Dottore* Vitali gestured, and the Emersons walked to the doorway.

They stood side by side, facing the crowd and blinking amid the cameras and commotion, while Vitali made his introductions. Julia tried not to fidget, but she felt very conspicuous.

The director spent a long time explaining the history of the sixteenth-century illustrations—how they were copies of Botticelli's original images of Dante's *Divine Comedy*, and how, although eight of the originals had been lost, the Emersons had possession of the full complement of one hundred.

As Julia scanned the crowd, one face stood out. A young-looking, fair-haired man with strange gray eyes stared unblinkingly in her direction, his expression one of intense curiosity. His reaction was so different from the other guests, Julia couldn't help but return his stare, until Gabriel nudged her, drawing her attention back to their host.

Dottore Vitali painstakingly traced the provenance of the illustrations from the Emersons back to the nineteenth century, where they seem to have appeared out of nowhere.

The Uffizi was proud to display images that had not been viewed in public since, perhaps, their creation.

The audience murmured appreciatively and broke out into enthusiastic applause as Vitali thanked the Emersons for their generosity.

Gabriel moved his arm in order to take Julia's hand, squeezing it. They nodded and smiled their acknowledgments. Then he walked to the podium and offered a few words of thanks in Italian to Vitali and the Uffizi.

He turned his body sideways, his eyes fixed on Julia's.

"I would be remiss if I didn't mention my wife, Julianne. The lovely lady you see before you is the reason why this evening came about. Without her, I would have kept the illustrations to myself. Through her words and her deeds, she has shown me what it is to be charitable and good."

Julia blushed, but she could not look away. His magnetic gaze was focused entirely on her.

"This evening is only one small example of her philanthropic work. Yesterday, we spent the day at the Franciscan orphanage, spending time with the children. Earlier today, my wife was on a mission of mercy with the poor and homeless, in the city center. My challenge to you this evening is to enjoy the beauty of the illustrations of Dante's *Divine Comedy*, and then to find it in your hearts to celebrate beauty, charity, and compassion in the city Dante loved, Firenze. Thank you."

The crowd applauded, with one exception. No one seemed to notice the fair-haired man's cynical reaction to Gabriel's call to virtuous living, or the contempt he expressed when Dante was mentioned.

Gabriel returned to Julia and kissed her cheek chastely before facing the applauding crowd. They posed for photographs and cut the ribbon that was strung across the doors that led into the exhibition. The exhibit was declared open, to the sound of much applause.

"Please." Vitali gestured to the room, indicating that the Emersons should be the first to view the collection.

Gabriel and Julianne entered the room and were immediately awestruck. The space had been renovated, its normally pale walls painted a bright blue to better display the pen-and-ink illustrations, only some of which were in color.

The illustrations were arranged in order, beginning with Botticelli's famous Chart of Hell. In viewing the collection, one was able to witness the journey of a man's soul from sin to redemption. And of course, there was the inevitable reunion of Dante with his beloved Beatrice.

"What do you think?" Gabriel held Julia's hand as they stood in front of one of their favorite images, Dante and Beatrice in the sphere of Mercury. Beatrice was wearing flowing robes and pointing upward while Dante followed her gesture with his gaze.

"It's beautiful." She linked their pinky fingers together. "Do you remember the first time you showed it to me? When I came to dinner at your apartment?"

Gabriel lifted her hand to his lips, pressing a kiss to her palm. "How could I forget? You know, I showed them to you on impulse. I hadn't even told Rachel about them. Somehow, I knew I could trust you."

"You *can* trust me." Her dark eyes grew serious.

"I know." He appeared conflicted and for a moment Julia thought he was going to confess his secrets, but they were interrupted.

The attractive, fair-haired man approached, angling to view the illustration.

As if in a dream, Julia watched the stranger move. His body almost appeared to float across the floor, his footsteps light and fluid. He appeared tall but was actually an inch or two shorter than Gabriel. Julia perceived that although the man was trim, his elegant black suit hid muscles that rippled beneath the fine material.

The Emersons politely retreated, but not before Gabriel locked eyes with the other guest. Wordlessly, Gabriel placed his body between the stranger and Julianne, blocking her from his view.

"Good evening." The stranger addressed them with a British accent, bowing formally.

To Gabriel's trained ear, the accent sounded Oxonian.

"Evening," Gabriel clipped, his palm sliding down Julia's wrist in order to grasp her hand.

The guest's eyes followed the path of Gabriel's hand, and he smiled to himself.

"A remarkable evening," he commented, gesturing at the room.

"Quite," said Gabriel, gripping Julia's hand a little too tightly.

She squeezed back, indicating that he should release the pressure a little.

"It's generous of you to share *your* illustrations." The guest's tone was ironic. "How fortunate for you that you acquired them in secret and not on the open market."

The stranger's eyes traveled from Gabriel's to Julia's, pausing briefly. His nostrils flared and then his eyes appeared to soften before he turned to the drawing nearby.

"Yes, I count myself lucky. Enjoy your evening." With a stiff nod, Gabriel moved away, still gripping Julia's hand.

She was puzzled by Gabriel's behavior but elected not to ask him about it until they reached the opposite end of the gallery.

"Who was that?"

"I have no idea, but stay away from him." Gabriel was visibly agitated, and he passed a hand over his mouth.

"Why? What's going on?" Julia stopped, facing him.

"I don't know." Gabriel's eyes were sincere. "But there's something about him. Promise me you'll stay away."

Julia laughed, the sound echoing across the gallery. "He's a bit odd, but he seemed nice."

"Pit bulls are nice until you put your hand in their cage. If he moves in your direction, turn around and walk away. Promise me." Gabriel dropped his voice to a whisper.

"Of course. But what's the matter? Have you met him before?"

"I don't think so, but I'm not sure. I didn't like how he was looking at you. His eyes could have burned holes in your dress."

"It's a good thing I have Superman to protect me." Julia kissed her husband firmly. "I promise to avoid him and all the other handsome men here."

"You think he's handsome?" Gabriel glared at her.

"Handsome the way a work of art is handsome, not the way you are. And if you kiss me now, I'll forget him entirely."

Gabriel leaned forward and caressed her cheek with the backs of his fingers before pressing their lips together.

"Thank you." She chewed at the inside of her mouth. "I'm afraid you embarrassed me in your introduction. I don't like the attention."

"You're the true benefactor. I'm merely your escort."

Julia laughed again, but this time the sound barely echoed. The room had filled with other guests, who were waiting a respectful distance away.

"You make a charming escort, Professor."

"Thank you." He leaned over to whisper in her ear. "I'm sorry I embarrassed you with my introduction. I was hoping to motivate some of our guests to consider donating to the orphanage."

"Then embarrass me all you like. If one person decides to support the orphanage, this entire exhibit will have been a success. Even if they hate the illustrations."

"How could anyone hate something so exquisite?" Gabriel gestured at the room.

Julia couldn't argue. Several different artists had illustrated Dante's work over the centuries, but Botticelli had always been her favorite.

They continued through the room, pausing in front of each picture. Gabriel noted with satisfaction that the stranger seemed to have disappeared.

When they'd reached the one hundredth and final illustration, Julia turned to her husband.

"An incredible exhibit. They did a fantastic job."

"It isn't finished." Gabriel tried to smother a smile, his sapphire eyes sparkling.

"Really?" She looked around, confused.

He took her hand in his and led her to the second floor and into the Botticelli room.

She stopped short, as she always did, when she passed through the doors. Seeing *The Birth of Venus* and *Primavera* in the same room always left her breathless.

It was the location of Gabriel's lecture during their first visit to Florence. He'd spoken of marriage and family then, things that at the time seemed as ethereal as a dream.

As she stood in front of *Primavera*, she felt happy. Something about the painting comforted her. And it was never as magnificent to view a copy as it was to see the original.

If she closed her eyes, she could feel the silence of the museum, hear the echoes from the distant corridor. If she concentrated, she could conjure Gabriel's voice, lecturing on the four loves of *eros*, *phileo*, *storge*, and *agape*.

All of a sudden, she opened her eyes, her gaze drawn to the image of Mercury on the far left. She'd seen the painting a thousand times. But at this moment, his figure disquieted her. There was something about his appearance, something about his face that seemed strangely familiar . . .

"They've made an addition to this room since your last visit." Gabriel's voice interrupted her musings.

"Where?"

He grasped her elbow, moving her to the right so she could see a large framed black-and-white photograph that hung on the wall opposite *The Birth of Venus*.

She covered her mouth with her hand.

"What's that doing here?"

Gabriel tugged her until she was standing in front of a photograph of herself. She was in profile, her eyes closed and her long hair held up by a pair of man's hands. She was smiling.

The picture was one that Gabriel had taken back in Toronto, when she'd first agreed to pose for him. She looked at the tag underneath the photograph and read the following,

«Deh, bella donna, che a' raggi d'amore
ti scaldi, s'i' vo' credere a' sembianti

che soglion esser testimon del core,
vegnati in voglia di trarreti avanti»,
diss'io a lei, «verso questa rivera,
tanto ch'io possa intender che tu canti.
Tu mi fai rimembrar dove e qual era
Proserpina nel tempo che perdette
la madre lei, ed ella primavera».
—DANTE, PURGATORIO 28.045-051.

"Ah, beauteous lady, who in rays of love
Dost warm thyself, if I may trust to looks,
Which the heart's witnesses are wont to be,
May the desire come unto thee to draw
Near to this river's bank," I said to her,
"So much that I might hear what thou art singing.
Thou makest me remember where and what
Proserpina that moment was when lost
Her mother her, and she herself the Spring."

"Those are the words Dante speaks when he sees Beatrice for the first time in Purgatory." Gabriel touched her face, and his eyes met hers with searing intensity.

"It was the same for me. When I saw you in Cambridge after being separated from you, I remembered those words. Just seeing you, standing in the street, made me remember all I'd lost. I was hoping you'd see me and come to me."

Gabriel pulled her against his chest as Julia's eyes filled with tears. "Don't cry, my sweet girl. You're my Beatrice and my sticky little leaf and my beautiful wife. I'm sorry I've been such a bastard. I wanted to show you how important you are to me. You are my most precious masterpiece."

Julia gazed up at him.

He swiped his thumbs under her eyes before pressing his lips to her forehead.

"You're my Persephone; the maiden to my monster."

"No more talk of monsters." She brushed his tuxedo with her hand, worried that she'd transferred tears and makeup to the wool.

Then he was kissing her until she was breathless, arms wrapped tight around her back. When he released her, she giggled.

"I take it you're impressed with the exhibition, Mrs. Emerson?"

"Yes." Her face grew grave. "But I'd like you to take the photograph down. It's a magnificent gesture, but I don't want to be on display."

"You aren't."

Julia looked from Gabriel to the photograph and back again.

"I'm hanging there for all to see."

"Vitali wished to give us a gift to thank us, but I refused. When I asked if I could do something—ah—unusual for you, he agreed." Gabriel gestured to the room. "Vitali is an old romantic and it pleased him to be able to do something special for us. He agreed to display the picture and give us an hour on this floor, all to ourselves."

Julia's eyes widened. "We have the Botticelli room all to ourselves?"

"Not just that." His blue eyes danced with amusement as he brought his lips to her ear. *"We also have the corridor."*

"You're kidding."

"No. This floor is off limits until"—he glanced at his Rolex—"forty-five minutes from now, when we have to go downstairs for the reception and dinner."

With one quick movement, she grasped his lapels with both hands and pulled him to her, pressing a long, hard kiss against his lips.

"I take it you're pleased?" he said, when she finally released him.

"Let's go." She grabbed his hand and began tugging him toward the door.

"Where?"

"Makeup sex, museum sex, corridor sex. I don't care what you call it, but now is our chance."

Gabriel found himself chuckling and trotting after a very determined, very fast-moving Julianne, who was tottering on high heels.

"You surprise me, Mrs. Emerson."

"How so?" She lifted her voice slightly so it could be heard above the tapping of her stilettos.

"You're supposed to be shy. You're supposed to be the seduced, not the seducer."

She turned around, her eyes glittering.

"I want a heart-stopping, mind-blowing orgasm against a Florentine wall, Professor. You've just told me we have what I never thought we'd have—privacy in a public space. Screw shyness."

Now Gabriel laughed, tipping his head back.

He marched her swiftly down the corridor and around the corner to the opposite side, where he positioned her in a dark corner between two high marble statues perched atop plinths.

"This time, I won't stop," he whispered, his large hand pulling up her dress in order to rest on her thigh.

"Good."

"There's no air conditioning in here, so things might get a little . . . hot." He stroked the skin of her thigh with the back of his hand.

"I would expect nothing less, Professor."

She wrapped her arms around his neck and pulled him close.

He lifted her and her legs surrounded his waist, pressing their lower bodies together. Her back came into contact with the glass of the museum windows and she shivered a little at the cool sensation.

"Now tell me who is handsome." He spoke against her lips.

"You are." Julia captured his mouth just as a groan escaped him.

She kissed him determinedly, her tongue tracing the seam of his lips. He opened to her, and her tongue eagerly entered his mouth.

They kissed as if they'd been separated for years, lips eager and wanting.

He slid his hand up and down her thigh before pulling the skirt of her dress higher. The taffeta sighed its approval.

As he pressed against her more tightly, his fingers moved to the flare of her hip, where he caressed back and forth and back and forth. When he came to rest on her hip bone, he pulled back.

"Where are your panties?"

"I like my body when it is with your body, remember? Panties just get in the way."

Gabriel groaned, the sound traveling down the empty corridor. "You've been walking around like this all evening?"

She winked at him provocatively.

"No wonder that man was staring at you."

"Stop talking about other men." She tugged at his bow tie.

He leaned forward to taste her lips again, stroking her tongue with his own.

Julia shifted in his arms, the heels of her shoes catching on his tuxedo jacket. She undid his bow tie, tossing it to the floor, and hastily unbuttoned his shirt. She began kissing his neck and chest, her lips whispering across the surface of his skin, before sliding a hand down to his waistband.

But Gabriel would not be rushed. He moved her hand back to his shoulder, then reached between her legs, touching her gently. He was barely able to contain his joy at her reaction to him.

Julia moved and writhed, moaning in his ear.

"Don't make me wait," she begged, trying in vain to pull him closer.

Gabriel rummaged in his pockets.

"It's a good thing I brought this." He held up a square foil packet triumphantly.

She opened her eyes, fixing on the item. "Where did that come from?"

Gabriel chuckled.

"I thought you'd be uncomfortable all evening otherwise."

She blinked. "Did you plan this?"

"Absolutely." His left hand squeezed her backside for effect.

She moved to take it from him, but he shook his head.

"Allow me, Mrs. Emerson." He held the packet in his teeth while he unzipped his trousers. Then he ripped the foil before swiftly rolling it over himself.

Gabriel teased her, sliding back and forth before easing inside. She exhaled in satisfaction, tightening around him.

There were no words. Indeed, they were beyond speech. Gabriel knew his wife's body as she knew his, and the two of them moved and responded to one another with an increasing pace.

Muffled groans and grunts of satisfaction echoed down the corridor, so much so that a group of statues covered their ears. Julia's back thumped against the window as they moved in concert.

"I'm close," she managed, the last word cut off as her orgasm overtook her.

Gabriel quickened his thrusts, filling her deeply until he, too, was overcome.

Julia clung to him as if she were dying, her arms wrapped around his shoulders, her face buried in his neck.

They were motionless for some time. Gabriel's breath left his body in a long, relaxed exhalation.

"Okay?" he asked, kissing her cheek.

"Fantastic."

They remained in one another's arms, holding each other tightly as their hearts and breathing slowed. Gabriel gently placed Julia on her feet, and pulled her dress down to cover her. His hand found her waist and he squeezed.

"Can you walk?" He eyed her, and her expensive shoes, with concern.

"I think so. I might be a little wobbly."

"Then allow me." He lifted her into his arms and carried her to a nearby bathroom.

"Is it very different when you wear one of those?" Julia nodded at the condom that Gabriel threw into a trash can.

"I can't feel as much, so it's frustrating." Gabriel proceeded to wash his hands. "For most of my life, it was all I knew. But knowing what it's like to be inside you without it makes a condom a kind of torture."

"I'm sorry."

He dried his hands and leaned over to press a kiss to the top of her head. "Don't be. I'm not so selfish that I want you to be uncomfortable or messy simply so I can have better sex."

She frowned.

He brought their foreheads together. "Sex with you is always magnificent. But that's because it's more than just sex. Now I think you'll have to fix your hair and your face. Or everyone will know that you've just had museum sex." He looked a good deal more than proud of himself.

She arched an eyebrow. "And you're all set to return to the party?"

"Of course." Gabriel buttoned his tuxedo jacket.

"You don't need to make any—adjustments?"

"No." He cocked his head to one side. "Of course, I don't mind if people realize I just had museum sex with my wife."

"Oh, they will."

"How?"

"Because you're forgetting something, Professor."

"And what's that?"

"Your tie."

Gabriel reached up to his neck, a look of surprise flitting across his face. He began buttoning his shirt.

"Where is it?"

"On the floor where I left it."

"Temptress," he muttered, shaking his head.

She leaned over the vanity, attending to her hair and makeup. "So how good was the sex we just had? On a scale of one to transcendent?"

"Earth-shattering and tie forgetting."

Smugly, she reapplied her lipstick. "Don't you forget it."

Chapter Thirty-six

I love exhibition openings," Julia murmured, as they rejoined the other guests. "They're the best."

"You never cease to amaze me." Gabriel's hand hovered at her lower back.

"I could say the same. I think you can see an outline of my body on the window upstairs."

He chuckled, his hand sliding down to pat her bottom.

Someone cleared his throat behind them.

Julia and Gabriel turned to find *Dottore* Vitali standing a few feet away.

"Forgive me for interrupting, but would you be willing to speak to a potential donor?" He eyed the Professor hopefully.

Gabriel looked at Julia. "Vitali asked me earlier if I would try to persuade someone to part with a few paintings. But I can delay."

"No, you go."

"Are you sure?"

"Persuade the person to donate. I'm just going to wander around for a while."

Gabriel kissed her cheek. Then he and his old friend joined a group of well-dressed men and women who were standing near the entrance to the exhibition.

Julia retraced her steps through the gallery, leisurely admiring the collection. She was standing in front of one of the more colorful illustrations of Dante and Virgil in Hell when an oily voice addressed her in English.

"Good evening."

She whirled around and found herself face to face with Professor Pacciani.

Her eyes darted around the room, relieved to discover that they were not alone. Several couples were nearby, also admiring the art.

He held up his hands. "I have no wish to disturb your evening. All I require is a moment."

Julia's eyes flickered to his. "In a moment, my husband will return."

"In a moment, my wife will return. I had better speak quickly." He grinned, exposing his teeth. "I regret what happened in Oxford. If you will recall, I was not the one behaving badly."

He stepped closer.

Julia took a step back.

"I remember. But I must be going." She tried to walk around him, but he sidestepped her.

"Another moment, please. Professor Picton was unhappy with my friend's behavior. So was I."

Julia observed him incredulously.

"I told Christa to stay away from you. But as you know, she didn't listen."

"Thank you, Professor. If you'll excuse me."

He stood in front of her again, far too close.

Julia had no choice but to step back.

"Perhaps you could mention this to Professor Picton. I am applying for a job with Columbia University in New York. A former student of Katherine's is the chair of that department. I wouldn't want any—bad feelings to interfere."

"I don't think Katherine would interfere in another department's search process."

"I would consider it a favor. I've already done you a favor."

Julia's eyes flew to his. "And what would that be?"

"I prevented my friend from sleeping with your husband."

Julia felt the world grind to a halt.

"What?" Her question was far too loud, and so the other attendees turned to stare in their direction.

Julia's cheeks flamed.

"I'm sure you wish to express your gratitude." He leaned closer.

"Are you kidding?"

"Your husband was going to meet Christa at her hotel. I persuaded her to turn her attention elsewhere. Favor done."

"How dare you," Julia hissed. She leaned forward at the waist and Pacciani took a surprised step back. "How dare you come to this place of beauty and say these ugly things to me."

Pacciani's face clouded in confusion, as if he were witnessing the impossible transformation of a kitten into a lion. He lifted his hands in surrender.

"I mean no harm."

"Oh, yes you do." Her voice grew louder. "You and your *friend*, or whatever she is to you, mean nothing but harm. I don't care what she told you or what her plans were. You didn't prevent my husband from doing anything. Do you hear me?"

Pacciani scowled, as he became conscious of the fact that all eyes were on them. Julia's exclamation could be clearly heard by the other guests.

Then his angry expression morphed into a condescending smile.

"All men require a little—how do you say? Recreation. It is too much to expect one woman to be enough." He shrugged his shoulders as if he were reciting a commonly known fact.

"Women are not items on a buffet. And my husband doesn't share your misogyny." She lifted her chin defiantly. "I won't be telling Professor Picton anything, other than that you accosted me with lies. Now go away and leave me alone."

When he made no movement to comply with her instructions, she pointed an angry finger toward the door.

"Get out." Her steely voice filled the room.

(It was, perhaps, not the most polite strategy for removing a guest at a lavish event.)

Julia ignored the looks of incredulity and censure, glaring determinedly at Pacciani, whose face was a mask of fury.

He lunged toward Julia but was caught at the last moment by a woman who took hold of his arm with an iron grip.

"I've been looking for you." Mrs. Pacciani scolded her husband, but not before giving Julianne a hostile glance.

Pacciani cursed in Italian, trying to shake off his wife.

"Let's go." Mrs. Pacciani tugged at her husband's arm. "There are *important* people we need to speak to."

With a threatening look, Pacciani turned and accompanied his wife to the hallway.

Julia watched their retreating backs with no little relief. And more than a little anger.

(Which effectively ruined her afterglow.)

"Darling?" Gabriel smiled as he entered the room, striding confidently in his tuxedo. As usual, all eyes were on him and his handsome form as he moved smoothly across the floor.

A few whispers were exchanged by some of the other couples as they watched Gabriel rejoin his wife.

His smile disappeared. "What's wrong?"

Julia pursed her lips, trying to control her anger. "Professor Pacciani cornered me."

"That bastard. Are you all right?" Gabriel placed a light hand on her shoulder.

"He offered an apology for Christa's behavior in Oxford. I lost my temper and made a scene."

"Really?" Gabriel squeezed her shoulder as he fought back a smirk. "Tell me more."

Julia began to shake, the aftermath of a rush of adrenaline.

"I called him a misogynist and told him to go. And I pointed at him." She lifted her index finger, staring at it in disbelief.

"Excellent." Gabriel brought her index finger to his lips, where he kissed it.

She shook her head. "Not excellent. Embarrassing. Everyone heard me."

"I doubt very much that anyone would blame you. The female guests probably despise him for his lechery, and the male guests probably despise him because he's slept with their wives."

"He wanted me to tell Katherine that he dealt with Christa. He's after a job at Columbia and Katherine is a friend of the chair."

"He'll never get it," Gabriel scoffed. "Katherine was Lucia Barini's supervisor. She's a friend of mine, as well. She'll see through him.

"Perhaps Pacciani wants the job at Columbia in order to be with Christa."

Julia appeared disgusted. "I wonder what his wife thinks about that.

"He also told me that he prevented you from having a tryst with her."

"With whom?" Gabriel's tone was sharp.

"Christa. He said you were going to meet her at her hotel, but that he distracted her. That's why I lost my temper. I'm afraid the other guests heard everything." She glanced around the room uncomfortably.

Gabriel cursed, shifting his gaze toward the door. Pacciani and his wife were nowhere to be seen.

"There's something I need to tell you." Gabriel linked their hands and piloted her to a quiet corner. He looked over her shoulder to be sure that no one was eavesdropping.

He brought their faces close together, dropping his voice. "Christa propositioned me right before your lecture. I should have said something at the time, but I didn't want to upset you."

Julia gazed at him reproachfully. "And afterward?"

"I didn't want to upset you."

"Which is why you didn't tell me about your secret conversation with Paul."

A muscle jumped in Gabriel's jaw, and he nodded.

Julia released his hand. "You should have told me."

"Forgive me."

"I'm not fragile. I can handle disturbing news."

"You shouldn't have to."

Julia rolled her eyes heavenward, taking a moment to examine the gallery's ceiling. "Gabriel, until we enter the next life, things will disturb us. It's part of the human condition. When you keep things from me, it puts a wedge between us." She gave him a look, heavy with meaning.

When he didn't respond, she gestured to the room. "Others can exploit that wedge."

He nodded, his expression tight.

"I think I deserve to know who is making a play for my husband. And when." She arched an expectant eyebrow.

"Agreed."

She watched him for a minute, taking in the expression in his eyes and the tightness around his lips. He looked very unhappy. But he also looked protective, and that was not a posture she wanted to disappear.

"You are going to tell me things, aren't you?" Her voice grew soft.

"Yes." He was being truthful, but they both knew he was holding on to his secrets. At least for the present.

"So," she said brightly. "You're forgiven. But since my good mood from my first foray into museum sex has been ruined, you're going to have to fix that."

Gabriel bowed, not taking his eyes off hers. "I am yours to command."

"Good." She leaned forward, grabbing his silk bow tie. "Because my command is pleasure. And I think I'd like it now."

He pushed her hair behind her shoulders and brought his lips to her ear.

"Then come."

Chapter Thirty-seven

August 2011
Cambridge, Massachusetts

When Julia and Gabriel returned home the last week in August, they arrived to find a plethora of unopened mail. Gabriel gazed at the envelopes that Rebecca had stacked neatly on his desk and decided he'd forgo opening them in order to unpack instead.

While he was in the bedroom, Julia remained in the study. She glanced at the open door apprehensively before quietly moving to close it.

She knew that what she was going to do would be a violation of Gabriel's trust. But, she reasoned, her actions were justified by his silence and his continued reticence to disclose what was troubling him. She'd hoped he would talk to her while they were in Florence. But he hadn't.

Simply put, she was afraid and she was having difficulty coping with the fear.

There was a drawer in his desk that he never opened. She was vaguely aware of it, although she'd never had the nerve to look through its contents.

Gabriel had caught her opening it one day while she was in search of some printer paper, and he'd closed it under her hand, saying there were memories in that space that he did not wish to relive. Then he'd distracted her by pulling her onto his lap on the red velvet chair and making love to her.

Julia hadn't touched the drawer since. But today, frustrated and concerned, she sat behind his desk, examining its contents. If Gabriel would not give her answers, perhaps his collection of memories would.

The Botticelli illustrations, which he'd kept in a locked wooden box in that same drawer, were no longer there, displayed as they were now in the Uffizi. Julia quickly and quietly retrieved the first item, holding it in her hand.

It was his grandfather's pocket watch. He'd worn it on occasion, back in Toronto, but since they'd moved to Cambridge it had remained in the drawer. The watch was made of gold and attached to a long chain that had a fish-shaped fob on it. She opened it carefully and read the inscription:

To William,
My beloved husband
Love, Jean

She closed the watch, placing it on top of the desk.

The next item she retrieved was an old cast-iron train engine that had clearly seen better days. She imagined Gabriel as a little boy, clutching his train, perhaps demanding that he take it with him when he and his mother left New York.

Her insides twisted.

She placed the train on the desk and returned her attention to the drawer.

There was a wooden box, which she opened. In it, she found a string of large South Sea pearls and a ring with diamonds set into the band. Julia picked up the ring to look for an inscription, but there wasn't one. She saw two silver bracelets and a necklace, all of which were marked from Tiffany.

The jewelry had to have been his mother's. But she wondered about its source. Gabriel had told her several times of the poverty they'd lived in. How could someone who was so poor have such expensive jewelry? And why didn't his mother sell the jewelry when money grew short?

Julia shook her head. Gabriel's childhood was tragic, to be sure, but so was his mother's life.

She closed the box and turned her attention to the photographs, which had been sorted into envelopes. She leafed through them quickly, finding pictures of Gabriel and his mother, and a few snapshots of a man and a woman who must have been Gabriel's parents. Surprisingly, however, there were no photos of Gabriel's parents together.

Like Gabriel, his mother had dark hair, but her eyes were dark too, against pale, milky skin. She was fine featured and very beautiful.

In contrast, Gabriel's father was gray haired with piercing sapphire eyes. He was attractive for an older man, but there was an overall harshness to his expression that Julia didn't like. In the pictures, he rarely smiled.

At the back of the drawer, underneath a worn teddy bear, was a diary. Julia opened it and looked at the flyleaf.

This is the Property
of
Suzanne Elizabeth Emerson.

On impulse, she opened it to a random page. Her eyes alighted on the sentence written at the very top:

I'm pregnant.
Owen wants me to have an abortion.
He gave me money and said that he'd make the appointment.
He said that if I did this for him, he'd find a way for us to be together.
But I don't think I can do it.

Julia slammed the book shut and hurriedly shoved it to the back of the drawer.

Gabriel could come looking for her at any moment. He'd be incredibly angry at what she'd done.

She already regretted it. Suzanne Emerson's words flashed before her eyes. If Gabriel were to read them, he'd hate his father even more.

She placed the teddy bear back where she found it, along with the photographs and the jewelry box. She was about to return the train to the drawer when she noticed what was next to it, sitting atop the pile of unopened mail.

It was a letter.

She hadn't recognized the handwriting, but it didn't matter. Paulina's name and address were neatly written in the top left corner of the envelope. Somehow, she'd discovered Gabriel's address and sent the letter to their home.

Their home. The home Gabriel shared with his wife.

Julia wanted to fling the letter into the fireplace.

She was already beginning to keep secrets—reading his mother's diary when he wasn't looking. She couldn't throw Paulina's letter away, too.

Holding the envelope away from her body, she walked to the bedroom and handed it to him.

"Thanks, but I'll go through the mail later." He moved to toss the envelope on the bed, but she stopped him.

"Look at the return address."

Gabriel glanced at the letter.

He cursed.

"Why is she writing to me? Not even Carson, my lawyer, hears from her now."

Julia remained motionless, watching him.

He ripped open the letter, expecting to find a long, handwritten missive. He was surprised to find a single piece of cardstock.

He read the printed words quickly.

"It's a wedding invitation." He turned the card over, finding Paulina's flowing script on the back.

> *Gabriel,*
> *I would never be gauche enough to invite you to my wedding.*
> *I simply wanted you to know that I'm getting married.*
> *After all these years, I'll finally be a wife and a mother, to two wonderful girls.*
> *Now that we're both happy, things are as they should be.*
> *XO,*
> *P.*

He handed the invitation to Julia for her perusal.

Julia skimmed it.

"She's getting married."

"Yes."

"How do you feel?" Julia searched his face.

He placed the invitation back in the envelope. Then he tapped it against the open palm of his left hand.

"She expressed it correctly—we're both happy. She's found the family she wanted."

His blue eyes trained on Julia's.

"She has you to thank."

"Me?"

"You were the one who persuaded me to let her go. That she'd never find her own happiness while she was dependent on me. You were right."

Julia shifted her weight at his praise, all too conscious of the fact that she'd been snooping through his personal effects only minutes earlier.

"You were right about Maria, too." Now his eyes were sad.

Julia went to him, wrapping her arms about his waist.

"I wish I weren't right about Maria. But sometimes loving someone means that you have to let them go."

"I'll never let you go. I'd challenge anyone to try to take you away from me." He sounded fierce.

Julia pressed her fingertips to his lips. "Remember that when you're working things out in your own mind. No matter what your troubles are, I'm here. And I'm not going anywhere."

She kissed him again, then she disappeared into the hall.

Gabriel looked at the invitation, his mind wandering into the past.

Chapter Thirty-eight

January 2010
Toronto, Ontario

Paulina Gruscheva entered the lobby of the Manulife Building, her high-heeled boots clicking against the marble floors, her cell phone pressed to her ear. She'd been resident in Toronto for some time, but Gabriel had refused to see her, speak with her, or entertain any communication with her at all.

She'd grown tired of waiting.

When she reached Gabriel's voice mail, she hung up and dialed his landline. She prayed silently that Julianne wouldn't answer. It was bad enough that he was sleeping with her. She didn't have to have their affair thrown back in her face.

Again.

Undeterred by the fact that he wasn't answering his phones, she approached Mark, the security guard, demanding that he contact Professor Emerson immediately. When he refused, she fluttered her eyelashes and tried to cajole him. He was immune to her tall, blond, blue-eyed charms.

She raised her voice, creating a scene.

Within minutes, Mark contacted the Professor and asked that he please meet his guest in the lobby.

Paulina smiled triumphantly.

But her smile disappeared when she saw him, his expression furious, his eyes snapping, as he walked toward her. He grabbed her elbow roughly and half-dragged her through the lobby and out to the semicircular driveway in front of the building.

"What do you think you're doing?" he spat, releasing her.

Paulina retreated a step, surprised by his fury.

"Well?" he demanded.

"I wanted to talk to you. I've been here for weeks. You wouldn't see me!"

"We are not having this conversation again. I said all I had to say to you back in Selinsgrove. You know where you stand."

He turned to go back into the building, but she caught his arm.

"Why are you doing this to me?" Her voice faltered as she blinked back tears.

Gabriel's expression softened. Marginally.

"Paulina, it's over. It's been over for a while. I'm not trying to do anything to you other than persuade you to move on with your life. And to let me move on with mine."

She looked up at him as the tears began to fall.

"But I love you. We have a history!"

Gabriel closed his eyes for a moment, and a pained look spread across his face.

He opened his eyes.

"I'm in love with someone else. I'm sleeping, exclusively, with someone else."

"Yes, you are. And she's your student."

"Careful," he growled.

She tossed her hair behind her shoulders.

"It's remarkable the kind of information you can gather in a city of this size. Antonio from Harbour Sixty was quite forthcoming."

He stepped closer. "You didn't."

"I did. Funny how you took her to the restaurant you always take me to when I'm in town."

"I haven't taken you there in a very long time, Paulina. Even after we stopped—" He paused, struggling.

"After we stopped—fucking, Gabriel? Why can't you say it? We've been *fucking* for years."

"Keep your voice down!"

"I'm not your dirty little secret. We were friends. We had a relationship. You can't just ignore me and treat me as if I were trash."

"I'm sorry for how I treated you. But listen to yourself. Don't you think you deserve to be the center of someone's universe? Instead of chasing after someone who wants someone else?"

She tore her eyes from his. "You always wanted other women. Even when I was pregnant. Why should now be any different?"

He flinched. "Because you deserve to be with someone who wants you as much as you want him. It's time to move on. It's time to be happy."

"You make me happy," she whispered. "You're all I want."

"I'm in love with Julianne and I'm going to marry her." He sounded determined.

"I don't believe you. You'll come back. You always come back." She wiped a few tears away with the back of her hand.

"Not this time. In the past, I was weak and you held my guilt over me. But no more. We can't see each other and we can't speak. I've been patient with you and I've tried to help, but I'm done. As of today, your trust fund is frozen."

"You wouldn't!"

"I will. If you go back to Boston and begin seeing a therapist, I'll see that you continue receiving support. But if you contact me again, or if you do anything to hurt Julianne, you'll be cut off. Permanently." He leaned forward menacingly. "And that includes doing anything to hurt her life as a student."

"You'd do that? You'd just throw me away? I've sacrificed my life for you. I lost my academic career!"

Gabriel's jaw clenched.

"I never wanted you to do that. I did everything I could to help you stay at Harvard. You dropped out."

"Because of what happened to me. Because of what happened to us!"

His hands fisted at his sides.

"I don't deny that I've behaved abominably and you have every reason to be angry. But my admission doesn't change the fact that this has to end. Today."

He leveled his gaze on her and for a moment, he wore a look of compassion.

"Good-bye, Paulina. Be well."

He moved toward the sliding doors.

"You can't. You won't!"

His face wore a look of steely resolve.

"I already have."

Gabriel walked into the Manulife Building without a backward glance, leaving Paulina outside, crying, and standing in the snow.

Chapter Thirty-nine

May 2010
St. James the Apostle Cemetery
West Roxbury, Massachusetts

Gabriel stood in front of the stone angels, their twin forms positioned like sentries on either side of the memorial. The angels were made of marble, their skin white and perfect. They faced him, wings spread wide, with a name etched on the marker that sat between them.

The monument reminded him of the memorials in Santa Croce, in Florence. The likeness was intentional, since this monument was crafted after his own design.

As he regarded the angels, he thought back to his time in Italy, of his volunteer work with the Franciscans. Of his experience next to St. Francis's crypt. Of his separation from Julianne.

If only he could wait until July first, there would be the possibility of reunion. But Gabriel wasn't sure that she'd forgive him. He wasn't sure anyone would forgive him, but he had to try.

He reached into his pocket and retrieved his cell phone, dialing a number from the contact list.

"Gabriel?"

He took a deep breath. "Paulina. I need to see you."

"What's wrong?"

He turned his back on the monument, somehow unable to speak to her while staring at the name that was carved in stone.

"I just need to see you for an hour, to talk. Can we meet tomorrow?"

"I'm in Minnesota. What's this about?"

"I'll fly to Minneapolis tonight. Can we meet?" He was insistent, his voice tense and thin.

She sighed heavily. "Fine. Let's meet at a Caribou Coffee tomorrow morning. I'll email the address."

She paused, and Gabriel could hear her fidgeting in the background.

"You've never flown across country to talk to me."

He clenched his teeth. "No, I haven't."

"Our last conversation wasn't exactly pleasant. You left me outside your building, crying."

"Paulina." His tone was slightly pleading.

"Then you cut off all contact."

Gabriel began to pace, the phone pressed tightly to his ear.

"I did. And then what happened?"

She was quiet for a moment.

"I went home."

He stopped pacing.

"You should have gone home years ago, and I should have encouraged you to do it."

Silence reverberated between them.

"Paulina?"

"This is going to hurt, isn't it?"

"I don't know," he confessed. "We'll talk tomorrow."

He ended the call and hung his head before returning to the grave of their child.

❧❧

Paulina was nervous. She'd been utterly humiliated during her confrontation with Gabriel in the lobby of the Manulife Building. Acutely aware of her dependence on prescription sleep aids and alcohol, along with her dependence on her trust fund, she did what she'd sworn she would never do. She went home.

She found a job. She moved into a modest but nice apartment. Even more incredibly, she met someone. Someone kind and loving, who wanted her and only her. Someone who would never look at another woman for the length of their relationship, and possibly, beyond.

Now Gabriel wanted to talk, in person.

Paulina loved Gabriel. But she also feared him. He'd been elusive and unattainable, even when she was pregnant and they'd lived together. There was always a part of him that he would never let her touch. She knew it. She accepted it. But she never liked it and she always felt his distance hanging over her, like a dark cloud that might pour rain at any moment.

In the aftermath of their final confrontation, she realized he would never love her. She'd thought that Gabriel was simply incapable of love. But when she heard him speak about Julianne, it became clear that he was capable of loving someone and being faithful. How tragic that the woman he was capable of loving was someone other than her.

Once she accepted it, a degree of freedom accompanied the inevitable pain and longing. She was no longer a slave trying to win her master's affection. She was no longer someone with limited aspirations, putting her future on hold in order to keep herself available for him.

As she entered the Caribou Coffee shop, she felt strong for the first time in years. It would be difficult to see him but she'd made so much progress in other areas of her life, surely she could make progress in her relationship with him.

She found him sitting at a table for two in the back of the shop, his long fingers wrapped around a coffee mug. He was wearing a jacket and a button-down shirt but no tie. His trousers were clean and pressed and his hair was tidy. He was wearing his glasses, which surprised her, since he only wore them while reading.

When he saw her, he stood.

"Can I buy you a coffee?" He offered her a restrained smile.

"Yes, please." She smiled in return but felt awkward. In the past he'd usually greeted her with a kiss, but now he maintained a polite, proper distance.

"Still taking your coffee with skim milk and sweetener?"

"That's right."

He moved to the counter as she took the chair opposite his.

As he waited for Paulina's order to be filled, Gabriel scratched his chin. She looked different. She still moved like a ballerina, her spine straight and her limbs controlled. But her appearance had changed.

Her long blond hair was pulled into a low ponytail, her beautiful features free of cosmetics. She looked fresh and young, and much of the hardness that was evident in her expression the last time he'd seen her was gone.

Her clothes were different, too. She'd always dressed well, with a preference for skirts and high heels fashioned by the latest designer. But today, she was clad in a long-sleeved blue top that was casual and plain, and she wore dark jeans with sandals. It had been years since Gabriel had seen her in casual clothes. He wondered what it meant.

He placed the drink in front of her and took his seat, his hands moving once again to wrap around his coffee mug. He focused on the black liquid, trying to figure out what to say.

"You look tired." Her blue eyes fixed on him with concern.

Gabriel avoided her gaze, turning to look out the window. He wasn't particularly interested in the Minneapolis scenery. He simply didn't know how to begin.

"We were friends once." She sipped her coffee and followed the path of his eyes, watching the cars that drove past. "You look as if you could use a friend."

He turned his head, his eyes starkly blue behind the black frames of his glasses. "I've come to ask for your forgiveness."

Her eyes widened and she placed her mug down on the table quickly, so as not to spill it.

"What?"

He swallowed loudly. "I never treated you the way a friend or a lover should be treated. I was callous and selfish." He sat back in his chair and looked out the window again. "I don't expect you to forgive me. But I wanted to see you and say that I'm sorry."

Paulina tried unsuccessfully to pry her focus from his face and his clenched jaw, but she couldn't. She was almost shaking, she was so surprised.

He watched the traffic pass and waited, waiting for her to say something. But she didn't. At last, he met her gaze.

Her mouth was open, her eyes wide. Then she closed her mouth.

"We were involved for years, Gabriel, and you never once said you were sorry. Why now?"

He didn't answer, just leveled his eyes, the muscle in his jaw the only movement in his face.

"It's because of her, isn't it?"

Gabriel said nothing. Facing Paulina was difficult enough. He couldn't speak of what Julianne meant to him—of how much she'd changed him, and of how much he feared the possibility that she wouldn't forgive him when he returned to her.

He accepted Paulina's censure without argument. In his current state, he craved punishment and disapproval, for he was all too conscious of his own sin.

She watched his reaction, the emotions that moved across his face. He was in evident distress, something she'd not seen for some time.

"I moved home," she volunteered, quietly. "I enrolled in a treatment program and I'm going to meetings. I've even been seeing a counselor."

She looked at him carefully. "But you knew that, didn't you? I've been sending reports to Carson's secretary."

"I knew, yes."

"She changed you."

"Sorry?"

"She's changed you. She's—tamed you."

"This isn't about her."

"Oh, yes, it is. How long have we known each other? How long were we sleeping together? Never once did you ask me to forgive you for anything. Not even for—"

He interrupted her quickly. "I should have. I tried to make up for things with money. By taking care of you."

Gabriel winced, even as he said the words. He was familiar, all too familiar, with the type of man who would act in such a way so as to cover up his sexual indiscretions.

Paulina picked up her coffee mug once again. "Yes, you should have. But I was a fool to settle for what we were. I couldn't see my way out of it. But now I can. And I swear to God, Gabriel, I'm not going back."

She pressed her lips together, as if she were trying not to say any more. Then, unexpectedly, she continued.

"All these years, I was worried that my parents would slam the door in my face. I made sure that the taxi waited in the driveway while I rang the doorbell." She looked down at the table. "I didn't make it that far. I was trying to navigate through the snow in my high heels when the front door opened and my mother came outside. She was still in her slippers." Paulina's voice caught and her eyes welled up with tears. "She ran to me, Gabriel. She ran to me and wrapped her arms around me. I realized before I even entered the house that I could have come home years ago and she would have greeted me exactly the same way."

"The prodigal daughter," Gabriel murmured.

"Yes."

"Then you can understand my desire for forgiveness."

She regarded him, his eyes, his expression. There was nothing about him that seemed insincere.

"Yes," she said slowly. "I'm just wondering why you're asking for this now."

He retreated back into his chair, his hands clutching his mug.

"You were my friend," he whispered. "And look at how I treated you."

Paulina wiped at her eyes.

Gabriel leaned forward.

"And there's Maia."

An involuntary cry escaped Paulina's lips.

She was like him, in this respect. The mention of their child's name caused immediate anguish. When the name was used without warning, the pain was especially sharp.

"I can't talk about her." Paulina closed her eyes.

"She's happy now."

"You know I don't believe that. When you're dead, you're dead. You go to sleep and never wake up."

"I *know* that isn't true."

At Gabriel's tone, Paulina's eyes snapped open. There was something in his eyes. Something he was trying to hide, but that he clung to with more conviction than she'd ever seen him manifest before.

"I know I have no right to ask you. I know that I'm troubling you by being here." He cleared his throat. "But I had to say these things in person. I wronged you. I was monstrous. I'm sorry. Please forgive me."

Now she was crying, tears slipping from her eyes and down her perfect face.

"Stop."

"Paulina. We did this one, beautiful thing together. Let's not mourn her by living empty, wasted lives."

"How dare you! You come to me to ease your conscience and say something like that!"

Gabriel ground his teeth together.

"I'm not here to ease my conscience. I'm here to make amends."

"My baby is dead and I can't have another. Make amends for that."

He tensed. "I can't."

"You never loved me. I wasted my life on a man who merely tolerated me. And only because I was good in bed."

A muscle jumped in Gabriel's jaw.

"Paulina, you have many admirable qualities, not least of which are your intelligence, your generosity, and your sense of humor. Don't sell yourself short."

She laughed mirthlessly. "In the end, it didn't matter. No matter how smart I am, I was dumb enough to try to change you. I failed."

"I'm sorry."

"I moved on with my life and you come here to dredge it all up."

"That wasn't my intent."

"But you did it just the same." She wiped her eyes with her hands, shifting her body away from him. "You get to go home to your young, pretty girlfriend knowing that she could give you a child, if that's what you want. Vasectomies are easily reversed, but what happened to me can never be undone."

Gabriel hung his head.

"I'm sorry. For everything."

Reluctantly, he stood to his feet. He moved to walk past her, but she caught his hand.

"Wait."

Gabriel looked down at her, his eyes wary.

"I met someone. He's a professor. He helped me get a job teaching English literature while I finish my PhD by extension."

"I'm glad."

"I don't need your money. I won't be withdrawing from the trust fund again.

"Keith is a widower with two little girls. One is seven and the other is five. Can you imagine? They call me Auntie Paulina. I get to dress them and do their hair and have tea parties with their dolls. I met someone who loves me. And his girls need me. So even though I can't have a child, I'm still going to be a mother. Or at the very least, an auntie. I forgive you, Gabriel. But I won't have this conversation again. I made my peace with the past, as much as I can."

"Agreed."

She gave him a genuine smile, and he brushed his lips against the top of her head.

"Good-bye, Paulina. Be happy."

He released her hand and walked away.

Chapter Forty

August 2011
Cambridge, Massachusetts

Going for a run?" Julia glanced up from the breakfast table to see Gabriel clad in his jogging clothes and shoes. He was wearing a crimson Harvard T-shirt and black shorts that hung loosely from his hips.

"That's right." He crossed the room in order to kiss her.

"So—are we going to talk soon?"

Gabriel turned away and began disentangling the earphones that connected with his iPhone. "About what?"

"About what's bothering you?"

"Not right now, no." He removed his sunglasses from their case and quickly cleaned them with the fabric of his shirt.

Julia bit her tongue, for her patience was almost at an end.

"Have you made an appointment to see your doctor?"

"Here we go," he muttered, placing his palms flat on the kitchen island and leaning into them, head bent and eyes closed.

"What's that supposed to mean?" She crossed her arms over her chest.

He didn't move.

"No, I haven't called the doctor."

"Why not?"

"Because I don't need to see him."

She uncrossed her arms. "But what about the vasectomy reversal? You'll need to speak with him about that."

"No, I won't." He straightened, nonchalantly picking up his sunglasses and placing them on his face.

"Why not?"

"I'm not having my vasectomy reversed. I'd like us to pursue adoption. I know we can't adopt Maria, but I'd like us to look into adopting a child when you graduate."

"You've decided," she breathed.

A muscle jumped in his jaw.

"I'm protecting you."

"But what about all our conversations? What about what we talked about in the orchard?"

"I was wrong."

"You were *wrong*?" She scrambled to her feet. "Gabriel, what the hell is going on?"

"Can we please not do this right now?" He began walking toward the door.

"Gabriel, I—"

"When I get back," he interrupted. "Give me thirty minutes."

She bit back an angry response.

"Just tell me one thing."

He paused, looking at her through his sunglasses.

"What's that?"

"Do you still love me?"

His expression grew pained. "I've never loved you more."

And with that, he opened the door and fled into the warm morning air.

❧❧

"How was your run?" Julia greeted a hot and sweaty Gabriel as he entered the kitchen.

"Good. I'm just going to take a shower."

"Care for some company?"

He gave her a half-smile. "After you."

Julia preceded him up the stairs and they entered the master bedroom together.

He sat on a chair, pulling off his shoes and socks and peeling away his shirt.

"Did running clear your head?" She studied him intently. The sheen of perspiration was visible on his tanned skin, his muscles rippling with every movement.

"Somewhat."

"Tell me what's troubling you."

He sighed loudly, squeezing his eyes shut. Then he nodded and she sat on the edge of the bed, waiting.

He placed his forearms on his knees, leaning forward. "My whole life I've been self-centered. I don't know how anyone could stand to be near me."

"Gabriel," she reproached him. "You're eminently lovable. That's why women fall at your feet."

"I don't care about that. It's all based on appearances. They wouldn't care if I was selfish so long as I gave them a good fuck."

Julia grimaced.

"I know you. I know all of you and I don't think you're selfish."

"I pursued you when you were my student. I was terrible to my family and to Paulina," he countered.

Julia looked over into darkened, tortured eyes.

"That's in the past. We don't need to speak of it."

"Of course we need to speak of it." He placed his head in his hands, gripping his hair. "Don't you understand? I'm still being selfish. I could hurt you."

"How?"

"What if Paulina's miscarriage was my fault?"

Julia's stomach lurched.

"Gabriel, we talked about this. It wasn't anyone's fault."

"It was my fault I was out on a bender all weekend. If I'd been home to care for her, I could have taken her to the hospital."

"Please don't go down that road again. You know where it leads."

He kept his eyes on the floor. "It leads to the conversation we had in the orchard."

"The orchard?"

"I've been talking to you about having a baby. But I never stopped to think about it in light of what happened with Paulina."

"Gabriel, please. I—"

He interrupted her. "What if her miscarriage was the result of a genetic abnormality? Something I contributed?"

Julia was stunned into silence.

"I told you I wanted a child. But I never stopped to think about the risks."

"Miscarriages are common, Gabriel. It's tragic, but it's true. Have mercy on yourself. There's a reason why you had that dream about Maia. Accept the peace she offered you and let it go."

"What if the same thing happens to us?" His voice broke on the last word. "Look at what your father and Diane are going through."

"It would be devastating. But this is the world we live in. There's illness and death. We can't pretend we're immune."

"We can avoid unacceptable risks."

Julia's eyes grew sad. "So now you don't want a baby with me?"

He lifted his head to see tears in her eyes.

"All this talk of Paulina." Julia swallowed hard. "I know I shouldn't be jealous, but I envy her. You shared a life-changing experience with her that we might not be able to have."

"I thought you'd be relieved."

"Nothing in what you've said brings relief." She searched his eyes. "And you certainly don't look happy."

"That's because I want what I can't have. I can't go through what I went through with Paulina again. I can't and I won't. I won't let that happen to you."

"No children," she whispered.

"We'll adopt."

"So that's it."

He nodded.

Julia closed her eyes, letting the implication of his words wash over her. She thought of their future, of the images she'd daydreamed about. She thought about telling Gabriel that she was pregnant, about carrying his child inside her body, about holding his hand while she gave birth to a son . . .

All the images vanished as if in a puff of smoke. Julia felt the loss immediately. She hadn't realized how much she wanted to have those experiences and to share them with him. Now that he was telling her she couldn't, she felt pain.

"No."

"No?" His eyebrows lifted.

"You want to protect me, and that's admirable. But let's be clear, there's something else."

"I don't want to see you hurt."

"It goes deeper than that, doesn't it? It's wrapped up in what happened between your father and your mother."

Gabriel stood up, dropping his shorts to the floor. He turned away, standing naked before her.

She cleared her throat. "Sweetheart, I know that you have scars. You can't even look at the things in your desk drawer."

"This isn't about that. This is about choosing the risks I'm willing to take. Your father could lose Diane and the baby. I'm not prepared to take that risk."

"Life is risk. I could get cancer. Or get hit by a car. You could wrap me in bubble wrap and keep me indoors and I could still get sick. I know that I could lose you too. And as much as I don't want to say it, someday you're going to die." Her voice broke on the last word. "But I choose to love you now and I choose to build a life with you knowing I could lose you. I'm asking you to make that same choice. I'm asking you to take the risk, with me."

She moved to him and took his hand in hers.

He looked down at their entwined fingers. "We don't know what the risks might be. I have no idea what's in my medical history."

"We can be tested."

He squeezed her hand before releasing it.

"That isn't enough."

"Some of your relatives are still alive. You could try to speak with them, find out about the medical history of your parents and grandparents."

He scowled. "Do you think I would give them the satisfaction of crawling after them, begging for information? I'd rather burn in Hell."

"Listen to yourself. You're right back where you started—thinking that you aren't good enough to reproduce. And refusing to find out if there are any obvious issues in your family tree. What about your dream about Maia? What about Assisi? What about me, Gabriel? We prayed for a child. We've been praying that God would give us our own child. Are you taking back that prayer?"

He clenched his fists at his sides but didn't respond.

"All because you don't think you're good enough," she whispered. "My beautiful, broken angel."

She wrapped her arms around his neck.

Gabriel let out an anguished sound as he returned her embrace.

"I'm making you dirty," he whispered, his sweat-slicked chest pressing against her blouse.

"You've never been cleaner." She tenderly kissed his stubbled jaw.

They held one another before Julia led him to the bathroom. Without words, she turned on the shower and quickly divested herself of her clothing.

He followed her inside the shower.

The water was warm and it fell like rain, bouncing and dancing over their bodies and down to the floor. Julia poured soap into her hands and began to wash Gabriel's chest, her palms gliding lightly over his pectorals.

He wrapped a hand around her wrist. "What are you doing?"

"I'm trying to show you how much I love you." She pressed her lips to his tattoo and then continued, lathering his abdomen with her hands. "I seem to remember a beautiful man doing this for me once. It was like a baptism."

They were silent as she explored the steel and sinew of his arms and legs, the firmness of his backside and the bumps of his spine. She took her time, gently touching him until all the suds had rinsed away.

His eyes pierced hers. "I've hurt you, again and again. Yet you're so giving. Why?"

"Because I love you. Because I have compassion for you. Because I forgive you."

He closed his eyes and shook his head.

Julia began washing his hair, coaxing him to lean forward so she could reach every dark strand.

"God hasn't punished me yet," he murmured.

"What are you talking about?"

"I keep waiting for him to take you away."

She brushed the shampoo from his eyes so he could open them.

"That isn't how God works."

"I've lived an arrogant, selfish life. Why shouldn't he punish me?"

"God isn't hovering above us waiting to punish us."

"No?" His eyes were tortured.

"No. Did you ever once feel that way when we were in Assisi? When we were sitting near St. Francis's crypt?"

He shook his head.

"God wants to rescue us, not destroy us. You don't have to be afraid of being happy, thinking that he wants to take that happiness away from you. That's not who he is."

"How can you be sure?"

"Because when you've had a taste of goodness, it helps you recognize the difference between good and evil. I believe that people like Grace and St. Francis and a whole host of other kind, loving people show us what God is like. He isn't waiting to punish you and he doesn't give you blessings just to strip them away."

She slid her hands up his chest until they rested on either side of his face.

"I'm not going to let you delay having your vasectomy reversed. Whatever you discover, whatever happened, you're my husband. I want a family with you and I don't care what your DNA says."

His fingers encircled her forearms.

"I thought you weren't ready to have a baby."

"I'm not. But I agree with what you said in the orchard. If we want to have a baby, we need to start discussing it with the doctors."

"What about adoption?"

"We can do both. But please, Gabriel, you need to have the procedure reversed if only to show that you believe you will be a good father. And that you aren't a prisoner of your history. I believe in you, sweetheart. How I wish you believed in yourself."

He stood under the spray of the shower, closing his eyes and letting the water run over his head. He released her, running his hands through his hair before stepping aside.

Julia took his hands in hers.

"These hands are yours. You can use them for good, or for evil. And no amount of nature, biology, or DNA determines those decisions for you."

"I'm an alcoholic because my mother was. That wasn't a choice."

"You chose to go into recovery. Every day, you choose not to drink or to use drugs. It isn't your mother or AA that's making that choice—it's you."

"But what will I pass on to our children?" His voice sounded desperate. "I have no idea what's in my family tree."

"My mother was an alcoholic. If you're going to focus on family history, you should ask what I'm going to pass on."

"The only things you could pass on would be beauty and kindness and love."

She smiled sadly. "That's what I was going to say to you. I saw how the children at the orphanage reacted to you. I saw you laughing and playing with them. And taking Maria for a pony ride. You will give our children love, protection, and care. You will give them a home and a family. And you won't cast them out when they make a mistake, or stop loving them when they sin. You will love them so desperately you'd die for them. That's what a father does. And that's what you will do."

His eyes lasered into hers. "You're very fierce."

"Only when I'm protecting someone I love. Or when I'm fighting to stop an injustice. Your giving in to those old lies would be unjust. You've done so much to help me, Gabriel. Now it's my turn. If you want to forget about your family, I'll support you. If you want to trace every branch of your family tree, I'll help. But don't let guilt and fear rob you of your choices. You made the decision to have the procedure reversed. I think you should stick to it. Even if we decide we want to expand our family through adoption."

"It would be easier for me to forget about my family. But I can't try to have a child with you without knowing more about them—at least to discover any obvious health concerns."

"It won't be easy. But you'll have someone beside you, supporting you. Right now your past has power over you because you don't know what's there. Once you know, you won't have to worry about it anymore. Take a risk with me, Gabriel."

He buried his face in her neck.

Of all the gifts God gave me, he thought, *the greatest one is you.*

Chapter Forty-one

Although Gabriel's concerns were not entirely assuaged by Julianne's words, he felt relieved. Her belief in him, her love for him, chipped away at his self-doubt. Truly he was blessed beyond all reason to find such a lover, such a wife. When she'd looked into his eyes and said she wanted him to reverse the procedure whether they planned to have a baby or not . . . Gabriel would remember that moment for the rest of his life.

A proverb from the Hebrew Bible came to his mind: *Whoso findeth a wife findeth a great good.*

It was at night, when he felt tortured by his past and fearful for his future, that his hope was shaken. Rather than leaving her side to haunt the house in search of alcohol, Gabriel resolved to wrap his arms around her and hold on. His brown-eyed angel didn't eliminate his concerns. But she gave him the strength he needed in order to fight.

The day after their shower, she'd found him in his study on the second floor, poring over a pile of books, his laptop open on the desk.

"Hi." She entered the study, carrying a glass of Coke. "I brought you a drink."

He regarded her appreciatively. "Thank you, darling."

He patted his lap and she placed the drink on the desk before joining him.

"Did you put this here?" He gestured at the toy train engine, which was now sitting atop a stack of files.

"Yes." She squirmed, wondering how she was going to explain herself.

"I'd forgotten about it. It makes a good paperweight."

"I should have asked before I went through your things."

He shrugged. “It was time. The train was one of my favorite toys as a child.”

“It looks like an antique. Where did it come from?”

Gabriel scratched at his chin. “I want to say that it came from my father. I seem to remember him giving it to me. But that can’t be right.”

Julia offered him a sympathetic look.

“What are you working on?”

“My book. I’m writing a section on Hell. I think I’ll include some remarks on the Guido story. I’ll cite your paper as an authority, of course.” He kissed her.

“That will be easier to do now that my paper is being published.”

“Really?”

“I received an email from the conference organizers telling me that a European press has agreed to publish a few of the papers. They want me to submit mine.”

“Your first publication. Congratulations.” Gabriel hugged her tightly, a feeling of pride washing over him.

“It will be a great line item for my CV.” She toyed with his glasses. “But I’m going to need a favor.”

“Anything.”

She lifted her eyebrows. “Anything?”

“For you, my love, I would endeavor to pluck the stars from the sky, only to shower them at your feet.”

Julia pressed her hand over her heart. “How do you do that?’

“Do what?”

“Say things like that. That’s beautiful.”

He offered her a half-smile. “I’ve spent years studying poetry, Mrs. Emerson. It’s in my DNA.”

“It certainly is.” She wrapped her arms around his neck and kissed him determinedly.

Their embrace grew heated. Gabriel was about to sweep his books from his desk and lay Julianne out on top of it when she remembered she was there to ask him a favor.

“Um, sweetie?”

“Yes?” His voice was a half groan as his hands roamed up and down her sides.

“I need to ask you something.”

"Go ahead."

"My paper is going to need some revisions before I send it in. They want the manuscript the first week of December. Will you read it and make some suggestions?"

Her expression telegraphed her trepidation. They'd had a fight about that paper a few months previous. She didn't want to fight with him about it again.

"Of course. It would be my pleasure. I'll try not to be a bastard when I give you my comments."

She grinned wryly. "I'd appreciate that."

"Now, can we have desk sex or do you want to chat all afternoon?"

"Desk sex, please."

"Your wish is my command."

Gabriel removed his glasses, tossing them aside. He closed his laptop and placed it on a nearby shelf before carefully removing the train engine. Then with one sweep of his arm, he sent all the books and papers to the floor before placing Julia on top of the desk.

Then they spent the next hour engaged in a new kind of marital bliss—desk sex.

(Desk sex can be very, very good, but it's important to remove the staplers first.)

Later, Julia began packing for their trip to Tom and Diane's wedding, while Gabriel remained in his office, trying to write. He found it difficult to concentrate on Guido da Montefeltro at the site of his most recent (and very passionate) encounter with Julianne.

I might never be able to work at this desk again.

Frustrated, he closed the document he was working on and pulled up his email. He typed a short note to Carson Brown, his lawyer, asking that he begin making inquiries about his biological parents and their families.

Then he lifted his cell phone and dialed a number.

Julia entered the bedroom after spending the evening revising her conference paper. Her eyes hurt. She had decided that Paul was right—she was suffering from some kind of eyestrain and needed to see an optometrist. She resolved to make an appointment when she and Gabriel returned from Selinsgrove.

"What's the matter?" Gabriel's voice reached her from the bed.

She pulled her hands away from her face. He was sitting up, wearing his glasses, and reading.

She gave him a sheepish look.

"I was on the computer too long and now my eyes hurt. I'm going to have them checked when we get back."

"Good. Your eyes are so beautiful, it would be shame for them to be injured." He put a finger in the book that he was reading and extended his other hand to pat the area beside him. "Come here."

Julia joined him on the bed, noticing that he'd been reading his mother's diary.

"What made you decide to read that?"

"Since I'm beginning my investigation of my family, I thought I shouldn't put it off."

"Is it making you sad?"

He put the diary aside and rubbed his eyes behind his glasses.

"It's tragic more than anything else. She graduated from high school and moved into the city to share an apartment with a girlfriend. Her first job was working for my father's company. One of his secretaries went on maternity leave and she filled in temporarily. That's how they met."

"She was young." Julia clasped her hand in his.

He glanced down at their connection. "Almost as young as you when I met you. Funny how history repeats itself."

"Don't," Julia said, in a low voice. "You could have gone down that road. But you didn't. We're different."

"I went down that road with someone else."

Julia felt her anger flame. "You didn't abandon Paulina. You cared for her for years. You are not the kind of man who would abandon your child."

"Say that again." Gabriel's voice was a cross between a growl and a plea.

Julia reached up to remove his glasses, lying across his body to place them on the nightstand. Then she lifted her face, still reclining over him.

"Gabriel Emerson, you are not the kind of man who would abandon your child. And as much as you might think of yourself as the seducer, we both know our seduction was mutual."

He stroked her hair lightly before lifting her chin and bringing their lips together.

"Our seduction was most definitely mutual. You're the only woman who ever persuaded me to give my heart. And you still seduce me, Mrs. Emerson. Every day."

Gabriel stroked her hair again.

"It sounds as if my parents' affair started while they were working long hours together. One night, he kissed her. Things progressed . . ."

"Did he love her?"

"He said he did. He bought her extravagant gifts. He wouldn't be seen in public with her, but they'd meet at hotels."

Julia fingered her necklace unconsciously.

"I saw some of the jewelry in your desk. There are things from Tiffany and what looks like a wedding band."

Gabriel scowled. "He gave her that ring when I was born. She used to wear it and pretend she was married. What a farce."

"It's possible he did it to protect her."

"Julianne, nothing my father did protected her." His voice was cold. "She was young and had lived a sheltered life with her family. She expected he'd leave his wife and family for her. Obviously that didn't happen."

Julia tightened her arms around him. "What have you done to find out more about your family?"

"I sent an email to Carson, asking him to make inquiries about the Emersons and about my father." He cleared his throat. "I made a few phone calls today and was able to schedule an appointment with Dr. Townsend. And a urologist."

"I'm proud of you. I know you're anxious. But no matter what you discover, we'll face it together."

He sighed and brought his hand up to cup the back of her head.

"If you're serious about learning more about your mother, I'll help you."

She turned to lie on her back, staring up at the ceiling.

"My father has her stuff. I don't think it's a good idea to ask about it. He's got a lot on his mind."

"You're right. Have you heard from him?"

"Diane sent me an email about my bridesmaid dress. I'm supposed to pick it up when we arrive."

Julia was quiet for a moment, thinking. Then she spoke.

"Do you think God has forgiven you?"

His brow furrowed. "Why would you ask me that?"

"Because of our conversation in the shower. You seem to think your past hasn't really been forgiven."

He shifted next to her.

"When I was in Assisi, after we'd been separated, it felt as if God forgave me."

"But you still look at yourself and don't like what you see?" Her tone was gentle.

"Why should I? I have so many faults."

"So do all human beings, sweetheart."

"Maybe I'm more conscious of my own sin."

"Maybe you haven't accepted the grace and forgiveness you've been offered."

He looked at her sharply.

She moved closer to him.

"I'm not saying this to grieve you. I see how far you've come, and it's nothing short of a miracle. But part of that miracle is recognizing the magnitude of the grace."

"I did so many terrible things," he whispered.

"And God's forgiveness is so small." Julia glanced at him out of the corner of her eye.

"I don't think that."

"But you act like that sometimes—as if you're still in Hell. As if God couldn't forgive you."

"I want to be better."

"Then be better. Accept the fact that God didn't bring you this far only to abandon you. He isn't that kind of father. And you won't be, either."

Gabriel pondered her words for a moment.

"If what you say is correct, then you have no reason to fear being a mother. No matter what happened with Sharon or what's in your past, grace is available to you too. I guess we both need to overcome our fears."

He caressed her cheek before rolling her beneath him.

"You will be a wonderful mother," he whispered before bringing their lips together.

Chapter Forty-two

Labor Day Weekend, 2011
The Hamptons, New York

Holy fuck!" Simon exclaimed, collapsing on top of her.

"Holy fuck is right." She giggled, wrapping her arms around him. "That was amazing."

Simon couldn't disagree. He could barely feel his body, his orgasm had been so strong.

Of course, the fact that he and April Hudson were several mojitos past being drunk might have had something to do with it.

In the back of his mind, there was something he was supposed to remember. Something important. Something regarding April.

She climbed on top of him. "Let's do it again," she slurred, leaning over him. "It barely hurt. I don't know why I was waiting . . ."

Chapter Forty-three

Labor Day Weekend, 2011
Selinsgrove, Pennsylvania

"Your dad has been using this room as the guest room, but we were thinking of making it the nursery." Diane opened the door to the small room that was next to the master bedroom.

Julia entered the room behind her, carrying a blue-and-white gift bag.

It was a few days before the wedding and she was helping Diane with things around the house.

"I wanted to paint the walls and have the room ready before the baby came. Now . . ." Diane moved her hand over her abdomen, back and forth.

"I don't see why you can't get the nursery ready." Julia looked around the room, eyeing three familiar-looking boxes on the floor of the closet.

"He might not come home," Diane whispered, close to tears.

Julia put an arm around her shoulders.

"The hospital and the doctors are familiar with cases like this. And there are a number of children who've gone through the surgeries that little Peanut will have to go through."

"Peanut?"

"Since we don't have a name for him, I've been calling him Peanut."

Diane pressed her hand over her stomach. "I like that. Peanut."

"We're all hoping and praying that Peanut will be okay. Decorating the nursery could be an expression of that hope—that you believe he's coming home." Julia fidgeted with the bag she'd been carrying. "I bought you and the baby a present."

"Thank you. That's the first gift we've received."

"Since he's my little brother, I wanted to be the first. Open it."

Diane carefully pulled back the tissue paper, revealing a rectangular wrapped object. She placed the bag on the floor and unwrapped the gift. Inside, she found a print of a cherub playing a guitar, housed in an ornate gold frame.

She held it up in order to admire it.

"I know that you've been hesitant about preparing for the baby." Julia's voice was soft. "But I thought that the angel would be an expression of hope. The painting is called *Angelo Musicante* and it's housed in the Uffizi Gallery in Florence."

"Thank you, honey." Diane hugged her. "That's very sweet."

She walked over to the window and placed the frame on the wide windowsill, leaning against the glass. It looked as if it belonged there.

"Your dad was talking about using your room as the guest room, once the baby comes."

"It isn't really my room. I grew up in Dad's old house."

"You're my daughter. You'll always have a room in my house." A gruff voice sounded behind them.

Diane and Julia turned to see Tom standing in the doorway.

"That's nice, Dad, but you don't have to save a room for me."

"It's your room." His tone and expression brooked no argument.

Julia merely sighed and nodded.

She gestured to the walls, which were white. "Have you picked out colors?"

Diane smiled. "Pale blue and red. I was thinking about having a sailboat theme. Maybe painting a mural of a boat on the wall. I thought it would be soothing."

"That sounds beautiful. I'll look for some bedding and things with sailboats on them."

"Thank you."

"I'll make sure my little brother has everything he needs. I'm looking forward to spoiling him."

Tom's eyes watered. But he would never admit it.

"So you're going to decorate?" he asked his fiancée.

"I think we should do a few things. Maybe not everything. After the honeymoon we could paint the walls." Diane looked up into his face, her eyes cautiously hopeful.

"Whatever you want." Tom leaned over to kiss her, pressing his palm lightly over where their child was growing.

Julia moved to the door, wanting to give them some privacy. "I'll just go downstairs and see what Gabriel and Uncle Jack are doing."

"Sorry, sweetie." Diane pulled away from her fiancé, but not before moving her hand gently over where his hand had rested.

"Would you like to take those with you? I think they belonged to your mother." Diane pointed at the boxes that were sitting in the closet.

The air in the room swiftly changed as Tom and Julia followed the path of her finger.

"What?" Tom's tone was sharp.

"They're just sitting there. Maybe there's something she'd like to take home with her to Massachusetts. But if you don't want them or you don't want them now, that's fine. I opened them just to see what they were, but I closed them back up again. I came across them when I was emptying this room out."

"I'd like to look at Mom's stuff." Julia was conscious of her father's fists opening and closing.

"I'm not all fired up about having this conversation three days before my wedding," Tom growled.

"Honey," Diane reproached him.

"All right. Why don't you ask Gabriel to come up and help me carry them down to your car?"

Julia nodded and exited the room, but not before seeing her father pull Diane into his arms.

As she descended the staircase to the front hall, she heard voices coming out of the living room.

"You tell her yet?" Julia's Uncle Jack, Tom's brother, was speaking.

"No." Gabriel's tone was clipped.

"You going to?" Jack's gruff voice grew louder.

"Since everything has been quiet, I haven't seen the need. She's been upset enough recently. I'm not about to add to it."

"She better not be living in fear."

"She isn't." Gabriel sounded impatient.

"I find she is, you and me got a problem."

Julia's footsteps echoed across the hardwood floor and the voices stopped.

She entered the living room and saw Jack standing by the far wall, his form menacing.

Gabriel was standing a few feet away, having adopted a similar posture.

"What's going on?" she asked.

Gabriel lifted his arm and she went to him, curling into his side. "Nothing. Did you help Diane?"

"A little. But I need your help now. I have a few boxes I need to carry out to the car."

"Absolutely." Gabriel gave Jack a significant look as he followed Julia into the hall.

❧❧

The day before the wedding, Julia agreed to help Diane's sister, the maid of honor, by running errands. She visited the florist to double-check the order, she visited the church hall to inspect the decorations, and she stopped in at Kinfolks restaurant.

Kinfolks would not have been her choice as the location of the rehearsal dinner, but since it was a place that held sentimental value for both the bride and groom, she kept her opinion to herself.

She'd just finished her meeting with the owner and the manager, ascertaining that everything would be ready for that evening, when she ran into Deb Lundy, her father's ex-girlfriend, and Natalie, her daughter.

Julia tried to plaster an artificial smile on her face as Deb approached her.

"Hello, Jules. I haven't seen you in a long time."

"Hi, Deb. How are you?"

"Just fine. Natalie is home for the weekend and we've been doing some shopping." Deb lifted the numerous bags that she was carrying.

Julia's gaze moved nervously from the tall blond woman to her daughter, who was standing some feet away with a sour expression on her face. Both women were dressed in expensive clothing and obviously designer sandals. Both women clutched large Louis Vuitton handbags.

Natalie was an attractive young woman, with red hair and green eyes. She and Julia had been roommates at Saint Joseph's University. They'd even been friends. But that was before Natalie decided to sleep with Julia's then-boyfriend, Simon, and invite her to join them in a threesome.

"Natalie was supposed to be in the Hamptons this weekend with her boyfriend. You remember him, don't you? Simon Talbot, the senator's son?"

"I know who he is." Julia resisted the urge to comment further. Deb knew exactly who Simon was to Julia and that he'd been arrested for assaulting her two years previous. Sadly, the arrest had yielded only a plea agreement and community service.

Ignoring Julia's obvious discomfort, Deb prattled on.

"Mrs. Talbot became ill and so their trip to the Hamptons was canceled. But I'm glad Natalie was able to come home. We see so little of her now that she's working for the senator's presidential campaign. She has a very important job."

"Congratulations," said Julia, trying to keep the contempt out of her voice.

Natalie ignored Julia and turned to her mother. "We need to go."

Julia watched her former roommate curiously. The last time they'd seen one another was in this very restaurant. Natalie had cornered her and shown her a clip from a video that Simon had made. A video that showed Julia in a compromising position. Natalie had threatened to post the video on the Internet if Julia didn't withdraw the assault charges against Simon.

In a surprising turn of events, Julia had stood her ground. She even threatened to go to *The Washington Post* and tell them that Simon had sent his new girlfriend to blackmail her. The senator would not have been pleased.

At the time, Natalie seemed skeptical that Julia would carry through on her threat. But she must have changed her mind. There was no evidence that the video had been shared or posted anywhere. It was as if they'd given up.

Julia wondered occasionally why she hadn't heard from them. But she decided to count herself lucky and simply accept her good fortune.

Seeing Natalie now, Julia expected her to be rude or aggressive. She expected Natalie to offer veiled threats or innuendo. Instead, she appeared agitated, shifting her weight back and forth and glancing at the door. It was as if she were afraid of something.

Julia didn't see any intimidating people in the restaurant or outside on the sidewalk. She wondered what was bothering Natalie. And why her smugness and superiority had been magically eliminated.

Deb gestured to her daughter to wait.

"It was good seeing you, Jules. I hear your dad is getting married again."

"Tomorrow, yes."

"Never thought he was the marrying kind. I guess old age will do that to you."

Julia lifted an eyebrow. Deb was at least as old as her father, if not a year or two older. But she had no wish to be drawn into a confrontation.

"Let's go." Natalie tugged on her mother's arm, and the two women walked toward the door.

Julia watched their departing backs with the distinct sense that she was missing something. Something important.

❧❧

"Aren't you exhausted?" Rachel leaned over the kitchen island two days later and rested her head on her outstretched arm. "We were out late the night of the rehearsal dinner, and out late last night at the wedding. I need more sleep."

Julia laughed as she shucked corn for dinner. "I guess it's a good thing I had a nap this afternoon."

Rachel rolled her eyes. "Sure you did. Gabriel said he napped this afternoon, too, but he's never napped a day in his life. I doubt he naps when you're in bed with him."

The color rose in Julia's cheeks, and she focused intently on the corn as she changed the subject. "The wedding was beautiful. I can't believe I got to dance with my dad at his wedding."

"I don't think I have the energy to celebrate your birthday tonight, Jules. I'm sorry I'm a bad friend." Rachel's voice was muffled by a yawn.

"Why don't you go and take a nap?"

"I tried. Like you, my husband followed me. Ergo, no nap but lots of babymaking."

Julia snickered. "How is that coming along?"

Rachel slumped forward dramatically. "I need a vacation."

"From babymaking?"

She groaned, eyes shut.

"Yes, damn it. We're having sex all the time but I'm not getting pregnant. It's depressing." She opened her eyes and rested her head on an upturned hand. "I need a break. Let me come and visit for a few days. I won't be a bother, I promise."

"I thought you wanted a baby."

"I do, but at what cost? I never thought I'd say this, but we're having too much sex. I'm beginning to feel like a machine."

"Good God, what have I wandered into?" Gabriel's eyebrows knitted together as he entered the kitchen from the back porch.

"Nothing. Your sister is just worn out. Rachel, skip dinner and go lie down in our room. You can join us for dessert."

"Really?"

Julia waved a cob of corn in the direction of the stairs. "Go."

Like a shot, Rachel was off her stool and flying through the door.

Gabriel watched her departing form and shook his head. "Tell me we aren't going to be like that."

"We aren't going to be like that." Julia pressed a kiss to his temple.

"Promise?"

"Promise."

"You convinced me to pursue a reversal, no matter what. And you've almost convinced me that my family history doesn't matter."

"It doesn't, sweetheart. Believe me."

He took the corn out of her hand and set it aside before clasping her hands in his.

"We can't get our hopes up. It's been almost ten years since my vasectomy."

"I'd be happy adopting. But for your own sake, I want us to try. Eventually. And with less drama than what we're seeing with Rachel and Aaron."

Gabriel laughed and pulled her into his arms.

Julia snuggled against him, her mouth opening wide into a sustained yawn.

Gabriel eyed her with concern. "Why don't you go and take a nap?"

"There's too much to do."

"Nonsense. Richard is reading a book on the back porch and Aaron is snoring in front of the television. I think we'll be having a late dinner."

"I gave our room to Rachel."

"Then use the couch in the study." He pressed his lips to her forehead. "They worked you pretty hard at the rehearsal and the wedding. You could use a nap." He winked. "Since you didn't have one this afternoon."

Julia kissed him and exited the kitchen.

Left to his own devices, Gabriel retrieved a small leather book from his briefcase and went outside to join Richard on the porch.

"It's a beautiful day," Richard remarked, closing his crime novel.

"Yes." Gabriel sat down in the Adirondack chair next to his adoptive father's.

"What are you reading?"

Gabriel showed him the book, on which the word *Journal* was embossed on the front in gold lettering. "It's my mother's diary."

The two men exchanged a look.

"I found something in it from Grace." Gabriel unfolded two pages that had been tucked inside the journal.

Richard gazed on the papers with interest.

"What are they?"

"Names, addresses, and telephone numbers. One is for my father. The other is for Jean Emerson of Staten Island. She's my grandmother."

"Is this the first time you've seen those pages?" Richard made eye contact with his son.

"Yes. Grace gave me my mother's things when I was a teenager. But I never looked at them."

Richard nodded, a look of recollection on his face.

Gabriel peered at Grace's handwriting. "I'm wondering why she did this."

"I'm positive we spoke to you about this when you were a teenager. Don't you remember?"

Gabriel's attention momentarily fixated on the woods behind the house.

"Only bits and pieces."

"When your mother died, social services located your grandmother and asked her to take you. She refused. Grace telephoned her, trying to figure out what the problem was. After she spoke to your grandmother, she placed her name and address with your mother's things, thinking that you might want to contact her one day."

"I don't remember Grace telling me that she spoke with my grandmother, just that social services located my relatives and they didn't want anything to do with me."

Richard frowned.

"You were only a boy. There was no point in burdening you with everything that happened. I thought that we disclosed the details when you were older."

Gabriel shook his head.

Richard's mouth tightened. "I apologize. We should have told you."

"You don't have anything to apologize for. You and Grace took me in when my own flesh and blood disowned me."

"You are our son." Richard's voice grew husky. "You have always been our son."

Gabriel's hands gripped the journal more tightly.

"Will it—offend you if I try to find out more about my biological parents?"

"Of course not. It's your heritage and you have a right to know about it."

"You're my dad," Gabriel observed quietly.

"Always," said Richard. "And no matter what."

"I put you and Grace at risk. You mortgaged your home to rescue me."

"A parent's love isn't conditional. No matter what you did, you were always our son. I simply prayed that one day you'd come back to us. And you did."

Gabriel's knee began to bounce in agitation.

Richard's gray eyes grew very intense as he watched him.

"We didn't give birth to you, but you are our son. You belonged with us."

"What did Grace say to my grandmother?"

Richard sat back in his chair.

"I think she explained who she was and what happened to your mother. I know she talked about you. She hoped she could reason with your family."

"And could she?"

"No." Richard appeared grim. "Your grandmother was too blinded by her own morality and her anger with her daughter. She disowned your mother when she became pregnant, and I doubt they saw one another after that."

"What about my father? Did Grace call him too?"

Richard shifted his weight. "I know we spoke to you about this because it came up in connection with your birth certificate. Your father persuaded your mother not to list him, which is why it only names your mother."

"So how did Grace find him?"

"Through your grandmother. She wasn't in a hurry to help her grandson, but she was eager enough to name your father. She had his address and telephone number, which is probably what you have there." Richard gestured toward the diary. "Grace knew better than to call him at home. She called him at the office. He refused to speak with her."

"I can recall Grace saying that my father knew where I was but that he wasn't coming to get me."

"She hoped your relatives would welcome you, which is why she called them."

"Grace thought the best of everyone."

"She did. But she was no fool. After speaking with your grandmother and trying in vain to talk to your father, she let it go. You've been with us ever since." He looked at Gabriel sadly. "Grace expected that she would be here when you found those pages. I know she would have wanted to talk to you about them."

"I should have looked at them earlier."

He thought for a moment about the vision he had of Grace and how she'd forgiven him. He still mourned her.

"Julianne is very fond of you." Gabriel changed the subject, if only to free himself of his painful musings.

"As I am of her. I have her and you to thank for allowing me to come home."

"This will always be your home." Gabriel shifted in his chair. "She thinks that if God is like a father, he must be like you."

Richard chuckled. "A high compliment, but an unwarranted one. I'm imperfect like everyone else."

"Would that I could have one quarter of your imperfection," Gabriel muttered, lowering his head.

"Grace and I always thought of you as a gift. But since she died, I've realized something even more profound."

Gabriel lifted his head, turning to look at his father.

"I know that you feel some sort of gratitude to us for adopting you—as if we did you a favor. But you're looking at things the wrong way."

Richard's eyes met Gabriel's.

"God gave you to us because he knew we needed you."

The two men exchanged a long look before gazing out at the orchard and losing themselves in silence. And if anyone had commented on the fact that Gabriel's eyes were wet, he would have said it was because of his allergies.

Chapter Forty-four

September 9, 2011
Durham, North Carolina

April Hudson exited her apartment building with the intention of driving to campus, but she was stopped abruptly by a man carrying roses.

"Hi," he said, smiling.

"Simon!" She ran to him, wrapping her arms around his neck and squealing. "What are you doing here?"

"I came to see you. And to give you these." He lifted the dozen long-stemmed red roses he held in his left hand.

"They're beautiful. Thank you." She jumped up and down and hugged him.

He laughed at her exuberance and returned her embrace, burying his nose in her long, blond hair.

"I was worried I wouldn't see you again. Do you want to come in?" she murmured against his neck.

He nodded, and she led him to the elevator.

"These are really beautiful." She held the bouquet close to her face, inhaling the scent. "And you chose red this time. The first time we went out, you bought white."

"White symbolizes virginity." He reached out to touch her long, straight hair. "That doesn't apply anymore."

She cringed as if he'd struck her and quickly handed him back the flowers.

He was going to ask what the problem was when the elevator door opened. She stepped around him and walked quickly to her apartment, her flip-flops snapping down the hall.

"April? Wait up." He jogged after her, still clutching the bouquet.

She pulled her keys out of her backpack and opened the door to her apartment. She moved behind the door as if she were going to close it in his face.

"Wait a second." He placed his palm against the door, holding it open.

"Look, you didn't have to fly all the way down here and give me flowers just to gloat. I know I'm not a virgin anymore."

"What are you talking about? I'm not here to gloat."

"Did you tell all your friends? I'm sure they had a big laugh over it. Take the nice Christian girl out a couple of times and she gives it up like it's prom night."

"That isn't what happened." Simon glared.

"After we spent the weekend together, you didn't contact me. No phone calls, no texts. Now it's the weekend and you show up on my doorstep. Did you fly all the way down here for a booty call?"

"Of course not. If you'd let me explain, I—"

"I'm not a booty call, Simon. Take your red roses and go back to Washington. I can't keep you from bragging about what happened, but it would be nice if you let me tell my parents first. I don't want my father reading in the newspaper about how I got drunk and slept with you on our second date."

She started to close the door, but he flexed his arm, stopping her.

"Just hold on. Can I come in?"

"No."

He leaned closer, dropping his voice.

"I came here because I wanted to see you. And I chose red roses because I thought you'd like them."

April clutched the edge of the door tightly but didn't respond.

"Let me take you to dinner and we'll talk. If you don't like what I have to say, I'll get back on a plane and you'll never see me again."

Her green eyes narrowed suspiciously. "What's your angle?"

"I like you."

"That's it?"

"That's it. Isn't that reason enough?"

"What about your father and the presidential campaign?"

Simon's eyes widened. It took a moment for him to recover himself.

"He asked me to take you out. I did. That's where the politics ended."

"I don't believe you." Her voice was soft and she looked like she was about to cry.

"Have a little more confidence in yourself, April. You're pretty, you're sweet. I wouldn't have invited you to the Hamptons and taken you out for mojitos simply for politics."

Her expression telegraphed her disbelief.

"I mean it. Now put those things in water and let me take you to dinner." He handed her the roses and flashed a smile.

She hesitated, looking at the flowers.

"Okay." She opened the door wider so that he could come in. "But no mojitos."

"Scout's honor." He saluted her before closing the door behind them.

Chapter Forty-five

At the end of the Labor Day weekend, Julia and Gabriel returned to Cambridge in order to begin the academic year. Gabriel was teaching a graduate seminar and an undergraduate class at Boston University, while Julia attended Harvard.

In the second week of September, Gabriel visited a well-respected urologist. He didn't want Julia to accompany him, since the appointment conflicted with one of her classes. So he went alone.

When he arrived home for dinner, she pounced.

"Well?"

"Good evening to you, too." He brushed his lips against hers and pulled back, staring at her.

"I'm still getting used to these." He touched the frames of her tortoiseshell glasses.

She adjusted them self-consciously before taking them off. "I only need them for reading. At least, that's what the optometrist said."

"You look like a sexy librarian. In fact, I think we should take them into the study and introduce them to the wonders of desk sex."

Julia laughed. "You aren't going to distract me with desk sex, Professor Emerson. I want to hear about your appointment."

Gabriel's smile faded.

"What if I promise you consecutive orgasms?" he whispered, grasping her wrist and bringing it to his mouth. He kissed her, nipping at the skin.

She swallowed hard. "That sounds—great. But I still want to hear about the doctor."

He took a step closer, walking her toward the kitchen table.

"And if I promise you kitchen table sex, the likes of which you've never experienced before?"

He placed her on the edge of the table, spreading her legs so that he could stand in between them.

She raised her hand to his face. "I'd say you're worrying me because you're trying to distract me with sex. Please tell me what happened."

Gabriel pulled away and sat down heavily on a nearby chair.

"Did you cook or did Rebecca leave something?"

"Rebecca made lasagne." Julia hopped off the table to retrieve a can of Coke from the fridge. She poured it over ice in a glass and handed it to him. "I hope you're hungry."

"The doctor isn't sure it will work." Abruptly, Gabriel placed the glass on the table.

"Oh, sweetheart." She sat in the chair next to him and placed a hand on his arm.

"He's pretty confident we could do artificial insemination if the reversal is unsuccessful, but I have to be tested to see if I'm producing viable sperm. When he has the results, he'll determine if we should schedule a reversal or not. My test is scheduled for next week."

"And?"

"Even if he performs the reversal, the probability of success is low." He cleared his throat. "Since the procedure was done almost ten years ago, the chance of pregnancy is thirty percent. There's a possibility of antibodies, scar tissue, and a secondary blockage point."

"I didn't realize it was so complicated."

He rubbed a hand over his eyes. "It's far more complicated than I expected. But it's a credit to the doctor that he was thorough in his explanation. He also forbade me to smoke."

"Well, that's a good thing. When will we know if the procedure is successful?"

"He says I could be fertile within a few months or it could take a year." He hesitated. "Or never."

Julia sat in his lap, wrapping her arms around his shoulders.

"I'm sorry, Gabriel. I wish I'd gone with you. I could have supported you."

"You were there in spirit." He gave her a half-smile.

"If the sperm production is fine, then we could pursue artificial insemination. If we want, he'll gather sperm at the time of the reversal and freeze them for us." He toyed with her hair. "The doctor suggested you visit a gynecologist, in case there are fertility issues on your side."

Julia grimaced.

Gabriel watched her expression carefully. "Is that a problem?"

"No. I don't like those kinds of checkups, but I can see why it would be necessary. I'm due for one."

"Unfortunately, the doctor also said that we'll have to abstain from sex for three weeks after my procedure. He told me that there cannot be any ejaculation."

Julia's eyes widened. "Three weeks? *Scheisse.*"

"Exactly. Are you still sure we should do this?"

"I'm not happy about having to be celibate for three weeks." She shuddered. "But I was celibate a lot longer than that before."

"Quite." A smile played at the corners of Gabriel's lips. "This will be new for both of us—marital celibacy. Who knew there was such a terrible thing?"

"I certainly didn't. Except for, you know, one week a month."

"That reminds me. We'll have to ensure that one of the three weeks coincides with your cycle. Otherwise we might have to be celibate for four weeks."

"You think of everything, Professor."

Gabriel's eyes appeared to darken. "I have needs."

She pressed their chests together, bringing her mouth inches from his.

"As do I, Professor. I'm sure we can attend to some of those needs without involving your injured parts."

"Injured parts?"

"I'll take very good care of you and all your parts. You'll need me to be your nurse."

Gabriel slid his hands down to cup her backside.

"I like the sound of that. A nurse, a librarian, a student, a professor—is there no end to your talents, Mrs. Emerson?"

"None. In fact, I have another secret identity."

"Oh, really?"

She brought her lips to the curve of his ear, "I'm also Lois Lane."

"I think I'll need to pick up my Superman suit from the dry cleaners."

"Merry Christmas to me."

"It will be." He gave her a heated look, heavy with promise. "So we'll schedule a few more appointments, but we've agreed to pursue this?"

"Yes."

"And we've also agreed that we aren't going to start a family until you graduate. This is all—preliminary."

She smiled and kissed him, and then they decided to delay dinner in favor of celebratory kitchen table sex during which Gabriel pretended to be Superman, coming home after a long day of fighting crime.

(It must be said that superhero kitchen table sex was an even better domestic coupling than regular kitchen table sex.)

❧❧

A few hours later, Julia and Gabriel sat on the floor in their bedroom, going through Sharon's boxes. They found photo albums filled with baby and toddler pictures. They found toys and the bracelet Julia had worn in the hospital when she was born.

She was surprised that her mother kept the baby memorabilia. She was even more surprised to find a copy of her parents' wedding picture, along with a series of photos from their courtship. There were even a few family pictures that predated the divorce.

One box held costume jewelry and scarves and photos of Sharon with different men. Gabriel watched as Julia disposed of those pictures with barely a glance. Given what he knew about Sharon's behavior with her boyfriends, he understood why Julia would want all memory of them destroyed.

He ran a finger across the back of her hand, caressing the knuckles. "You have a home and family now."

"I know." She gave him a little smile, but it didn't touch her eyes.

She looked in vain for her mother's engagement and wedding rings. But they'd likely been pawned long ago. She couldn't remember the last time she'd seen them.

If Julia had expected to find answers among her mother's things, she was sorely disappointed. The materials they found didn't explain why Sharon decided that the baby girl she initially loved to distraction became an annoying household presence. They didn't explain how alcohol and sex became more important than flesh and blood.

"Darling?" Gabriel's voice broke into her thoughts.

"A whole life. Three boxes. What a waste."

Gabriel rubbed her back sympathetically.

"Why didn't she love me?" Julia croaked.

Gabriel felt as if his heart were being torn apart. He sat behind her, pulling her back against his chest.

"I wish I had an answer. All I can say is that I understand. Believe me, Julianne, I understand."

"It's hard for me to believe she ever loved me."

"She kept the photographs. It's clear she loved you when you were born. You can see it in her face. She loved you after that, too, when you were little."

"But she loved alcohol more."

"It's an addiction."

"I'm not without compassion, Gabriel, but I can't contemplate choosing alcohol and men over my child."

Gabriel's grip on her tightened. "That's as it should be. But you've never struggled with addiction, Julianne. That's something I know too much about.

"I'm sure there were times your mother wanted to stop."

"There were times she went into recovery, yes."

"There but for the grace of God go we," he whispered.

When she didn't respond, he continued in a whisper, "This is my fault. I'm the one who insisted on looking into our parents, and now see what's happened."

"You aren't the one who hurt me.

"I suppose it was silly to think I'd find an explanation in one of these boxes. If my dad doesn't have one, how could there be an explanation in a pile of junk?"

"Your baby things aren't junk. We'll frame the photos and put the other things on a shelf. Someday, if we have a little girl, you can show her how beautiful her mama looked when she was a baby."

Julia pressed her face into the crook of his neck. "Thank you."

He gave her a tight squeeze, holding her until she was ready to pack up the boxes.

Chapter Forty-six

"I'm sorry, could you repeat that?" Julia stared wide-eyed at her gynecologist.

It was the third week in September and Julia had just had her yearly physical exam. It was supposed to be routine, with a view to uncovering any fertility issues. But the doctor's remarks indicated that the exam had been anything but routine.

"I want you to have an ultrasound. My secretary will contact radiology at Mount Auburn Hospital and schedule the appointment. I want you seen immediately, and I'm noting that in my referral." Dr. Rubio scribbled hastily in Julia's chart.

Julia's stomach flipped. "So it's serious?"

"Potentially serious." The doctor paused, her dark eyes meeting Julia's. "It's good that you came in when you did. I found something on one of your ovaries. We need to know what it is. You'll have an ultrasound, the radiologist will write up a report and send it to me, and we'll go from there."

"Cancer?" Julia could barely pronounce the word.

"That's a possibility. It could be a benign growth or a cyst. We'll know more soon." Dr. Rubio returned to her writing. "But don't miss your ultrasound appointment. It's imperative that we have you looked at right away."

Julia sat very, very still.

All she could think about was Grace.

"Darling, I'm in the middle of my seminar. Can I call you back?" Gabriel's voice was low as he answered his cell phone.

"I'm so sorry. I forgot. I'll just see you at home." Julia was flustered and fighting back tears. She could hear footsteps on the other end of the line and the closing of the door.

"I'm in the hallway now. What's going on?"

"I'm on my way home. I'll see you soon. Please apologize to your students for me." Julia disconnected before she began sobbing. Somehow the sound of his voice, patient and sweet, made everything worse.

She buried her face in her hands just as her cell phone rang. She didn't have to look at it to know who was calling.

"H-hello?"

"What happened?"

"I'll tell you at dinner." She hiccuped.

"No, you'll tell me now, or I'll cancel my seminar and come and find you. You're worrying me."

"The doctor found something during my exam."

Silence emerged from the other end of the line.

She could hear Gabriel inhale sharply.

"Found what?"

"The doctor doesn't know. I'm supposed to go for an ultrasound at Mount Auburn Hospital as soon as possible."

"Are you all right?"

"Yes." Julia did her best to lie convincingly.

"Where are you?"

"I'm walking home from the doctor's office."

"Stay where you are. I'll come and get you."

"You'll have to cancel your seminar."

"I can't teach a class knowing that you're alone and crying. Stay there and I'll call you back in a minute."

"I'll be fine. I'm just in shock."

"You aren't fine. Just give me a minute."

"I'm almost home. I'll see you soon."

She disconnected the phone.

Gabriel cursed, then opened the door to his seminar room to cancel his class.

In the days between Julia's appointment with her doctor and her ultrasound, Gabriel received a call from his urologist indicating that his sperm production was normal. Professor Emerson was gloriously fertile.

(Parenthetically, it should be noted that he never doubted his fertility.)

His relief was overshadowed by the anxiety he felt over Julia. He put on a brave face, not wanting to upset her, but inwardly, he was afraid.

She was young. She was healthy. Of course, Grace had been young and healthy prior to her diagnosis. She'd had breast cancer for some time before it was discovered.

Gabriel's virility and strength was such that he rarely, if ever, felt helpless. But gazing at his beloved wife while she tossed and turned night after night made him feel impotent. She was light and life and love and goodness. And it was possible she was very, very sick.

Gabriel closed his eyes and prayed.

"Sweetie?" Her voice came out of the darkness.

"Yes?"

"I want you to promise me something."

He rolled to his side so he could see her better.

"Anything."

"Promise that if anything happens to me, you'll take care of yourself."

"Don't say such things." His tone was unnecessarily sharp.

"I mean it, Gabriel. Whether my time is soon or when I'm old and gray. I want you to promise that you'll continue on the path that you're on. That you'll be a good man, that you'll live a good life and that you'll try to find happiness."

Gabriel felt as if he were choking as a myriad of emotions bubbled up into his throat.

"I won't find happiness without you."

"You found peace without me," she whispered. "You found peace in Assisi. You can live without me. We both know that you can."

He placed his palm on top of her stomach, his fingers stroking her naked skin.

"How can a man live without his heart?"

She pressed her hand over his.

"Richard does."

"Richard is a shell of his former self."

"I want you to promise me. I worry that you've made so much of me that if something were to happen, you'd . . ." She trailed off.

"I will always struggle with addiction, Julianne, but I don't think I could go back to my old life." His voice dropped. "Then I truly would be alone."

"I promise that wherever I am, I'll do all that I can to help you. I swear." Her voice was a desperate whisper.

"If you were Francis to my Guido da Montefeltro, you'd come for my soul, wouldn't you?"

"I swear it. But I don't believe your soul is in mortal danger."

He lifted his hand and traced the curve of her cheekbone with his thumb. "No more morbid talk. If it's necessary to your peace of mind to make this promise, then I promise. But don't you dare leave me."

Julia nodded against his hand, her body relaxing.

Chapter Forty-seven

On the day of Julia's ultrasound, Gabriel canceled his classes in order to accompany her.

"I'm sorry, sir, but you aren't allowed inside the ultrasound suite."

Gabriel stood to his full height, a scowl distorting his handsome features. He looked down at the much shorter technician. "Excuse me?"

The technician pointed at a notice board that was affixed to the wall. "Only the patient is allowed. Family must wait out here."

Gabriel placed his hands on his hips, fanning his jacket out angrily. "She's my wife. I'm not leaving her."

"The average ultrasound only takes thirty minutes. She'll be with you soon." The technician nodded at Julia. "Mrs. Emerson, if you'll follow me."

Gabriel tugged on Julia's arm, stopping her. "We'll go to another hospital."

Julia shifted her weight from foot to foot, practically dancing in the hallway. "They made me drink five cups of water. I have to pee like crazy. Don't make me go through this again."

"I'm not letting you go in there alone." His eyes, flashing blue fire, rested on hers.

"This can't wait." Her tone pierced him.

He blinked a few times.

"What if there's a problem?"

The technician cleared her throat and nodded toward the same sign. "I'm not allowed to discuss what I find. Only the radiologist can write up an official report, and that will be sent directly to your doctor."

Gabriel muttered a few choice expletives and gave the technician a glare that nearly knocked her over.

"I'll be fine, sweetie. But if you don't want to see my bladder explode right in front of you, you have to let me go." Julia crossed her legs.

Gabriel watched her walk away, feeling furious and helpless simultaneously.

❧❧

Two days later, Julia was summoned to Dr. Rubio's office to discuss the radiologist's report. Gabriel accompanied her.

"Fibroids," the doctor announced triumphantly. "I read the report and I saw the ultrasound. I concur with her findings."

"What's a fibroid?" Julia clutched Gabriel's hand.

"A fibroid is a benign growth on or in the uterus. They're very common. According to the report, you have two of them."

"Two?" Julia sounded panicked. "But I thought you only found one."

"I found the bigger one during your pelvic exam. Because it's attached to the exterior of your uterus, I thought it was part of your ovary. There's also a small one lower down on the front of your uterus." Doctor Rubio quickly sketched Julia's insides while Gabriel tried valiantly not to faint.

(One must remember that his vast knowledge of uteri was primarily experiential rather than visual.)

"The larger one is about five centimeters. The smaller one is about three centimeters." She pointed to her drawing with a pen.

Julia felt queasy and looked away.

"Will she need surgery?" Gabriel ignored the sketch and made eye contact with the doctor.

"Not necessarily." Dr. Rubio turned to her patient. "If they aren't bothering you, we're inclined to leave them. We'll put you on birth control pills. The hormones in the pill slow the growth of the fibroid."

"What about fertility?"

Doctor Rubio glanced at the chart. "Ah, yes. You want to try to start a family in a few years. We'll monitor your fibroids, but since they're located on the outside of the uterus, I don't think fertility will be a problem. However, once you're pregnant we'll have to keep an eye on them. Fibroids tend to grow during pregnancy because of the rise in hormone levels. They can crowd the uterus and cause premature delivery. We'll monitor all of that when the time comes. But for now, I take this to be good news. I'm going to ask that we schedule you for another ultrasound in about six months, simply to check the fibroids. I'll write up a prescription for you to go on the pill. And we'll go from there."

Julia and Gabriel exchanged a look, then thanked the doctor and exited the office.

Later that night, Gabriel lay awake, staring at the ceiling, an inexplicable feeling of dread hanging over him.

Careful not to wake Julia, he crept out of bed and walked down the hall to the study. He switched on the light, closed the door, and went to his desk.

Within a few minutes, his laptop was on and he was Googling "fibroids." He clicked on a page that looked promising and began viewing a few photographs of fibroids being removed during surgery.

Then he promptly passed out.

Chapter Forty-eight

Gabriel was fortunate enough to have his vasectomy reversal scheduled for the first week in October. Now it was Julia's turn to miss a class and accompany him to the hospital.

The morning of his surgery, she awoke to the sound of Peggy Lee singing "Fever." It wasn't Gabriel's normal choice of morning music, but it sounded promising. She pulled on her robe and walked to the bathroom.

Gabriel was standing in front of the vanity, shaving. His dark hair was damp from the shower, its edges curling. He was naked to the waist, a dark blue towel slung low on his hips. Julia wanted to trace the top of the V that extended below the towel.

As was his custom, he used a shaving brush to mix soap into a lather, spreading it over his face. His sapphire eyes were focused behind his glasses as he lifted the safety razor and began.

"Lurking about in doorways, Mrs. Emerson?" He spoke without turning his head.

"I came to see what was giving you a fever."

He paused and gave her a searing look. "I think you know the answer to that."

"I know what raises *my* temperature. There's nothing sexier than watching the man you love shave."

He rinsed his razor. "I'm glad you think that, because it's a daily essential." His eyes gleamed. "Unless you've grown attached to my stubble. As I recall, you seemed to enjoy it last night."

His eyes darted in the direction of her thighs.

She felt her cheeks flame. The memory of lying flat on her back, Gabriel's stubble rubbing against her . . .

He waved a hand in front of her face. "Penny for your thoughts."

"Sorry, what?"

He chuckled. "I asked how you were feeling this morning."

"I'm fine. How about you? Are you nervous?"

"Not really. But I'm glad you're coming with me. I'm supposed to be at the hospital at ten. That gives us plenty of time for some extracurricular activities after I've finished shaving. You'll have to give me something to tide me over for the next three weeks."

He continued his ritual, the razor moving expertly.

"I can do that." She approached him and pressed an openmouthed kiss between his shoulder blades.

"I think we should wait until after I've finished. You're distracting me."

"Really?"

She kissed him again, this time wrapping her hands over the tops of his shoulders, feeling the muscles tense beneath her fingers.

"I can't help myself, Professor. I love touching you."

She traced the lines of his biceps, moving to his forearms, admiring muscle and sinew. She pressed her lips to the hills and valley of his spine before tracing the dimples that winked at her above the edge of the towel.

He placed a heavy hand on top of the vanity.

"I can't shave while you're touching me."

"Then maybe I should do it for you."

"Oh, really?" A heated look passed between them.

"You enjoy feeding me. Perhaps I'd enjoy shaving you."

"You're very provocative this morning."

"Maybe I need a sexy memory to get me through our marital celibacy."

Gabriel put his razor aside and gestured in front of him, a look of amusement on his face.

She moved into the gap, facing him. In one swift moment, he lifted her to sit on the counter.

He spread her knees, pushing her robe out of the way. Then he stood between her legs.

His eyes drifted down. "No panties this morning?"

"I haven't gotten that far yet."

"Lucky for me." He smiled while his fingers fumbled with the knot at her waist. "Lucky for us your cycle hasn't started yet."

She placed her hands over his, stopping him.

"Will you teach me to shave you?"

"Shaving is overrated."

"I'd like to do this for you."

He made a show of sighing, as if his patience were being tested. Then he picked up the razor. "Shave with the direction the hair grows, but don't apply pressure. The blade is very sharp."

He stepped away, looking in the mirror as he demonstrated his technique. Satisfied with his display, he rinsed the razor before placing it in her hand.

She looked at him. Then she looked at the razor, at the blade that gleamed in the halogen light.

"Stage fright, Mrs. Emerson?"

"I'm afraid I'll make you bleed."

His eyes bore into hers. "Then you know how I felt your first time."

Julia's heart rate increased at the memory. He'd been very worried that night, but very, very gentle.

He pressed his lips to her wrist, drawing on the skin. "You'll be careful."

He separated the edges of her robe before pushing the silk over her shoulders. Then he placed his palm between her breasts, feeling her heartbeat.

Julia arched an eyebrow. "You want me to shave you, half-naked?"

"No." He moved his mouth to her ear and dropped his voice to a throaty whisper. "I want you to shave me completely naked."

He took his time unfastening her belt, as if he were unwrapping a gift. Then he stood between her knees again.

"There's nothing sexier than having the woman you love shave you, while you enjoy her body."

Julia shuddered as the cooler air swirled around her heated skin. She placed her left hand on his shoulder to steady herself.

He nodded and she began.

The safety razor glided simply and easily over his skin without any need for pressure. All the while, two sapphire eyes focused on her.

He placed his hands at her waist and began stroking her hip bones with his thumbs.

"I'm not sure that's a good idea." She rinsed the razor. "I'll nick you."

"Perhaps it would be an exercise in self-control for both of us."

His fingertips traced a path up to her breasts, circling them lightly. When she moaned, he slid his hands back to her waist.

"I like the feel of your skin under my hands."

She met his gaze. "So do I."

She swallowed hard and returned to what she was doing, trying to ignore the feel of his fingers gliding over her abdomen and between her breasts. He began to tease her nipples, which were extremely sensitive.

"I guess you must trust me," she ground out, trying to keep her hand steady.

He stroked a finger over the prominent peaks. "I do, Julianne. More than I've ever trusted anyone."

His eyes were tender, their blue intensity communicating far more than his words could. "But I can't see you and not touch you."

He cupped her breasts, cradling them gently in deference to her forthcoming cycle.

Patiently, she worked the razor over the parts of his face that were yet unshaven while he fondled and teased her. Her breathing grew shallow.

He dropped his hands to her inner thighs, where the skin was slightly sensitive from being teased by his stubble. He moved higher, inch by tantalizing inch.

With a few last strokes of the razor, she pulled back to admire her handiwork. "I think we're finished."

He kissed her lightly. "Thank you."

"You're welcome." She put the razor aside, leaning back on her hands.

"But I don't think we're finished yet." His eyes glinted as he moved to the juncture of her thighs. His thumbs tangled in her curls.

She licked her lower lip.

"Then drop the towel, Professor."

Gabriel's procedure was unremarkable. What was remarkable, however, was the grimness of the surgeon's face when he came to see Julia in the waiting room.

"Mrs. Emerson." He greeted her, moving to sit in the empty chair beside her.

She closed her laptop. "How is he?"

"The surgery went well. It was complicated, but nothing unexpected. We also retrieved some sperm and froze it, as your husband directed."

"Gabriel said that you have a very high success rate." Julia sounded hopeful.

"I do. Some of my patients have conceived a child as early as three months after the procedure. But every case is different." The doctor's expression grew serious. "During surgery, your husband had a reaction to the anesthesia."

"A reaction? Is he all right?" Julia's heart began to race.

"He'll be fine, but he's been vomiting. He's on intravenous and I want him to stay overnight. He's in recovery now, then they'll move him to a room. I'll make sure someone comes to get you so you can stay with him."

The surgeon eyed Julia's worried expression.

"These kinds of reactions to general anesthesia are not uncommon. We'll monitor him as a precaution, and he'll probably be ready to go home tomorrow."

The doctor patted her hand and disappeared through a set of swinging doors.

❧❧

"Gabriel?" Julia whispered.

He'd been moaning and thrashing a little in his hospital bed. She leaned over to take his hand.

"Sweetie? The surgery went well. You're going to be fine."

His eyes opened suddenly.

She pushed his hair back from his forehead.

"Hi, baby."

He closed his eyes. "I feel like a baby. I feel like hell, actually. Dizzy."

"Are you going to be sick?"

He shook his head. "Tired."

"Then go to sleep, darling. I'm here."

"Pretty baby," he mumbled, before drifting into sleep.

Julia pressed her lips to his forehead.

I love this man with all my heart. I'd give my life for him. I'd give anything for him.

It was unusual to see Gabriel as he appeared in the hospital bed. He rarely, if ever, got sick. When he wasn't asleep, the strength of his presence dominated his surroundings.

Now his personality was muted. Quiet. Vulnerable.

She thought back to the time when she'd cared for the Professor while he was drunk. She'd helped him to his apartment and he'd vomited all over her.

(And his British racing green cashmere sweater.)

She remembered dragging him to the bathroom and cleaning him up. She ran her fingers through his hair, wondering what it would be like to have a baby to care for. At the time, such musings seemed so remote, so unattainable.

Gazing down on the handsome face of her beloved husband, she knew that something inside her was shifting. Something had changed.

❧❧

"How is he?" Rebecca eyed Julia with concern as she entered the kitchen the following afternoon.

Julia placed a tray on the counter. "He's asleep. He says he's uncomfortable, but he wouldn't take his pain pills until I threatened him."

Rebecca laughed. "How did you do that?"

Julia placed the dirty dishes in the sink. "I reminded him that the longer he took to heal, the longer he'd have to wait for sex. He grabbed the pill bottle out of my hand. I don't think we'll have trouble getting him to take his medication anymore."

Rebecca shook her head, smothering a smile.

"Chicken soup for dinner with homemade rolls. How does that sound?" She moved to the stove, where she was simmering an entire chicken in a stockpot.

"Delicious. Thank you."

"Will you need me to stay this weekend?"

"No. I'm sure we'll be fine." Julia looked at Rebecca with interest. "Would you do that?"

Rebecca placed the lid back on the stockpot. "Of course. I can be here whenever you need me, except during the holidays. And even then, if I had advance notice, I could work something out. It might sound silly, but I think of you two as family."

"It isn't silly. We think the same." Julia leaned against the counter. "It's so much easier when you're here. Dirty clothing disappears and clean clothing appears in its place. There's always food in the fridge or freezer and the house is immaculate. I'd never be able to do what you do."

"Sure, you could. But you couldn't be a student, too. You'd have to choose one or the other. Are your brother-in-law and his family still coming to visit?"

Rebecca wiped her hands on her apron and moved to the kitchen island. An iPad was propped up on a stand, like a cookbook. She opened the iCalendar application and scrolled through it, looking at the Emersons' appointments.

"No. Between my ultrasound and Gabriel's surgery, we decided it would be best if they came after Christmas. We'll be going home for Thanksgiving, anyway." Julia winced in remembrance. "I thought I mentioned it. I'm sorry."

Rebecca waved her hand in the air. "No problem. I'll adjust the calendar."

"I didn't expect Gabriel to be so weak after his procedure. He insists he's going to work tomorrow, but I don't see how he can. He's in pain."

"Men make the worst patients. They don't take their medication, they don't do what they're told, and they never, ever admit they're sick. They're like cats."

Julia chuckled. "I'll remember that."

"In fact, it's probably easier to give a pill to a cat than to a man. Then again, a man can't scratch you."

Now Julia was laughing.

"It's a good thing he's upstairs. He'd be cross with us for comparing him to a cat."

Rebecca winked. *"Meow."*

Chapter Forty-nine

The week following Gabriel's surgery, he was almost back to his old self. Except that he was grumpy and cross because of the lack of sex.

(One might observe that being grumpy and cross was precisely his old self.)

Julia bore his grumpiness as she usually did, with saintlike good humor. Of course, the fact that she was getting regular orgasms courtesy of her husband might have had something to do with her mood.

"There's a letter from Katherine." Gabriel waved in the direction of the kitchen table, where the day's mail was stacked.

Julia picked up the small white envelope. Sure enough, the letter was from Professor Katherine Picton of All Souls College, Oxford.

"She's still in England. I would have thought she'd be back in Toronto by now."

Gabriel pulled up a chair and began going through the rest of the mail, hoping that there wouldn't be any surprises among it.

"She's a fellow at All Souls for the year. Open it and see what she says."

Julia put on her glasses, opened the envelope, and began to read.

Dear Gabriel and Julianne,

I hope that this letter finds you both well.

Oxford is enjoyable and I'm pleased with the research I've been able to accomplish. I look back fondly to the conference this past summer and hope to see you soon.

I mentioned this before, but Greg Matthews has invited me to give a series of lectures at Harvard at the end of January. I'm told he's also invited Jeremy Martin to give a paper.

I'm hoping to see you both during my visit.

I'm also hoping you'll save me from Greg's dreadful culinary predilections.

As ever,
Katherine.

"What does she say?" Gabriel looked at his wife over the rims of his glasses.

"She says she's coming to Harvard in January. I haven't heard anything about that in the department. Have you?"

"I haven't heard a formal announcement. What else does she say?"

Julia handed him the letter.

Gabriel perused its contents quickly.

He grimaced. "Jeremy."

"Yes."

He tossed the letter back onto the table.

"I'm not looking forward to that confrontation. He's still angry I resigned."

"Can you smooth things over with him?"

"I don't know. We were friends for a while, and then we weren't. We'll see." He pushed her hair behind her shoulder. "Don't worry about it. The important thing is that we'll be able to see Katherine and have her over for dinner. She doesn't like Greg's choice of restaurants."

Julia folded her glasses and placed them on the kitchen table before climbing into Gabriel's lap.

"I can't imagine Katherine having a tawdry affair with an old, desiccated Oxford professor."

Gabriel chuckled. "Neither can I. But Old Hut was considered handsome in his day. I've seen photographs."

"But the two of them together. She had to know it was wrong—not only because of her career but because he was married."

Gabriel tapped the end of her nose. "I think she loved him."

"That doesn't make it right."

"What we did was wrong as well, if you remember." He lowered his voice, his eyes focused on hers intently.

"Yes." She placed her arms around his neck. "I suppose it's easy to point fingers and forget one's own failings."

"If she felt one tenth the love I felt for you, well, I can understand how she was led astray. Now that I'm married, however, I feel sympathy for Mrs. Hutton. If someone were to try to lure you away—" He cursed.

"I love you more now than I did before we were married." Julia wore a contemplative expression. "Marriage is the strangest thing. Almost without realizing it, I feel as if our lives and our hearts became knitted together. I don't know how it happened."

"Marriage is a sacrament." Gabriel's tone was solemn. "And of course, there's the sex we're no longer having."

"The three weeks are almost up."

Gabriel moved his mouth to her ear.

"You'd better inform your professors that you won't be in class that day."

She shivered at his nearness.

"I won't?"

"Do you think I'll let you leave the house after going without you for three weeks?" He nipped at her ear. "You'll be lucky if I let you leave the bed."

"I like the sound of that." She rested her head on his shoulder. "I know that alongside our medical appointments, you were making inquiries about your family history. Have you found out anything?"

"I asked Carson to look into things. He was supposed to get a copy of the coroner's report on my mother, and also health information about her parents and my father and his parents. But I haven't heard anything."

"No one is going to give your lawyer that kind of information."

"Probably not," said Gabriel grimly. "But he's been known to hire private investigators that tend to be persuasive. They'll find out what I need to know."

"Persuasive?"

"In this case the information can probably be bought. Failing that, people can be made to talk."

"Gabriel." Julia's tone was reproachful. "Have you ever bought information like that?"

"Yes."

His swift, unblinking answer surprised her.

"Did you feel remorse?"

"Absolutely not."

"Why?"

"Because I was doing it for you. That's why."

She pulled away from him. "I don't understand. What kind of information did you get?"

He sighed. "It's a long story. You'd best get comfortable."

Julia resisted the urge to move and remained where she was, in his lap.

"I should mention that although I didn't intend to tell you what happened, for the past few months it's been nagging at me that I should."

"Tell me what?"

"How I ensured that Simon and Natalie would never bother you again."

Julia's eyes widened as Gabriel began his story.

Chapter Fifty

April 2010
Selinsgrove, Pennsylvania

Gabriel's cell phone rang. He reached over to pick it up so he could see who was calling. Julianne had called several times since he'd left her in Toronto. Although he listened to her voice messages in an effort to torture himself, he couldn't risk answering and actually speaking with her.

July first. If I can just hold on until July first, she'll be safe.

The display indicated that the number was blocked. Gabriel had a fair idea who was calling.

"Jack," he rasped.

"Found the girl. Found her boyfriend. We need to meet."

Gabriel rubbed at his eyes.

"Can't you look after this? That's what I'm paying you for."

Jack cursed.

"Don't trust you. Tom tells me you broke my niece's heart. I should be tuning you up rather than doing a job for you."

"This isn't for me. It's for her," Gabriel snapped. "The girl tried to blackmail her. The boy fucking bit her and threatened to rape her. How is it in those scenarios, I'm the villain?"

"Melrose Diner, South Philly, tomorrow at nine A.M."

Jack hung up.

"Fuck," said Gabriel.

❧❧

Jack Mitchell was a private investigator. At least, that was the occupation he put on his tax forms. He was an ex-Marine who also worked in private security, investigations, and enforcement.

Simply put, he helped rich individuals stay safe from all kinds of threats, including blackmail.

Jack was Tom Mitchell's younger brother and the man that he turned to when his friend Richard Clark needed to pay off the drug dealers his son owed. Jack and a few of his contacts took the money Richard provided (money that was gained by mortgaging the family home in Selinsgrove) and persuaded the dealers to forget the name of Gabriel Emerson.

Jack could be very persuasive.

When Gabriel needed someone to persuade a certain couple to stay away from Julianne, he immediately thought of Jack. Contacting him wasn't easy, but a few well-placed phone calls put them in touch.

Despite Jack's initial resistance, when he saw the photographs of Julianne's injuries at the hands of the senator's son, he agreed to take the job. He followed Simon and the redhead he was banging as they cut a wide swath through Philadelphia and Washington, D.C. In a short period of time, Jack had a dossier thick enough to share with Emerson. And damning enough (he thought) to ensure that his niece would no longer have to worry about the rich boy and the redhead.

Jack would make suggestions about how to use the information to its greatest effect. And he hoped that he'd be able to call his shot at a few minutes alone with the rich kid. Someone needed to teach that motherfucker a lesson.

❧❧

Jack slid a manila envelope across the table to Gabriel.

"Leverage to get them to turn over the stuff they have on Jules. I'll have a conversation with them about what will happen if they don't. Senator Talbot is making a bid for the White House. They'll comply. End of story."

"What am I looking at?" Gabriel flipped through a set of black-and-white photos, all of which featured the senator's son involved in some kind of sex act. Some of the photos featured him and two women. All of them turned Gabriel's stomach.

"Debutantes, Capitol Hill brats, and an intern from the senator's office." Jack placed his index finger over the pale, shadowed face of a young woman.

Gabriel frowned in distaste. "College student?"

"High school."

"Underage?"

Their eyes met.

"Seventeen."

"Fuck," Gabriel muttered. "The guy is a predator. Is the senator implicated?'

"His people are aware the kid is a problem. They've been tailing him."

"But they haven't done anything?"

"Nothing on radar. Don't see how they can let this continue. The kid gave alcohol and drugs to a seventeen-year-old and then slept with her. It's all on film."

"Motherfucker." Gabriel placed the photos back in the envelope and slid it across the table.

"Returning your fee." Jack tucked the photos inside his leather jacket and then took a business-sized envelope from one of the pockets. He held it out.

Gabriel waved it aside.

Jack dropped the envelope next to Gabriel's coffee mug.

"She ain't your problem anymore."

Gabriel leveled angry blue eyes on the man sitting across from him.

"She will always be my problem."

Jack squinted.

"Man like you, spends thousands on white stuff that goes up his nose. Nearly gets himself and his father killed. Shit." He shook his head. "I'm fucking delighted you aren't with her anymore."

"Then take the money." Gabriel clenched his fist and inhaled deeply, resisting the urge to bounce Jack's head off the table.

"Tom should have solved this problem. Way I look at it, he fell down on the job."

"It isn't the first time. If you're so sympathetic to Julianne, why the hell didn't you rescue her from her mother? You could have saved her the scar on the back of her head."

Jack's face grew very red. "She told you?"

"Of course."

"Fuck."

Gabriel glared. "I don't expect you to understand, but for reasons I won't delineate, we can't be together. I'd still walk through Hell for her. And I'll be damned if I'm going to let some motherfucker with a senator for a father embarrass and humiliate her. You don't want the money of a cokehead who broke your niece's heart? Fine. Do your job and do it right, or I'll find someone who will." Gabriel stuffed the envelope into his pocket and moved to stand.

Jack held out his hand to stop him.

"I'll call you when it's done."

"Good. I expect you to keep this conversation between us."

Jack looked up at him in surprise. "Don't you want her to know?"

Gabriel's expression tightened. "The important thing is that she's safe. No blackmail, no blowback. They stay out of her life forever. And she gets to sleep peacefully at night."

A long look passed between the two men before Gabriel strode out of the diner.

Chapter Fifty-one

October 2011
Cambridge, Massachusetts

Scheisse," said Julia.

"Quite," said Gabriel.

"I can't believe you hired my uncle Jack."

"He's good at what he does. He's gotten me out of scrapes before."

A sudden realization came upon her. "Is that what you were arguing with him about back at my dad's house?"

"He was angry I'd never told you."

"He never mentioned anything."

"He's a man of few words."

"Why didn't you tell me?" She looked at him reproachfully.

"My actions were justified, but not legal. I didn't want you knowing anything about it if there was a chance Simon or Natalie decided to go to the police. Or the feds. Before we were married I told you I'd looked into them and was satisfied that they wouldn't bother you again."

"I didn't think you threatened them."

"Is it really so bad?" he whispered.

Julia met his gaze and saw thinly disguised disappointment in his eyes.

"I told you I hadn't confessed everything from my past, Julianne. We agreed that was fine."

"But my father was so angry with you. Didn't you want him to know that you protected me?"

"The fewer people who knew about it, the better. I doubt he would have changed his opinion."

"So while we were separated, you were working hard to make sure I was safe?" She blinked back tears. "Thank you."

He hugged her tightly. "You're welcome. You should know that when I recovered the photos and videos of you I destroyed them without looking at them."

Julia's shoulders sagged in relief. "But Uncle Jack saw them."

"I think he took pains not to look. And they're gone now."

"Simon and Natalie probably kept copies."

"Jack said he got everything that included you. And he has a few other things in case he needs to motivate Natalie or Simon in the future."

"How did he get everything?"

"That's not important. The important thing is that you don't need to worry about them. They won't bother you again."

Julia hugged him, crying relieved tears on his shoulder.

Chapter Fifty-two

October 2011
Durham, North Carolina

"What are you doing?" April padded into her kitchen on bare feet, clad only in her boyfriend's dress shirt.

He was standing at the stove cooking bacon and eggs in a single pan.

"Making us breakfast." He smiled at her and reached over to peck her lips. "How did you sleep?"

"Good." She stretched her arms over her head, then giggled. "I sleep better with you than without you."

"Me, too," he admitted, more to himself than to her.

She grabbed a container of orange juice from the refrigerator and poured them each a glass.

"I sleep better with you, but I feel guilty."

"Guilty?" Simon turned, holding the spatula in his hand. "Why?"

April ducked her head, focusing on her orange juice. "Because we're sleeping together and we aren't married."

Simon froze.

Chastity was as foreign to him as Eastern Europe. He'd encountered it before, in Julia, but it had always been something annoying and stupid, something he'd wanted to destroy through either seduction or manipulation.

With April, he found himself feeling something entirely different. Something that might have been the twinges of remorse.

It was a new experience for him.

"Sex isn't bad."

"That's a funny thing to say." She tapped her finger against her juice glass. "You've taught me sex is very, very good. I love it and I love being with you."

"Then what's the problem?"

"I was taught to wait. And I didn't."

Simon turned back to the stove, at a loss as to what to say. For a moment, he continued cooking breakfast, then turned off the burner and put the pan aside.

He wiped his hands on the seat of his boxer shorts and walked over to her.

"You were taught to wait because your parents didn't want some asshole taking advantage of you."

"Simon." Her tone was scolding. "Don't cuss."

"Sorry. Your parents were trying to protect you."

"It isn't just my parents. It's my church."

"Well, they were trying to protect you, too. And that's a good thing. But our situation is different."

She lifted her head. "Is it?"

"Yes." He put his arms around her.

"How is it different?" She sounded cautious. "Tell me."

"I'm not just having fun here. I like having sex with you, but I also enjoy your company. I can let my guard down when I'm with you. I don't have to be Senator Talbot's son. I can just be myself." He smiled somewhat hesitantly.

"That's how I feel, too." She snuggled into his chest. "But every time you leave, I feel bad."

"That's because we care about each other."

"I wish we could stay like this forever," she whispered, her arms tightening around his waist.

"Me, too," he admitted. He was stunned to discover that his words were true. That even in the short time he'd known her, he'd come to care for her, deeply. Their relationship was easy and good and he couldn't imagine ending it.

"I love you, Simon."

Simon felt his heart jump into his throat.

He was not a stupid man. He knew what he had in his arms—a beautiful, gentle, amazing young woman. She didn't have the baggage that he carried. She wasn't jaded and intent on social climbing, like Natalie. And she wasn't fearful and self-righteous, like Julia. Julia had always made him feel as if he were an animal, something unworthy to touch her.

April probably woke up that morning, decided she loved him, and simply told him. No deliberation, no head games, no social climbing through sexual means.

Without warning, Simon found his lips moving.

"I love you, too."

April hugged him as tightly as she could, almost bouncing on the balls of her feet.

"This is great!" she shrieked. "I'm so happy."

"So am I." He smiled down at her youthful, uninhibited exuberance and kissed her.

Chapter Fifty-three

Cambridge, Massachusetts

As October came to an end, the date Gabriel was waiting for drew near. He'd been fantasizing about what he was going to do to Julianne once their required celibacy ended, planning their activities meticulously.

The afternoon before the date, Julia stood in the kitchen of their home and called him. The phone rang only twice before he answered.

"Hello, gorgeous."

She flushed. It never ceased to amaze her how, with a word or two, he could increase her heart rate and cause her skin to heat.

"Hello, handsome. Where are you?"

"Just picking up a few things. Where are you?"

"At home."

Gabriel paused, and Julia could hear the sound of a car door slam. "You're home early. I wasn't expecting you until six."

"Professor Marinelli canceled her seminar because she has laryngitis. I think I'm going to go upstairs and have a shower. Then I might take a nap until you get home. I was up really early this morning."

The sound of the Range Rover roaring to life filled Julia's ears.

"You do that. I'll be home soon. See you then."

"I love you."

"I love you, too."

Julia heard what sounded like a chuckle before Gabriel disconnected. She wondered what he found so funny.

She poked around in the kitchen for a few minutes, noticing that Rebecca hadn't prepared anything for dinner. She wondered why.

Perplexed, she climbed the stairs to the second floor. She didn't bother to hang up her clothes but simply dropped them in the bedroom before entering the shower.

A hot shower would revitalize her after an exhausting day.

She'd almost finished her shower when she heard the shower door open.

"Why, hello there."

Gabriel stood in front of her, naked and smiling. He leaned forward to kiss her.

"Did you need a shower too?" she asked, trying not to ogle him and failing miserably.

"No. I just wanted to be where you are."

She kissed him again. "Thanks."

She ran an appreciative hand down the center of his chest to the deep V that bracketed his hips. Then she switched off the shower, squeezing the water out of her hair.

Gabriel retrieved a towel and handed it to her.

That was when she noticed the way his eyes were alit in anticipation, his smile growing wider.

"What?"

"Did you forget what day it is?" He trailed a finger down her arm.

"No. Our special day is tomorrow."

"We're starting early."

"Do you think that's wise?"

"I don't give a damn. I've waited long enough. A man can only stand so much."

"Oh, really?" She cocked her head to one side.

"So prepare to be pleasured, my dear."

She quickly ran the towel over her body, drying herself, then wound it over her hair.

Gabriel picked up a glass jar and held it out to her.

"*Chocolate Body Paint*," she read. She glanced up at him. "Now?"

"Now." He wiggled a small paintbrush under her nose. "You said that you enjoyed our foray into body painting while we were in Selinsgrove. I decided we should try it again."

"But I thought you'd want to do other things. You've been doing things for me for three weeks. I've been able to do very little for you."

"Foreplay is for me as well as you," he whispered, his eyes darkening. "And I have plans for both of us."

"Wow." She breathed.

"I thought about trying it in the bedroom, but things could get messy."

He crouched in front of her, his face level with her navel, and opened the jar. He dipped the paintbrush in the chocolate, spreading the confection liberally over the delicate strands of the brush, before winking up at her.

"Shall we begin?"

She nodded, her eyes half closed.

Slowly, he began to draw a heart around her navel.

The feel of the chocolate and the brush gliding across her warm skin caused her to fidget. And of course, despite the fact that it almost tickled, Gabriel would not be rushed.

"There." He put the jar and brush aside and licked his lips. "Now comes the fun part. Ready?"

"Yes." The word came out as more of a squeak than a statement.

She reached out a shaking hand to grasp a railing when Gabriel's tongue made contact with her skin, swirling through the chocolate and dipping into her navel.

He steadied her by splaying one of his hands across her backside.

"It tastes better than I expected." He nibbled at her. "Then again, that's probably because I like how you taste."

His tongue blazed a trail to her hip bone, where he began placing openmouthed kisses.

"I think we need more chocolate. What do you think?"

"Yes, please." Julia nodded furiously. "Definitely, more."

Gabriel picked up the chocolate and the brush.

"Then you'd better hold on tight, darling, because I'm planning to be thorough."

She leaned forward, cupping his chin.

"As am I."

Chapter Fifty-four

As November progressed, Diane and Tom continued to receive positive reports about their baby's health. Surgery would still be necessary, but the baby was developing and Diane was also healthy.

Julia received the reports about her brother with a combination of relief and cautious optimism.

She hadn't told her family about her fibroids or about Gabriel's vasectomy reversal. His family didn't know that he'd had the procedure in the first place. And she didn't want to worry anyone about her own health issues, especially since Dr. Rubio assured her that fibroids were common and, at least at this point, not serious.

The Emersons bore one another's health burdens, sharing only some of the information with Rebecca. But Julia seemed to bear the burden of her graduate career alone.

(Or so she thought.)

Late one November evening, Gabriel awoke with a start. He was instantly alert, straining his ears for the slightest sound. In the distance, he heard a woman crying.

He reached for Julia in the darkness, but she was gone.

Without even bothering to switch on the light or to grab his bathrobe, he sprang to his feet, naked, and exited the bedroom.

A shaft of light shone from underneath the study door.

He quickly walked toward it, the sound of crying growing louder.

Behind the door, he found Julia, her head on her desk. Her shoulders were shaking, her glasses discarded on her open laptop. A large pile of books was scattered across the desk and down on the floor.

"Darling." He placed his hand on her head. "What's the matter?"

"I can't do it."

"You can't do what?" He crouched beside her.

"I can't catch up. I'm behind in my reading for all my classes. I should be working on my seminar papers, but I've been trying to read. I should have started the revisions on my lecture, but I haven't had time. And I'm just so tired." Her voice cracked.

Gabriel eyed her sympathetically. "Come to bed."

"I can't!" she wailed, throwing her hands up. "I need to stay up all night and finish my reading. Then tomorrow, I need to spend the day in the library working on my papers. I don't know when I'm going to revise my lecture for publication."

"You can't do anything more tonight. Even if you stayed up, you're too tired to focus. Come to bed now and you can get up early. You can tell me about your readings over breakfast and I'll see if I can give you the CliffsNotes version of them." He gestured to her with his hand.

She shook her head. "CliffsNotes won't cut it."

"Julianne, it's two o'clock in the morning. Come to bed." His tone grew commanding.

"I have to stay up."

"Sleep now and I'll help you. I can go with you to the library and help you with your research. That should save you some time."

"You'd do that?" She wiped her nose with a tissue.

He frowned. "Of course. I've been volunteering to help you all semester. You wouldn't let me."

"You're busy with your own stuff. And then you had surgery." She wiped her eyes hastily.

"You're going to get sick if you don't take care of yourself. Come on." He placed a hand on her elbow and helped her to her feet before closing her laptop firmly.

He followed her down the hall to their bedroom.

"I'm so tired," she sniffled, resting her head on the pillow. She was even too tired to spoon.

"All you have to do is ask. I'd do anything for you. You know that."

"I'm supposed to do this by myself."

"Bullshit." He placed an arm around her waist. "The program is designed to be grueling. Everyone else is probably getting help from someone."

"You didn't need help when you did it."

"Think about what you're saying. I was doing coke when I was in grad school. And I had P—someone to look after me."

He sighed, lowering his voice. "You looked after me when I came home from the hospital. That's probably when you fell behind. Let me help you catch up. But the first thing you need is a good night's sleep. We'll talk tomorrow."

She was too weary to argue. Within minutes, her breathing deepened and Gabriel knew that she'd fallen asleep.

Chapter Fifty-five

That Saturday, Julia and Gabriel planned to spend most of the day in the library, researching her seminar papers. As a way of showing her appreciation, she prepared pancakes while he sat at the kitchen table, clad in his pajama pants and glasses, reading *The Boston Globe*.

She poured the batter onto a hot griddle before turning to him.

"There's something I've been wondering."

"And what's that?"

"Will you tell me what you wrote in the card that you left at my apartment, back in Toronto?"

He lowered his newspaper.

"What card?"

"The one that didn't survive my loss of temper."

He pretended to search his memory.

"Oh, that card."

She rolled her eyes. "Yes, that card."

He folded the newspaper and put it aside. "Do you really want to know?"

"Of course."

"But you tore it up."

She gave him a look.

"I thought you forgave me."

"I did." He smiled ruefully. "It was a simple card. I apologized for being an ass."

"That was nice," she prompted. "What did you say?"

"I called you my Beatrice and said that I'd wished for you my whole life, even though I was convinced that you were a hallucination. I said that now that I'd found you, I'd fight to make you mine."

Julia smiled to herself as she flipped the pancakes.

"And there might have been poetry."

She looked over at him. "Might have been?"

"Shakespeare's twenty-ninth sonnet. Do you know it?

"'*When in disgrace with fortune and men's eyes*
I all alone beweep my outcast state,
And trouble deaf heaven with my bootless cries,
And look upon myself, and curse my fate,
Wishing me like to one more rich in hope,
Featured like him, like him with friends possessed,
Desiring this man's art, and that man's scope,
With what I most enjoy contented least;
Yet in these thoughts my self almost despising,
Haply I think on thee, and then my state,
Like to the lark at break of day arising
From sullen earth, sings hymns at heaven's gate;
For thy sweet love remembered such wealth brings
That then I scorn to change my state with kings.'"

Julia pressed her hand over her heart. "That's beautiful, Gabriel. Thank you."

"What's even more beautiful is the fact that I don't have to content myself with memories anymore. I have you."

Julia quickly turned off the burner and moved the griddle from the heat.

"What are you doing?" Gabriel appeared puzzled.

She tossed the spatula aside.

"We're having ripped-up-note-revealed sex. I've been waiting for this forever." She grabbed his hand, tugging him toward the hall. "Come on."

He planted his feet. "What kind of sex is that?"

"You'll find out." She gave him a saucy look and raced toward the stairs, the Professor at her heels.

❧❧

Having spent a very long day conducting research, Gabriel and Julia returned to a dark house. Julia ordered pizza for dinner while Gabriel flipped through the Saturday mail.

He came across a blue envelope that was addressed to him in a spiky, unfamiliar hand. The return address was in New York City.

Intrigued, he opened the envelope and read,

Dear Gabriel (if I may),

Recently, I was contacted by Michael Wasserstein, our family attorney, telling me that you were making inquiries about our father, Owen Davies. I was told that you wanted to learn more about his family history.

My name is Kelly Davies Schultz and I'm your half-sister. We also have a younger sister, Audrey.

I always wanted a brother. I mention this because I feel badly about how my mother and sister behaved with respect to our father's will and I want you to know that I was not a party to contesting it. At the time, I wanted to write to you to tell you so, but my mother was being difficult and I decided not to antagonize her. I made the wrong decision.

Since my mother died this past spring, I've been thinking about you and wondering if I should get in touch. I think it's Providential that you reached out when you did.

Michael tells me you live in Massachusetts, that you are a professor, and that you are recently married. I'm wondering if you and your wife would like to come to New York to meet me and my husband, Jonathan? We'd be delighted to take you to dinner. I think that would give us a chance to get to know one another.

You're unlikely to hear from Audrey, for reasons I'll explain in person. But I'm eager to meet you and to share what I know of our family history.

I'm enclosing my business card with my home number and email written on the back. Please don't be alarmed by the fact that I'm a psychiatrist. I promise that I don't practice on family members, and also my specialty is children. So even at your young age you're far too old to be my patient . . .

I look forward to hearing from you and hopefully, to meeting you. Please don't hesitate to call or to write.

Your sister,

Kelly

Gabriel lowered himself into a chair and sat, staring at the pages.

Chapter Fifty-six

After dinner, Julia reread the letter from Kelly Davies Schultz.

"What do you think?" She folded it neatly and handed it back to Gabriel.

"I'm skeptical."

"She sounds nice. And funny, too. Why are you skeptical?"

"They tried to have me disinherited. How do I know this isn't a ploy?"

"A ploy for what? The money was distributed years ago."

He folded his arms across his chest. "Information."

"Sweetie, she's the one with information. You wanted the opportunity to find out more about your family history, especially your parents' health. Now you have it. I thought you'd be happy." She sat on the chair next to him. "When would we go?"

Gabriel's expression tightened.

"The sooner I put all of this behind me, the better."

"We're supposed to be in Selinsgrove for Christmas and New Year's. I'll want to go earlier if Diane has the baby."

Gabriel looked at her closely.

"You have a lot going on right now. I've tried to help you catch up, and I promise I'll do more."

Julia gave him a half-smile. "I feel as if there's a 'but' coming up."

"Would it hurt you if I said this was something I wanted to do right away? Maybe after classes are finished the second week in December? I can have a graduate student deal with the exams."

Julia scratched at the surface of the kitchen table with her fingernail.

"That's when I have to submit my lecture for publication. I'll be finishing up my seminar papers and turning them in. That's the worst time for me to go away."

"I was thinking this might be something I should do on my own."

Julia examined her fingernails as if they were fascinating.

"You have no idea what you're going to find out. I think you'll need me."

Gabriel smiled slowly.

"I will always need you, Julianne. But I think the first time I meet Kelly it should be the two of us. Then if there's anything unpleasant, I'll deal with it."

"If that's what you want. Can't we visit her over Christmas or something?"

"I don't think it's wise to put this off. She might change her mind. Certainly, the sooner I know about my medical history, the better." He gazed at her significantly. "I wouldn't ask you to do anything that would put your program in jeopardy."

"Okay." She did not sound enthusiastic.

"We can ask Rebecca to stay while I'm gone. Then you won't be alone. It will be a short trip. Two or three days, tops. I'll see if I can schedule an appointment with the lawyer who handled my father's estate and I'll meet Kelly. Then I'll come home."

He took her hand, tracing her lifeline with his thumb.

"I can't bring myself to call her my sister."

"I think I should come with you."

"You just said that you don't have time. You need to get some work done. And I know that I'm distracting." He gave her what he hoped might be a provocative look.

"You can be very distracting."

"Good." He lifted her into his arms and walked toward the stairs. "Prepare for some extensive distracting."

She placed her hands on his biceps, stilling him.

"Put me down."

"I'll put you down when we get to bed."

"I have something to say that you aren't going to want to hear."

"Then say it quickly and get it over with." He tensed.

She wriggled in his arms, so he set her down on the stairs.

"Your trip to New York is going to open up a lot of memories. Of course I'll do whatever I can to help. But one thing we haven't talked about is forgiveness."

"Forgive my parents?" he spat. "That's a laugh."

"Forgiveness frees you. It's for you, as much as for them."

He pulled away from her. "I can't forgive them. They don't deserve it."

"Who deserves forgiveness, Gabriel? You? Me?"

"You, for one."

"Apart from God, the only person who can forgive me is the one I've wronged. That's the power we have. We can use that power for good—to forgive someone. Or we can use it to hold on to old wrongs and hurts so that they never heal."

She reached out to him, grasping his hand.

"I'm not saying they deserve it. I'm certainly not asking you to forget or to pretend nothing ever happened. Just think about it."

"I've already thought about it. The answer is no."

"How can you ask Paulina to forgive you if you aren't willing to forgive your parents?"

Air escaped Gabriel's lungs as if she'd struck him.

"Don't," he whispered.

"Just think about it, my love. Think about your reconciliation with Maia and what that meant to you. And imagine what it would mean to your father to hear that you forgive him."

Gabriel led her upstairs but did not speak.

Chapter Fifty-seven

While Julia finished her seminar papers and revised her lecture for publication, Gabriel met with his urologist for a checkup on December fifth, then flew to New York.

As soon as he'd checked into his room at the Ritz-Carlton, he realized his mistake. He should have brought Julia with him. The large and beautiful bed would be cold that evening. He hated sleeping alone. It always reminded him of their separation, a memory he loathed.

He placed a few phone calls—to Lucia Barini at Columbia, to his father's lawyer, and to Julia. He was disappointed when his call went to voice mail.

"Julianne, I'm in New York. I'm staying at the Ritz-Carlton, room four eleven. I'm having dinner with Kelly tonight, and then I'll be in my room. Talk to you later. I love you."

Gabriel ended the call with a huff of frustration. Then he prepared to meet his sister.

Upon arriving at the Tribeca Grill, he was ushered to a table for two, at which sat an older, blond woman. When she looked up at him, he saw a pair of blue eyes that matched his own.

She fanned a hand to her mouth before standing. "I'm Kelly."

"Gabriel Emerson." He shook her hand awkwardly.

Her eyes filled with tears. "You look just like him."

"Like whom?"

"Dad."

Without thinking, Gabriel pulled his hand back.

Kelly managed a smile. "I'm sorry. Please." She gestured to the empty seat across from hers.

She sat down and dabbed at her eyes with a napkin.

"It was just such a shock, seeing you there. You look just like Dad did when he was young. How old are you, if you don't mind me asking?"

"Thirty-five."

"I remember being thirty-five. I won't play coy and make you guess my age. I'm forty-nine."

Gabriel nodded, his jaw clenching and unclenching. He tried to formulate something to say but found himself at a loss. Mercifully, they were interrupted by the waiter.

They ordered drinks and made small talk until the waiter returned. Then they placed their dinner orders, waiting almost impatiently for the waiter to leave again.

Kelly leaned forward in her chair.

"I'm so pleased to meet you. Thank you for accepting my invitation."

"Not at all." Gabriel tried to force a smile.

"I owe you an apology."

His smile disappeared. "For what?"

"As I said in my letter, I should have reached out to you when I learned of your existence. I should have done the right thing rather than worrying about upsetting my mother."

Gabriel's hands drifted to his silverware. "That was a long time ago. We don't need to speak of it."

"Thank you. I should mention that my mother knew about you but would never discuss you, even after Dad died. She never forgave him for having a mistress."

Gabriel's body visibly tightened.

"So you didn't know about me before?"

"No, but I knew your mother. I'm sorry to hear that she passed away." Kelly offered a sympathetic look.

"Thank you." Gabriel straightened in his chair. "She died when I was nine. But the family who adopted me are very good."

"Michael mentioned that. He told me that our father had kept apprised of you and your doings for years."

Gabriel's eyebrows shot up. "What?"

"Didn't you know that?"

"No. We left New York just before my mother died. I didn't have contact with your father after that." Gabriel ground his teeth. "Not a phone call, not a letter, nothing."

"I'm so sorry. I assumed there was some contact between you and Dad, based on what Michael said." Kelly sipped her wine thoughtfully. "He told me that Dad was aware of the family who adopted you, and that he knew you went to Princeton and Harvard. Apparently, you were a topic of conversation between them over the years."

"If he was interested enough to discuss my life with his lawyer, why wasn't he interested enough to pick up the telephone? Or to write a letter?"

Kelly looked down at the tablecloth. "I think I can shed some light on that. Dad was the kind of man who made a decision and stuck to it." She lifted her face, surveying Gabriel's body language with concern. "But I'm worried this conversation is upsetting you."

"I'm here for answers," he clipped. "I knew they weren't going to be pleasant."

"Yes, of course. So you knew Dad?"

"I met him, yes."

"But you grew up in Pennsylvania, after you left New York?" she prompted.

"I was fortunate that when my mother died, a family connected with the hospital agreed to take me in."

"And your mother's family?"

He grimaced and said nothing.

"I don't mean to pry. But it's something I wondered. I met your mother a few times, and she seemed to be close to her parents. So I wondered why you didn't go and live with them."

"My grandfather died before I was born. My grandmother became estranged with my mother over the circumstances surrounding my conception. When my mother died, my grandmother told social services they couldn't take me. My adoptive mother contacted my father, but he disowned me. I would have ended up in foster care were it not for the Clarks." Gabriel's expression was shuttered.

"I'm so sorry." Kelly leaned forward in her chair. "You haven't had it easy, have you?"

"You knew my mother?" He swiftly changed the subject.

"She was one of the secretaries in my father's office. She was young and pretty, and whenever I went to visit my dad, she was always kind to me. I liked her very much. Around the time you were born or maybe shortly thereafter, my parents had a series of fights. And then everything calmed down. But a few years later, my mother left my father and moved in with my grandparents on Long Island. Six months later, my parents reconciled and she moved back to Manhattan. I'm speculating, of course, but I'm guessing the separation had something to do with you. One of the things I overheard my mother yelling about was 'that child.' Of course, Audrey and I had no idea who she was talking about. We assumed they were fighting over one of us."

Gabriel pressed his lips together. "How old were you when they separated?"

"Um, let me see." Kelly looked up at the ceiling. "I'd say twenty-three? Thereabouts."

"I would have been nine. That was when we left New York."

"My mother probably gave Dad an ultimatum and that's why your mother decided to leave."

"Did you ever speak to your mother about any of this?"

Kelly's eyes widened in horror. "Absolutely not. My parents fought, but they never told us what their fights were about. I wouldn't have had the nerve to ask Mother about it, even as an adult."

"Can you tell me anything else about my mother?"

Kelly regarded their place settings thoughtfully. "She was beautiful and very sweet. She was young and full of life. My mother was a bit of a social climber and she could be very difficult. I don't know if you realize this, but the age difference between your parents would have been considerable. Dad was born in 1936. Your mother must have been twenty years younger."

"I gathered that. What can you tell me about him?"

"I loved Dad, but he worked a lot. I have happy memories of going for walks with him in the city and having pancakes with him on Saturday morning. He was a pretty good father, even if he wasn't a very good husband."

"But your mother loved him."

"Of course." Kelly sounded offended. "He was handsome and charming. He had a great sense of humor and he was very accomplished.

He just happened to be a philanderer. As surprising as it may sound, he adored my mother." At this, Kelly's eyes watered. She was quiet for a moment as she fought to control her emotions.

"I see this is upsetting for you, too. I'm sorry." Gabriel's tone was gentle.

Kelly waved a Kleenex in the air before drying her eyes.

"It was a shock when we found out he'd had a mistress and that we had a brother. Audrey hasn't quite gotten over it."

"And you?"

Kelly put on a brave face.

"I try to practice what I tell my patients and their parents. You can't control all of life's circumstances, but you can control your reactions to them. I could stay angry at my father for cheating on my mother. And I could be angry with my mother for being so hard-hearted that she kept me apart from my only brother. Or I could choose to forgive them, and myself, and try to make things better."

Her eyes fell to her hands, which were resting in her lap. "I always wanted a brother. I just didn't expect him to be so young."

"For what it's worth, I'm sorry. I'm sorry my mother and your father were . . . involved." Gabriel's expression softened in sympathy.

Her eyes met his. "Thank you, Gabriel. Don't the strangest sort of miracles come out of the worst of circumstances? Here we sit, after all these years. Knowing Dad, as I did, I'm sure he must have cared for your mother. And you. He wouldn't have watched you from afar or included you in his estate if he didn't."

"I'm not sure." Gabriel pushed his meal aside.

"I can't imagine him fighting with my mother over something he didn't care about. And it was no secret in our family that he always wanted a son. But my mother didn't want another child."

Kelly's head bent so she could stare at her dinner plate. She'd barely touched her food.

"I wish you'd had more time with him. I know that in wishing that, Audrey and I would have had less time." She gave Gabriel a sad smile. "But I would have shared him."

"And Audrey?"

"Audrey." Kelly sighed. "Audrey sided with my mother. She sees you as a gold digger."

"I didn't want the money." Gabriel's tone was harsh. "I only accepted it because I found myself and my adoptive family in dire circumstances."

Kelly reached out to him across the table, placing her hand over his.

"I don't begrudge you a penny." She patted his hand before withdrawing. "Dad made a series of choices that had consequences for all of us. But he's dead. Our mothers are dead. It's time to forgive and move on. Certainly, Gabriel, you did nothing to hurt us. You could have sued the estate for more. You could have appeared at the reading of the will and embarrassed my mother. You could have called a press conference or spoken to a tabloid. But you didn't. Your actions show that you are a man of character, and that was another reason why I wanted to meet you. I think God brought us together." She gazed at her brother cautiously.

He blinked a little. "My wife tends to think like that. She sees Providence in everything."

"I would agree with her." Kelly finished her wine. "Do you mind if I ask what prompted you to write to Michael?"

"I don't think it was Providence. Although perhaps it was." Gabriel toyed with his water glass. "I'm afraid my curiosity was practical more than anything else. Eventually my wife and I would like to have a family. I wanted to know more about my parents' medical history."

"That's a problem easily solved. Dad died of a heart attack. He didn't exercise, he was a workaholic, and he ate whatever he wanted. I'm not sure he was born with a tendency for high cholesterol, although it's possible. Certainly, Audrey and I don't have that problem. As for his parents, as far as I know, they died in old age of natural causes. Did you know about them?"

"Not at all. Not even their names."

Kelly's expression saddened.

"I'm sorry to hear that. We're very proud of our grandparents. Grandfather was a professor, like you. He taught Romantic literature."

"What was his name?"

"Benjamin Spiegel."

Gabriel sat bolt upright. "Benjamin Spiegel? Professor Benjamin Spiegel?"

"Yes. You know of him?"

"Of course. He was the leading American expert in German Romanticism. We read his work in graduate school." Gabriel rubbed at his chin. "He was my grandfather?"

"Yes."

"But he was . . ." A look of realization came over Gabriel's face.

Kelly tilted her head, watching him closely. "Jewish, yes."

Gabriel looked confused. "I had no idea our father was Jewish. It was never mentioned."

"I can't speak for your mother, of course, but there's a long story behind Dad's silence. He had a youthful falling out with his father and changed his last name to Davies, leaving his family and heritage behind. By the time he met and married my mother, in 1961, he presented himself as an agnostic. So Judaism wasn't part of our household."

Gabriel sat very still, his mind working.

"Benjamin Spiegel," he muttered. "I admire his writing very much."

"He was a good man. He was a rabbi, you know, before he left Germany in the twenties. He was also a much-beloved professor at Columbia. There's a building named for him, as well as a number of scholarships. When he died, our grandmother, Miriam, founded a charitable organization in his name here in New York. I'm on the board, along with several of our cousins. I'm sure they'd welcome your involvement, if you're interested."

"What does the organization do?"

"We promote literacy and reading in the New York public school system and donate books and supplies to classrooms. We also fund a lecture series at Columbia and at his former temple. Jonathan and I always attend." She smiled. "We like to say that we're part of the Presbyterian wing of Reform Judaism."

Gabriel returned her smile. "I didn't know I was German. Or Jewish. My mother's family was English, I think."

"Many people would be surprised at what they find in their family tree if they look back a generation or two. Which is why all this hatred between races and religions is so foolish. We're all family, in one way or another."

"I agree."

Kelly smiled. "Since you're a professor of literature, I think it would be fitting for you to deliver the lectures at Columbia one year."

"That's very kind of you to say, but I'm afraid I'm a Dante specialist."

"Grandfather was interested in everything, judging from the books in his library. I'm sure Dante was there somewhere."

Gabriel wiped his lips with his napkin. "Won't it be an embarrassment to the family?"

Kelly's sapphire eyes grew momentarily fierce, rather like that of a lioness.

"You *are* family. And if anyone dares to object, well . . ." Her voice trailed off as if she were contemplating something particularly nasty. "Apart from Audrey, I think you'll find everyone to be civil."

"In that case, please tell the committee it would be an honor." He bowed his head slightly.

"Excellent. I'll mention you to the cousins."

Kelly pushed her plate of food away and signaled to the waiter to remove it.

"You've barely eaten." She looked with some distress at his full plate.

"I'm afraid I'm not hungry." He indicated that the waiter take his meal, as well. Then he ordered coffee.

"Have I upset you?" Kelly's voice was low.

Gabriel paused.

"No. It's just a lot to process." His expression shifted and his eyes grew alight. "The revelation that Professor Spiegel is my grandfather is a welcome surprise."

Her mouth widened into a smile.

"I'd like to introduce you to Aunt Sarah, Dad's youngest sister. She can tell you all about her parents and your aunts and uncles. She's a wonderful lady. Very bright." Kelly regarded him for a moment. "Did your mother ever explain why she called you Gabriel?"

"No. My middle name is Owen, after our father."

Kelly's blue eyes sparkled. "His birth name was Othniel. Be grateful he rid himself of it before you were born."

"Does my name have any significance to you?" Gabriel waited with anticipation for her answer.

"I'm afraid not. Except that when Audrey was a teenager and my parents bought her a dog for her birthday, she wanted to call him Gabriel. Dad threw a fit and said no." Kelly looked off into space. "I'd forgotten about that until this very minute. My parents had a fight about that, too." She made eye contact with Gabriel again. "In the end, she called the dog Godfrey, which was a very silly name for a Pomeranian. But Pomeranians are a silly breed, I think. Jonathan and I always had Labradors."

Gabriel was silent, not knowing what to say.

After a moment, he spoke.

"His name isn't on my birth certificate. And I wasn't granted his surname, obviously."

Kelly appeared uncomfortable. "I'm afraid I already knew that. When my mother and sister decided to contest the will, that was one of the pieces of evidence they cited. But Dad had signed an affidavit before he died, affirming that he was your father and stating that he persuaded your mother not to name him on your birth certificate. I don't know what kinds of promises Dad gave to your mother. But he must have felt guilty over what he did. Eventually."

"Humph," said Gabriel.

"In fact, I think he must have felt something more than guilt." She picked up her large handbag and went through it. "Here." She placed an old photograph on the table, next to Gabriel's empty coffee cup.

The picture was of him and his mother. He looked to be about five years old.

"I don't remember this picture. Where did you find it?" He peered at it closely.

"Dad kept a box of things on his dresser. When my mother died, it came to me. I was looking at it the other night and I noticed there was a place where the fabric on the inside of the box had been ripped. Inside the hole, I found the picture. He must have been hiding it from my mother."

"I don't know what to do with this." Gabriel gestured to the picture.

"Keep it, of course. I have some other things for you, too."

"I couldn't."

"Do you read German?"

"Yes."

"Good." She laughed, the sound soft and musical. "I understand a little German because Dad used to speak it now and then, but I don't read it. So Grandfather's books are of no use to me. And I won't wear Dad's cuff links. So you see, you'd be doing me a favor by taking them off my hands. In fact, given the size of our apartment and the amount of things in it, it would be a mitzvah."

"A mitzvah," he mumbled, as the waiter served their coffee.

"I've been very rude, Gabriel, doing most of the talking and not asking about yourself or your wife. I hope I'll be able to meet her."

"I'd like that." Gabriel finally cracked a smile. "Her name is Julianne. She's a graduate student at Harvard."

"She has a lovely name. How long have you been married?"

"Since January."

"Ah, newlyweds. Do you have a picture?"

Gabriel wiped his hands with his napkin before pulling out his iPhone. He quickly scrolled to a recent photograph of Julia sitting behind his desk at their house in Cambridge. Unthinkingly, he stroked the curve of her cheek with his thumb as he gazed at the photo.

He handed the phone to his sister.

"You must love her very much." Kelly had been watching him intently.

"I do."

"She looks young."

Gabriel barely suppressed a frown. "She's younger than me, yes."

Kelly chuckled. "At my age, everyone looks young."

She was about to return the phone when she stopped. She peered closely at the photo. Then she tapped at the screen to enlarge it.

"What's that on your desk?" She held the phone out to Gabriel, pointing to a small, black object.

"That's a train engine. I've had it since I was a boy. Julia thought it would make a fine paperweight."

Kelly stared at the photo again.

Gabriel frowned. "What is it?"

"It looks familiar."

"Familiar?"

She lifted her head to look at him.

"Dad had one, from when he was a child. He kept the engine, one car, and a caboose on his dresser. Then one day, the engine disappeared. When Audrey asked him about it he said that it got broken. We thought at the time it was a feeble excuse. The engine was made of iron. Where did you say you got it from?"

"I don't remember. I've always had it."

"Interesting," she breathed.

"Why?"

"The train was his favorite toy when he was a child. I think his initials were scratched into the bottom of the engine." She gave Gabriel a significant look. "When you get home, you should check. I'd be interested in knowing."

"Would it make a difference?"

"If it's the one I'm thinking of, then he must have given it to you. Since it meant so much to him, I think you must have meant a lot to him, too." She returned his phone to him.

"I can't believe that."

She toyed with her coffee cup, swirling her spoon in the brown liquid before placing it on the saucer. "But you see, I knew him. I knew him for years. He was a complicated man, a driven man, but he wasn't cruel. He found himself caught between your mother and you, and my mother and us. I'm not saying he made the right choice. If he'd been stronger or my mother had been more forgiving, he could have had all his children living in the same city. The whole thing reminds me a little of the story of Hagar and Ishmael from the Bible. I can't help but suspect my mother played the part of Sarah. Even though her name was Nancy. I want to believe that he loved you. That he cared about you and that's why he kept tabs on you and included you in his will."

"I can't believe that." Gabriel's tone was cold.

"But it's possible, brother. He wasn't a monster. And, 'There are more things in Heaven and earth, Horatio, than are dreamt of in your philosophy.'"

"Hamlet," said Gabriel, begrudgingly.

"I like to think our grandfather would be proud of both of us. You went to Harvard. I went to Vassar." She smiled. "Is your wife—is Julianne religious?"

Gabriel tucked the photograph Kelly had given him in the inner pocket of his suit jacket.

"Yes. She's Catholic and her faith means something to her. Certainly, she tries to live it."

"And you?"

"I converted to Catholicism prior to our marriage. I believe, if that's what you're asking."

"I don't think we have a Catholic on the foundation's board. You'll be the first." Kelly signaled to the waiter to bring the check. "Wait till the cousins learn that there's now a Catholic wing of Reform Judaism."

"It was a mistake." Gabriel huffed into his cell phone, as he connected with Julia's voice mail. *"I shouldn't have come without you.*

"Julianne, I wish you wouldn't switch off your phone. It's the best way for me to get hold of you. It's after midnight and I've just gotten into my hotel room after having dinner with Kelly.

"Sorry I couldn't call you earlier. Our conversation went longer than expected. She's very nice. You were right, as usual. Funny how you're almost always right. [exhaling slowly]

"The portrait Kelly painted of our father is very different from the one I remember. I didn't have the heart to tell her that the man she adored hit my mother. [sigh]

"I wish you were here. By the end of dinner I was beginning to doubt my memories. To doubt myself.

"I need you to do something for me. Can you look at the train engine on my desk and see if there is anything scratched into the bottom of it? It's important.

"I'm going to have to extend my visit. There's an aunt Kelly wants to introduce me to on Friday. This means I won't be leaving until Saturday. I'm sorry about that but I think it's best to tie up all the loose ends before I come home.

Call me when you get this message, no matter what time it is." [another pause] "Apparuit iam beatitudo vestra. *I love you."*

Gabriel tossed his cell phone on the large, empty bed.

He was still processing his conversation with his sister. Much of what she'd said surprised him. It was clear that her relationship with her father was loving and good. In this respect, as in others, it appeared that he and Kelly had two very different fathers.

It had been a relief to have some of his questions answered, even if the answers led to more questions. Certainly, the news about his grandfather was good. A warm feeling spread in his chest at the thought.

At least I have one blood relative I can be proud of, in addition to my sister.

How he wished he could have come home to a sleeping Julianne and tell her what had happened. How he wished he could crawl into her arms and erase the day. He'd made a colossal error when he determined to do things alone. And now, as usual, he was forced to live with the consequences.

Cursing himself, he strode to the shower, hoping that the hot water would clear his head. Then he was going to finish reading his mother's diary, to see if he could discover the truth about his parents' relationship.

Chapter Fifty-eight

December 5, 2011
Washington, D.C.

Natalie Lundy stared at the photograph in shock.

She heard a strange buzzing sound as her world suddenly came to a halt. She looked at the black-and-white picture—at the man and the young blond woman holding one another and smiling for the camera. At the large diamond solitaire glittering on the woman's finger. At the announcement of the union of two powerful political families.

Natalie's stomach rebelled. She heaved over the wastepaper basket, emptying herself of that morning's breakfast. Shakily, she wiped her mouth and stumbled to the bathroom.

She drank a cup of water as her mind worked. She'd just lost everything. She'd heard the rumors, of course. But she also knew that Simon was only with Senator Hudson's daughter for political reasons. Or so he'd said the last time he'd been in her bed, at the end of August.

She'd done what he told her to do. She'd worked for his father and kept her mouth shut. She'd emailed or called Simon on occasion, but his responses had become fewer and fewer until they ceased altogether, sometime in November.

He'd been playing her. He'd been playing her for years. Always panting after someone else while satisfying himself with her body.

And she'd done things for him. Things she hadn't wanted to do, such as various sexual acts and pretending not to care while he fucked other women.

She stared at her reflection in the bathroom mirror as a terrible idea took hold.

She had nothing to lose, but everything to gain. He had everything to lose and God damn it, she'd see that he lost it.

She put the water glass aside and wiped her mouth, darting into the bedroom on surer feet. She crouched on the floor and pried aside one of the floorboards underneath her bed. She withdrew a flash drive and carefully put it in her jacket pocket. Then she replaced the floorboard.

Grabbing her coat and purse, she headed to the door. As she hailed a taxi, she didn't notice the dark car parked across the street. So she didn't realize that it pulled into traffic behind the cab, following at a safe distance.

Chapter Fifty-nine

Gabriel, are you getting my messages? This is the third time I've called and gotten your voice mail.

"I left you a message this morning about the train engine. There are letters scratched into the bottom of it and they say 'O.S.' I don't know what that means, do you? And how did you know to look for them? I never noticed them before.

"I'm sorry you have to extend your trip but I understand. I hope that your meeting with your aunt goes well.

"I'm at the library working on my last seminar paper. You know we're not allowed to talk on the phone here. Text me and I'll step outside and call you back. I love you. And I miss you."

Julia groaned as she ended the call. Gabriel's messages had been melancholy and sad, and growing more so. Somehow, between all his errands and her attempts at completing and submitting her lecture for publication, they'd missed one another. She worried about him.

At least if she could complete her final seminar paper, she'd be finished for the semester. Then she and Gabriel could begin their Christmas holidays.

She began typing on her laptop in earnest.

"What do you think of Giuseppe Pacciani of Florence?" Lucia Barini, chair of the Department of Italian at Columbia University, gazed at Gabriel over her desk.

He snorted. "Not much. He's published a few things in addition to his book, but nothing of consequence, in my opinion. Why do you ask?"

"We're conducting a search to replace one of our retiring professors and he's on our long list."

Gabriel lifted his eyebrows. "Oh, really?"

"However, a graduate student has made serious allegations against him, dating all the way back to when she was his student in Florence. You know her—Christa Peterson."

Gabriel grimaced. "Yes, I know her."

"I heard the rumors about what happened in Toronto. I also heard that Christa started those rumors and that she's one of the reasons why you and Julianne are no longer there."

"Julianne was admitted to Harvard. We were getting married. I was eager to leave Toronto." Gabriel's affect was decidedly flat.

Lucia gave him a friendly smile. "Of course. I only realized what a problem Christa had been after Jeremy Martin persuaded me to take her. Otherwise, I wouldn't have been inclined to admit her. We receive a lot of applications and can afford to be choosy."

Gabriel simply sat, immobile like a statue.

Lucia removed her glasses. "It's come to my attention that Christa is a troublemaker and that she takes her troublemaking tendencies wherever she goes. She had trouble with Pacciani in Florence, she had trouble in Toronto, and apparently, she had trouble with Katherine Picton in Oxford this summer. Katherine telephoned to tell me to start teaching etiquette to our graduate students since it's obvious they don't know how to behave in public." Lucia's tone was absent any amusement. "I don't like receiving calls like that from anyone, especially from her. This semester, my faculty informed me that no one wants to serve on Christa's examination committee. They're worried about being slandered for harassment."

Gabriel's look was pointed. "They're right to be worried."

"That was my thought, as well. Now I'm in the awkward position of either having to agree to supervise Christa myself, and offending Katherine, or having to tell her to go elsewhere." Lucia tossed her glasses on the desk in front of her. "I don't suppose you have any suggestions?"

Gabriel paused, knowing in that instant that Christa's academic career rested in his hands. He could explain, in detail, what really happened in Toronto and Oxford, and demonstrate the lengths to which

Christa would go for a sexual conquest. Such information would no doubt make up Lucia's mind for her.

He pulled his glasses out of his pocket and then put them back again, acutely aware of the words Julia (and St. Francis) would whisper in his ear.

Exposing Christa would also expose himself and Julianne. She didn't want the rumors fed. And she deserved to be able to stand in a room filled with academics and be seen for herself, and not as part of a scandal.

Lucia was a friend, but not a close one. Gabriel didn't want to revisit every encounter he'd ever had with Christa Peterson, embarrassing himself and his wife. For her sake, and the sake of her reputation, he decided to try a different tack.

"If we put the personal issues aside, I can tell you that Christa's work for me was mediocre."

"That's been my impression. If you couple that with her behavior . . ." Lucia shrugged. "She's a liability."

"I doubt Pacciani is blameless. I've seen him in action."

"He represents another difficult situation." Lucia gestured to a file that was sitting open on her desk. "Christa is making allegations about his past behavior, but there are reports that he beds his students and that's why he's eager to leave Florence. I don't want that in my department for obvious reasons, not least of which is because it invites lawsuits."

"Yes," said Gabriel, tapping his foot unconsciously.

Lucia placed her glasses in a case, which she then tucked into her purse. "Enough of my troubles. Let me take you to lunch. I have reservations at Del Posto."

She pushed back from her desk. "We have a lot of catching up to do. Is it true that Julianne told Don Wodehouse that the question he asked wasn't germane to her thesis?"

Gabriel laughed uproariously. "No, that isn't true. At least, not exactly."

He followed Lucia out of the office, proudly describing Julianne's presentation and the way she handled her questioners, including Professor Wodehouse of Magdalen College.

❧❧

"Damnation." Gabriel cursed his iPhone, which appeared to be dead.

As if he had the power of resurrection, he shook it, pressing the *on* button repeatedly. He'd almost decided to fling the item into Central Park out of frustration when he remembered that he'd neglected to charge it the evening before.

"Julianne will be worried," he muttered, as he walked the streets of New York to Michael Wasserstein's office.

Mr. Wasserstein was retired, but since he'd been Owen Davies's attorney from the time he penned a prenuptial agreement for him in 1961, he'd agreed to meet Gabriel at his former law firm.

Gabriel looked at his watch. He had just enough time to make a quick call to Julianne from a pay phone before his meeting.

He located an obliging phone at Columbus Circle, swiped his credit card, and dialed her cell phone. After several rings, he received her voice mail, once again.

"Damnation," he muttered (once again).

"Julianne, for God's sake, answer your damn phone. I'm going to have to buy you a pager. [loud exhale] I'm sorry. That was rude. Would you please answer your phone? I'm calling from a pay phone because I forgot to charge my phone last night and now it's dead. When I get back to my room I'll charge it. [brief pause] Now I'm wondering if I brought the charger cord with me. I can't seem to remember a damn thing. See what happens when I'm away from you? I'm lucky I'm not homeless and panhandling. I'm on my way to see my father's attorney. Apparently, he has some things he wants to say in person. [longer pause] I wish you were here. I love you. Call me when you get this message."

Gabriel hung up the phone, then continued walking, his thoughts on his upcoming appointment.

❧❧

"So how's it going, Rach?" Julianne asked her friend that evening, connected as they were by long distance.

"It's fine." Rachel's normally cheerful demeanor was decidedly subdued.

"What's wrong?"

Julianne could hear a door open and close.

"I'm just going into the bedroom so Aaron can't hear me."

"Why? Is something wrong?"

"Yes. No. I don't know." Rachel sounded exasperated.

"Can I help?'

"Can you get me pregnant? If so, I'll book you the next flight to Philadelphia. And I'll see that you're canonized for performing a miracle."

"Rach." Julia's tone was gently reproachful.

"What's wrong with me?" Rachel began to cry.

Julia's heart tore at the sound of her best friend's sobs. Rachel's tears were the soul-baring cries of a woman who desperately wished to become a mother.

"Rachel, sweetie. I'm so sorry." Julia felt her own eyes water as she listened, not knowing what to say.

When Rachel's tears subsided, she spoke. "We've both been to the doctor. The problem isn't Aaron. The problem is me. I'm not ovulating. So I'm going to have to start having hormone injections in the hope that they can jump-start my ovaries. Or else . . ."

Rachel sniffled.

"I'm so sorry. Are the hormone injections a big deal?" Julia's question was hesitant.

"You could say that. Damn it, I don't know why my body won't cooperate! The one time I want it to do something important, it fails me. I just don't understand."

"What does Aaron say?"

Rachel laughed. "It's what he doesn't say. He keeps telling me that it's all right, that everything will work out. I'd rather he told me that he was pissed off and disappointed."

"Is he?"

"How could he not be? I am."

"I'm sure he's upset because you are."

"That doesn't help me."

"Then talk to him."

"Why, so I can discuss how much of a failure I am? No thanks."

"Rach, you aren't a failure. And it sounds like you have options. So don't give up hope."

Rachel didn't respond.

"Do you want to come up for a visit?"

"No. Work is really busy right now. But you're coming home for Christmas, right?"

"That's right. We'll be home next week, I think. Sooner if Diane goes into labor."

"Have you heard from them lately?"

"I talk to them on the phone every Sunday, and Diane sends me email updates. So far everything is okay, but they're still worried about the stress of delivery on the baby. She's going to deliver at the Children's Hospital, which means they'll have to drive into Philadelphia when she goes into labor. Or get a hotel in the city around her due date."

"When is she due?"

"December twenty-third."

Rachel was silent again.

Julia heard the sound of a door opening and then Aaron's voice.

"Jules, I'm going to have to go." Rachel's voice was muffled. "But I'll call you later, okay?"

"Sure. I love you, Rachel. Don't give up hope."

"That's all I have left." Rachel sniffed again before hanging up the phone.

Julia placed the handset back in its cradle on the desk before saying a long prayer for her friend.

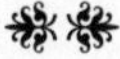

"This is ridiculous." Julia pushed her cell phone away from her the following evening.

"What's the matter?" Rebecca breezed into the kitchen with a stack of dish towels, fresh from the laundry room.

"Gabriel. I'm receiving his messages, but we haven't been able to speak since he left. I keep calling and calling and all I get is voice mail—on his cell phone and in his hotel room." She placed her head in her hands. "I found the charger cord to his phone upstairs. He's going to have to buy another one. Or call me from the hotel. But he seems to be out *all the time*."

"They took most of the pay phones off the streets of New York. He'll have trouble finding one while he's out." Rebecca folded the dish towels and placed them in a drawer.

Julia drummed her fingers on the granite countertop while staring daggers at her cell phone.

"I should have gone with him."

"Why didn't you?"

"I had papers to finish. I still have one left to do, but now I can't concentrate." She lifted her face to look at Rebecca. "I'm worried about him."

"I'm sure he's all right. Although it isn't like him to forget something." Rebecca gestured toward the phone cord. "He's usually so—fastidious."

"That's a polite word for it."

Julia glanced at the mail that Rebecca had stacked on the kitchen island and noticed an envelope addressed to Gabriel from JetBlue.

She stood up straight.

"Do you think I could get a flight to New York tonight?" Julia reached for her laptop.

"It won't be cheap, but you could try." Rebecca smiled gently. "Gabriel has only been gone two days."

"It seems like forever," muttered Julia.

Rebecca's face wore a knowing look. "That's because you're still newlyweds."

Julia pulled up the JetBlue website and began typing furiously.

"The prices are a fortune," she lamented, as she scrolled through several pages.

"Think of it as an early Christmas gift."

"It isn't as if I spend a lot of money on things," she rationalized. "Gabriel is the one who insists on paying top dollar for everything."

"He'll be glad you bought the ticket when he sees you." Rebecca glanced toward the stairs. "I can pull out your suitcase and help you pack. If your flight is tonight, you'll probably have to leave right away. You don't want to be stuck in rush hour traffic on the way to the airport."

Julia lifted her arm and gave Rebecca a hug. "Thank you. He'll be so surprised."

"He's probably in worse shape than you," Rebecca observed, as she headed toward the stairs.

Within two hours, Julia was at Logan Airport, waiting for the last flight to John F. Kennedy Airport in New York. She left a message for Gabriel with the concierge at the Ritz-Carlton, telling him that she would be checking in later that evening, and she ordered sparkling water, strawberries, and truffles to be delivered to their room.

Rebecca had been in the middle of packing her carry-on when she'd flown into the bedroom, telling her that the taxi was on its way. Julia was in such a hurry, she'd quickly grabbed her makeup and toothbrush, leaving her other essentials behind.

She packed up her laptop and research (which were far more important than personal items, since she needed to finish her seminar paper), located her purse, and made it to the front door just in time to greet the arriving taxi.

Gabriel was going to be surprised.

**

The Professor ordered the cabbie to wait for him before exiting the taxi. They'd parked down the street from the house he was interested in, so as not to attract attention.

He walked down the street slowly, noting the numbers on the houses. It was a residential neighborhood on Staten Island, populated by old, small homes.

Then he saw it.

The house itself was unremarkable—small and white with a detached garage and a short, paved driveway. It was situated on a very small lot, with a tiny fringe of lawn that separated the front of the house from the sidewalk. A new-looking black Mercedes was parked at the curb.

Gabriel stood, two houses down, watching.

To his surprise, the front door opened and a man with gray hair exited. The man turned his body, coaxing an elderly woman. After she'd closed and locked the door behind them, he took her arm and painstakingly escorted her down the front steps.

Gabriel approached.

The woman must have been hard of hearing because the man's voice was raised, but not in anger. Gabriel heard something about a doctor's appointment and Joey's birthday party.

The woman caught sight of Gabriel and stopped, staring over at him.

He slowed his pace, finally pausing on the sidewalk across the street.

This was his moment.

Now was his opportunity to speak to her, to demand answers to questions, to reveal himself.

The man she was with glanced in Gabriel's direction, then began tugging at the woman's arm, his voice still raised.

The woman turned away from Gabriel and obediently followed her escort to the Mercedes, where he opened the door and patiently waited while she situated herself.

The man seemed oblivious to the Professor's presence as he closed the car door and rounded the vehicle. He started the car and drove away.

Gabriel watched the Mercedes turn the corner and disappear out of sight.

Chapter Sixty

It was well after midnight when Gabriel entered his hotel room. He was world weary and tired, his hair disheveled, his tie askew.

Without bothering to switch on a light, he threw his winter coat over a chair and kicked off his boots.

(It should be mentioned that his boots were almost, but not quite, bad-assed, given that they were worn with a suit.)

Just as he was removing his tie, light streamed from the lamp on one of the nightstands.

"What the—"

Gabriel's curse was interrupted by a feminine voice. "Sweetie?"

His eyes focused on the sight of Julianne, naked in bed with tousled hair. Her dark eyes were soft and sleepy, her ruby lips parted, her voice deliciously husky.

She looked like a sex kitten.

"Um, surprise." She waved.

With a cry, Gabriel ran toward her, crawling across the bed and placing his hands to her face so he could kiss her. He kissed her long and he kissed her well, their tongues touching until they were both breathless.

"What are you doing here?" He pushed her hair lovingly back from her face.

"Delivering the charger cord for your iPhone." She pointed to the forgotten item sitting on the nightstand.

His long fingers slid to the back of her neck, where they massaged her skin. His eyes gleamed.

"You flew to New York to give me my phone cord?"

"Not just your phone cord. I also brought the attachment that plugs into the wall. You know, in case you wanted to charge it through an outlet."

He kissed her nose. "I really missed that cord. Thank you."

"Did you miss the attachment?"

"Absolutely. I was very, very lonely for it." His lips curved into a half-smile.

"I was worried about you. We kept missing each other on the telephone."

Gabriel's expression shifted and his eyes looked tired. "We need a better form of communication."

"Smoke signals, perhaps?"

"At this point, I'd accept passenger pigeons."

She gestured to the table that held the strawberries and chocolates, some of which had already been consumed. "I ordered room service. I'm afraid I started without you. I didn't expect you to be so late."

He moved so that his back was against the headboard and pulled her into his lap, tucking the sheet around her naked body so she wouldn't catch cold. "If I'd known you were waiting, I'd have come home hours ago. I was on Staten Island and then I went to Brooklyn to see our old apartment."

"How did it go?"

"Everything seemed smaller than I remember it—the neighborhood, the building." He brought their foreheads together. "I'm glad you're here. I regretted my decision to come on my own almost the moment I left the house."

She breathed deeply, inhaling his scent. She smelled Aramis and coffee and something that could have been soap. But she didn't smell smoke.

"You're quite the secret agent, Julianne. I had no idea you were coming."

"I left a message for you with the concierge. When I arrived, he had one of the porters escort me." She gazed around the room. "It's a beautiful room."

His lips twitched. "I would have booked a suite if I'd known you were coming."

"This is far nicer than I could have imagined. And it has a breathtaking view of Central Park."

His arms tightened around her. "So now that you're here, what am I going to do with you?"

"You're going to kiss me. Then you're going to take off your suit and show me just how much you missed your phone cord."

"And the attachment."

"And the attachment."

"I hope you napped on the plane." Gabriel grinned before bringing his eager mouth to hers.

Chapter Sixty-one

Gabriel was still inside her, their bodies entwined. Julia was running her fingers lazily up and down his back as he held himself above her.

"You're my family." His thumb traced the curve of her cheek.

Julia's eyes met his.

He continued, his voice a husky whisper. "All this searching, all this anxiety, when what I was looking for was right here."

"Darling." She pressed her palm against his jaw.

"I'm sorry I got lost in my head and shut you out."

"Sweetie, you needed to find out more about your family. It was part of your healing."

"What I needed was you."

She gave him a heartbreaking smile, as if he'd handed her the world.

"I need you, too, Gabriel. I was sad while you were gone, even though Rebecca stayed with me. The house was so empty. And sleeping alone sucks."

He laughed, and her body reacted to his movements.

"Remind me of this conversation the next time I'm determined to go off on my own."

"*A man has to do what a man has to do.* But he should bring his wife with him." She pushed his hair back from his forehead.

"I'd never argue with a naked woman."

Her pretty features grew pensive.

He stroked her cheek again, his blue eyes darkening. "Have I made you sad?"

"I was just thinking about what Grace used to say."

"And what's that?"

"That marriage is a mystery. That two people somehow become knitted together until they're one. When we're separated, I feel as if part of me is missing." She shifted slightly beneath him. "I'm glad you feel it, too."

"I felt it before we were married, but it's different now. The ache is more intense."

"For a long time, I didn't see how marriage could be something over and above love. But it is. I just can't explain it."

"Neither can I. Perhaps that's why she called it a mystery."

He looked down the length of their bodies.

"I suppose I should let you go."

"I like this. It's postcoital-cuddling-while-you're-still-inside-me."

"That's the technical description, yes. If we wait long enough, we'll be able to start up again."

Julia flexed her muscles around him, and he twitched in response.

"As I recall, Professor, your recovery time is minimal."

"Thank God for that," he murmured, beginning to move inside her once again.

❧❧

It must be said that in general, the Emersons slept better when they were together than they ever did apart. That evening was no exception.

(When they finally stopped making love long enough to sleep, that is.)

The following morning, Gabriel awoke, noticing that Julianne was still slumbering, her face pressed against one of his pectorals. He studied her profile without moving, resisting the urge to lift her chin so he could kiss her.

Instead, he memorized the skin of her back and shoulders with his fingers.

A great burden had been lifted from him. He hadn't received exactly the answers he'd wished, but he'd received something better—the gift of his sister and his grandfather. Professor Spiegel was erudite and noble, well known for his intellectual insight and charity. He was a man Gabriel desired to know better. He was an ancestor whose blood he would be glad to pass on to his children.

The thought comforted him.

Kelly had introduced a seed of suspicion that their father was not the monster he'd thought. Gabriel's memories and dreams were mixed to such a degree that it was possible he'd confused one with the other. Still, the facts he knew for certain about his father were damning enough.

What kind of man abandons the mother of his child and disowns his son?

His throat tightened as he thought of himself.

"Did you see your grandmother?" Julianne blinked up at him sleepily.

"Only from a distance. She was walking from her house to a car, with someone who is probably an uncle. At least, I think she was my grandmother. She lives in the same house."

"You didn't speak to them?"

"No." He moved his hand to the small of her back, spanning the twin dimples that were above the curve of her backside. It was one of his favorite parts of her body.

(Privately, he contemplated planting a flag there in an act of corporeal colonialism.)

"Why not?" Julia was puzzled.

"They aren't my family. Standing there, I realized I might as well be an alien to them. There was no connection. Nothing." He sighed. "At least when I met my sister I recognized her eyes."

Julia gave him a questioning look.

"She and I have our father's eyes."

"Don't you need to speak to your grandmother to find out about your mother's medical history?"

"Carson was able to get the autopsy report for my mother. He was also able to get information about her medical history, through dubious means."

"And?"

"Heart disease and high blood pressure run in her family, but there wasn't anything especially worrisome."

Julia visibly relaxed under his fingers.

"That's good news, isn't it?"

"Yes." Gabriel sounded strangely underwhelmed.

"What about your father's side?"

"Kelly told me there was some heart disease on their side."

"So you don't want to meet your grandmother or your other relatives?"

"I have my mother's diary and a few anecdotes from Kelly. That's enough."

"Kelly knew your mother?" Julia sat up next to him.

"She remembers meeting her when she worked for our father. And she recalls her parents fighting, presumably over my mother and me. I'd like to introduce you to Kelly. She and her husband have invited me to dinner tonight and then Friday night we're supposed to go and visit our Aunt Sarah in Queens."

"I'd love to meet your sister. But you might have to take me shopping for something to wear to dinner. Rebecca packed for me, so I have a carry-on full of lingerie and only one dress."

Gabriel's eyes grew heated. "Clearly, she doesn't know you very well."

"Why do you say that?"

He leaned forward, brushing her ear with his lips. "Because you sleep naked."

Julia thrilled to his nearness. She began playing with the few strands of his chest hair.

"Did you finish your mother's diary?"

"Yes."

"And?"

"It's about what you'd expect. As time wore on and she realized she would never have a life with my father, she grew more and more despondent, until finally, she stopped writing altogether."

Julia rested her hand over his tattoo, gently pressing into the skin.

"Are you glad you came to New York?"

"Yes. Because of Kelly, I have some good news. Professor Benjamin Spiegel of Columbia was my grandfather."

"Benjamin Spiegel," she murmured. "I don't recognize his name. Was he a Dante specialist?"

"No, he specialized in Romanticism. We read some of his work in grad school."

"Katherine Picton despises the Romantics. She accused me once of giving a Romantic reading of Dante."

Gabriel chuckled. "Not everyone appreciates the Romantics. But Professor Spiegel did. His writings were the gold standard for decades. He published in German, mostly, but a few of his articles are in English."

"And he was your grandfather?"

"Yes." Gabriel wore a look of pride. "Kelly tells me he was much loved at Columbia and well known for his charity work and his leadership in the Jewish community."

Julia's eyebrows lifted. "Why didn't you know about him?"

"He and my father had a falling out. My father changed his name, turned his back on Judaism, and didn't speak of his family. Kelly knew, of course. She's in touch with our cousins."

"Did she know him?"

"Unfortunately, he died before she was born."

"I guess we know where your passion for literature came from. And your interest in kosher sex."

He laughed. "My interest in kosher sex is derived from other things, but maybe there's a connection."

His face grew serious. "Learning about my grandfather was the saving grace of my visit."

Julia's smile faded. "What about your sisters?"

"Audrey won't have anything to do with me. Kelly is wonderful, but she views my father in a very different light." Gabriel grimaced. "I don't know where the truth lies. Was he the loving dad she remembers or the man who hit my mother?"

"Maybe he was both."

"Impossible."

"I hope that he didn't hit your mother or you, but it's possible his relationship with his wife and other children was very different."

"That isn't comforting."

"I'm sorry."

Gabriel buried his face in her hair.

"Why didn't he want us?"

Julia's heart clenched.

"I think he wanted you, along with his other family. That was the problem. He wanted to have it all and he couldn't. Any failure on his part is his, not yours." She kissed Gabriel forcefully. "Will you tell me more about your sister? So much has happened and I've only been hearing pieces of it."

"I will, but can it wait? There's something *kosher* I'd rather do instead." Gabriel rolled to his back, pulling her on top of him.

❧❧

After room service had been delivered and eaten, Julianne returned to bed, covering herself with a sheet.

"Let's just stay here all day and have sex."

Gabriel sat at her feet, his eyes sparkling. "Now that's the Julianne I know and love. But don't you have a paper to finish?"

"I'd rather finish you." She crooked a finger.

He was just about to pull the sheet from her naked body when his iPhone rang.

He glanced at it.

Then his eyes traveled to Julia's.

"Who is it?" she asked.

Gabriel wore a sour expression. "Your uncle Jack."

"Why is he calling you?" She sat up, tugging the sheet with her. "Do you think something's wrong with my dad? Or the baby?"

"I hope not."

He unplugged his phone and held it to his ear. "Hello?"

"Emerson. I'm standing in a Fed Ex depot in Washington, D.C." As always, Jack came straight to the point.

"And?"

"I'm holding a flash drive that contains videos and photographs, some of which are of my niece. And they aren't exactly G-rated."

Gabriel sat down on the edge of the bed.

"You told me you got everything," he growled.

"Thought I did. The girl must have had a backup hidden somewhere. She tried to send it to Andrew Sampson at *The Washington Post*."

"Then fix it. This is your problem."

"Know that. Just called to discuss the play."

Gabriel's eyes darted to Julia's.

What's going on? she mouthed.

He held up a single finger, indicating that she should wait.

"What do you suggest?"

"The girl is angry with her boyfriend because he dumped her to marry someone else. She wants to embarrass him and his father. I say we help her. I'll copy everything having to do with the girl and her boyfriend to a new flash drive and send it."

"Isn't that risky?"

"It implicates them and keeps my niece out of it."

Gabriel looked at Julianne—at the way her eyebrows were knitted together, a wrinkle forming in between them.

"Your niece is here. Let me speak to her about it and I'll call you back."

"I don't have a lot of time."

"I'm not making this decision for her." Gabriel disconnected the call, tossing the phone on the bed.

He scrubbed his face with his hands.

Julia moved closer. "What's going on? Why is Jack calling you?"

"Apparently Natalie had a flash drive of photos and videos hidden somewhere. She tried to Fed Ex it to *The Washington Post*."

"What?" Julia screeched. "It's going to be on the Internet. It's going to be in the newspapers. Oh my God. Oh my God."

She buried her face in her hands and began rocking back and forth.

Gabriel reached out to touch her shoulder. "Not so fast. Jack intercepted it. He wants to know what he should do with it."

Julia dropped her hands. "Tell him to destroy it. Ask him to find all the copies and destroy them, too."

"Are you sure? He can delete the photos involving you and send the rest. They'd get what they deserve."

Julia pulled the sheet up to her chin.

"I don't want revenge."

Gabriel's eyes glinted dangerously. "Why the hell not?"

"Because I've moved on. I rarely think of them and I want to keep it that way. I don't want to watch their lives implode and know that I'm responsible."

"You wouldn't be responsible. They're the ones responsible."

"I'm accountable for my actions." Julianne's voice grew steely. "I don't understand why Natalie is doing this now, after you and Jack sorted her out."

"Simon is marrying someone else."

Julia's eyes grew round. "What?"

"I expect Natalie is hoping his fiancée will leave him if his past is exposed."

Julia seemed shocked. "He finally dumped her. I would have thought he'd keep her on the side, but perhaps his father told him to cut her loose."

"That wouldn't surprise me. The election is next year."

"Now there's a wedding." Julia shook her head. "Nothing like a little matrimonial window dressing to make the campaign appear more family friendly. I just wish Natalie would leave me out of it."

"You're in it. At least for now." Gabriel's mouth settled into a grim line. "I think it's safe to say that Jack will be paying Natalie and her apartment another visit. What do you want me to tell him about the flash drive?"

"Ask him to destroy everything."

Gabriel huffed in frustration, running his fingers through his hair. "They don't deserve your mercy."

"His fiancée does, whoever she is. She'll be humiliated."

"She's a stupid girl if she's involved with him."

Julia winced.

"I was a stupid girl once." Her voice was so soft, Gabriel had to strain to hear her.

"You weren't stupid; you were manipulated. Come on, don't you want them to suffer?"

"Not this way."

He rose to his feet, placing his hands on his hips.

"I do! Think about what he did to you. Think about what she did. They made you suffer for years. They nearly destroyed you!"

"But they didn't," she said quietly, to his retreating back.

He walked toward the window and moved the curtains, staring out over Central Park.

"I broke his jaw, and it still didn't give me satisfaction." Gabriel examined the bare, snow-covered branches of the trees. "I wanted to kill him."

"You acted in self-defense. If you hadn't come to my rescue . . ." She shuddered in remembrance of the day she was almost raped. "But what you're asking me to do isn't self-defense."

He glanced at her over his shoulder. "No. It's justice."

"We spoke once, about mercy seasoning justice. We spoke about penance and forgiveness."

"This is different."

"That's right. Because even though I could demand justice, in this case, I decline. To quote one of our favorite novels, *to God I respectfully return the ticket*."

Gabriel snorted. "You're misquoting Dostoyevsky for your own Franciscan purposes."

Julia smiled at his indignation.

"I know you're angry with me for not wanting to punish them. But, darling, think of his mother. She was kind to me. This will kill her."

Gabriel didn't take his eyes from the trees.

"You threatened to go to the press yourself."

"To tell them the truth, not to share the pictures. And only if Natalie gave me no other choice."

Gabriel's right hand formed a fist, which he brought to rest against the window, resisting the urge to punch through the glass.

It wasn't fair.

It wasn't fair that someone as sweet as Julianne was neglected by her mother and father and left to a cruel and manipulative boyfriend.

It wasn't fair that Suzanne Emerson was left to cling to the scraps her lover fed her, while he lavished love on his family.

It wasn't fair that Grace and Maia died while others lived.

It wasn't fair that Tom and Diane were expecting a baby with a damaged heart.

No, the universe wasn't fair. And if that weren't lamentable enough, when the opportunities came for justice, Franciscans like Julianne turned the other cheek and spoke of mercy.

Damn.

He closed his eyes.

She'd turned the other cheek to him.

As had Grace.

As had Maia.

With a deep sigh, he focused his attention on Assisi and what had happened to him when he visited the crypt. God had met him there, but not with justice. With mercy.

"Call your uncle."

"Gabriel, I—"

He opened his eyes and unclenched his fist but didn't turn around. "Just call him. Tell him what you want him to do."

Julianne tugged the sheet free, winding it around her petite frame. She went to him, bringing her front to his back.

"You want to protect me. You want justice. I love you for that."

"I still wish I'd killed him."

"You have." She pressed her cheek against his shoulder blade.

His muscles tensed. "How so?"

"You love me, you're kind to me, and you treat me with respect. The longer I'm with you, the more everything having to do with him seems like a bad dream. So in many ways, you have killed him. You've killed his memory. Thank you, Gabriel."

Gabriel closed his eyes as a great wave of love and something he couldn't quite name washed over him.

Julia kissed his shoulders and went to call her uncle.

Chapter Sixty-two

That evening, Julia and Gabriel dined at Kelly's Manhattan apartment with her husband, Jonathan, and their daughters, Andrea and Meredith.

Julia felt welcomed by Gabriel's family. By the end of the evening, they were visiting like old friends rather than strangers.

Kelly gave Gabriel a pair of cuff links and an old Brooklyn Dodgers cap that had belonged to their father, along with several books that had been written by their grandfather.

Gabriel gave Kelly the knowledge that the train engine he had, was, in fact, their father's. He'd carved the initials "O.S." into it as a boy, when his name had been Othniel Spiegel.

The Emersons invited the Schultzes to visit in Cambridge or Selinsgrove, and there was talk of a joint holiday in the Hamptons the following summer. Kelly made sure that Gabriel promised to attend the next meeting of the Rabbi Benjamin Spiegel Foundation. She was looking forward to introducing her brother to the cousins.

Back at the Ritz before bedtime, Julia checked her email. She was wearing the Dodgers cap, since it was almost too small for Gabriel's head.

(A fact she pointed out with no little amusement.)

She stared at her laptop screen from behind her tortoiseshell glasses.

"*Scheisse.*"

"I really need to start teaching you to curse in a different language. I've heard that Farsi has some particularly colorful expletives." Gabriel smirked as he walked toward her, clad in a plush hotel bathrobe.

"I'm not sure Farsi could capture what I feel when I look at this." Julia pointed to the screen.

Gabriel picked up his glasses and put them on. He gazed at the scanned black-and-white engagement photo, recognizing Simon Talbot immediately.

He resisted the urge to curse. "Who's the woman?"

"Do you know Senator Hudson from North Carolina? That's his daughter. She's a senior at Duke."

Gabriel and Julianne exchanged a look.

"Her family is very conservative. How did she end up with him?" Gabriel sounded contemptuous.

"I have no idea. But I can understand why Natalie is upset. Simon dumped her for the Jacqueline Bouvier of fiancées. Look at her."

"Who sent you the photo?"

"Rachel. It was published in *The Philadelphia Inquirer*."

Julia turned back to her laptop, gazing sadly at the photograph of the smiling couple.

"I feel sorry for her. She has no idea what she's getting into."

"Perhaps she does but doesn't care." Gabriel tugged on the brim of her ball cap. "This looks good on you. I didn't take you for a Dodgers fan."

She grinned. "I'm embracing your Brooklyn heritage."

The next day, Julianne finished her seminar paper while Gabriel attended to business, researching his grandfather in the Columbia University archives. That afternoon, they joined Kelly and Jonathan in paying a visit to Aunt Sarah at a nursing home in Queens.

After an evening spent shopping and then dining at the Russian Tea Room, they returned to the hotel. The room was bathed in candlelight as Julia moved atop him. Her hands rested on his chest, stroking him.

He gripped her hips, urging her to increase her pace.

"Say my name," he whispered.

She gasped as he thrust up inside her.

"Gabriel."

"Nothing could enflame me the way your voice does when you say my name."

"Gabriel," she repeated. "That's beautiful."

He pulled her closer, his lips moving across her breasts.

"You inspire me."

"You're very intense."

"Of course I'm intense. I'm with my beautiful wife, having fantastic sex."

"I feel like we're the only ones in the world."

"Good," he mumbled, watching her as she moved up and down and up and down.

"You make me feel beautiful."

In response, he licked her breast until she began to groan.

"I love you."

Gabriel's eyes grew determined as he urged her to go faster.

"I love you too."

"I'd be proud to have a baby with you," she managed, just before lifting her chin and closing her eyes. Her body shook as the pleasure coursed through her.

He continued thrusting, watching as she climaxed. Then he quickened his pace, planting himself with one great thrust before he came.

❧❧

"I'm glad you joined me in New York." Gabriel held Julia's hand as they waited to check in for their flight back to Boston. "I'm sorry we didn't get to see a show, but at least we saw some of the sights."

"Gabriel, you braved the crowds to take me Christmas shopping. I don't have anything to complain about." She pressed a kiss to his lips. "They're going to charge us for having overweight bags."

"I'd like to see them try. It's Christmas, damn it."

She laughed. "So it is. Somehow, I can't imagine you sitting through an entire Broadway show."

He sniffed. "I'd see Shakespeare."

"The musical?"

"Very funny. I'd sit through a performance of *Les Misérables*." His gaze leveled on hers. "Your interpretation of that novel changed my life."

Julia looked down at her feet, at the new high-heeled Manolo Blahnik boots Gabriel had insisted on buying her at Barneys.

"I think a lot of things conspired to change your life. I can't take credit for what happened to you in Assisi."

"No." He lifted her hand, stroking his thumb over her knuckles before toying with her wedding band.

"But I wouldn't have made it to Assisi if you hadn't helped me first. And I wouldn't have had the joy of discovering my grandfather if you hadn't agreed to have a child with me. You've given me so much."

"Tammy said that fatherhood does something special to a good man. I'd like to see what it does to you."

Gabriel blinked twice, hard. "Thank you, Julianne."

He captured her smile with his mouth, kissing her until a throat cleared behind them.

Embarrassed, they moved ahead in line, hands woven together.

The Emersons had just cleared security when Julia's cell phone rang.

"Jules." Tom's gruff voice echoed in her ear.

"Dad. Is everything okay?"

The pause on the other end of the line caused Julia to stop walking. Gabriel stood at her side, a questioning look on his face.

Tom cleared his throat. "I'm at the Children's Hospital in Philadelphia."

"Oh, no. Are Diane and the baby all right?"

"Diane woke up in the middle of the night feeling funny and so we drove here right away." Tom paused. "Right now, they have her hooked up to a bunch of monitors but she and the baby are fine. However"—he paused again—"she started going into labor a little while ago."

"She's early," Julia breathed.

"That's right." Tom's voice was tight. "They won't know how he's doing until he's delivered. The doctors say there are lots of things they can't see on an ultrasound. They might have to work on his heart immediately."

"Will he need surgery?"

"The corrective surgery is scheduled for three days after delivery, give or take. I suppose he might need surgery before, depending on what they find."

Julia looked at Gabriel. "We're at JFK in New York, getting ready to fly back to Boston. Would you like me to come home?"

"Yes. If you can. She'll probably still be in labor when you arrive, but it would be good to have you here. It's going to be a long three days and I don't know if—" He began coughing.

"I'm coming. Okay? I'll change my flight and head straight to the hospital. I'll call you when I arrive so you can tell me where to meet you."

"Okay." He sounded relieved. "Jules?"

"Yes, Dad?"

"Thanks. See you soon."

"Bye, Dad. Give my love to Diane."

Julia disconnected the call and looked up at her husband. His expression was grim.

"I guess I should have spoken to you before I promised I'd go to Philadelphia." She chewed at the inside of her mouth.

"It's an emergency. We have to go."

"*We?*"

"The baby will be my nephew. And I'm not letting you go by yourself." He pulled her into his side, leading her through the crowd.

Chapter Sixty-three

Jules?"

Tom's hand was on her shoulder, trying to awaken her. She was seated in a chair in the Special Delivery Unit waiting room. Gabriel was standing nearby, nursing a very bad coffee.

(Fortunately, he'd restrained himself and elected not to complain to the hospital administration about the sad state of their vending machines.)

Julia opened her eyes, squinting against the overhead light.

Her father crouched in front of her. "We had the baby."

"Is he all right?"

"They had to do a procedure right away, but now he's recovering and Diane is with him." Tom pulled his cell phone out of his pocket and held it out to her. "He's a good-looking boy."

Julia scrolled through a series of pictures of a tired but glowing Diane and a mocha-skinned boy who had black, curly hair.

"He's beautiful, Dad. I'm so happy for you." She handed the phone back.

Tom looked at the last picture for a moment, his thumb grazing across the baby's head.

"Thomas Lamar Mitchell. Seven pounds, ten ounces. Born today, December eleventh."

"I didn't know you were naming him after yourself."

"A boy should have his father's name," Tom's voice was gruff. "Anyway, Diane wants to call him Tommy. For now."

"Then Tommy it is." Julia glanced over at her husband, who was frowning into his coffee cup.

"You kids should go back to the hotel. I'll call if anything changes. You won't be able to see him today. They're keeping an eye on him, and hopefully they'll operate on his heart in a few days."

"Okay, Dad." Julia wrapped her arms around her father, hugging him. "Congratulations."

Chapter Sixty-four

"So how's the baby?" Rachel leaned across the dining room table in her parents' former house.

It was two nights before Christmas. Julia had just rejoined Gabriel's extended family at the table, after speaking with her father on the telephone.

"He's fine. I guess it's normal practice for the baby to remain in the hospital until a month after surgery. He'll be able to come home in January."

"That must be hard on your dad and Diane."

"It is, but they're staying with the baby. Dad was going to take a leave of absence from Susquehanna, but they gave him family leave with pay." Julia smiled. "How's that for a caring employer?"

"What about the hospital bills?" Rachel lowered her voice.

"A guardian angel is taking care of what the insurance doesn't cover." Julia's eyes flickered in the direction of her husband, then returned to her friend.

"Some guardian angels are so damn sweet."

"What are you two whispering about?" Gabriel leaned into their conversation.

Julia grinned. "My new brother. I can't wait to buy him his first Red Sox cap."

Gabriel made a face. "Your father will burn it. He's a Phillies fan."

"He won't burn a gift from me. I'm the big sister."

"Sisters are very important," said Rachel, solemnly. "Remember that when you go shopping for my Christmas gift."

"I'll try to do that." Gabriel pushed his chair back from the table and stood. He lifted his water glass.

Everyone stopped what they were doing, including Quinn, who sat still in his high chair, staring at his uncle.

"We have a lot to be thankful for." Gabriel's eyes met Julianne's and held them. Then he took his time, making eye contact with his siblings and their spouses, and finally, with his father, who sat at the foot of the table.

"Mom had a habit of forcing everyone to say what they were thankful for, during dinners like this. I thought I'd cut to the chase and announce that I'm thankful for my beautiful wife, my new job, and my new nephew, Tommy."

The adults lifted their wine glasses in response, drinking to Tommy's health.

"I know that everyone heard the toast I made to Mom at Rachel and Aaron's wedding." Gabriel's voice suddenly grew hoarse. "But I'd like to repeat part of it."

As everyone at the table indicated their agreement, Julia saw Gabriel's hand tremble slightly. She quietly slipped her hand into his and was gratified when he squeezed her softly.

"This evening would be incomplete if we didn't acknowledge the absence of our mother, Grace. Grace was gracious and beautiful, a loving wife, and a devoted mother. Her capacity for goodness and compassion knew no bounds. She was generous and kind and very, very forgiving. She welcomed me into her home. She mothered me when I had no mother, even when I was difficult. She taught me what it is to love someone selflessly and absolutely, and without her and Dad I'd probably be dead."

Gabriel paused and looked at Richard and Julia.

"Recently, I had the opportunity to find out more about my biological parents, including my Jewish heritage through my father. When I chose to read a passage from the Hebrew Bible at Rachel and Aaron's wedding, I didn't know about my background. Now the Scripture is even more meaningful and I can say, as I said before, that it expresses Grace's love for her family."

He freed himself from Julia's grasp and pulled a folded piece of paper from his pocket and began to read.

"'Who can find a virtuous woman? for her price is far above rubies.
The heart of her husband doth safely trust in her, so he shall have no need of spoil.
She will do him good and not evil all the days of her life.'"

Gabriel's eyes sought Julia's, and for a moment the world stopped as he saw amazement and love radiate from her face.

"'She seeketh wool, and flax, and worketh willingly with her hands.
She is like the merchants' ships; she bringeth her food from afar.
She riseth also while it is yet night, and giveth meat to her household, and a portion to her maidens. . . .
She perceiveth that her merchandise is good: her candle goeth not out by night. . . .
She stretcheth out her hand to the poor; yea, she reacheth forth her hands to the needy.
She is not afraid of the snow for her household: for all her household are clothed with scarlet.
She maketh herself coverings of tapestry; her clothing is silk and purple.
Her husband is known in the gates, when he sitteth among the elders of the land. . . .
Strength and honor are her clothing; and she shall rejoice in time to come.
She openeth her mouth with wisdom; and in her tongue is the law of kindness. . . .
Her children arise up, and call her blessed; her husband also, and he praiseth her.
Many daughters have done virtuously, but thou excellest them all. . . .'

"I ask you all to drink to the memory of our mother, Grace."

By the time everyone drained their glasses, there was barely a dry eye among them.

Chapter Sixty-five

December 2011
Near Essex Junction, Vermont

Two nights before Christmas, Paul was working in the barn, deep in thought.

(Parenthetically, it should be noted that he was also deep in something else. Something *organic.*)

"Hey."

His sister Heather had wandered almost silently into the barn and was now staring at him, arms folded across her chest.

"Hey yourself." He continued working, speaking to her over his shoulder. "What are you doing?"

"Chris had to look at one of the Andersons' horses. They think it has colic. He'll be out most of the night, so I asked him to drop me off. How are you?"

"Fine."

"You don't sound fine." She stared at him until he met her gaze.

"I'm just preoccupied with my upcoming interviews. I'm meeting with six different colleges at the Modern Language Association convention in January. That's a lot of pressure."

"Right." Heather gazed at her big brother skeptically.

"I have an interview with St. Mike's. If they hire me, I could help Dad out on the weekends."

"That's great news. I'll put in a good word with St. Michael, himself, asking that he see to it that you get the job."

Heather cocked her head to one side and listened to the music that was playing in the background. It was a cover of "In the Sun" and Paul was listening to it on repeat, over and over again.

"If you're excited about your job prospects, then why the hell are you listening to *this*? I'm ready to slit my wrists already and I just got here."

He glared at her and began walking in the opposite direction.

She followed.

"I ran into Ali the other day at Hannaford's."

"Mm-hmm."

"Why don't you ask her out?"

"We go out once in a while."

"I mean on a date, not as friends."

"We broke up." He laid emphasis on the words. "A couple of years ago."

"Chris wants to go snowboarding in Stowe for New Year's. He's going to rent a place so we don't have to drive back and forth. Invite Ali and come with us."

"That's not a good idea."

Heather reached out and caught her brother's arm, stopping him midmotion. "Yes, it is. It will be like old times. *Ask her*."

"We can't leave Mom here by herself."

"That's why you hired extra help. *Virgil.*" Heather gave him a toothy grin.

"I'm not Virgil. I'm Dante," he mumbled.

"What?"

"Nothing." He turned away.

"Look, big guy, you need to blow off some steam. You're letting things fester. I can see it." She grinned at him impishly and tried to tickle him. *"Fester, fester, fester."*

Paul swatted her hands away. "If I say yes, will you bug off?"

"Absolutely."

"Fine. Now get lost."

"*Fine.* I'll make coffee. And when you come to the house, I'll expect you to call her."

Heather disappeared from the barn and Paul stood still for a moment, wondering what he had just agreed to.

Chapter Sixty-six

December 27, 2011
Selinsgrove, Pennsylvania

Richard, his children, and their spouses were gathered around the dining room table enjoying dessert and coffee. Rachel was updating everyone on her fertility treatments.

"Yeah, I'm on hormones. But I feel better than I did on the pill. It made me emotional."

Aaron lifted his eyebrows behind Rachel's back, and everyone laughed at his incredulous expression. Everyone, save Rachel and Julianne.

Gabriel's eyes drifted to his wife, noticing that her eyes had narrowed. She began staring so hard at the table that he wouldn't have been surprised if the wood started to blacken and burn under her gaze.

Suddenly, she pushed herself back from the table and bolted, her chair toppling over. Gabriel righted the chair and excused himself, climbing the stairs two at a time in an effort to catch up with her.

When he reached their bedroom, Julia was pawing through the contents of her nightstand. She pulled the drawer out and dumped the contents on the bed, spreading the items out into a single layer.

"Damn it!" She cursed.

"What's the matter?" His hand caught only air as she brushed past him.

He followed her into the en-suite, watching her empty her makeup case onto the counter. She tossed items aside frantically, an expression of distress breaching her lips.

"Julianne, what's the matter?"

"I can't find them."

"Find what?"

When she didn't answer, he grasped her arm. "Julianne, *find what*?"

"My birth control pills."

For an instant her panic traveled through him, but only for an instant.

"I'm sure they're here somewhere. When's the last time you saw them?"

She blinked, her eyes flickering to the side.

"In Cambridge," she whispered.

Now his eyes widened.

"Not in New York? Not here?"

"I was on my period just before you left for New York, remember? I should have started a new pack of pills that Wednesday."

"And did you?"

She shook her head. "I was on my way to see you. I was in such a hurry to make it to the airport, I forgot them. And then while we were in New York . . ."

"Darling." He reached for her but she turned away, covering her face with her hands.

"I can't believe I've missed almost an entire month of pills and only realized it now. I'm such an idiot."

"You aren't an idiot." He pulled on her wrist and moved so that he was encircling her with his arms. "You were in a hurry to meet me in New York. Then we had the call from your father at the airport. You've had a lot on your mind."

"I guess it's a good thing your surgery hasn't kicked in yet."

A shadow passed over Gabriel's features, but then it was gone, like an errant cloud on a summer's day.

❧❧

"So I just need a replacement package of pills until I get back to Boston." Julia explained her situation to the pharmacist the following morning.

The pharmacist nodded. "That shouldn't be a problem. I'll call your pharmacy back home. It should only take a few minutes. Just have a seat."

"Thank you."

Julia rejoined Gabriel in the waiting area that was nestled inside the small Selinsgrove pharmacy.

"Is everything all right?" He gave her a concerned look.

"Yes." She breathed a sigh of relief. "It shouldn't take too long."

Gabriel pulled out his iPhone and began pressing some buttons.

"What are you doing?" She looked over at him with interest.

"While you were talking to the pharmacist, I was checking our messages. My urologist's office called."

"Should you call him back?"

"If you don't mind."

"I don't mind." Julia frowned. "Why is he calling you over Christmas vacation?"

"I don't know. I was expecting a call a couple of weeks ago about my latest test results. There probably hasn't been a change." He looked unhappy.

"The doctor said it could take up to a year. Don't worry." Julia took his left hand in hers.

He kissed the back of her hand before standing and walking to the front of the store.

By the time he returned, Julia had already received her prescription, paid for it, and taken the first pill.

Gabriel planted his feet, staring at her prescription bag.

She looked up into wide, conflicted eyes.

"What's the matter?"

"Let's go home." He moved to touch the small of her back, guiding her toward the door.

"Is everything all right?"

"We'll talk in the car."

Julia dutifully walked with him to the Jeep, which was parked outside. It was the vehicle that Gabriel kept in Selinsgrove simply for convenience.

"You're scaring me," she whispered.

"No need to panic." He opened the passenger door, waiting until she was situated before closing it.

When he climbed into the driver's seat, he didn't bother placing his key in the ignition. He simply put his iPhone on the dashboard and turned to her.

Julia could see by his expression that he was struggling.

"Was it bad news?"

"I don't think so."

"Then what is it?"

Gabriel took her hand in his, tracing the hills and valleys of her knuckles with his thumb. He stopped at her wedding band.

"Look at me."

She met his eyes, her heart beginning to pound in her chest.

"I don't want you to panic, all right?"

"Gabriel, I'm panicking. Just spit it out."

He pressed his lips together.

"The doctor's office called to give me my latest test results. They were supposed to call two weeks ago, but there was an—anomaly."

"An anomaly?"

"The test results were positive." He was speaking slowly, very slowly, his eyes searching hers.

Then he waited for the import of his revelation to sink in.

She blinked. Several times. "So you're—?"

"Yes."

"But that's impossible. It's hasn't been three months yet."

"I know. They repeated the test and received the same results. Apparently, the doctor would like to use my story as a testimonial."

Gabriel's proud smile disappeared when he saw Julia's face.

"Even if I'm fertile, it doesn't matter. You've been on the pill since September. It would take more than a month for your system to get back to normal, wouldn't it?"

"I don't know. They warn you to use backup birth control if you miss a couple of pills. And I missed a whole package." Julia lifted a shaking hand to her mouth.

Gabriel wrapped his arm around her shoulder, drawing her close.

"I'll go back into the drugstore and buy a pregnancy test. Then we'll know for sure."

Julia's eyebrows shot up. "Right now?"

"Would you rather wait?"

"This can't be happening." She dropped her face into her hands.

Gabriel flinched.

"Would it really be so terrible?" he mumbled, rubbing his chin.

When she didn't answer, he touched her shoulder. "I'll be right back."

Julia leaned back against the headrest and closed her eyes, calling on all deities named and unnamed to come to her aid.

Chapter Sixty-seven

December 28, 2011
Washington, D.C.

Natalie Lundy stared at her cell phone and cursed. She'd placed call after call, leaving message after message, but now the number she'd been dialing for several weeks was no longer in service. Simon had changed his number. And her emails had gone unanswered.

She gazed at the cardboard box that sat on the floor, its contents silently mocking her. She was jobless.

The day after the announcement of Simon's engagement, she'd been summoned to the office of Senator Talbot's campaign manager. At least Robert had had the good sense to be embarrassed about what he was about to do.

"We have to let you go," he said, avoiding her eyes.

"Why?"

"We're overstaffed. The senator wants us to make some cuts, and personnel are the first thing to go. I'm sorry."

Natalie lifted a single eyebrow at him. "This wouldn't have anything to do with my relationship with Simon, would it?"

"Of course not," Robert lied smoothly. "It's business, not personal."

"Don't give me that *Godfather* bullshit. I've seen the movie."

Robert's eyes moved to the space behind her, and he nodded. "Alex here will walk you out. If you want, I can make a phone call to Harrisburg and see about getting you a position with one of the state senators."

"Go fuck yourself." She stood to her feet. "You can tell the senator and his son to do the same thing. They want to be rid of me, fine. But this isn't over. I'm sure Andrew Sampson at the *Post* would be interested in hearing what I have to say about the way the Talbots do business."

Robert lifted his hand. "Now don't get carried away. As I said, I can get you a job in Harrisburg."

"I don't want to be in fucking *Harrisburg*, Robert. I'd like to know why I'm getting screwed. I did my job and I did it well. You know that."

Robert's eyes flickered to Alex. "Give me a minute."

Alex withdrew, closing the door behind him.

"Listen, Natalie. You don't want to make threats that you aren't prepared to carry out."

"But—I am prepared to carry them out."

"That wouldn't be prudent."

"To hell with prudence."

Robert shifted in his seat. "Of course, the campaign will provide you with a generous severance package. The details will be sent to your apartment."

"Hush money?"

"Severance for being terminated due to financial exigency."

"Whatever." She picked up her purse and headed to the door. "Tell Simon he has twenty-four hours to call me. If I don't hear from him, he's going to be sorry."

And with that, she opened the door and stomped into the hall.

It had been more than two weeks, and Simon hadn't called. The damning evidence she'd sent to *The Washington Post* had been delivered. Fed Ex gave her confirmation of the fact. But she hadn't heard from Andrew Sampson or anyone else. Perhaps he'd decided not to run the story. Perhaps it was too tawdry.

The day after her trip to Fed Ex, her apartment had been trashed. It didn't take a great deal of intelligence to figure out that the thief had been someone from the senator's campaign. They'd taken her laptop, her digital camera, her files, and her flash drives. She no longer had anything that she could use to blackmail Simon or anyone else.

She'd received the hush money—twenty-five thousand dollars. It was enough, she thought, to help her start a new life in California. It wouldn't hurt for her to move away and start anew, using Senator Talbot's money. She could plot her revenge on the Talbots from Sacramento.

She didn't have any evidence for her allegations, so it was unlikely that any respectable journalist would take her seriously. But she could bide her time and sell her story to a tabloid as an October surprise. That should do it.

She smiled to herself, as she began packing her worldly goods.

Chapter Sixty-eight

December 28, 2011
Selinsgrove, Pennsylvania

Julia and Gabriel were standing in the en-suite of their bathroom in Richard's house, eyeing two different pregnancy tests that were sitting on the vanity. Both tests displayed the same result.

"Julianne?" Gabriel's voice was a heartbreaking whisper.

She wasn't looking at him; she was staring at the tests. She stood still, like a deer trying to evade a predator.

"This is my fault." He lifted a hand to touch her but then thought better of it.

She turned her head, as if she were suddenly aware of his presence. "How is it your fault?"

He paused, struggling for words.

"I didn't protect you. I knew how anxious you were about getting pregnant. I should have worn a condom. I should have asked you about your pills." His voice dropped. "I failed you."

Julia closed her eyes and drew a very deep breath. "Gabriel, you didn't fail me. I'm the idiot who forgot her pills." A tear slid from the corner of her eye and down her face.

He caught it with his fingers.

"That's enough. You aren't an idiot. You were in a hurry because you were trying to get to me. As usual, you were worrying about someone other than yourself."

More tears traced the planes of her pretty face, and her shoulders began to shake.

"It's too late."

He moved into her and her fingers gripped his shirt, clutching him as if she were drowning.

Chapter Sixty-nine

That night the Emersons had difficulty sleeping. Julia was plagued by fear and guilt—fear about what would happen to her academic aspirations and guilt at placing such a high priority on them. Gabriel was conflicted. On the one hand, he was ecstatic that they were expecting a child. But Julianne's concern and evident distress prevented him from displaying his true feelings. He, too, was mired in guilt for not having protected her.

Of course, neither one of them expected that the vasectomy reversal would be successful so soon, if at all.

While everyone else in Richard's household spent the day in leisurely community, Julia stayed in bed. She was exhausted. Certainly, she wasn't prepared to face Rachel and Aaron, even though she and Gabriel had agreed that they would wait until the three-month mark to announce their pregnancy.

Gabriel spent the day trying to pretend that he hadn't received what was potentially the best news of his life. He resolved to give Julianne the time and space she seemed to need to come to grips with what was, for her, a startling disappointment.

Late that evening, she was curved into a ball, lying on her side in the large bed. Everyone else in the house was fast asleep. Everyone except her husband.

Gabriel was spooned behind her, his arm wrapped loosely about her waist. She'd slept most of the day, so of course she wasn't tired now. Even though he skirted the edge of exhaustion, his concern for her prevented him from resting.

Her deepest fear had been realized. She was pregnant and only midway through her second year of a seven-year doctoral program.

She sniffled at the thought.

Instinctively, Gabriel drew her closer to him, his hand splaying across her lower abdomen.

For a few moments, he allowed himself the luxury of wondering what his life would have been like if Maia had been born. He'd barely had time for Paulina when she was pregnant. He doubted his attitude would have changed when she had the baby.

His stomach rolled. He could see himself hurling expletives at her to keep the baby quiet as Maia cried, disrupting his writing. Paulina would have had to bear the burden of parenthood alone. He wouldn't have taken the time to feed the baby, or rock her to sleep, or, God forbid, change a diaper. He'd been a self-centered, drug-using bastard back then. It would have been negligence on Paulina's part to leave Maia in his care.

He would have moved out, leaving Paulina to cope with Maia by herself. Oh, he might have given her money. But his addiction would have eaten all his funds until it eventually killed him. Then Paulina and Maia would have been alone.

Even if he'd gone into treatment and miraculously made it through, he still couldn't imagine being an active, involved father. No. The old professor would have been too busy writing books and trying to further his career. He would have sent birthday cards and money, or, more probably, had his secretary or maybe one of the many women in his life send them for him.

In short, he would have been like his father, fighting with Paulina on the telephone over his lack of involvement until he finally tired of the conflict and ceased contact altogether. His vision of what his life would have been like was very clear.

He grounded himself by tightening his hold on Julianne. He was no longer the old professor; he was a new man. He resolved with everything that was in him to be the best, most active, attentive husband and father he could be.

The first thing he needed to do was to comfort his wife. Then he needed to take steps to ensure that she didn't lose everything she'd worked for since she was in high school.

He opened his mouth to begin whispering to her, but Julia extricated herself, tossing the blankets aside and moving toward the closet.

He heard her switch on the light and start rummaging through some clothes.

Gabriel followed. By the time he made it to the closet, she'd pulled on a pair of jeans and one of his old cashmere sweaters and was searching for socks.

"What are you doing?"

"I can't sleep." She didn't look at him as she leaned over to put on a pair of his argyle socks.

"Where are you going?"

"I thought I might go for a drive. Clear my head."

"Then I'm going with you." He reached over to pull a shirt off a hanger.

She closed her eyes. "Gabriel, I need time to think."

He lifted a pair of jeans and a sweater from one of the shelves.

"Remember what I said in New York?"

"You said a lot of things in New York."

"I said that being apart was a bad idea. You agreed with me. We're partners, remember?"

She kicked at the hardwood beneath her argyle socks. "I remember."

"Don't shut me out." His tone was almost pleading.

"I have no idea what to say to you. This is my darkest nightmare come true!"

Gabriel rocked back on his heels, almost as if he'd been struck.

"Nightmare?" he whispered. *"Nightmare?"*

Julia couldn't look at him.

"This is why I need time to think. I don't know how to express what I feel without hurting you. I'm going to lose everything I've worked for because of this. You can't imagine how much this hurts."

A muscle jumped in his jaw.

"I'm the one who was hesitant for us to have a baby." His voice was low. "This has brought up all my old anxieties, too."

She lifted her head, her eyes flashing.

"You know me, Gabriel. You know I won't do anything to take this away from you."

They exchanged a look before she bent her eyes to the floor.

"Let me go with you. We don't have to talk. I just want to be near you." His tone grew gentle.

Julia realized that he was trying very hard to be considerate, even though his first instinct was to take charge and take over.

"Fine," she said, reluctantly.

They walked downstairs and bundled up against the cold, winding scarves around their necks. In the hall closet Gabriel retrieved his beret and Julia found an old knitted cap that belonged to Rachel.

"What would you think of a walk?" He toyed with the keys he'd left on the hall table.

"A walk? It's freezing out there."

"We don't have to walk long. The fresh air will help you sleep."

"Fine." Julia followed him through the living room and into the kitchen, where he retrieved a flashlight.

Then she was following him out the back door and onto the snow-covered patio.

He didn't offer his hand but kept close to her, as if he were worried she might fall.

They walked in silence into the woods, their breath making ghost-like ribbons in the air. When they arrived at the orchard, Julia leaned against the old rock, hugging her arms tightly around her middle.

"We keep coming back here."

Gabriel stood in front of her, shining the flashlight beam to the side.

"Yes, we do. This place reminds me of what's important. It reminds me of you."

Julia turned away from the concern that she saw on his face.

"I have a lot of happy memories from here." His voice took on a wistful tone. "Our first night together, the night we made plans to consummate our love, our engagement . . ." He smiled. "That night back in the summer when we made love just over there."

She followed his gesture to the space on which they'd lain entwined. Images and emotions crashed over her. She could almost feel his arms about her, skin against skin.

"Several months ago I was apprehensive about having a child. You persuaded me to have hope; to look forward and not to the past. Our hope was rewarded with the knowledge that my family tree is not entirely cursed."

"God is punishing me," she blurted.

His forehead furrowed. "What are you talking about?"

"God is punishing me. I wanted to graduate from Harvard and become a professor. Now—"

"God doesn't work that way," Gabriel interrupted.

"How do you know?"

He removed one of his leather gloves and brought his hand to the side of her neck, just under her ear.

"Because a young woman, wise beyond her years, told me so."

"And you believed her?" She looked up at him, eyes brimming.

"She's never lied to me," he whispered. "And when a brown-eyed angel speaks to you, it's best to listen."

Julia laughed mirthlessly. "I think your brown-eyed angel screwed up."

Gabriel's face grew pained before he exerted control over his features. But she saw his expression.

"I'm sorry. I don't mean to hurt you." She reached for him and he moved closer, moving his other hand to cup her neck as well.

"I don't know what to say that won't make me look like a patriarchal, unfeeling asshole."

"Oh, really, Professor?"

He pressed his lips together, his eyes guarded. "Really."

"Try me."

His thumbs stroked her jaw synchronously.

"I know this isn't what you want. I know the timing is terrible. But I can't help it." His thumbs stilled. "I'm happy."

"I'm terrified. I'm going to be a mother twenty-four hours a day, seven days a week. I'll never be able to study for my general exams and research my dissertation. Not while I have to look after a baby. This is exactly what I was afraid was going to happen."

She squeezed her eyes shut and two tears escaped, trailing down her cheeks.

Gabriel wiped them away.

"You're speaking as if you'll be a single parent, Julianne. But you won't. I'll make sure that all the responsibility for the baby doesn't fall to you. I'll speak to Rebecca and ask her to move in with us. Maybe I could take a paternity leave or use my sabbatical. I'll—"

"Paternity leave? Are you serious?" Her eyes widened.

"Deadly." He shifted his boots in the snow. "It would be a nightmare for the baby, I'm sure, to be left with me. But I'll do whatever it takes to guarantee that you finish your program. If that means taking a paternity leave or using my sabbatical, I'll do it."

"You've never looked after a baby before."

Gabriel gave her a look that could only be described as prim.

"I went to Princeton, Oxford, and Harvard. I can certainly learn how to look after a baby."

"Looking after a baby is not like conquering the Ivy League."

"I'll do research. I'll buy all the relevant books on newborns and study them before the baby arrives."

"Your colleagues will ridicule you."

"Let them." His blue eyes grew fierce.

The edges of Julia's mouth turned up.

"You'll be up to your elbows in dirty diapers and burping cloths, surviving on a few hours' sleep, and trying to soothe a cranky, colicky tyrant by reading *Goodnight Moon* over and over. In English. Because I don't think Dante successfully completed his Italian translation of it."

"To quote a common, urban saying: *Bring it on.*"

She grasped his wrist with her hand. "Your department will marginalize you. They'll say you aren't serious about your research. Their opinions might diminish the likelihood of you winning grants or further sabbaticals."

"I'm a full professor with tenure. Fuck them."

For one impetuous moment, Julia was seized with the urge to laugh.

But she didn't.

"I'm serious, Julianne. Fuck them. What can they do to me? Barring anything Apocalyptic, they're stuck with me. How I choose to order my family life is none of their business."

"Why are you so determined to do this?" She searched his eyes.

"Because I love you. Because I love our child already, even though he or she is probably smaller than a grape." He stroked her cheeks with his thumbs. "You are not alone. You have a husband who loves you and is happy we're having a baby. You won't go through this by yourself."

He lowered his voice to a whisper. "I'm standing right here. Don't push me away."

She closed her eyes, clutching his forearms.

"I'm frightened."

"So am I. But I swear to God, Julianne, it will be all right. I will make it all right."

"What if something goes wrong?"

He brought their foreheads together. "I hope nothing like that happens. But we shouldn't start this journey by thinking of all the terrible outcomes. You're the one who taught me to hope. Don't despair."

"How could this happen?"

He rummaged in his coat pocket for a handkerchief and gently wiped her face.

"If you don't know how this happened, darling, then clearly I'm not doing it right."

He tried to smother a smirk and failed. Completely.

Julia opened her eyes to see his own, slightly darkened with masculine pride.

"Superman," she muttered. "I should have known you had magic in your genes."

"Why, yes, Mrs. Emerson, I do have magic in my jeans. I'd happily put on a magic show for you at any time. All you need do is ask."

Julia rolled her eyes. "Very funny, Superman."

He kissed her then, tenderly. It was the kiss of a man who'd just received what he desired most from his beloved. A most desired, most unexpected gift.

"I . . . I prayed for this," he said hesitantly.

"I did, too. More than once. I should have known that St. Francis would not have rested until he persuaded God to give us a baby."

"Oh, I don't know about that." He tapped her nose with his finger. "A certain Dante scholar convinced me that St. Francis tended to get his point across with silence. Maybe he didn't say anything. Maybe he just stood there."

"Oh, he said something," Julia complained. "This is his way of showing me my lecture was wrong and he actually fought with the demon for Guido's soul."

"I doubt that most sincerely. And so would Professor Wodehouse. In fact, I think St. Francis is probably bragging about you among the circle of the blessed."

"I didn't give him much to brag about these last few days. I've been spoiled and selfish."

"You're neither." Gabriel's tone grew severe. "You've been taken by surprise, just like me, but you have more at stake. As I said before, I promise I'll take on more in order to even things out."

He hugged her tightly.

"I didn't expect my prayers to be answered. I still can't get used to the idea that God would even listen to me, let alone decide to grant my requests."

"Maybe this is the lavishness of God's grace, given unexpectedly."

"Fun dayn moyl in gots oyern."

Julia lifted her eyebrows. "Yiddish?"

"Exactly. It means, 'From your mouth to God's ears.'"

A warm feeling expanded in her middle.

"We'll be able to teach the baby Yiddish. And Italian. And about his famous great-grandfather, Professor Spiegel."

"And his famous mother, Professor Julianne Emerson. You will finish your program, Julianne, and you will become a professor. I swear to it."

She burrowed her face in the wool of his winter coat.

Chapter Seventy

January 1, 2012
Stowe, Vermont

Paul found himself sitting next to the fireplace in a chalet in the wee hours of the morning. Heather and Chris had already retired to their bedroom, having rung the New Year in already, leaving Paul and Allison to drink their beer in companionable silence.

They were both seated on the floor. Allison was gazing at Paul with an inscrutable expression on her pretty face.

"Do you remember our first time together?"

He sat bolt upright and nearly expelled his beer.

He coughed.

"What? Why are you asking me that?"

She looked away, visibly embarrassed. "I was just wondering if you ever thought about it. I'm sorry. I shouldn't have brought it up."

He began peeling the label from his bottle of Samuel Adams as he waited for his heart to start beating again.

"Is that something you think about a lot? Our first time?" Paul cared about Ali and didn't want to make her feel bad. He didn't want her to be ashamed of their past. He sure as hell wasn't.

"Um, don't you?"

"You broke up with me, remember?" He picked at his beer bottle again. "Where are you going with this?"

"I just wondered if you ever thought about me that way."

"Of course I do. But what are you trying to do—torture me? I had to stop thinking about you like that, otherwise . . ." Now it was his turn to look embarrassed.

"I'm sorry." She wrapped her arms around her legs, resting her cheek on her knees. Her eyes found his in the firelight and she looked so lost. So sad.

Paul shifted to stare into the flames.

"What do you think about?" he asked at last.

"The way you smell. The way you sound when you whisper in my ear. The way you used to look at me when we . . ." She gave him a half-smile. "You don't look at me like that anymore.

"I understand why. It was my fault and I have to live with that."

"Maybe everything happens for a reason." Paul kept his eyes fixed resolutely on the fire.

"Maybe. I just wish I could take it back. That I wasn't so stupid."

"The long-distance thing was tough for me, too. We were arguing."

"They were stupid arguments."

"Yes, they were."

"I'm sorry."

Now he was looking at her.

"Stop saying that, okay? You did what you thought you should do. I got over it. End of story."

"But that's what I'm most sorry about," she whispered.

"What?"

"The fact that you got over it."

Their eyes met, and Paul swore he saw tears swimming in her eyes. She brushed at them quickly.

"Don't get me wrong, they're good memories, happy memories. But after you and I broke up and I started dating someone else, I couldn't help but think about it again."

"You dated a guy named Dave, right?"

"Yeah. We worked together but not anymore. He moved to Montpelier."

"You didn't date him for very long."

She pillowed her cheek on her knees again. "He was nice enough, but not as nice as you."

"Did he hurt you?" Paul's tone was wary.

"No. But when we had sex he wouldn't look at me. He always kept his eyes closed. I never felt like he was really there, you know? I felt like

I could have been anybody. Any girl he'd taken home with him, rather than his girlfriend."

"Ali, I—"

She interrupted him. "I couldn't help but compare him to you. That's why I brought up our first time. How you insisted that we get to know each other really well before we had sex. How you booked a hotel just down the road for our first time." Her expression was wistful. "You always made me feel special, even before you told me you loved me."

"You *are* special."

She looked at him steadily.

"Do you think we could pick up where we left off?"

"No."

She cringed.

He reached over to grasp her hand. "I still have feelings for you. But I'm not ready to jump into something right now. Even if I were, we can't just pick up where we left off. We're both different people."

"You don't seem that different."

"I am. Trust me."

Allison squeezed his hand. "I've never trusted anyone more. I was jealous of Julia. Of the way you said her name. Because that's how you used to say my name. But I broke up with you and you fell for someone else. I would have kept my mouth shut if things worked out between you two. But they didn't."

Paul took another long pull from his beer and shook his head.

On January second, Paul had to leave for the Modern Language Association's annual convention, which was being held in Seattle. All his interviews for prospective jobs would take place during the convention.

Allison drove him to the airport in Burlington. Before he exited the car, she gave him a small gift bag.

"It's just some chocolate chip cookies I made. There might even be a book in there."

Paul thanked her with a smile.

"What's the book?"

"Sense and Sensibility."

He looked at her quizzically. "Why are you giving me that?"

"I thought you might find it meaningful."

"Thanks," he said. "I think."

"You're welcome. I'll miss you."

"I'll miss you, too. Come here."

He tugged her into a warm embrace.

By way of response, she pulled back slightly before pressing a gentle but insistent kiss to his lips. She was surprised but elated when he didn't recoil but rather deepened their connection.

"I'll be home soon," he managed, when they finally pulled themselves apart.

She answered him with a hopeful grin, waving until he disappeared into the terminal.

Chapter Seventy-one

January 10, 2012
New York, New York

Christa Peterson breezed into the Department of Italian at Columbia University. She'd enjoyed a very pleasant winter break at her parents' home in Toronto and had even met someone with whom she'd enjoyed a brief affair. Now she was eager to resume her studies and continue her journey toward becoming a Dante specialist.

With interest, she emptied her pigeonhole of all its mail, sitting on a chair nearby in order to peruse it. Much of the mail was junk, with the exception of a single typewritten announcement. Christa scanned it quickly.

The announcement listed the names of three senior Dante specialists who would be visiting the department over the course of the next two weeks, as candidates for the vacant professorship. Christa read the names twice before relaxing in her chair.

She smiled. But not because of the names listed.

No, she smiled because a particular name had not been listed. It would seem that her plan to revenge herself on Professor Giuseppe Pacciani was already bearing fruit.

With that delightful thought in mind, she pocketed the announcement, threw the junk mail into the wastepaper basket, and was preparing to exit the department when Professor Barini stopped her.

"Miss Peterson, I need to speak to you."

"Of course." Christa obediently followed the professor into her office.

Professor Barini left the door ajar before sitting behind her desk.

"I'd like to thank you for taking my advice about Professor Pacciani. I noticed that he didn't make the short list." Christa made no attempt to hide her exultation.

Lucia ignored the comment and retrieved a file, quickly leafing through its contents. Then she looked at Christa over the rims of her glasses. "You've run into a problem."

"A problem? What kind of problem?"

"You're supposed to choose three professors to sit on your oral examination committee, but I've been notified by the faculty that no one is willing to do so."

"What?" Christa's dark eyes grew wide.

"This has never happened before. As the chair, I cannot compel a faculty member to serve on your committee. And even if I could, I wouldn't. Their lack of willingness to participate indicates that they don't think you'll perform to their satisfaction."

Christa couldn't quite believe her ears. It was unthinkable that every faculty member in the department would refuse to work with her. No one had given her even the slightest indication of that kind of antipathy.

(At least, to her face.)

"What does that mean?"

Lucia sighed. "It means that, unfortunately, we will be granting you a terminal MA as of May and that you will need to apply elsewhere to pursue your studies."

"You can't do that!"

Lucia closed Christa's file with a snap of her wrist. "There are regulations about a student's satisfactory performance in the M.Phil program. According to the faculty, you are not performing satisfactory work."

"But, but, this is outrageous!" Christa sputtered. "I've completed all my assignments. I've been getting decent grades. No one has offered me any critical feedback. You can't simply push me out of the program on a whim!"

"We don't have whims here at Columbia, Miss Peterson. We have standards. While it's true you've been passing your seminars, you still have to take the oral exam. As I mentioned, no one is willing to serve on your testing committee. That means you won't be able to complete the program."

Christa gazed around the room helplessly, trying to figure a way out of her predicament.

"Let me talk to them. I'll go see the professors on my own and plead my case."

Lucia shook her head. "I can't let you do that. At this point, they've added a letter to your permanent file. If you go to them after the fact, they'll view it as harassment."

Christa scowled at the implication.

"That's ridiculous. I'm not going to harass them."

Lucia gave her a long look. "Be that as it may, I can't let you speak to them."

Christa felt the control she thought she'd regained slip through her fingers.

(It didn't occur to her that this must have been how Professor Emerson and Julianne felt when they'd been brought before the disciplinary committee in Toronto.)

"It's too late for me to apply to other programs. This will ruin me." Her chin began to wobble.

"Not necessarily. Many programs receive applications until March. My assistant can help you identify those programs. Perhaps you should consider returning to Canada."

"But I want to stay here. Professor Martin said—"

"Professor Martin is not the chair here; I am." Lucia nodded at the door. "I realize this is a disappointment, but perhaps at another university, you will be successful."

"There must be something I can do. Please." Christa sat forward in her chair, begging.

"You can appeal to the dean, if you wish, but university regulations prevent her from demanding that faculty serve on specific examination committees. I'm afraid she can't help you." Once again Lucia nodded at the door. "My assistant will help you research other programs. I wish you good luck."

Christa stared across the desk, in complete and utter shock. But as she exited the office, she remembered something, something Pacciani had said to her back in Oxford.

Be careful, Cristina. You don't want Professor Picton as an enemy. . . .

Departments around the world are filled with her admirers. Your chair at Columbia was her student.

It angered her sorely that in the end, Pacciani had been correct. But as quickly as the realization came to her, so did a possible solution. She would simply have to pursue her education outside the patronage system of Professor Picton. And that meant that she would need to research every single professor in every department that offered a doctoral program in Dante studies.

She had days of work ahead of her, simply to find a possibility of enrolling in a doctoral program.

(It must be said parenthetically that karma had been served.)

Chapter Seventy-two

Fear and anxiety are not so easily managed, especially by people who have struggled for years with both. When the Emersons returned to Cambridge, they each made appointments to see their respective therapists, immediately.

Dr. Walters suggested several different strategies for Julia to cope with the anxiety over her pregnancy, but she stressed the fact that Julia needed to ask for help and that she also needed to accept it and not try to do everything on her own.

Dr. Townsend painstakingly addressed Gabriel's worries over the health and welfare of his wife and unborn child. But he was pleased with the progress Gabriel had made since the summer.

The Emersons also visited Dr. Rubio, who confirmed the pregnancy, estimating the due date would be around September sixth. A series of appointments were scheduled, including ultrasounds to monitor the progress of the baby and any issues relating to the uterine fibroids. Julia was urged to modify her diet and to take supplements, in order to ensure her health and the health of the baby.

She was also instructed to avoid oral sex with her husband.

"Come again?" The Professor's voice boomed in the small room.

"No male-on-female oral sex during pregnancy," Dr. Rubio repeated briskly.

"That's ridiculous."

Dr. Rubio gazed at him coolly.

"And where did you become board certified in obstetrics, Mr. Emerson?"

"It's *Professor* Emerson, and I went to Harvard. Where did you go, an anti–oral sex college?"

"Darling." Julia placed a restraining hand on his arm. "Dr. Rubio is trying to help us and the baby. We want to be healthy."

"Cunnilingus is healthy," he huffed. "I can prove it."

Dr. Rubio cursed obliquely in Spanish. "If air enters the vagina, it could cause an air embolism, which might harm the baby. I advise all my patients not to engage in that kind of oral sex. I'm not picking on you especially, *Professor* Emerson. Now, I'll see you at your next appointment. Don't forget—no caffeine, no raw milk products, no Brie or Camembert, no alcohol, no shellfish, no sushi, no peanut butter, and certainly, no oral sex." She glared in Gabriel's direction.

"One might as well say 'no pleasure.' What the hell is left?" he complained, moodily.

Julia giggled nervously. "I'm sure we can find something. Thanks, Dr. Rubio."

And with that Gabriel drove Julia to the nearest Barnes and Noble, whereupon he bought no less than three pregnancy books, all of which stated that cunnilingus during pregnancy was fine, so long as air didn't enter the vagina.

Then the Emersons retired to their home, whereupon the Professor commenced proving his point.

❧❧

"I'm not sure you should come with me to my next doctor's appointment," Julia mused as she dressed one morning.

It was January twenty-first, the date of their first wedding anniversary. Rebecca (who was delighted at the prospect of becoming a nanny in addition to her housekeeping duties) had rented out her house in Norwood and moved into one of the guest bedrooms. Julia found her presence comforting, especially since she and Gabriel no longer had mothers to guide them through pregnancy.

"I'm going to all your appointments. Rubio doesn't scare me." Gabriel sounded impatient as he buttoned up his dress shirt. "And she doesn't know everything, either."

Julia didn't bother arguing.

She was in her second month of pregnancy and was already feeling the effects. Her breasts had enlarged and were very tender. She was exhausted most of the time, and she'd become sensitive to various scents.

She'd had to request that Gabriel no longer wear Aramis because she couldn't stand the smell. And she'd gotten rid of all her vanilla-scented products and replaced them with grapefruit-scented items because it was one of the few smells she could still tolerate.

To Gabriel's delight, however, Julia's hormones were such that she wanted sex several times a day. He was happy to accommodate her.

(For in this respect, as in several others, he was the consummate gentleman.)

"Are you all right?" Gabriel observed her face, which had taken on a greenish cast.

She continued buttoning up her jeans. "Look, Gabriel, they still fit."

He reached over to kiss her forehead. "That's great, darling. But we should probably start shopping for maternity clothes."

"I don't want to spend my anniversary shopping."

"We don't have to. But I thought we'd spend some time walking around Copley Place before we check into the Plaza for the weekend."

"Okay," she said softly. "That sounds good."

By the time she reached the kitchen her stomach had begun to roll. She eyed the platter of scrambled eggs on the breakfast table as Gabriel helped himself to a few strips of bacon.

She felt a funny sensation in the back of her throat.

"Why don't you start with a slice of dry toast? That's what I used to do every morning." Rebecca picked up a loaf of bread and motioned toward the toaster.

"I don't feel good," Julia announced, closing her eyes.

"I bought more ginger ale. Sit down and I'll get you one." Rebecca put the bread aside and moved toward the fridge.

Before Julia could respond, she felt her stomach heave. She covered her mouth and ran for the nearest bathroom.

Gabriel followed, the sounds of her retching echoing down the hall.

"Sweetheart." He crouched next to her, reaching around to lift her hair out of the way.

She was on her knees, head hanging over the toilet.

She vomited again and again, her stomach emptying.

Gabriel rubbed her back with his other hand. He fetched her a towel to wipe her mouth and a glass of water.

"This must be love," she murmured, in between sips of water.

"What's that?" He sat behind her, cradling her in his arms.

"You held my hair, Professor. You must love me."

He reached a tentative hand to her lower abdomen. "I seem to recall you looking after me once, when I was sick. And that was before you loved me."

"I always loved you, Gabriel."

"Thank you." He kissed her forehead. "We made this little one together. You aren't going to scare me off with bodily fluids."

"I'll remember that when my water breaks."

❧❧

The Emersons spent a few hours leisurely walking around Copley Place before driving to an Italian restaurant in the north end for dinner.

That evening, in their suite at the Copley Plaza hotel, Julia undressed, dropping her clothes carelessly on the floor. Gabriel surveyed her body, his eyes fixing on her breasts, which were full and ripe.

"Your beauty always takes my breath away."

Julia felt her skin heat under his gaze. "Your compliments always surprise me."

"They shouldn't. Perhaps I don't say them often enough." He paused, staring at her. "We aren't newlyweds anymore."

"No, we're not."

"Happy anniversary, Mrs. Emerson."

"Happy anniversary, Mr. Emerson."

He reached into his jacket pocket and removed a distinctive blue box, tied with a white satin ribbon.

Julia stammered.

"I'm sorry, Gabriel. I have a card for you but I forgot your gift back at the house." She rubbed at her forehead. "I hope I'm not getting pregnancy brain."

"Pregnancy brain?"

"Dr. Rubio says it's common for pregnant women to experience short-term memory problems. It's probably due to hormones."

"I don't need a gift, but I'm grateful you thought of me."

"It's a Star of David on a silver chain. I know you don't wear jewelry." She gestured to his wedding ring. "Except for that. But I thought maybe . . ."

"Of course I'd wear it. Thank you, Julianne, that was very thoughtful."

"I'm sorry I forgot it. Thank you for your present." She gazed at him warmly as he handed her the box.

When she opened it, she found a diamond solitaire pendant suspended on a long platinum chain. She looked up at him quizzically.

"It matches Grace's earrings." He stood behind her, gesturing toward the necklace.

"It's beautiful." She touched the stone as he fastened the chain around her neck. "Thank you."

"Thank you for putting up with me," he whispered, kissing the place where her neck flared into her shoulders.

"I wouldn't say it's a hardship. We have our ups and downs like any couple."

He straightened, taking her hand in his. "Let's try to make sure our ups are greater than our downs."

❧❧

After they'd spent time loving one another, they curled together on the bed.

Julia fingered the necklace that rested just above her expanded breasts.

"Are you scared?" she whispered.

The corners of Gabriel's lips turned up. "Terrified."

"Then why are you smiling?

"Because part of me is growing inside you. I get to see my beautiful wife carry my child."

"In a few months, we'll have a family."

"We're already a family." He reached out to stroke her hair. "How are you feeling?"

"I'm tired. I nearly fell asleep in one of my seminars this week. I'm finding it difficult to stay awake in the afternoon without caffeine."

His expression grew concerned. "You need to get more rest. Maybe you should come home and take a nap before your seminars."

Julia yawned.

"I'd love to, but there isn't time. I just need to start going to bed early. Which means we'll need to have sex right after dinner."

"And so it begins," he mumbled.

"Don't start with me." She pushed at him playfully and he grabbed her wrist, pulling her into a tender kiss.

"I hope it's a girl."

Julia was surprised. "Why?"

"I want someone I can spoil, like you. A little brown-eyed angel."

"That reminds me. Until we find out the sex of the baby, I don't want to call the baby *it*. I know some people do that because there's no gender-neutral pronoun in English. But I don't like that."

"I love it when you talk about grammar. It's sexy." He kissed her. "We'll just call her *her* or *the baby*."

Julia's hand drifted down to her abdomen. "What makes you so sure the baby is a girl? I think we're having a boy."

"He's a she. And we'll have to come up with an appropriate name."

"Such as what? Beatrice?"

"No," he said softly. "There's only one Beatrice. We could call her Grace."

Julia was thoughtful for a moment.

"I'm not ready to decide on a name, although Grace is a possibility. I think he's going to be a boy, though. So for now, we'll just have to call him Ralph."

"Ralph? Why Ralph?"

"It's a good, all-purpose nickname. I would have called him Peanut, but that's what we called Tommy before he was born."

Gabriel chuckled. "Your mind is fascinating. Now go to sleep, little mama. Morning comes very early these days."

He kissed her forehead before turning out the light. Then he held his wife in his arms.

❧❧

A few hours later, he awoke to the feel of a hand stroking his naked chest.

"Darling?" His voice was thick with sleep.

"I'm sorry I woke you." She moved closer, pressing her thigh in between his.

He felt her lips press light kisses over his pectorals and up to his neck.

"Can't sleep?"

"No, I can't."

Her hand brushed over his abdominal muscles before descending lower.

She kissed him and he responded warmly. His sleepiness and fatigue seemed to melt away as she moved her hand up and down.

"You have something I need."

"Are you sure?" His hand caught her wrist, pausing her movements.

She hesitated.

"Julianne?"

"I'm sorry for waking you up, but I really need to have sex. Right now."

"Right now?"

"Right now. Please."

He removed his hand and threw back the bedclothes.

"Do with me as you will."

Instantly, she moved to straddle him. He reached up to cup her heavy breasts as she leaned down to kiss him.

"*Invite me inside*," he murmured, as he pressed up against her.

"Do you need an invitation?"

Gabriel stared into her eyes, which had widened with excitement.

"I could spend the rest of my life inside you and die happy. You're my home."

Julia paused at the sudden vulnerability that flashed across her husband's face. She lifted her hands to cover his, pressing into her breasts.

"You'll make me cry. And I'm emotional already."

"No tears, please." He squeezed her more tightly.

"*Then come*," she whispered, bringing their hips into alignment.

He slowly entered her.

"*Home*," he whispered.

Julia didn't try to blink back the tears. She let them fall.

"I love you so much."

He responded by licking and sucking her breasts, teasing her and spurring her on. Within minutes they were pushing and pulling, their skin warm and alive with excitement.

"Is it good?" Gabriel ground out, his hands dropping to her hips.

Her eyes were closed, her rosy lips parted. When she didn't answer he placed a tender hand to her face. "Julia?"

Her eyes fluttered open. "It's good," she panted. "So good."

His large hands gripped her hips, urging her on.

"Faster," he murmured.

Julia responded by lifting herself and quickly slamming down, over and over again, until they both collapsed from near exhaustion.

Chapter Seventy-three

January 31, 2012
Cambridge, Massachusetts

Professor Katherine Picton stood in the lecture hall at Harvard, surveying the crowd. She'd delivered her paper presentation a half hour after Professor Jeremy Martin offered his. And she'd fielded questions from the audience and received a very smart paperweight as a gift from Professor Greg Matthews, on behalf of the Department of Romance Studies.

She hadn't had the opportunity to greet the Emersons yet. She was eager to do so. They'd invited her to their home for dinner so she could escape Greg's more experimental culinary choices.

"Ah, there you are!" Professor Picton's crisp British accent cut through the hum of a dozen or so conversations.

She strode quickly down one of the aisles, straight to where Julia was still seated, while Gabriel stood next to her, chatting amiably with Julia's supervisor, Professor Marinelli.

"Katherine." Gabriel greeted her smoothly, kissing her cheek.

"Gabriel and Julianne. Good to see you both."

She turned to Professor Marinelli. "Cecilia, delightful to see you, as always."

"And you." The two women embraced.

"Now then, have you spoken with Jeremy?" Katherine turned her blue-gray eyes on Gabriel.

"No." Gabriel was terse.

"I think it's high time you two buried the hatchet. Don't you?"

Cecilia gazed between the two other Dante specialists and politely made her excuses, choosing to flee to another part of the room where an argument was not about to break forth.

"I don't have a problem with Jeremy." Gabriel sounded offended. "Jeremy has a problem with me."

Katherine's eyes snapped.

"Then you won't mind if I bring him over here."

She marched her small figure up to Jeremy Martin and spoke to him rather directly.

Julia stood uneasily, wondering what was about to happen.

It was obvious that Professor Martin did not wish to speak with Gabriel. Julia watched as he looked in their direction, then looked back at Katherine, shaking his head.

Katherine appeared to scold him, but only for a moment, before the two professors walked in the direction of the Emersons.

"Here we go," Julia whispered, taking Gabriel's hand.

"Emerson." Jeremy's voice was stiff, as he approached.

"Jeremy."

Katherine looked between the two men and frowned. "Well, get on with it. Shake hands."

Gabriel released Julia's hand in order to shake the hand of his former friend.

"For what it's worth, Jeremy, I'm sorry."

Julia looked up at her husband in surprise.

Professor Martin appeared taken aback as well. He shifted his weight, his eyes traveling from Gabriel's to Julia's and back again.

"I understand that congratulations are in order. You've been married about a year, I think. Is that right?"

"That's right," Julia interjected. "Thank you, Professor Martin."

"It's Jeremy, now."

"I know we owe you a debt. I won't forget it." Gabriel lowered his voice.

Jeremy stepped back.

"This isn't the time or the place."

"Then perhaps we could talk in the hall? Come on, Jeremy, we were friends for years. I'm trying to apologize."

Jeremy grimaced. "All right. Ladies, excuse me." He nodded at Katherine and Julia before following Gabriel into the hallway.

"That went well." Julia turned to Katherine.

"We'll see. If they return without having spilt any blood, I'll agree with you." Katherine's eyes sparkled impishly. "Shall we watch through the door?"

❧❧

Over dinner at their home that evening, Gabriel and Julia were determined not to announce her pregnancy to Katherine. They'd resolved not to tell anyone until she was in her second trimester.

(However, they did nothing to hide the telltale sign of the Volvo SUV that Gabriel had recently purchased, which was parked in the driveway.)

While Gabriel was in the kitchen making coffee, Katherine turned her all-seeing eyes on Julia and tapped a single finger on top of the linen tablecloth.

"You're expecting."

"What?" Julia faltered, putting her water glass down so she wouldn't spill.

"It's obvious. You aren't drinking. You declined coffee. Your husband, who by all accounts is very solicitous, is hovering over you as if you were made of china, while simultaneously trying to hide his extreme, testosterone-laden pride. You can't fool me."

"Professor Picton, I—"

"I thought we'd agreed you'd call me Katherine."

"Katherine, I'm not very far along. We aren't telling anyone, including family, until I'm in my second trimester."

"That's wise. It might be good for you to put off telling your department until the last possible moment." Katherine sipped her wine thoughtfully.

"I'm afraid to tell them."

Katherine put her glass down. "Can you tell me why?"

Julia's hand went to her abdomen. "There are several reasons. I'm worried they'll think I'm not serious enough and that Cecilia will drop me as a student."

"Nonsense. Cecilia has three children, two of which she had while she was a graduate student in Pisa. Next problem."

Julia paused, her mouth open.

"Um, I didn't know that."

"I've known her for years. She's a working mother who is determined to carve out time for her family. That's why they spend their summers in Italy, so the children can be with their grandparents. Next problem."

"Um, I'm worried they'll take away my funding and I'll lose my fellowship."

"Universities are very different from when I was a student. There are legal issues that would prevent your department from doing that. You're entitled to a maternity leave just like everyone else. In fact, if I'm not mistaken, Harvard has a committee on the status of women that would ensure you are treated fairly. Even if your department were chaired by a fool, and it isn't, he'd have to follow the guidelines. Next problem."

"I'm not asking for a maternity leave. But I was told by my doctor I'd need to take at least six weeks off after the baby is born. I'm worried my chair will force me to deregister for the semester."

Katherine frowned. "Not take a maternity leave? Are you mad?"

Julia started to protest, but Katherine lifted an aged, wrinkled hand.

"I might be an old maid, but I know you won't be able to do justice to your program, or your newborn, if you don't take a maternity leave. You are allowed one. You should take it."

"Won't the department frown on it?"

"Some of the old fossils might, but if you have the support of your supervisor, what does it matter? My advice is to speak to Cecilia and ask for her advice. She'll know best how to guide you. Don't let the misogynists drive you into an impossible situation."

Katherine tapped her chin thoughtfully. "I'm always eager to fight injustice. Let them try to injure you. In fact, I have half a mind to accept Greg Matthews's offer to join his department just to ensure that they don't."

Julia's jaw dropped. "You'd consider that?"

"I've decided to sell my house and leave Toronto. All Souls is eager to have me join them in Oxford on a more permanent basis, but the truth is there are only a few fellows in that college that I can tolerate. It's making my meals in college most unpleasant."

"It would be wonderful to have you at Harvard."

"I'm beginning to think so, too." Katherine's eyes shone. "This is where all the action is. Greg promised me he'd move my library personally. I want to accept his offer simply to see him hand-packing my books."

Julia laughed at the thought of Professor Matthews, who was very distinguished, moving Professor Picton's extensive private library by hand.

"I'm happy you and Gabriel are having a baby. Whether I move to Harvard or not, I'm hoping you'll let me be the aged, eccentric godmother who purchases outrageous gifts and feeds the child things that aren't good for him."

"I'd like nothing more." Julia squeezed Katherine's hand just as Gabriel returned with coffee.

He glanced between the two women. "What's going on?"

Katherine lifted her wine glass, saluting him. "I was just telling Julianne that I accept the distinguished appointment as your baby's godmother."

❧❧

Just before bed, Julia asked Gabriel about his conversation with Professor Martin.

Gabriel stared up at the ceiling.

"It went better than expected, but I doubt he'll ever forgive me."

Julia rested her head on his chest. "I'm sorry."

"He thinks I stabbed him and the entire department in the back. Although the fact that I married you seems to have ameliorated his low opinion of me. Perhaps once he learns we're pregnant, his anger will cool a little more."

"How do you feel about him?"

Gabriel shrugged. "He was a friend. I'm sorry we had a falling out, but I'm not sorry for what I did. I'd do it again."

Julia sighed. "Well, the day wasn't a total loss. I enjoyed watching my fellow graduate students react to your arrival."

Gabriel's lips twitched. "Oh, really? And how did they react?"

Julia rolled onto her stomach. "Like they'd never seen a hot professor before. You made quite an impression in your turtleneck."

"Ah, yes, the turtleneck. Turtles have that effect on people."

"It's the man they were admiring. And I was proud to be with you."

She laced the edges of the sheet between her fingers. "But there are still rumors going around."

"Oh, really?" Gabriel lifted her chin so he could make eye contact.

"Zsuzsa told me that some of the grad students have been saying that you got me into the program."

"Bastards," Gabriel spat. "This is Christa's fault."

"Not entirely. We made our choices and we have to live with them."

"The reality of what happened and what they're saying is poles apart."

"That's true. But you'll be interested to know that now they're gossiping about Christa."

Gabriel gazed at her with cautious interest. "Christa? Why?"

"Sean, one of the PhD students in my department, has a friend at Columbia. He said that the department forced Christa out. None of the faculty would agree to supervise her."

Gabriel's eyebrows lifted. "Really? When I was in New York, Lucia mentioned that Katherine complained about Christa's behavior in Oxford. But I doubt her dismissal had anything to do with us. Lucia also said that her work wasn't very good."

"It's possible she didn't get along with the Dante specialists in that department. They can be mercurial." Julia winked at her husband slyly.

"I have no idea what you're talking about." Gabriel sniffed.

"Sean said that Christa is on her way to do her PhD in Geneva."

"Geneva doesn't have its own doctoral program in Italian. They're part of a consortium."

"That's where she's headed, if the rumors are to be believed."

Gabriel shook his head. "If she'd just focused on her work at Toronto and not become fixated on me, she'd probably still be there. Her original application and writing sample were very good. It was her machinations that were her downfall. Then she made the colossal error of going up against Katherine. That made Lucia nervous."

"Why?"

"Katherine is one of the best in her field. If anyone wants to publish in Dante studies, or write a grant for support, or try to get a job, people look to her for her opinion. If she approves of you, she'll say so. If she doesn't, she'll say that, too. No one wants to alienate her in case they need her support some day. That includes Lucia and her department."

Julia pursed her lips.

"I didn't want Christa's life to be ruined. I just wanted her to leave us alone."

"She did this to herself. She had several opportunities to rethink her choices, and she didn't. No one made her go to Oxford and try to sabotage you, or to do mediocre work at Columbia."

"I suppose you're right." Julia rested her head on the pillow. "Academia is the strangest place."

"Bit like Mars, really. Except with more sex."

Julia laughed. "I'm glad Katherine approves of me. I shudder to think what would happen if she didn't."

"Me, too. But in any case, I'll speak to Greg Matthews and make sure the rumors about us are quashed."

"Don't call in a favor for that. I might need his help with something else."

"Like what?"

"Katherine thinks I need to take a maternity leave. She wants me to speak to Cecilia about it."

Gabriel stroked the arches of her eyebrows with his fingers.

"And what do you want?"

"I have to talk to Cecilia. But I was hoping to wait until I'm in my second trimester. Most mis—" She caught Gabriel's eye and stumbled over the word. "—problems occur in the first trimester."

"If you want to take a maternity leave, you should. If you don't want to, you don't have to. I'm going on leave regardless. After the paternity leave, they owe me a sabbatical. I could be home with the baby for two years."

"Isn't there some rule about not taking a leave and a sabbatical back to back?"

"Probably." Gabriel began caressing her lower back. "But I have it written into my contract that they give me a sabbatical the year after next. It was part of their job offer."

"I'd hate to see you waste your sabbatical," she said quietly.

His hand rested in the hollow of her lower back.

"What part of spending time with the baby would be wasted?"

"You won't be able to finish your book."

"I'm sure I'll have time to write. Even if I didn't, it would be worth it. Talk to Cecilia and see what she says. But whatever you do, don't worry. I made promises to you, and I intend to keep them."

Julia smiled. "That's the only reason why I'm not freaking out."

He gazed at her intensely. "Good."

Chapter Seventy-four

April 2012

So, Julianne, what can I do for you?" Cecilia Marinelli ushered her graduate student into her office, gesturing to a comfortable chair near the large desk.

Cecilia was just under five feet tall, with bobbed dark hair and blue eyes. She was from Pisa, originally, and spoke English with an accent.

"I came to ask your advice." Julia began wringing her hands.

"Ask." Cecilia gave Julia an encouraging look.

"Um, I'm going to have a baby."

"Congratulations! This is good news, yes?" Cecilia switched to Italian, smiling widely.

Julia answered her in Italian. "Yes. Very good news. Uh, but I'm due in September, right at the beginning of the semester."

Cecilia shrugged. "Then you take maternity leave and return the next year."

"I don't want to fall behind in my program, so I'm not going to take a maternity leave."

Professor Marinelli shook her head. "This is not the best idea. Normally, in your third year, you would teach in the fall and take your linguistics course plus another class. Then you would write your general exams in the winter. Since your baby comes in September, I think your teaching and coursework would have to be delayed until January. Then you will be studying for your exams at the same time. This is too much." Cecilia's tone was not unkind.

"I didn't realize that." Julia's voice sounded shaky and small.

"You do what you like, but certainly, I would take maternity leave."

"Really?"

Cecilia sat back in her chair for a moment. "It will be too much for you to put all these things in one semester. Your colleagues will have the advantage of you in their general exams. And you cannot fail. So, to make things fair, you take maternity leave for one year. Then, you teach and take your classes the following September, and take your exams in the winter. Yes, you will be behind a year. But you are a good student. I think you will catch up when you are writing your dissertation. It will be better to be behind a year than to realize midsemester you cannot do everything."

Julia's heart sank as all her plans fell to pieces. Frantically, she searched for another solution.

"Aren't some of the courses offered in the summer?"

Cecilia noted her student's reaction and switched to English. "No, I'm sorry."

Julia's hands twisted in her lap.

"It's just that Gabriel was going to take a leave from BU so that I wouldn't have to."

"Gabriel? With a baby?" Cecilia laughed, chattering to herself in Italian.

(Apparently, she found the thought of the Professor looking after a baby highly amusing. In this, she was not alone.)

"This, I did not expect. But it shows he will be a good father, yes? If he is willing to help. But Gabriel's leave doesn't solve the problem of the schedule. It isn't realistic to think you can have a baby, then return to class the next day. God forbid you have complications and need to take time off before the baby is born."

Julia winced. "I hadn't thought of that, either."

Cecilia smiled patiently. "This is why we have advisors, to offer advice and maybe a little caution. My advice is to take maternity leave. You won't lose your place in the program or your funding. If you want, I can give you a reading list for your dissertation prospectus and you can work on that while you're on leave. You could also work on your other languages. But let's not be too ambitious. And there's one more thing, but you must promise to keep it secret. Professor Matthews is waiting to make the formal announcement." She switched back into Italian, as if that language afforded them more privacy.

"Of course." Julia responded in Italian, looking at her supervisor with interest.

"Professor Picton has decided to come to Harvard."

"Really? That's wonderful." Julia's heart leapt with joy.

"Yes, it is. She's committed to stay in Oxford one more year, then she will arrive next September, when you return from maternity leave. I cannot speak for her, but I believe she would be a reader on your dissertation. This is very good news for your project."

Julia smiled as the wheels began turning in her mind.

"So," said Cecilia, reverting to English once again. "I won't tell you it will be easy, being a mother and a student. But you can do it. Please give Gabriel my congratulations. I'm happy for you both."

Julia thanked her professor and exited the office.

❧❧

When Julia arrived home for dinner, Gabriel was sitting on a bar stool at the kitchen island, reading the newspaper.

He immediately dropped the paper when he saw her.

"Why, hello, beautiful. How was your day?"

"It was okay." Julia put her messenger bag down on the floor and sat next to him at the island.

"What's wrong?" He placed his hand at the back of her neck and gently pulled her close so he could kiss her. "Are you ill?"

"I have good news and bad news."

The edges of his lips turned down. "What's the bad news?"

"Professor Marinelli said I have to take a maternity leave."

"Why did she say that?"

"Since the baby is due in September, she doesn't think I should register for courses in the fall. The way the schedule is, it would be too much if I tried to cram the third-year requirements into the winter semester. So she thinks I should just take the year off."

Gabriel rubbed at his chin. "I'd forgotten about how busy the third year is. What do you want to do?"

"What can I do? I have to take a maternity leave." She put her elbows on the counter.

"Julianne, you can do anything you want. If you want to take classes after the baby is born, we'll make it work. You'll just have to take incompletes while you catch up on what you've missed."

"The graduate school doesn't like students taking incompletes."

"No, they don't. But they allow it, in certain circumstances. I'm sure they'd allow it in this case."

"Then I'd be playing catch-up while studying for my general exams."

"That's true. Just because Cecilia thinks it might be challenging doesn't mean it will be impossible. As I said before, I will make this work. I promise."

Julia looked up at him, at his warm and earnest expression. "You will make this work?"

"Of course. But I'm not going to tell you what to do. You decide and I'll speak to Greg, if necessary."

"No, I'll talk to him. But—" She paused.

"What?"

"I need to tell you the good news. Cecilia said that Katherine is coming to Harvard."

Gabriel's mouth opened in astonishment. "What? I had an email from her last week. She never mentioned anything."

"Apparently, she's staying at Oxford next year and coming to Harvard the year after. That's another reason why Cecilia thinks that a maternity leave is a good idea—Katherine will arrive when I come back."

"That's great."

"It is. But—" Julia shook her head. "I don't want to take a maternity leave, but I'm worried about failing my exams."

"You won't fail."

"I won't be in tiptop shape either."

"Then we'll get you into tiptop shape. You're going to have Rebecca and me here to hold the fort. You can study for your exams and do what you need to do."

"I want to be a mother, too," she whispered. "I don't want to ignore the baby."

"I'm sure you can find a balance." He kissed the top of her head before crossing over to the refrigerator. He retrieved a bottle of ginger ale and quickly poured it over ice in a tall glass.

He handed it to her. "You don't need to decide right now. Register for the fall and if you feel like you need to drop the courses or take incompletes, you can."

"I don't want to start something and not finish it. I certainly don't want to risk failing my exams." She looked up at Gabriel, a worried expression on her face. "I don't want to be an absent mother, like Sharon."

"You won't be like her."

Gabriel looked down at the marble-topped island and traced a pattern on its surface.

"Truthfully, I don't know what to expect when we have the baby. But as I said, I'm taking leave regardless."

"Cecilia mentioned that she could give me a reading list for my dissertation prospectus. I could work on that while I'm on leave, along with my languages."

He lifted his head. "I'm sure the baby will be delighted to learn about Dante and also to be able to do more than just curse in German."

Julia laughed and wrapped an arm around his waist. "I think I'd be missing out if I didn't take part of a maternity leave. Who knows what kind of mischief you and the baby will get into?"

"Oh, you can be sure we will get into all kinds of mischief." He winked. "And there is a strong possibility that shenanigans and hijinks of various sorts will also occur, with regularity."

"Perhaps you and the baby will need me." Julia glanced at him.

Gabriel's eyes locked on hers.

"Of course we'll need you. But I'll make it work if you can't be here." He brought the backs of his fingers to her face and gently stroked her cheek. "If you take maternity leave, we could spend part of the year in Umbria."

"Really?"

"Or Oxford, or Paris, or Barcelona. You name it."

"Selinsgrove?"

Gabriel pulled back. "Of all the cities in the world, you want to go there?"

"That's where your family home is. That's where my family is. It might be nice to be close to Diane. She could give me advice and we could schedule play dates."

"We can talk to her on FaceTime from Europe."

"The orchard is there."

Gabriel traced his thumb across Julia's lower lip and sighed. "Yes, the orchard is there."

"I'll look into registering for the fall and if I can't go back after the baby is born, I'll drop the classes. Then I'll go on maternity leave for the winter semester and start studying for my general exams."

"That sounds like a good plan. Katherine will be here by the following September."

"We can have the baby at Mount Auburn Hospital, and decide from there where we want to go. I'm not sure about taking a newborn on a transatlantic flight."

"Hmm. I hadn't thought about that."

Julia wrapped her arms around his waist. "We haven't thought of a lot of things."

"Ah, but I have a book." Gabriel reached over to pick up a copy of *What to Expect When You're Expecting* that was sitting nearby.

"Make sure to mark the place where it talks about transatlantic flights and the likelihood of writing a book on Dante's concept of Hell while caring for a baby. I'd be interested in reading those sections."

He tossed the book aside. "Very funny, Mrs. Emerson."

She pressed herself against him. "If we go to Europe, we'll be able to visit some museums."

"That we will."

"We'll be able to tango against the wall."

"We'll have to bring Rebecca with us if we ever want to have a tango in a museum again." He pressed an openmouthed kiss to her neck.

"Museums aren't as accommodating as they used to be."

His eyes shone.

"Except for our last visit to the Uffizi."

Now she was blushing.

"That's what I want for our next anniversary."

"What? A museum?" He smirked.

"No. Another tango against a wall."

"Shall we try the Louvre next time?"

Julia felt her insides flame. "That sounds promising."

He kissed her neck, fluttering his lips against her skin. "We have a lot of good things to look forward to, Mrs. Emerson. But I think we both need to read that book."

Chapter Seventy-five

Selinsgrove, Pennsylvania

"You're *what*?"

A pile of silverware slid from Rachel's fingers, clattering onto the kitchen island. She stared openmouthed at her best friend.

Gabriel had his arm around Julia as they stood in the kitchen of the Clark family home. Scott, Tammy, and Quinn sat on stools nearby, while Richard and Aaron were deep in conversation near the stove.

"I'm pregnant," Julia repeated, her eyes searching Rachel's face.

The room fell silent.

"But, but, I didn't know you were trying. I thought you were going to wait," Rachel sputtered.

"The news was unexpected but not unwelcome." Gabriel pressed his lips to Julia's temple.

"That's great news, Julia. When are you due?" Tammy interjected.

"September." Julia's hand curved over her slightly protruding abdomen. "We told Dad, Diane, and my uncle Jack last night."

"I think this calls for cigars. I'm very proud of you both." Richard shook Gabriel's hand and clapped him on the back before kissing Julia's cheek. "It will be nice to have another baby around. Quinn and Tommy will have a new playmate."

"Exactly." Tammy followed, hugging Julia, and so did Scott.

Julia looked over at her best friend apprehensively. "Rach?"

"I—" Rachel suddenly closed her mouth. She looked as if she were about to burst into tears.

Aaron wrapped an arm around her shoulders. He murmured something in her ear.

"I'm happy for you," Rachel managed. After a moment, she embraced Julia and Gabriel together. "I am. I'm happy for you both."

Julia's eyes began to water.

"I think we should give the girls a minute. Isn't there a game on?" Aaron jerked his thumb toward the living room, where the wide-screen television was located.

Tammy, Quinn, and the men quickly retreated, leaving the best friends alone.

"This is a surprise." Rachel sat on one of the bar stools. "Was it an accident?"

Julia chewed at the inside of her mouth. "Gabriel doesn't want us using the word *accident*. He doesn't want the baby growing up thinking he wasn't wanted."

"Of course not!" Rachel appeared horrified. "I didn't think of it that way. I'm sorry."

"But, uh, clearly this was unexpected, because we were planning on waiting."

Rachel's eyes trained on her friend's.

"It must have been a shock for you. Are you all right?"

"I was upset at the beginning, but Gabriel has been great. He's really excited and his enthusiasm is infectious. Rebecca moved in with us, so she'll help with the baby. I've decided to take a maternity leave, and Gabriel is going to do the same."

Rachel snorted, resting her forearm on the top of the island. "Gabriel is taking a maternity leave? I'll believe that when I see it."

"Well, it's a paternity leave. It's available to him and so he's going to take it. They owe him a sabbatical anyway, but he's deferring it." Julia sat on the stool to Rachel's left. "We're even talking about moving here for part of the year, after the baby is born."

Rachel's gray eyes grew soft. "Dad would love that. Have you told him?"

Julia shook her head. "We were waiting until we told everyone we were expecting." She glanced in the direction of the living room. "Gabriel is probably asking him right now."

"Dad won't say no. Will Rebecca come too?"

"I haven't thought that far ahead. But it would be a bit ridiculous for one little baby to require three adults to supervise him."

Rachel regarded her friend. "You haven't been around babies much, have you?"

"No."

"You might need Rebecca to keep up the house and to cook for everyone." Rachel stared at her fingernails. "You and Diane will be able to commiserate about motherhood. We'll come home for weekends. The baby will be surrounded by family."

"That's what we wanted. I'm sorry about the timing. I know you and Aaron have been trying and I feel so—"

"Don't." Rachel forced a smile. "I'm happy for you. And I'm going to be the best damn aunt I can be. I'm hoping, someday, you'll have the chance to be the same to mine."

"Me, too."

Julia smiled, a sympathetic sadness twisting in her insides.

That evening, Aaron stood in his wife's childhood bedroom, which was still decorated with the awards and trophies she'd won in high school. He held her in his arms as she sobbed into his chest.

He felt helpless. He felt impotent.

"Rach," he whispered, rubbing her back.

"It's so unfair," she managed, her hands fisting his shirt. "They didn't even want a baby! Jules was going to wait until she graduated. I can't believe this is happening."

Aaron didn't know what to say. When Julia announced her good news, he was envious, but not to the degree that Rachel was. After a year of trying to conceive, she was battling depression. He didn't want to feed it by focusing on the unfairness of life and raising existential questions that might never be answered.

"I know you're upset, but I need you to calm down."

"I want my mom." She pressed her forehead into his shoulder. "She would know what to do."

"As much as I loved your mother, she wasn't a miracle worker."

"But she could give me advice. And I'm never going to see her again." A fresh round of sobs escaped Rachel's chest.

"You know that's not true," he whispered, rubbing her back once again. "This was a shock, but we have to get over it. People around us are going to have children. You don't want this to come between you and Julia."

"It won't."

"That's my girl. So no tears tomorrow." He pulled away, his face marked with concern.

"I can do that. I gave an Academy Award–winning performance earlier. I wanted to cry as soon as she told me."

"I don't want you to act, Rachel. I want you to appear to be okay and I want that to be the truth."

"But I'm not okay." She sat on the edge of her bed.

"I want to talk to you about that." Aaron joined her on the bed. "Instead of focusing on what we don't have, I'd like us to start thinking about what we have. We have our jobs, we have a nice place to live, we—"

"We have fertility treatments that aren't working." Rachel cursed under her breath.

"There are other options. We've discussed this."

"I'm not ready to give up."

"We don't have to give up. But maybe we should just relax for a while. Take a break."

"Take a break?" She peered over at him curiously.

"Stop the fertility treatments and forget about having a baby. Just for a while."

She crossed her arms around her middle. "No."

He took her hand in his. "I think the pressure is getting to you."

"I can handle it."

"No, baby, you can't. I know you like I know myself. And I'm telling you, you need a break. We need a break."

"We're supposed to try the fertility treatments for a year. We can't stop now." Her chin began to wobble.

"Yes, we can." He brushed his lips across hers. "We'll talk to the doctor when we're back in Philadelphia. Then we're going to take a long vacation. Gabriel promised he'd lend us their house in Italy. We can take some time and just be a normal couple again."

"What if this is it? What if we can't . . ." She couldn't bring herself to say it.

"Then we'll start looking at other options." He placed his arm around her. "Whether or not we have a baby, we have each other. That's something, isn't it?"

She nodded.

"We need to take care of each other. And I'm not taking care of you if I let you continue like this."

"I feel like a failure." Rachel wiped her face with the back of her hand.

"You aren't," he whispered. "You're the most incredible woman I've ever met. I would love to have a family with you but not if that journey is going to break you. I'm sorry, but I don't want kids that much."

Rachel looked at him, surprised. "I thought this was important to you."

"You come first. You've always come first." He squeezed her shoulder. "I want the woman I married. Once we get back to that, then we can start talking about kids again. Okay?"

Rachel was silent as she contemplated what he was proposing. She closed her eyes, and it felt as if a great weight had been lifted from her shoulders.

Suddenly, she felt as if she could breathe again.

"Okay."

Aaron pulled his wife into his arms. "I love you."

❧❧

Down the hall, Julia leaned her hip against the bathroom vanity, watching Gabriel brush his teeth.

"Your father is proud of us for having a baby."

Gabriel nodded, as he continued brushing.

"That means he's proud of us for having sex and you for impregnating me. Do you think they make T-shirts for grandfathers that express those sentiments?"

Gabriel made a strangled choking noise before he began spitting into the sink.

"Are you all right?" She tapped on his back. "Can you speak?"

He responded with more spitting and then raucous laughter.

"T-shirts," he managed, placing his hand on the counter to support himself. "How do you come up with this stuff?"

"It wasn't me who said it. I don't think anyone has ever told me that he's proud of me for having sex. My dad was happy for us, but he didn't say he was proud."

Gabriel deposited his toothbrush in the holder before straightening. "I did."

They exchanged a look.

"Yes, you did." Julia smiled to herself. "Uncle Jack seemed happy, when I told him. But he was acting weird on the telephone."

"What did he say?"

"He congratulated me, but he also gave me a lecture."

Gabriel's eyebrows lifted. "About what?"

"About my need to protect myself and the baby. I assured him I was doing so and then he asked me what you were doing to protect us."

"And what did you say?"

"I said you were very attentive and that you were coming with me to all my appointments. He muttered something about that not being enough."

Gabriel frowned. "Did you respond?"

"I asked him what he was worried about, but he kind of clammed up on me. Do you think something is up with Simon and Natalie?"

"I doubt it. If something were in the works, he'd tell us about it."

"Maybe." Julia shook her head. "He promised me he'd keep an eye on us, and I told him I'd welcome whatever help he could give us. It was a very strange conversation."

"Your uncle Jack is a strange person. Maybe he's decided to beat up Greg Matthews in order to ensure that you get a maternity leave."

"Professor Matthews already authorized it. I don't need Uncle Jack's help with that." She smiled and exited the bathroom.

She stood by the window, looking out into the starless night.

Gabriel could see the outline of her body through her old-fashioned linen nightshirt: her long slim legs, her rounded hips and bottom. He switched off the lights and stood behind her, his talented fingers lifting and toying with her hair.

"Your conversation with my sister was difficult, but she took the news well, I thought." He linked their hands together, bringing their connection to rest over where their child was growing.

"She and Aaron have been trying for so long and we weren't and boom! We're pregnant."

Gabriel chuckled and rested his chin on her shoulder. "It wasn't quite like that. There was divine intervention."

"Do you really believe that?"

"You don't?" His body tightened.

"I do, I just feel guilty. It seems unfair," she whispered.

"Perhaps we need to do a better job of supporting them. I'm sure this is hard on both of them." He kissed the nape of her neck, pressing his chest to her back. "Did you ever tell her how we met?"

"No. It was too precious and too painful to talk about."

"And now?" He pressed her.

"I like the fact that it's our secret. Your family is wonderful, but I don't think they'd understand. My father would come after you with a shotgun."

"Point taken."

He began to drag his fingertips over her scalp, touching her gently, when she suddenly flinched.

"I'm sorry," he murmured. "I forgot about your scar."

"It's all right. You only startled me."

Gabriel began to caress her again, this time avoiding the stretch of raised skin beneath her hair.

"Sharon could be nice sometimes, when she wasn't drinking and she was between boyfriends." Julia swallowed hard. "She would take me to the zoo and we'd have picnics. She let me play dress-up with her clothes and she'd do my hair. I liked that."

Gabriel stilled his hand, pausing thoughtfully before speaking. "I remember some good things about my mother, too. I'm sorry Sharon hurt you. I wish I could take it all away."

"I wonder why Sharon was nice to me at all if she was just going to turn around and be abusive again."

Gabriel continued toying with her hair. "I understand. The cycle of abuse interspersed with occasional bouts of kindness keeps you stuck, waiting and hoping for the kindness to return. And it does, on occasion, only to be swept away. I know all about that. Regrettably."

Julia turned to face him. "We've overcome a lot."

"That we have."

"What happened with Simon doesn't haunt me anymore. Not like it did. I feel as if I've moved past that."

Gabriel cursed under his breath. "That motherfucker is lucky he has a powerful family. I still wish I could beat him senseless and teach his girlfriend a lesson. Your uncle Jack didn't want us to let them off the hook."

Julia placed a hand on his chest. "It's over now. Simon is getting married, and Jack said that Natalie moved to California."

"The farther away the better."

"I don't know if I'll be a great mother, but I certainly have an idea of what I shouldn't do."

Gabriel touched her abdomen through her nightshirt.

"Part of being a good parent is being a good person. And Julianne, you are the best person I've ever met."

He kissed her softly.

"Standing in this house, I can't help but remember what life was like with my parents. *We can have a home like theirs.* A home filled with love and happiness. We've had so much grace lavished on us . . ." Gabriel's voice trailed off.

"I'm just relieved I don't have to do this alone."

"Me, too."

Gabriel took her hand and led her to the bed.

Chapter Seventy-six

Durham, North Carolina

April Hudson breezed into her apartment building Monday afternoon, stopping to check her mailbox. She'd just returned from a romantic weekend in the Hamptons with her fiancé, Simon Talbot.

She sighed as she thought about him. He was tall, blond, and handsome. He was smart and from a good family. And the things he could do with his body . . .

The Hamptons were a sentimental favorite. It was where she'd given him her virginity. It was where he'd asked her to marry him.

(Not, of course, in the same weekend.)

As she shuffled through her mail, her mind was a happy whirl of wedding plans and memories from the weekend. He treated her well. And she no longer had to feel guilty about sleeping with him, because they were getting married. She was going to wake up with him every morning, forever.

(Because her thoughts were so engaged, she didn't notice the ex-Marine from Philadelphia who was sitting in a dark car across the street, watching to see if she'd open his letter. She certainly didn't know that he was ensuring that no one would trouble his niece and her unborn child.)

At the bottom of her mailbox, she found a manila envelope. It had her name on it, but no address or stamp. Puzzled, she gathered her mail and took the elevator to the third floor. Once she'd entered her apartment and locked the door behind her, she abandoned her luggage and flopped onto the couch.

She opened the manila envelope first and was stunned to find that it contained a stack of large black-and-white photographs. They were all date-stamped *September 27, 2011.*

A strange buzzing filled her ears. As did the sound of her keys falling from her hand and crashing onto the hardwood floor.

Leafing through the photos, she saw two naked bodies entwined on a bed. The identity of the man was unmistakable. So was his body, his positions, his *technique.*

But the woman he was with didn't look like a woman. She looked young, like a teenager.

And the things they were doing . . .

April covered her face with her hands, a cry of anguish escaping her lips.

Chapter Seventy-seven

Washington, D.C.

That evening, Simon Talbot knocked on the door to his father's office in their family home in Georgetown. He'd been summoned by Robert, his father's campaign manager, and ordered to return home immediately.

He didn't know what was so urgent. That morning, he'd said goodbye to April at the airport after enjoying a quiet but sexually charged weekend. He intended to surprise her the following weekend by flying down to Durham. Soon her semester would be over and he'd help her pack her things and move her life to his apartment in Washington, where she belonged.

"Come in," the senator called.

Simon opened the door and walked toward the chair that was placed in front of the senator's desk.

"Don't bother sitting. This won't take long." As usual, the senator was gruff and to the point.

"Have you seen these?" He tossed a stack of photographs onto the desk. They fanned out into a random pattern.

Simon looked at the picture nearest him. Snatching it up, he stared at it. His face grew pale.

"Well? Have you seen them?" The senator raised his voice, angrily thumping on the desk with his fist.

"No." Simon slowly placed the photograph back on the desk, as the feeling of fear pricked the back of his neck.

"It's you, isn't it?"

"Uh—"

"Don't lie to me! Is that you?"

"Yes." Simon felt his chest tighten. He was having difficulty breathing.

"Did you take these pictures?"

"No, Dad. I swear. I have no idea who took them."

His father cursed.

"These are just copies. Do you know how I got them?"

Simon shook his head.

"Senator Hudson. Someone sent the originals to your fiancée. She told her father about them and he had copies made, which he delivered to me."

Simon's chest grew even tighter.

"April saw them?"

"Yes. She was hysterical. Her mother flew down to Durham to be with her. She had to take her to the hospital."

"Is she all right? What hospital?"

"Focus on the problem, boy, for God's sake! Do you have any idea what this means for my campaign?"

Simon clenched his fists. "Forget about your campaign for a minute. Did April try to hurt herself? What hospital is she in?"

"We're lucky the Hudsons have no interest in blackmail. They simply want you to leave their daughter alone. The wedding is off, obviously. They're going to make the announcement tomorrow."

Simon pulled out his cell phone and hit a button. He held the phone to his ear, but within seconds, he received a recorded message indicating that April's cell phone number was no longer in service.

"Dad, I can explain. Let me talk to April. It isn't what she thinks."

"Don't," his father barked. "Robert recognized the girl in the pictures. She was a high school student who interned in my office. Do you understand the damage you've done? How could you be so stupid!"

"It happened over a year ago. The date is wrong. I swear I wasn't fucking around on April. I love her."

"You love her," his father scoffed. "You had that red-headed whore on the side all the time."

Simon took a step forward. "I didn't. I broke things off with her. I'm telling you, April is different."

The senator waved his hand as if he were swatting a fly.

"It's too late. She doesn't want anything to do with you. And who could blame her? The girl in the photos was seventeen, she was working for me, you slept with her, and you encouraged her to drink and use drugs. And it's all in God damned black and white!" The senator swiped across his desk, sending the photos, pens, and papers flying into the air.

"Dad, I swear I can fix this. Just let me talk to April."

"No." The senator rose to his feet, glaring at his son. "The Hudsons want you to leave her alone, and that's what you're going to do."

"But Dad, I—"

"Do what you're told for once!" he bellowed.

Simon stood, but only for a moment before picking up a bronze statue of a horseman that his father kept on his desk and hurling it against the wall.

"You never listen!" he shouted. "My whole life, you give orders, you talk, but you never fucking listen. So fuck you. Fuck your campaign and fuck the family. The only thing I've ever cared about is her. And I'm not going to lose her."

And with that, he strode out of the office, slamming the door behind him.

❧❧

It was, Simon thought, the bitterest irony, as he sat in a police station in Durham.

(Unlike Gabriel, Simon did not know the actual meaning of the term *irony*.)

He'd tried repeatedly to see April, but with no success. He sent flowers and letters, but they were refused. He tried emailing her, but she'd blocked his email address.

He'd attempted to wait for her outside her apartment and had been arrested. Now he was sitting in a police station awaiting news of whether he would be charged. He didn't have a lawyer, and he knew his father wouldn't help him.

He'd deserved his last arrest—when he'd assaulted Julia. He'd been angry and looking to even the score between them. But with April, he'd acted out of love. He could only hope that if he accepted his arrest and pleaded guilty, perhaps he'd have the opportunity to make amends. Perhaps she, or her mother, who was a kind, sympathetic woman, would give him five minutes to explain.

He didn't know who took the pictures. Natalie had not been a party to that particular encounter, although she was familiar with the hotel room in which it occurred. It was possible she'd hired someone to film him.

It was obvious that Natalie had sent the pictures to April. She was the only one who stood to gain by breaking them up. And in one calculated act, she'd hurt him, April, and his father's campaign. And she was enough of a vindictive bitch to want to do so.

So while Simon was biding his time waiting for an opportunity to make amends with April, he was going to take a trip out to Sacramento and pay Natalie a visit.

Those were the plans that formed in Simon's mind as he waited to find out his legal fate. He had no idea that Jack Mitchell was sitting in his dark Oldsmobile outside the police station, thinking of his pregnant niece, and smiling.

Chapter Seventy-eight

Cambridge, Massachusetts

Once Julia's morning sickness subsided, she developed a strange fixation on Thai food. There was a restaurant near her old apartment in Cambridge that she favored, insisting it was the only place that satisfied her craving. Consequently, Gabriel or Rebecca ordered takeout from that restaurant almost daily.

Given her food intake, at one point Gabriel surmised that seventy-five percent of her body mass (and the baby's) was composed of spring rolls. So the child was no longer called Ralph. Gabriel, Rebecca, and eventually Julia referred to him as Spring Roll.

At the end of April, the Emersons visited Mount Auburn Hospital in order to have another ultrasound. They hoped that the picture would be clear enough to reveal the sex of the baby.

"Spring Roll is a boy," Julia whispered, trying to ignore the pain of her overfull bladder.

"No." Gabriel grinned. "Trust me. I know women. This baby is definitely a girl."

Julia couldn't help but laugh.

The technician called her name. Julia squeezed Gabriel's hand before following the technician into the ultrasound suite.

(At this juncture, Gabriel knew better than to argue with the technician about accompanying his wife.)

"Do you want to know the sex of the baby?" the technician asked as she placed a gown on the bed.

"Absolutely. My husband is waiting and I know he'd like to find out, as well."

"Of course. I'll let you get changed and be right with you. My name is Amelia." The technician smiled and left Julia to change into the gown.

In a few minutes, Julia's rounded abdomen was covered with a warmed but sticky gel, and the ultrasound began. She couldn't help but stare at the computer screen, watching image after image of her baby.

Truthfully, she couldn't make out much other than the head and the body. Poor Spring Roll looked like an alien.

"We're in luck," said Amelia, pressing a few buttons to capture some images. "Your baby is in the right position so I can have a good look."

Julia heaved a sigh of relief. She was excited but nervous.

"I'll just capture a few more images and then we can call your husband. Okay?"

"Thank you."

A few minutes later, Amelia went to fetch Gabriel. When he entered the room, he strode to Julia's side immediately and took her hand, kissing it.

"So?" He turned to Amelia, who was sitting at her computer screen once again.

She pointed to the screen. "Your baby is developing well. Everything looks good. Congratulations, you're having a girl."

Gabriel's face split into a wide, happy smile.

Julia's eyes filled with tears. She cupped her hand over her mouth in surprise.

"I told you, Mama. I know women." He kissed Julia's cheek.

"We're having a girl," she repeated.

"Is that all right?" His sapphire eyes darkened in concern.

"It's perfect," she breathed.

Gabriel made copies of the ultrasound snapshots and immediately had them professionally framed, but he resisted the urge to display them outside their bedroom and study.

"Now that we know that Spring Roll is a girl, we should probably think about setting up her room." Gabriel kept his eyes on the road as he drove the Volvo one Saturday in May. "We should also talk about names."

"That sounds good."

"Maybe you should think about what you want and we can go shopping."

Julia turned to look at him. "Now?"

"I said I'd take you to lunch, and we can do that. But afterward, we need to start thinking about Spring Roll's room. We want it to be attractive, but functional. Something comfortable for you and for her, but not juvenile."

"She's a baby, Gabriel. Her stuff is going to be juvenile."

"You know what I mean. I want it to be elegant and not look like a preschool."

"Good grief." Julia fought a grin as she began imagining what the Professor would design.

(Argyle patterns, dark wood, and chocolate brown leather immediately came to mind.)

He cleared his throat. "I might have done some searching on the Internet."

"Oh, really? From where? Restoration Hardware?"

"Of course not." He bristled. "Their things wouldn't be appropriate for a baby's room."

"So where then?"

He gazed at her triumphantly. "Pottery Barn Kids."

Julia groaned. "We've become yuppies."

Gabriel stared at her in mock horror. "Why do you say that?"

"We're driving a Volvo and talking about shopping at Pottery Barn."

"First of all, Volvos have an excellent safety rating and they're more attractive than a minivan. Secondly, Pottery Barn's furniture happens to be both functional and aesthetically pleasing. I'd like to take you to one of their stores so you can see for yourself."

"As long as we get Thai food first."

Now it was Gabriel's turn to roll his eyes. "Fine. But we're ordering takeout and taking it to the park for a picnic. And I'm having Indian food, instead. If I see another plate of pad Thai, I'm going to lose it."

Julia burst into peals of laughter.

Late that night, Gabriel retired to the master bedroom after a long evening spent putting together a wish list for the nursery. Some of the items he was going to place on a gift registry, since his sisters (Kelly and Rachel), Diane, Cecilia, and Katherine had all demanded that he and Julia register for baby gifts.

Gabriel had no idea parents did such a thing and found himself intrigued by the concept.

(He was distressed to learn that the Pottery Barn Kids gift registry did not extend to children's books in Italian or Yiddish.)

As he walked past the bed toward the bathroom, he noticed that Julia's feet were peeking out from under the duvet. The rest of her body was covered.

He smiled and reached over to pull the duvet over her feet.

Chapter Seventy-nine

May 2012
Sacramento, California

Natalie Lundy went about her daily life with a spring in her step. Simon and April had had a very public breakup, he'd been disowned by his family, and Senator Talbot's campaign was in shambles.

In short, she had no reason to jeopardize her new job by telling compromising tales to the tabloids. Someone had done the work for her—probably a jealous ex-lover of Simon's or a political opponent of his father's.

Natalie was blissfully unaware of Simon's plans for revenge. Or the fact that he'd abandoned those plans when April elected not to press charges against him. Natalie heard rumors that he was trying to win April back, but public opinion was such that she thought that outcome was more than unlikely.

Certainly, Natalie and Simon had no idea of Jack Mitchell's involvement, which meant that he slept well at night, secure in the knowledge that he'd done what he needed to do in order to protect his pregnant niece.

Chapter Eighty

July 2012
Boston, Massachusetts

I'm not sure this is a good idea." Julia hesitated outside the Agent Provocateur boutique on Newbury Street.

"Why not?" Gabriel gripped her hand.

"This isn't a maternity store. They won't have anything that fits me." Her cheeks colored.

"I've already spoken with Patricia. She knows we're coming." He smiled down at his pregnant wife. "In fact, I made a few requests."

Julia recognized the name of the boutique's manager, as they'd met once before. Gabriel was not the sort of man who was embarrassed by women's underthings. In fact, he preferred to choose them himself, at least for special occasions.

This was a special occasion. As her pregnancy progressed, Julia was uncomfortable sleeping naked. Since none of her sexy lingerie fit her anymore, she'd taken to wearing yoga pants and T-shirts to bed. For Gabriel, this was not a welcome change.

So of course, he did something about it.

Patricia greeted them warmly and ushered them to a private dressing room in which she'd placed a rack of nightgowns, underwear, and robes.

"Call me if you need anything." She gestured to the house telephone that was placed on a table nearby before closing the door behind her.

Julia fingered the transparent black chiffon of a babydoll nightgown as Gabriel watched her, the way a cat watches a mouse.

"I don't think I can do this." She glanced at the large trifold mirror balefully.

"It's just us. Look, Patricia provided us with drinks." He placed a few ice cubes in a glass and poured some ginger ale over them.

She took the drink gratefully. "This is not a good day for me. I feel like a cow."

"You are not a cow," Gabriel clipped. "You're pregnant. And beautiful."

She avoided his eyes. "I can't stand in front of that mirror. I'll look like a bus—from three different directions."

"Nonsense." He took the drink out of her hand, placing it on the low table nearby. "Take off your clothes."

"What?"

"I said take off your clothes."

She backed away from him. "I can't."

"Trust me," he whispered, stepping closer.

She looked up at him. His blue eyes were warm, but he looked very determined.

"Are you trying to make me cry?"

He stiffened.

"No, I'm trying to help you see what I see when I look at you." He beckoned to her and she moved to him.

He placed his hand on her shoulders and kissed her forehead. "Pick something you think is pretty and try it on. I'll sit over there with my back turned while you change. If you don't like anything here, we'll go somewhere else."

Julia leaned against him for a moment and he took her weight, stroking her sides up and down.

She sighed and picked a few satin hangers, carrying them to the far corner, where there was a series of hooks on the wall.

Gabriel smiled as he sat in a leather club chair, which was positioned a few feet away, facing the mirror. He made sure to keep his back to her while she undressed, not wanting to upset her.

He helped himself to some Perrier and began eyeing the clothes rack. In deference to Julia's modesty, he hadn't requested the more provocative items—items that lacked coverage over the breasts, for example. The point of this exercise was to purchase things that made her feel confident and sexy, not self-conscious and cold.

Although some of his choices might push her boundaries, he wasn't interested in upsetting her. This was supposed to be fun and, he hoped, inspirational.

"It's a little tight," she called to him.

"They're supposed to be tight. Come over where I can see you." He kept his eyes fixed on the mirror, almost breathless in anticipation.

"I think I need a larger size."

"I gave Patricia your measurements."

"You did *what*?" She almost shrieked. "But I'm massive."

"Julianne." His tone was commanding. *"Come—here."*

She took a deep breath and walked toward the mirror.

Gabriel felt his heart stutter in his chest.

Julia stood wearing a Syble babydoll, which was black chiffon and embroidered with small pink flowers. She'd kept on her black maternity panties but had added a pair of black seamed stockings, pulled up just to below her baby bump.

"Breathtaking," he said.

She stood to the side of the mirror, her hand traveling between the panels of black chiffon to her stomach. Then she turned around slowly, checking her backside.

"You look perfect."

She caught his eyes in the mirror.

He could no longer sit. He moved to stand behind her but resisted the urge to touch.

He knew that if he gave in, he'd have her in the dressing room in the leather club chair and their shopping trip would be over. Surely he could wait a few minutes while she tantalized him.

"What do you think?" he asked, his voice gruff.

"I like it. I still think it's a little tight." She tugged at the straps, exposing more of her large breasts.

He moved his hands to fit over them and squeezed.

"It fits you like a glove. You have a beautiful figure."

A soft look came into her eyes. "You really think that."

"I do." He caressed her breasts through the fabric, passing his thumbs ever so gently over her sensitive nipples.

Her lips parted as she watched him touch her, feeling the sensations tingle across her flesh while seeing the hunger in his eyes.

Here was a man hopelessly aroused and eager, plying his seductive trade.

Gabriel brushed her hair aside and brought his lips to her ear. "Just think how I'll make you feel when I remove it."

Throwing caution aside, he placed his lips to her neck, his tongue darting out to taste her skin.

"It's getting hot in here." She closed her eyes, leaning into his embrace.

"I'm just getting started." He pressed himself against the curve of her backside so that she could feel his prominent arousal. "I think we can agree that we'll take what you're wearing. Now choose something else."

She turned to kiss him, reaching up to tangle her fingers in his hair. She kissed him until they were almost ready to forgo shopping before returning to the clothes rack.

Gabriel walked to a nearby table and lifted the house phone.

"Patricia? We're going to need more ice."

Chapter Eighty-one

August 2012
Near Burlington, Vermont

As the winter months passed, Paul spent more and more time with Allison. They went to dinner and to the movies. They flirted via email and text message. And his cupboards at the Norris farmhouse were always filled with Dunkin' Donuts coffee and homemade cookies.

In fact, his friendship with Ali (for so he was still calling it) had become very important to him. He eagerly looked forward to spending time with her every weekend. And although their physical relationship hadn't progressed beyond a few chaste kisses, their connection continued to deepen.

However, neither of them could have anticipated the overwhelming joy that was to come in early March when Paul was offered the position of assistant professor in the Department of English at Saint Michael's College. He didn't waste time fussing over the salary or negotiating a lighter teaching load or other perks. He simply accepted the job. Gladly.

He emailed Julia about his job offer and they resumed their occasional, friendly correspondence. He was stunned when, in mid-April, she emailed him announcing that she was pregnant.

Given the fact that they'd had a gap in their correspondence, Paul didn't feel comfortable interrogating her about the timing of her pregnancy. He certainly didn't want to upset her, not only because he treasured their friendship but because he didn't want Gabriel to withdraw his approval of his completed dissertation. Consequently, Paul simply sent her a congratulatory message and promised that he would send the baby a gift from Vermont.

Having successfully completed and defended his dissertation, and having survived graduation from the University of Toronto in June, Paul moved into his new office on the campus of St. Michael's College at the end of August.

He was happy. He was going to live at home while he saved for a down payment on a house. He would help out on the farm when he could, but his father's hired hands seemed to have everything running smoothly. And his father's health had improved significantly.

As he unpacked his books in his new office, he found his Dante and Beatrice action figures. Alas, the company that produced them had ignored his repeated requests for a Virgil action figure.

(Once again, their official position was that Virgil was not worthy of action.)

He was just positioning Dante and Beatrice on top of his desk when he heard a knock.

"Come in," he called over his shoulder, not turning around. "The door's open."

"Hi."

Paul turned from Dante and Beatrice to see Allison standing in the doorway.

In that instant, although he'd seen her a thousand times, although he'd known her for years, Paul was struck by how pretty she was—her hair, her face, her eyes. She was beautiful.

"I thought you might be here. I wondered if you might need some help."

"There isn't much to do. I'm just arranging my books." He placed the empty box on the floor.

Her face fell.

"Oh. Well, I didn't mean to bother you. I'll let you get back to work."

She turned to go, and Paul's heart plummeted into his shoes.

"Wait."

He stood up and walked over to her, catching her hand in his.

"It's good to see you."

She smiled up at him. "It's good to be seen."

"You were gone for two weeks."

"My sister needed help with her kids. I only planned to be gone for a week, but you know how it is." She reached up and pushed some of his hair back from his forehead. "I missed you. I've been counting the days."

"I missed you, too. A lot."

They stared at one another for what seemed like an age before Paul found his words.

"I was going to take a break anyway. How about I take you to American Flatbread for pizza?"

"I'd like that."

She moved to exit his office, but he tugged on her hand.

She looked up at him questioningly.

"Roses," he whispered, stroking his work-roughened fingers over her knuckles.

"What?"

"Our first time together. Your skin smelled of roses."

Two patches of pink appeared on her face.

"I didn't think you'd remember."

He looked down at her intensely.

"How could I forget? To this day, every time I smell roses I think of you."

"I don't wear roses anymore. I thought I grew out of them."

He reached up to cup her face in his hand.

She leaned into it and closed her eyes.

"Would you wear roses again? For me?"

She opened her eyes, searching his.

"Only if you're serious."

"I am." He tried to show her with his expression that he was telling the truth.

"Then yes."

Allison moved into the gap between them and lightly pressed their lips together.

With a gentle push, Paul closed the door to his office and pulled her into his arms.

Chapter Eighty-two

September 9, 2012
Cambridge, Massachusetts

A strangled moan emanated from the bathroom.

Gabriel's eyes snapped open. He was confused. For a moment, he didn't know where he was.

When he heard the moan again, he stumbled sleepily through the darkened bedroom.

"Darling? Are you all right?"

When he entered the bathroom, he found Julia almost doubled over, clutching the marble-topped vanity with white-knuckled hands. She was breathing deeply.

"Do you want me to wake Rebecca?" Gabriel turned to go, readying himself to sprint down the hall.

"No, call the hospital."

"What should I tell them?"

"Tell them I think I'm in labor."

Immediately, he flew into a panic, hurriedly asking her questions, fumbling back into the bedroom to find his glasses and his cell phone, and hastily dialing the maternity ward of Mount Auburn Hospital.

"Has your water broken?" he asked, after he successfully reached a nurse.

"No. Your hardwood floors are safe."

"Very funny, Julianne. Are you in active labor?"

"I think so. The contractions are painful and regular." Julia tried to keep her breathing deep and relaxed, a technique she had practiced over and over again with her prenatal yoga teacher, who had promised success.

(Julia was contemplating asking for her money back.)

"How far apart are your contractions?"

"Six minutes."

She focused every ounce of her attention on her breathing and shut out the sound of his voice.

(She loved him, it was true, but he wasn't exactly helping.)

"The nurse said I should bring you in right now. I have your bag and the bag you packed for the baby. Are you ready?" He tried to sound calm and began to rub her back through her loose-fitting T-shirt.

"Yes. Let's go."

Julia straightened up and took a good look at her husband.

"You can't go like that."

"Why not?" He combed his hair with his fingers, trying to make himself look like someone who'd had a full night's sleep. Then he scratched at his stubbled face. "I don't have time to shave."

"Look at yourself."

Gabriel gazed at his reflection in the mirror. To his shock and dismay, he was clad only in his underwear, a cheeky pair of boxer shorts that had the phrase *Medievalists Do It in the Dark (Ages)* printed all over them in phosphorescent lettering.

"Damn it! Give me a minute."

Julia waddled after him into the bedroom, chuckling. "Scott will be very pleased that his Christmas present is coming with us to the hospital. At least if there's a power outage we'll be able to find you. You'll just have to drop your pants."

"You are the soul of comedy, Mrs. Emerson."

She giggled, finding his fashion faux pas slightly funnier than usual.

During the past couple of weeks, she'd forgone the expensive lingerie he'd bought her at Agent Provocateur, arguing that the items weren't warm enough. In response, Gabriel had declared that her maternity yoga pants and T-shirts "did a grave injustice to her sexiness" and suggested she rely on his body to warm her.

She hugged a body pillow instead.

"Those medieval boxer shorts do a grave injustice to your sexiness," she goaded him, clutching at her protruding abdomen as she cackled with delight.

He cast her a withering glance as he pulled on a pair of jeans and a shirt. Then he took her elbow and accompanied her down the hall. They paused just outside the nursery as another contraction seized her.

Gabriel switched on the pink-and-white chandelier so he could see her face. "Is it very bad?"

"Yes." She tried to distract herself by leaning against the doorpost and staring into the baby's room.

She would have been content to purchase all the furnishings for the nursery from Target, but Gabriel had insisted on Pottery Barn.

(Parenthetically, it should be noted that Julia referred to Pottery Barn as *Protestant Barn*, for it featured fine furnishings that were WASP-ish in the extreme. Furnishings that she was enamored of but thought were too expensive.)

Together, and with items generously given by their friends and family, they'd transformed one of the guest rooms into a tranquil space for a little girl. Julia chose sage green for the walls and a soft white for the woodwork and crown molding. A fanciful area rug that featured flowers in pink, yellow, and green pastels covered the oak floorboards.

"This is my favorite room in the whole world," she breathed, gazing at the classic Winnie the Pooh decals they had placed over the crib and changing table, in anticipation of wide and eager little eyes.

"It's waiting for her." Gabriel smiled. "It's waiting for our little Spring Roll."

When Julia's contraction subsided, he took her hand and helped her down the stairs and into the Volvo, in which he'd already installed the baby's car seat. He sent a text to Rebecca, explaining what was happening, and assured her he'd be in touch.

A short while later, they arrived at the Bain Birthing Center at Mount Auburn Hospital. By the time they were settled in one of the birthing rooms, Gabriel had managed to conjure a calm exterior. He didn't want Julia to see his anxiety or to feel the way his insides churned with unspoken fears.

But she knew. She knew what he was afraid of, and she held his hand and told him that she and Spring Roll were going to be fine.

They held hands during her internal exam, in which the obstetrician on call announced that Spring Roll was in a transverse position and that she hoped the baby would decide to turn when it was time for her to be born.

Nurse Tracy quickly distracted a nervous Gabriel from demanding a complicated, illustrated explanation of transverse positions, teaching him to read the monitor so he could tell Julia when a contraction was peaking and when it was coming to an end.

She was grateful for his distraction. But that didn't stop him from Googling transverse positions and their attendant information on his iPhone.

(It should be noted that at that point, Julia wished he'd left the damn thing at home.)

Fortunately, the pain medication relaxed her enough to allow her to nap, and she drifted into semiconsciousness.

"Julianne?"

She opened her eyes to see her husband standing over her, a concerned expression on his face.

She smiled at him weakly, and it almost broke his heart.

"You were moaning."

"I must have been dreaming."

Julia reached out to him and he took her hand, bringing it up to his lips so he could kiss it.

"My rings," she whispered, pressing against his wedding band. "Did I lose them?"

He stroked her naked finger. "You took them off months ago, remember? Your fingers were swelling and you were worried they'd get stuck. You started wearing them on the necklace I gave you a year ago, back in the orchard."

She reached up to touch her neck. "I forgot. I put them in my jewelry box yesterday."

"You had a premonition. Spring Roll is almost here."

She closed her eyes. "I didn't think anything would be more demanding than my program at Harvard. I was wrong."

Gabriel's heart clenched.

"You'll be back at the university soon enough. Rebecca and I will help."

Julia hummed in response.

"I know it was too soon." He brought his mouth to her ear. "I'm sorry."

"We talked about this. Sometimes surprises are the best things."

"I'll do whatever it takes to make it up to you."

"Having a child with you isn't a hardship. Except for the pain." She grimaced.

He pressed his lips to her brow. "I called my dad. He's going to speak to your dad and Diane. I doubt they'll be able to drive up with Tommy, but he's going to offer."

She nodded but didn't open her eyes. "Good."

While Julia was sleeping, the obstetrician attempted to reassure Gabriel that the transverse positioning of babies was not uncommon. A baby would sometimes reposition herself during labor or the obstetrician would simply turn her. It was nothing to worry about.

Gabriel was grateful for the doctor's encouragement but still anxious. What gave him strength was his hope for the future—the knowledge that soon he would meet his daughter and he could begin being a father.

As Julia lay in her bed half-asleep and dreaming, he paced the room. She looked so small in the big hospital bed, so fragile.

So young.

Chapter Eighty-three

Julia?" Gabriel held her hand as the next contraction gripped her. He kept a watchful eye on the monitor so he could announce when the contraction was beginning to subside, and then afterward he would gently stroke her knuckles or her forehead, praising her.

"You're doing so well."

Gabriel was not. He was disheveled and nervous and, if he were to take the time to think about it, extremely concerned. Despite the fact that they were in a well-respected hospital in Boston and enjoying excellent medical care, he was terrified.

He kept his fears to himself, silently praying over and over that Julia and Spring Roll would be all right.

Shortly before nine o'clock in the evening, Julia began to run a fever. By that time, Dr. Rubio was on call. She examined Julia and ordered an antibiotic added to her intravenous drip.

Gabriel chewed at his lip as he watched the nurse hang the bag next to the other fluids that slowly dripped into his wife's arm.

Dr. Rubio broke Julia's water and encouraged her to begin pushing. Her epidural succeeded in taking only some of the pain away, and much of it remained. Julia still had feeling in the lower half of her body.

Nurse Susan held one of Julia's legs while Gabriel held the other. She pushed with each contraction, and although Dr. Rubio and Gabriel cheered her on, very little happened. Eventually the obstetrician admitted what Gabriel had been afraid of—Spring Roll was stubbornly maintaining her transverse position, and she was situated too high up to be delivered with forceps.

Julia groaned weakly at the news, collapsing back on the bed in near exhaustion.

"What does that mean?" asked Gabriel quietly, his hands folding into fists.

Dr. Rubio pursed her lips.

"It means we need to do an emergency cesarean section. The baby's heart rate is beginning to increase, your wife is running a fever, and it's possible there's an infection. I'll assemble my surgical team, but we need to do this right away."

"That's fine with me," said Julia. She was tired. Oh, so tired. The idea of having an end to labor brought welcome relief.

"Are you sure?" Gabriel nervously clutched her hand.

"There really aren't any other options, Mr. Emerson. I can't deliver this baby in the position she's in." Dr. Rubio's voice was firm.

"As I told you before, it's *Professor Emerson*," he snapped, his frazzled emotions getting the best of him.

"Sweetie, relax. We're going to be fine." Julia smiled thinly and closed her eyes, willing herself to outlast the contractions that continued wracking her body.

Gabriel poured his apology into a chaste kiss and a few whispered words of comfort before Julia's room became an epicenter of activity. The anesthesiologist arrived and asked a series of questions. The nurse asked Gabriel to follow her so that he could change into surgical scrubs.

He did not want to be separated from Julia, not even for an instant. He'd spent hours at her side, feeding her ice chips and holding her hand. But since he wanted to be with her in the operating room and it was a sterile environment, he agreed to go.

Before he left, Julia extended her hand. He took it, pressing his lips to her palm.

"I don't regret this," she whispered.

He pulled back. The pain medication seemed to be affecting her thought processes.

"What don't you regret, darling?"

"Getting pregnant. After this is over, we're going to have a little girl. We'll be a family. Forever."

He gave her a tight smile and kissed her forehead. "I'll see you in a few minutes. You stay strong."

She returned his smile and closed her eyes, adjusting her breathing in order to deal with the next contraction.

Chapter Eighty-four

In his absence, Julia simply closed her eyes and focused on her breathing—that is, until she was lying in the obstetric operating room and Dr. Rubio began touching the area that had been prepped for incision.

"I can feel that," said Julia, clearly alarmed.

"Does it feel like pressure?"

"No. I can feel you pinching the skin."

Gabriel sat at Julia's side, above the screen that blocked her lower body from his view.

"Are you hurt?"

"No," she said, sounding panicked. "But I can still feel pain. I'm afraid that I'll feel the incision."

Dr. Rubio repeated her test, pinching and twisting at Julia's skin, and Julia insisted with increasing anxiety that she could feel every pinch.

"We have to put her out," announced the anesthesiologist, moving swiftly to prepare a general anesthetic.

"It's hard on the baby. Give her something else," Dr. Rubio objected.

"I can't give her any more. She's had an epidural and a top-up. I'm putting her out."

Julia looked up into the kind eyes of the anesthesiologist.

"I'm sorry," she whispered.

The anesthesiologist patted her shoulder. "Honey, you don't need to be sorry. I do this all the time. Just try to relax."

Gabriel began asking questions as the surgical team buzzed around him.

Julia squeezed his hand as if willing him not to lose his temper. She needed him to be calm. She needed him to watch over her while she slept.

She barely noticed what the doctors were doing, or the anesthesiologist's instructions. The last thing she heard before she drifted into the darkness was Gabriel's voice in her ear, assuring her that he would be with her until she woke up.

Chapter Eighty-five

Damn it." Dr. Rubio released a current of rapid-fire demands and instructions, and her team sprang into action.

"What's wrong?" Gabriel's grip on Julia's limp hand tightened.

Dr. Rubio jerked her head toward Gabriel, without making eye contact. "Get the husband out of here."

"What?" Gabriel stood to his feet. "What's happening?"

"I said get him out of here," Dr. Rubio barked at one of the nurses. "And get the surgeon on call down here. Stat."

The nurse began herding Gabriel toward the door.

"What's going on? Tell me!" He raised his voice, directing his questions at the medical team.

No one answered.

The nurse took his arm and tugged.

Gabriel took one last look at Julia, her eyelids taped shut. Her skin pale. Her body still.

She looked as if she were dead.

"Will she be all right?"

The nurse led him through the swinging door and out into the surgical waiting room.

"Someone will be out to speak to you soon." The nurse nodded encouragingly at Gabriel before returning to the operating room.

He slumped into a chair, his mind spinning. One minute they had been preparing for the cesarean section and the next . . .

He pulled the surgical mask from his face.

Panic and fear raced through his veins. All he could see was Julia's face, her arms stretched out from her body as if she were on a cross.

❧❧

In Gabriel's mind he was in the backyard of his house in Selinsgrove, walking toward the woods. He'd trod that path a thousand times. He could navigate it in the dark. Now it was daylight.

As he approached the woods, he heard a voice calling his name.

He turned around to see Grace standing on the back porch, beckoning him.

"Come back."

He shook his head, pointing in the direction of the orchard. "I have to go get her. I've lost her."

"You haven't lost her." Grace smiled patiently.

"I have. She's gone." Gabriel's heart rate quickened.

"She isn't gone. Come home."

"I have to go and get her." Gabriel scanned the trees for any sign of Julianne before entering the woods. His steps quickened until he was running, branches snapping and scraping at his clothes and face. He stumbled to his hands and knees just as he entered the clearing. He scanned the area quickly, and an anguished cry escaped from his lips as he realized Julianne was nowhere to be found.

Chapter Eighty-six

"I can't believe we lost one."

"Neither can I. Two emergency c-sections at the same time. At least only one went south." The voice sighed. "I hate nights like this."

"Me, too. Thank God our shift is over."

It took a few minutes for Gabriel to open his eyes. Had he been asleep or . . .

He rubbed at his chin. He didn't know. One minute, he was in the woods behind his house, the next he could hear nurses talking.

His head began buzzing as his memory of Julianne lying on the table, pale and unmoving, came back to him.

The nurses must have been talking about her.

I can't believe we lost one.

He fought back a sob as he heard footsteps, his eyes focusing on a pair of ugly shoes. It was grossly inappropriate, he knew, but he couldn't help but notice how thick and unflattering they were. As if they were made of wood.

What a waste of a perfectly good podiatric opportunity.

He lifted his head.

The nurse, whom he hadn't seen before, gave him a restrained smile. "I'm Angie, Mr. Emerson. Would you like to meet your daughter?"

He nodded and stumbled to his feet.

"I'm sorry you were sitting there so long. Someone should have brought you to her before, but things have been really busy and we've just had a shift change."

She led him into an adjoining room, where a bassinet was situated. Another nurse was standing nearby, writing on a chart.

Gabriel walked over to the bassinet and looked down.

A little bundle of white lay motionless. He saw a reddish face, and black hair that was partially covered by a tiny, purple knitted cap.

"She has hair."

Angie stood next to him. "Yes, lots of hair. She's almost nine pounds and nineteen inches long. She's a good-sized baby."

Angie picked up the child, cradling her. "We'll give you a wristband that matches hers so we know she's yours."

The second nurse affixed a white plastic wristband on Gabriel's right wrist.

"Would you like to hold her?"

He nodded, wiping his cold, clammy palms on his green surgical scrubs.

Angie gently placed the baby in his arms. Immediately, the child opened large, dark blue eyes and looked up at him.

Their eyes met and Gabriel felt as if his entire world stopped.

Then she yawned, her tiny rosebud mouth expanding greatly, before she closed her eyes again.

"She's beautiful," he breathed.

"Yes, she is. And she's healthy. It was a difficult delivery, but she's fine. You'll notice that her face is a bit swollen, but that will come down."

Gabriel lifted the baby so she was inches from his face.

"Hello, Spring Roll. I'm your daddy and I've been waiting to meet you for a long time. I love you so much."

He held her close, listening to her tiny breaths, feeling her little heart beat through the swaddling material.

"My wife," he croaked, not bothering to blink away the tears that had re-formed in his eyes.

The nurses exchanged a look.

"Did Dr. Rubio talk to you?" Angie asked.

Gabriel shook his head, holding the baby tightly.

Angie looked to the other nurse, who frowned.

"She should have spoken to you by now. I'm sorry about that. It's been very busy, as I said, and there was a shift change." Angie gestured to a nearby chair. "Why don't you sit down with your daughter, and I'll go see if I can find the doctor."

Gabriel did as he was told, holding his daughter close to his heart.

The nurses' expressions said it all.

There would be no happy reconciliation.

There would be no vision of Julia holding their child.

He'd lost her. As surely as Dante had lost Beatrice, he'd lost his beloved.

"I've failed you," he whispered.

Hugging his daughter close to his chest, Gabriel cried.

Chapter Eighty-seven

As Gabriel sat, holding Spring Roll, time seemed to have no meaning. Images flashed before his eyes. He saw himself taking the baby home from the hospital. Feeding her in the middle of the night. Walking down the hall to the empty master bedroom.

He was so alone.

He'd loved one woman in his life. At first, he'd loved her like a pagan, eager to make her an idol and worship her. Then he'd recognized that some things were more important than his love for her—her happiness, for example.

In his mind's eye he could see and hear her clutching his hand, whispering, "I don't regret getting pregnant."

She'd regret it now. He'd taken her life.

His shoulders shuddered as a sob overtook him.

His beautiful, sweet Julianne.

He had his cell phone but didn't feel like talking to anyone. From the texts he'd received, he knew that Richard and Rachel would be arriving soon. Rebecca was readying the house for the guests and the baby. Kelly had texted to say that she'd ordered flowers and balloons, which were on their way to the hospital.

He hadn't had the will to tell them Julianne was gone.

He stared at the face of his daughter, wondering how he was going to parent her alone. He'd relied on Julianne for so much. And ultimately, it was his selfishness that ended her life.

He was lost in his own grief and exhaustion when someone entered the room and stood before him. Once again his eyes focused on a pair of very ugly, sturdy shoes.

"Professor Emerson."

He recognized the voice of Dr. Rubio and lifted his head.

She looked tired.

"I'm sorry about what happened. We had several emergencies all at once and I couldn't get away. I'm sorry it took me so long to—"

"Can I see her?" Gabriel interrupted.

"Of course. But I just need to explain. Your wife—"

Gabriel couldn't hear the doctor's words. He was enveloped in pain. All his conversations with Julia about children flooded his mind.

This was his fault. He'd persuaded her to have a baby and then they'd gotten pregnant before she was ready.

He'd done this. He'd planted his child inside her, and the act had killed her.

He lowered his head despondently.

"Professor Emerson."

Dr. Rubio came closer.

"Professor Emerson, are you all right?" Her lightly accented voice sounded at his ear. She muttered to herself in Spanish, words that Gabriel identified, but dimly.

"Can I see her?" he whispered.

"Of course." Dr. Rubio gestured to the door. "I'm sorry someone didn't come to get you earlier, but the nursing staff was overwhelmed."

Gabriel slowly got to his feet, continuing to cradle his daughter in his arms.

Dr. Rubio directed him to place the baby in the bassinet, and then she wheeled the contraption in front of her.

He pulled a handkerchief out of his pocket and wiped at his face, ignoring the initials that had been embroidered on it. It had been a gift from Julianne "just because." She was like that—generous of spirit and generous of heart. How he wished he'd worn the Star of David she'd given to him as an anniversary present. Surely he could have derived some comfort from it.

Gabriel followed Dr. Rubio through a series of rooms, until they entered a very large space that had a number of hospital beds in it.

"Here she is."

Gabriel stopped abruptly.

Julianne was lying in a hospital bed and a nurse was leaning over her, giving her an injection.

He could see her legs shift beneath the blanket. He could hear her moan.

He blinked rapidly, as if the tears in his eyes had caused a mirage.

He felt his body sway.

"Professor Emerson?" Dr. Rubio took hold of his elbow in an effort to steady him. "Are you all right?"

She called to the nurse and asked her to place a chair next to Julia's bedside. They helped Gabriel to the chair and wheeled the bassinet so that it was next to him.

Someone pushed a plastic cup of water into his hand. He stared at it as if it were a foreign object.

Dr. Rubio's voice, which had been hazy in his ear, suddenly became clear.

"As I said, your wife lost a lot of blood. We had to give her a transfusion. When I made the incision for the cesarean section, I encountered one of her fibroids, and unfortunately it bled quite a bit. We had to do some surgical repair afterward, which is why the procedure took so long."

"Fibroids?" Gabriel repeated, his hand over his mouth.

"One of her fibroids was attached to the uterus right at the place where we make the incision. We stopped the bleeding and stitched her up, but it made the c-section more complicated than usual. Fortunately, Dr. Manganiello, the surgeon on call, scrubbed in. Your wife is going to be fine." She placed a hand on Gabriel's shoulder. "And there doesn't appear to be any permanent damage to her uterus. She'll be waking up soon but she'll be woozy. We'll be giving her medication to control the pain. I'll check on her tomorrow during my rounds. Congratulations on the birth of your daughter. She's a beautiful little girl." Dr. Rubio patted his shoulder and left.

Gabriel stared at Julia, noticing that the color in her skin had returned. She was sleeping.

"Mr. Emerson?" The nurse noticed his tears. "Can I get you something?"

He shook his head, quickly wiping his face with the back of his hand. "I thought she was dead."

"What?" The nurse's tone was sharp.

"No one told me. She looked like she was dead. I thought . . ."

The nurse came a step closer, a look of horror on her face. "I'm so sorry. Someone from the previous shift should have explained what was happening. There was another emergency c-section at the same time as your wife's, but that patient lost her baby."

Gabriel lifted his eyes to meet the nurse's.

"That isn't an excuse," the nurse said quietly. "Someone should have told you that your wife was all right. I've worked in labor and delivery here for ten years and we lose very few mothers. Very, very few. And when we do, there is an immediate inquest and everyone is extremely upset."

Gabriel was about to ask what "very few" meant when he heard a groan coming from Julia's hospital bed. He put the cup of water aside and stood over her.

"Julianne?"

Her eyelids fluttered open. She looked at him for only an instant, then closed her eyes.

"Our daughter is here. She's beautiful."

Julianne didn't move.

But a few minutes later, she began moaning again.

"It hurts," she whispered.

"Hold on. I'll get someone." Gabriel called the nurse.

After the nurse adjusted Julia's intravenous, Gabriel picked up the baby.

"Darling, meet your daughter. She's beautiful. And she has hair." He held the baby up so Julia could see her from her reclined position.

Julia's gaze was wide and unfocused before she closed her eyes.

He cradled the baby against his chest once again.

"Sweetheart? Can you hear me?"

"It will take a while for her to come around. But she'll wake up eventually." The voice of the nurse broke into Gabriel's musings, as he wondered anxiously if Julia was unhappy about how the baby looked.

He placed the child back in her bassinet and sat next to it, keeping a watchful eye on his wife. He was never going to let her out of his sight again.

His iPhone chirped with a couple of texts, and he quickly checked it. Richard and Rachel were making excellent time and would arrive soon. Tom and Diane sent their congratulations and their love.

And Katherine Picton restated her insistence that she be named godmother. She even promised a rare manuscript of Dante's *La Vita Nuova* as an inducement.

Gabriel snapped a few photos of Spring Roll with his phone and quickly emailed them to everyone, including Kelly, pausing to tell Katherine that no inducement would be required.

❧❧

"She has hair?" When Julia finally awoke, the first thing she noticed was the dark strands peeking out from under the baby's purple knit cap.

"She does. Lots of hair. Darker than yours." Gabriel grinned and placed the baby on Julia's chest.

She unwrapped the baby and peeled back her gown, placing her daughter skin against skin. The infant immediately snuggled into her mother.

In Gabriel's mind, it was the most incredible sight he'd ever seen.

"*She's beautiful*," Julia whispered.

"Pretty like her mama."

She pressed gentle kisses to the baby's head. "I don't think so. She has your face."

Gabriel laughed. "I don't know about that. I'm not sure she looks like either one of us, except that she seems to have my eye color. She has the biggest eyes you've ever seen, but she doesn't like to open them."

Julia lifted her head to examine the baby's face, cuddling her even closer.

Gabriel watched her with concern. "Are you in pain?"

She grimaced. "I feel as if I've been sawn in half."

"I think you were."

She peered up at him questioningly.

"No darling, I didn't look." He brushed a kiss against her hair. "We should probably talk about what we're going to call her. Her grandfathers are not going to be impressed with the name Spring Roll. And I've already heard from Katherine, who thinks the baby should be named after her."

"We talked about Clare."

Gabriel considered that possibility for a moment.

"I like Clare, but since we prayed at St. Francis's crypt, perhaps we should call her Frances."

"St. Clare was Francis's friend. We could call her Clare and make Grace her middle name."

"Grace." Gabriel caught Julia's eye and felt himself choking up. "How about Clare Grace Hope? She represents the culmination of so much hope, so much grace . . ."

"*Clare Grace Hope Emerson.* It's perfect." Julia kissed Clare on her tiny cheek.

"She's perfect." Gabriel kissed Julianne and Clare and wrapped his arms around them both.

"My sweet, sweet girls."

Chapter Eighty-eight

Julia slept soundly, her breathing deep and her form unmoving. When the nurse directed Gabriel to place Clare in the bassinet so that he could sleep, he refused. He held his daughter in his arms as if he were afraid she'd be taken away from him.

His eyes grew heavy and he reclined in the chair next to Julia's bed, placing his daughter on his chest. With a yawn, she seemed content, her cheek resting against him, her tiny bottom in the air.

"Faith, hope, and charity," he murmured to himself. "But the greatest of these is charity."

"What's that?" Julia shifted in bed, turning toward him.

He smiled. "I didn't mean to wake you."

Julia moved her legs tentatively, clutching the place where her incision was. "The pain is coming back. I'm probably due for a shot."

She looked over at him, at the way he was holding Clare in his arms, her body resting in the center of his chest.

"You're a natural, Daddy."

"I hope so. But even if I'm not, I'll work hard to become one."

"I didn't know," Julia whispered, her eyes filling with tears.

"You didn't know what?"

"I didn't know it was possible to love someone other than you so much."

Gabriel cupped Clare's head with his hand.

"I didn't know, either." He kissed his daughter's head. "In fact, I was just disagreeing with St. Paul."

"Oh?" She wiped away a tear. "And what did he say in response?"

Gabriel caught her eye. She grinned.

"I told him that the greatest virtue isn't charity; it's hope. I discovered charity with Richard and Grace, but also with you. And it helped me through some very dark days. I also discovered faith, when I went to Assisi. But without hope, I wouldn't be here. I would have taken my life. Without divine intervention in the form of a teenage girl in a Pennsylvania orchard, I'd be in Hell and not sitting at your side holding our daughter."

"Gabriel," she whispered, the tears flowing.

"Charity is a great virtue, and so is faith. But hope means the most to me. This is hope." He gestured to the baby girl on his chest, swaddled in white and wearing a tiny knit cap.

Gabriel's prayers of thanks were spontaneous and heartfelt. Here, in this room, he had an embarrassment of riches—a pretty, intelligent wife, who had a very large and giving heart, and a beautiful daughter.

"This is the culmination of all my hopes, Gabriel." Julia reached out to him and he strained to catch her pinky finger with his own. "This is my happy ending."

He looked to the future with hope and saw a house ringing with the laughter of children and the sounds of small feet running up and down stairs. He saw Clare with a sister and brother, one adopted, one not.

He saw baptisms and first communions and his family sitting with him in the same pew, Mass after Mass, year after year. He saw skinned knees, and first days of school, prom dates and graduation from high school, broken hearts and happy tears, and the joy of introducing his children to Dante, Botticelli, and St. Francis.

He saw himself walking Clare down the aisle at her own wedding, and holding his grandchildren in his arms.

He saw himself growing old with his beloved Julianne and holding hands with her in their orchard.

"*Now my blessedness appears*," he whispered, holding his wife's hand and Clare Grace Hope as she slept peacefully on his chest.

Fin.

Acknowledgments

I am indebted to the late Dorothy L. Sayers, the late Charles Williams, Mark Musa, my friend Katherine Picton, and The Dante Society of America for their expertise on Dante Alighieri's *The Divine Comedy*, which informs my work. In this novel, I've used the Dante Society's conventions of capitalization for places such as Hell and Paradise.

I've been inspired by Sandro Botticelli's artwork and the incomparable space that is the Uffizi Gallery in Florence. The cities of Oxford, Florence, Assisi, Todi, and Cambridge lent their ambience, along with the borough of Selinsgrove.

I've consulted the Internet Archive site for its version of Dante Gabriel Rossetti's translation of *La Vita Nuova* along with the original Italian. In this work, I've cited Henry Wadsworth Longfellow's translation of *The Divine Comedy*.

I am grateful to Jennifer for her feedback and support. This book would not exist without her encouragement and friendship. I am grateful also to Nina for her creative input and wisdom. And I owe a special debt to Kris, who read an early draft and offered invaluable constructive criticism at several stages. Thank you.

I've enjoyed working with Cindy, my editor at Berkley, and I look forward to working with her on my next two novels. Thanks are also due to Tom for his wisdom and energy in navigating my transition to Berkley. And thanks to the copyediting, art, and design teams who worked on this book.

My publicist, Enn, works tirelessly to promote my writing and to help me with social media, which enables me to stay in touch with readers. I'm honored to be part of her team.

I would also like to thank those who have offered encouragement, especially the Muses, Tori, Erika, and the readers who operate the

Argyle Empire and SRFans social media accounts. Special thanks are also due to Elena, who assisted in specifying the Italian pronunciation for the audiobooks. John Michael Morgan did a magnificent job reading *Gabriel's Inferno* and *Gabriel's Rapture*.

Finally, it is no great secret that I intended to end the story of the Professor and Julianne with *Gabriel's Rapture*. Thank you to everyone who wrote to me asking that their story be continued. Your continued support, and the support of my family, is inestimable.

—SR

Ascension 2013

Keep reading for a special excerpt from
Sylvain Reynard's new novel.
Coming soon from Berkley Books!

A lone figure stood high atop Brunelleschi's dome, under the shade of the gold globe and cross. His black clothing faded into the darkness, making him invisible to the people below.

From his vantage point, they looked like ants. And ants they were to him, an irritating if necessary presence in his city.

The city of Florence had been his for almost seven hundred years. When he was in residence, he spent every sunset in the same place, surveying his kingdom with Lucifer-like pride. These were the works of his hands, the fruits of his labor, and he wielded his power without mercy.

His considerable strength was magnified by his intellect and his patience. Decades and centuries passed before his eyes, yet he remained constant. Time was a luxury he owned in abundance and so he was never hasty in his pursuit of revenge. A hundred years had come and gone since he'd been robbed of one of his most prized possessions. He'd waited for them to resurface and they had. On this night, he'd restored the illustrations to his personal collection, the sophisticated security of the Uffizi Gallery causing him only the most trifling of inconveniences.

So it was that he stood in triumph against the clouded dark sky, like a Medici prince, looking out over Florence. The night air was warm as he contemplated the fate of those responsible for the exhibit of his stolen illustrations. He hadn't quite decided whether to kill the men, or merely torture them.

He had time and time enough to make his plans and so he stood, enjoying his success, as a warm, persistent rain began to fall. The ants below scattered, scurrying for shelter. Soon the streets were empty of human beings.

He clutched the case more closely under his arm, realizing that his illustrations were in need of a dry space. In the blink of an eye, he traveled down the side of the dome to a lower half dome, before running across the square and clambering up the side of an adjacent building. Soon he was on the roof of the Arciconfraternita della Misericordia.

There was a time when he would have served the Arciconfraternita, joining in their mission of mercy, rather than running over it without a thought. But he hadn't exercised the gift of mercy since 1274. In his new form, the concept of mercy never entered his consciousness.

He flew through the rain at great speed, heading toward the Ponte Vecchio, when the smell of blood filled his nostrils. There was more than one source, (or vintage as he called it), but the scent that attracted his attention was young and unaccountably sweet. It resurrected in him memories long forgotten. Instantly, he changed direction and increased his speed, moving toward the Ponte Santa Trinita. His black form was a blur against the night sky as he leapt from rooftop to rooftop.

Other monsters moved in the darkness, from all parts of the city, racing toward the place where her innocent blood cried out from the ground.

As he ran, the question uppermost in his mind was: Who would reach her first?

About the Author

Sylvain Reynard is a Canadian writer with an interest in Renaissance art and culture and an inordinate attachment to the city of Florence. (Parenthetically, it should be noted that the snarky narrator of *Gabriel's Redemption* was contracted to write this biographical description, and he can attest that SR is, in fact, real, and has an enviable collection of argyle socks).